THE MOMENT OF THE ROSE

THE
Moment
OF THE
Rose

LUCY KENNEDY

CROWN PUBLISHERS, INC.

NEW YORK

This is a work of fiction, its characters created by the author, their motivation, actions, and dialogue entirely imaginary.

For DUGALD

The moment of the rose and the moment of the yew-tree
Are of equal duration.   —T. S. Eliot

1

ABOUT AN HOUR AFTER THEY left the city Tom turned off the highway at a crossroad gas station. The real estate agent was to meet them here.

Tom's father and mother, Nick and Agnes Dorn, were in the back seat. Without turning his head he knew his mother would be leaning forward eagerly. Even with their early morning start from the flat, she'd taken the trouble to be a tidy credit to them. With her dark braids smooth under a tailored hat, her good blue gabardine dress bought at some sale, she appeared a well-thought-of school teacher.

He knew her eyes, in spite of shadows underneath, would be insistent with life.

And his father's slight form would be gathered in a knot to meet unforeseen difficulties.

Tom parked in the gas station lot.

The countryside, faintly spring green, had a used-up look. Some of its low hills were bare clay and gray shale. On others wild cherry and locust saplings wore festoons of honeysuckle like meager women arrayed in inexpensive finery.

When his father stepped out of the car, he did not look toward the business section of McRae beginning a block or two ahead. Instead he peered up at the feathering April shoots of a locust tree. His sparse hair was indented by the gold ear pieces of rimless glasses. With his head up, the pouch under his chin disappeared and his gesture toward the locust was hopeful. "Good blossoms for bees."

Tom smiled a little. Nick's certainly accumulated a lot of odd pieces of string. Hoarded for a life time. Maybe for today.

Across the lot shone a long chrome-decked trailer on cinder blocks. The door was open. Tom could see a heavy man about forty, his curly hair a thick mat, sitting behind a plywood desk.

1

At the door Tom said, "We're looking for a Mr. Krimmer. About some real estate?"

"Hube Krimmer? Haven't seen him today." Tom did not turn to go so the man motioned toward a chair. "Welcome to wait. Seavey's the name."

"Thanks."

Above the desk a calendar girl whose apricot flesh was bisected by a G-string won hands down over a sign reading "Seavey & Sons Pipe Lines."

"I suppose he's been in business around here quite awhile?"

"Who, Krimmer?"

A drawn-out shrill scream of tires from the highway. They stiffened for the crash. A moment full of silence and Seavey ran out. Tom followed him.

A delivery truck had swerved to avoid being hit by an old cream-colored Packard headed in from the side road. Seavey's smile was grim as he thumbed at the two in the Packard—a handsome dignified man with silvery hair and a young girl. "The Abels! And the daughter driving! Wouldn't you know it!"

From the truck, a frightened driver blinked out at the Abels. Finally, he started his stalled engine and drove, very carefully, across the intersection.

The girl drove up to the gas pump.

Seavey, adjusting his smile, walked toward the Abels.

Tom lit a cigarette, impatient they'd come before he'd had a chance to inquire about Krimmer.

As Abel walked around his car, polished brown shoes crunching the gravel, his voice, "Check the plugs, please," sounded resonant and positive. Seavey stood, eyes down but smile mocking.

The girl, about sixteen, was sitting on their running board. Below her dark blue shorts, her legs this early in spring were well tanned. Her hair, smooth and fine, was the delicate light brown of a trans-muted childhood blonde. Except for one high-boned cheek, her hair hid her face.

Tom catalogued them. Daddy, driven into the station by his spoiled darling daughter. From a white house back in the country. With a saddle horse for the girl. Except for the car. The car doesn't look prosperous.

The girl stood up, throwing away her cigarette. As she stretched yawning, he could see a slender tanned thigh curving up into her

2

shorts and her breasts strained against her white jersey. She's older than I thought. Perhaps twenty-five.

Abel was lifting out his traveling bag and brief case. She slipped a hand through her father's arm as they moved toward the edge of the lot.

They were passing Tom. She's beautiful, all right. Not that it means anything to me. No time. Time!

He heard her say, "You'll work it out, Father. I just know it."

Abel said, "I'm about due for some luck."

With bag and brief case swinging jauntily, he moved off.

By the time the girl slid behind the wheel, Seavey had reached her. "I have some beer in the cooler," he said. Well, he was trying.

Tom liked the way she closed the door and looked at Seavey as though he were the village idiot.

Gravel flew up as the car pulled away.

Seavey, watching her go, smiled cynically. "Anything makes me want to puke is a wench pretending she's icy. Don't tell me she don't put out plenty."

The sound of grapes souring. Tom stared curiously after the car. Then he began again. "Is this Mr. Krimmer supposed to be a straight guy?"

"Oh, Hube's all right. As I was saying about her—young Pansy Leland who clerks over in his old man's hardware, used to go to art school in the city and he— How about a beer while you're waiting?"

The compartment beyond the trailer office held a luxurious studio couch. Seavey did not miss Tom's glance at it. "I have to work late at the office some times." His laugh boomed out. "Well, as I was saying, Leland knew her when she was around that Drama School in the city, see—"

"This Krimmer—he been in business long?"

"About fifteen years. They say she—"

Agnes Dorn was eager to get out of the car. Maybe this would be it! The place where they would live. And when she knew they had to wait, she adventured away, safaried even to the hardware store.

Tell it's spring, the way the whole store's overflowing—hoes, fertilizer, bags of seed. What's that—reddish-brown, twisted, piled on the stand beside the door? Peonies! Wait. Slow. Your breath gets funny when you're too feeling.

3

Must be the sun, so warm on my back, right through my dress, but, how strange. Holding this one, I can see, plain as crystal, Aunt Flo. Aunt Flo's big back yard. A long ago spring. I must have been about thirteen.

Guess it's this place, this town, brings it back. The country sort of still and steady, and people running around making busy-ness, but not too worried, not too many of them, or too crowded together. It'd be nice.

Can see Aunt Flo's hand holding a long narrow tool, a trowel, making a deep firm-sided hole. Her bony brown hand and the long sleeve of her blue percale dress, faded, but starched and ironed the way she did them up. Her long skirts rustled with starch when she'd kneel, planting. Back of her, those lilacs, a cloud of bloom, and that big mock orange bush where the pollen'd yellow my nose when I smelled the fragrance. Those were flowers took their time growing. Like the peonies. Take two, three years to even get established. How bright and fine the grass was near the pump. When I went out to get a bucket of water, I'd see the cascade of white and crimson peonies—pineys, Aunt Flo called them.

This is a fine healthy one. A flower bed, big, five, six feet square, with dirty black soil. Kneeling beside it now in the spring. Putting in pineys.

If we get settled, I'm coming back here. Put it back now.

A window box collects so much soot. And it isn't the same, planting perennials in it. Probably wouldn't be living there the next year anyway.

Maybe this time we can put down roots. To put the feet down and stand steady. A little place in the country. Her chin lifted and she smiled at no one in particular.

And for Nick. It would be, maybe, at last, a chance to begin to live. But I mustn't push him, no matter how plain I see it would be good for him. He has that fear of debt. Never does to force people. Have to let them come to it.

She glanced back at the lot to be sure they weren't waiting for her.

What a pretty girl with all that fall of silky hair. Nice the way people wear shorts in the sun. Tom is looking at her, too. It's natural.

I wish we were settled, that he didn't feel he had us on his hands.

She moved along to another table with a heap of dried brown bulbs. Chinese Lilies—it says. Wonder if they come maybe from China. I don't know these. New and strange.

4

Her thin knobby hand cupped around the flaky dried brown skin delicately. A banked flower. A banked fire.

A bulb is a real wonderful thing. All that excitement and life, perfume even, stored in here somehow. Magic. How did it know when? Conditions knocked on the door. It surged out.

Tom—he moves in surges too. Right now, seems like he's in a long dark underground period. But, how could you know what riches were being stored up? Her hand caressed the round ball of stored life. It's all there, waiting some mysterious condition.

Like that lotus bloom she'd read about. She was just getting over a bad sick spell, and what joy it gave her, reading that piece in the newspaper. Life stored in a seed a thousand years old. She could see the scientist digging around in ruins—Egypt, was it? What if he'd said, seeing it lying there on stones, "Why, that's just some old brown skin, throw it away, burn it up." With a grain of faith, he'd carried it over the ocean, home, and when conditions were right, it bloomed. After a thousand years, a lovely delicate mauve, perfect, perfumed. All that time, waiting, stored up, holding its richness. Until the time came. There was faith for you!

Some people like that. All stored up, waiting to bloom. Tom. Maybe the whole Dorn family. Maybe this would be the time to put down the roots, to begin.

That man in the dark suit getting out of that shiny car, going toward Nick. That must be Mr. Krimmer.

With a generous motion, Mr. Krimmer ushered the Dorns toward his car.

About forty-five, everything about Hubert Krimmer seemed fixed, the gray in his copper hair, the splotches on his tightly drawn skin. His eyes, usually half-closed, had the wide spacing of shrewdness and intelligence. He looked rather like a sleepy snake wearing horn-rimmed glasses.

He drove them through the business center, angled off on Maple Avenue, and headed toward the lure—Stratford Heights.

"You folks care to give me an idea how much you wish to invest?" Nick hesitated. "That depends."

Lots of them didn't like to admit they were only in the eight or ten thousand dollar class. "Well, I think you're absolutely right there. When folks are buying a home," he intoned solemnly, "money is not the first consideration. Just helps me a little to have some figure." That put them on the defensive.

Although his face had long ago frozen into a look which said there was mighty little to laugh about in this world—laugh? to *smile* at— he turned to Agnes what was probably a smile. "Not as important as being near to the church of your choice, eh?" She sat silent. "Any church you want near to?"

But Agnes was looking at the street of new five-room frame houses, coming one after the other like hiccoughs, and shook her head no.

Now what kind of an attitude was that? But they were coming into Stratford Heights, and he turned his full attention on that. He liked to handle it just so.

The houses were larger here. "A hundred feet of ground between each and every house." Krimmer waited. Usually at this point, while the husband was wondering, how much? the wife would ask, how many bathrooms?

He liked to get hold of folks when they had reached the two bath-room level. These were people he understood and could really perform a service for, people worth going to trouble over. He looked down Canterbury Lane, with the neat house numbers set out beside the transplanted dogwood. There was not a single family—not one, in the whole development—that was a Jew. Not one that was less than second-generation American. All that care and trouble, that good handling, was due to his, Hubert Krimmer's, sense of public spirit. And did any of them living there, surrounded by fine folks, really appreciate what he had done?

Now Dorn—that was an odd name. He remembered the family who had come, slyly trying to get into Stratford Heights. Gave their name as Coin.

He stopped in front of a newly built French Provençal and per-suaded Agnes and Nick to alight and look at it.

While they were walking around it, Tom, in the car, turned to Krimmer. "Where do these people work?"

"Oh, businesses in town."

Tom stared at the barbered hedges, the tulips toeing the mark.

Krimmer gestured. "That house with the Spanish front, he runs the supermarket. That white colonial—I sold that—to the manager of the oil refinery outside McRae. Why? You looking for a position?"

"No." The silence hung a minute, as Tom looked at Nick and Agnes dutifully circling the house. "I'm going to medical school—if things get settled."

"Oh. That's fine. Guess you were in service then." He supposed the boys had to be taken care of, but his nostrils twitched and some deep gorge rose at the idea of a big lummox like that, must be all of twenty-six or seven, going to school—just because the tax-payers were sheep enough to hand it out free.

And after Nick and Agnes were back in the car, and they were driving on down the street slowly, he picked up the thread of his inquiry. "Odd name you folks have, Dorn. A hobby of mine, names. What country does it come from?"

Nick, looking at the magazine-cover houses, said, "Bohemia."

Bohunks!

"My great-grandfather married a Swiss woman," Nick said, "but their son married a Norwegian, and his son came to America and married into a Welsh family from up Kirtleton—so I don't know what that would make us. Guess we just thought of ourselves as Americans."

Krimmer drove down the hill now, away from Stratford Heights, along a clay bottom near a creek, and after awhile they came to Wesley Manor, two bedrooms, one bath. This was about where they belonged, he figured, though you never could tell. Sometimes people saved a long time for a house.

"You folks see anything you like?"

"Guess I didn't make it clear when I phoned. We don't want in the town. Your ad Sunday said you had country places. That was how I happened to—"

"Oh, a farm."

"No."

"Which of the companies here you going to be with? I can locate you near it."

"None of them. You see—"

"Oh, retired!" Then he added jocularly, "Looking for a gentleman's estate."

"No, I'm not retired." Nick was positive. "Not a farm exactly. A little—" a guarded look came over his face as if he were afraid to put words around the living idea "—little place in the country." He stopped.

Years of city streets full of people who were just feet walking, of elevators close-packed with the solitary, of street cars jammed with newspaper faces, of people living in row-houses unrelatedly joined together, made it seem unnatural to speak out to a stranger. In the country, they said it was different. But he was too used to *not* talking.

What if coming home from the paper company for the last time, his brief case full of the little mementoes that had collected in the desk—

7

what if on that street car he had said to the faces, "This was my last day. They got a new bookkeeping machine I'd have to go to night school to learn to run. Besides, we have to leave the flat, the building's being razed. I'm trying to decide whether to change my way of life. Maybe find a place out somewhere, be self-sustaining, raise pheasants, or strawberries or bees. We'd use up all our savings, though, and what if it didn't work?"

He could see the faces turning in anguished outrage, on necks held rigid balancing the load of stones in the crown of each hat.

"A place," Nick said finally, "with some ground. Off by itself."

"How much you planning to spend?"

He wished Krimmer would not keep trying to pin him down. He had not made the decision. To use their own savings, yes. But to use Tom's allotment money. No matter what had happened, they'd never used that, had saved it for him. Tom had strong feelings about it, wanted them to use it. He wouldn't even talk about medical school any more.

And if they didn't use it, it probably meant debt. No debt.

"Well, I'm not sure."

Krimmer didn't force the point then. The words "off by itself" had fallen in his mind on a certain culture of hostility he'd been nurturing there since last fall. In this culture Nick's words grew quickly into a really good idea.

He'd sell them, these Dorns or Dornskis or whatever their name was—the other part of Abel's Island! Krimmer sat a moment, enjoying his own brilliance. Then he swung the car around and headed for the black asphalt single lane road. "You came to the right man," he congratulated Nick.

He'd warned Abel the rest of the island was on the open market, hadn't he? All right, Abel was scratching around every which way trying to raise the money, but the last time he'd made an offer, it'd been only eight thousand. This Dorn might give ten.

Now, as if with diffidence, he threw out the bait. "There's a place out a-ways. Folks around here call it The Island. It isn't really, just a bend of Beaver Creek. It may be more land than you want—about thirty acres."

Dorn was rising all right. "An island?" he murmured with a beguiled look. "How much?"

Krimmer said, "The house isn't too modern. Only one bath. Guess I'll show you the McClure place—it's right down this way. It might be better for you."

8

When he finished taking them through the sixteen high-ceilinged rooms that would cost a thousand dollars a year to heat, he knew Nick would say:

"I'd like to see that place—that island."

"I guess I shouldn't have mentioned The Island. There's a man interested in it, and I half-promised to hold it for him. He's going to let me know Monday." The man who was to let him know Monday had come to seem almost real to Krimmer. Sometimes he could even picture what he looked like.

Krimmer took them next to the Link place with the caved front porch and the clogged plumbing, at the end of a street straggling away to nothing. And afterward Nick said, frowning, "Let's look at this island place anyhow."

"It's kind of far out. Mrs. Dorn might not like that."

He darted a glance from the father to the mother to the son.

First thing to find out was who was boss. If it was the man, sympathize that a smart man had to even consider a stupid woman's opinions; if the woman, tell her the woman occupied the house nine-tenths of the time and should pick it; that the kitchen was the most important room in the house, even if the man wouldn't admit it. This family seemed afraid to say what they wanted for fear of over-influencing the others. The meanest kind to handle.

But there were ways. It was the well that made him so confident. Let them think he hardly knew its value, then toss it in, just at the right moment.

He had them figured now. City people who thought they would come to the country and make a living raising strawberries or something. Yes, the well would cinch it.

They followed the asphalt road out of town.

Krimmer smiled a little now. Yessir, I think I'd be smart to get these people in there. Abel wants the whole island. If someone bought the other half—darned if I don't think he'd be disgusted enough to go back to the city. On account of the way he is. Can't be certain, but a mighty good chance! One thing—if he gets it all, he'll stay for sure.

The car mounted a low hill, crowned with a buff brick church. Its steeple was slate, trimmed with wooden commas. "That's the Beaver Presbyterian Church," Krimmer said over his shoulder to Agnes. "My wife'd be glad to introduce you to the Circle ladies if you want."

Hubert was a life-long member of that church. Everyone knew he would never go out of his way to hurt anyone—not if they didn't hurt

9

him. On the other hand, God had given a man a brain so he could defend himself.

Abel had interfered with Hubert Krimmer, seriously. Had—and might again.

The Dorns in the back seat talked in low tones he could not catch and Krimmer brooded a little about Abel, and what he had pulled last autumn.

It wasn't that Krimmer had anything against Abel personally. Krimmer prided himself on having no enemies. But he didn't like what Abel had *done*.

Abel, with barely the legal residence, had barged into the primaries last fall, where he had no business! Through some connections in the courthouse crowd back in the city, he'd managed to get his name on the primary ballot for county commissioner.

To win the primaries in this machine-run county meant election, and Krimmer could have taken the primaries if it hadn't been for Abel.

Krimmer had it planned so long. He knew the incumbent would have to retire at seventy-two, knew that would be last fall when this end of the county was rightly due for some recognition. He knew the old commissioner's gang would put up his henchman, Ealy, for the primaries, but Krimmer expected his own following here would balance that. Only he had counted on support from the courthouse crowd. Didn't he deserve it after all he'd done? His lips thinned as he thought of all his leg work over the years, his careful moving up to committeeman, even to getting appointed appraiser.

Then, just when he thought everything was in balance, Abel was up, and with their support. At Krimmer's protest, they said they'd already made Abel commitments. Krimmer tried at last to argue with Abel that in simple justice he ought not to pick another man's plum. Abel went right ahead.

In a three-cornered fight, Krimmer was smart enough to see that by a slight margin, Abel, the outsider, with no rights whatsoever, might win. Krimmer threw his support to Ealy.

Of course, Krimmer knew what he was doing. Ealy was not too bright and he hit the bottle. Now, Ealy, elected, was making a mess of it. The machine wouldn't take chances with him again. Come next primary, there'd be a re-shuffle. Krimmer would be ready.

But there sat Abel. A threat.

Unless in the meantime, he went back to the city.

Krimmer's commission would be five percent if he sold the Dorns, but he was thinking more of the justice of the thing. If someone interfered with you, you had to stop them before they got too strong. Or at least you ought to try.

Now they were in hills whose sparsely wooded sides did not give a feeling of gentle, round bulk. The land seemed still irritated by the ancient conflicts which had sheared and rent the steep gulleys.

They came now to the dirt road.

A stream ran along one side of it.

Krimmer slowed, as branches switched against the car windows. "What river is that?" Nick asked.

"It's wide enough here to be a river, at that," Krimmer answered. "It's called Beaver Creek." The car barely moved. He wanted them to come to the island slowly—look across and see it.

The road emerged from overhanging branches into the sun. He stopped the car and waited, to give them a chance to take it in before he said, motioning to his right across the stream, "Well, folks, there you are!"

They got out and stood looking across the water.

Along the shore at their feet the coves were emerald pools reflecting moving leaves.

On their right, at a narrow point of the stream, a little bridge with stone abutments and wooden flooring leaped across from the dirt road where they stood to the almost-island.

The gently moving stream, lustrous as burnished pewter, turned on itself like a lasso, enclosing ten acres or so of partly cleared flat, partly wooded hillock.

Krimmer pointed. "Beyond the rise on the island is a narrow neck of land. Can't see it from here. That's the way you get from the island to the rest of the acreage."

A graveled road led up a rise from the bridge and disappeared into shrubbery. On their right, on the lower and cleared part of the island, close to the water, stood a small gray shingle house.

Protected by the moat of the river, the island looked serene and aloof.

From the moment Nick saw it, he was helpless. All the niggling questions, the cool judgment, the common sense that should thrust forward now, all the caution and suspicion limed on the walls of his mind—all seemed to dissolve. He was defenseless. He wanted it.

If only he had enough money!

He felt young, strong, as if he could cope with anything. He'd use Tom's money if necessary! On that island, a man could be free, independent. He'd find ways to sustain them, to make it up to Tom. It could be done! With a place like that, he could—

Krimmer was looking at him intently. Nick forced a look of indifference and turned away.

Tom, noticing the mail box at the side of the dirt road near where they stood, crossed to look at it. "Glen J. Abel," it was lettered. Wasn't that the man in the gas station? And underneath, in lettering more recent, he read, "Mrs. Harry Winters."

"Someone from the island?" Tom touched the mail box.

"Yes, rural route out here, and the carrier delivers on this side. Mr. Abel lives up there." Krimmer motioned to the wooded hillock, where now they noticed a bit of roof. "With his married daughter."

Tom thought, She didn't *look* married.

Nick's face had reddened. He begrudged another house on the island. So, he thought, you not only want an island, but got to have it all to yourself. A neighbor can be nice. You can sit out in the garage, talk over projects, lend him your back numbers of *Popular Mechanics*.

"He selling part of the island?" Nick asked.

"No, Mr. Abel doesn't own this part. Folks around here still call this Abel's Island because his grandfather settled here, helped open the town. But he lost it all. After the panic of '93, they say."

Tom thrust a lower lip out doubtfully. "These houses must be pretty old!"

"The one on the hill was built around 1880, I guess, but the other was built much later, by a Dr. Purcell. The place stood vacant awhile after McRae Abel lost it. Then this Purcell made money speculating in gas wells around here, and he bought it. Purcell built the gray house there for a summer place for his daughter."

"She's the owner then?" Nick asked.

"Her heirs. They live in California. After Purcell died, she moved out there. The heirs divided the place so they could rent it easier. Abel bought the high side couple of years ago. The heirs decided to sell this part, too."

"How many acres'd you say?"

"The shingle house has four acres on the island and around twenty-five back in the woodland. Like to take a look?"

Nick shrugged. "Might as well, now we're here."

The planking on the narrow bridge rattled. Below the bridge was a small dock.

"Nice place to fish from," Krimmer said casually. Nick stared unbelieving. Fish!

They stopped where the lane branched off to the shingle house. The way was choked with blackberry bushes. They went in on foot.

Krimmer liked to step aside at this point. The father and son would go poking up and down, pretending they knew what they were doing. The woman would go into the kitchen.

Upstairs, Tom's brows knit as he said to Nick, "The paint's flaking from the outside trim."

"Look, a water mark on the ceiling."

"Maybe a roof leak."

Tom went to check the plumbing. "Seems okay."

"Floors in pretty good shape."

Outside, Tom pointed. A small crack in a foundation wall.

The five-room house was not specially inviting, except for a wide porch, where the glint of sun from the water made fish scales of light on the ceiling.

They found Agnes standing in the back dooryard. Her eyes were burning so, Tom moved quickly toward her, but she put a hand on his arm as if to say, "I'm fine."

She asked Krimmer her only question. "Who lived here before?"

"Oh, let's see, forget the name. Folks moved away from town. Just renters."

The men went on around the house, talking. Agnes stood.

So that's why nothing here but a ragged barberry bush. Renters. Ready to move on. She tried to keep calm and steady but her hands clutched her handbag. She could not keep herself from smiling. Her eyes seemed to penetrate the black soil.

When she joined the men, she heard Nick say disparagingly, "Probably hard to get drinking water."

"No, a fine well, and a good cistern, too."

"How much is it?" Nick tried to look away, but his eyes flew involuntarily to Krimmer's mouth.

Usually, Krimmer could guess when he was going to be too high. Now he couldn't. The son and his father and mother stood silent, expressionless.

"Ten thousand." Krimmer saw the father's jaw tighten but he couldn't tell what it meant. "Of course, that includes the woodland and the well." He dropped that as if he himself were too dumb to know the value, but they might see something in it. "Oil well."

"Oil well?" Tom asked.

13

"Come on, we'll walk back that way. I'll show you."

A path led up a slight rise in back of the house, then down a slope, to a narrow neck of land, twelve or fifteen feet wide, that held the so-called island to the mainland.

They crossed it and followed the path up another rise. About halfway down the other side, Krimmer, stepping gingerly along the narrow path, paused. "Poison ivy," he said with a petulant old-womanish air. "I have a very sensitive skin. Mrs. Krimmer is always warning me. They say you can get it from the old berries."

At the bottom of the slope, a meadow stretched away, full of succulent-stemmed jewel weed, and the green umbrellas of May apples. At its far edge rose an oil derrick, its well-aged planks blending into the landscape. Some distance away, to the left, through trees, they could see part of another derrick.

Krimmer pointed. "That one's on the Abel place. It was shut down, too, when he bought in here couple years back. He had it reconditioned."

"Reconditioned?" Tom sounded excited.

"Yes, a company comes in and does it. I hear he gets a couple barrels a day out of it now. Crude sells around four fifty at the pipe line."

The Dorns gazed, incredulous. Tom was skeptical. "He hasn't got it pumping now."

"They only pump a couple times a week. He has a production fellow comes around and does it."

Krimmer pointed. "That path through the woods hits an improved road finally. Gives you another way out."

Beyond the road, seemingly far off, in a haze, rose a great gray cone, its sides as even as an Egyptian pyramid, and as dead looking.

"What's that?" Nick asked.

"Culm pile." Krimmer turned away. There it was. They asked. He answered. If they asked more, he would answer.

But Tom was moving quickly waist deep in last fall's burdocks, toward the derrick.

He stood beside it, sniffing the strong gassy smell of crude oil dripping. He could see the inch pipe line now, leading back into the woods toward a small wooden tank.

Krimmer said Abel got two barrels. There must be some joker in it! Why would the place be selling? Questions flashed into his mind. He hurried back up the hill.

"How much does it cost to recondition one of these wells?"

14

"Oh, in round numbers, roughly, say in the neighborhood of five hundred dollars." It had cost Abel seven fifty.

"Trouble is," Nick said, "I don't know anything about oil wells."

"If you get it reconditioned and producing, you can lease it out. There's a small pipe line operates around here. Run by the Seavey family."

"That's the fellow in the gas station?"

"His family. They won't bother to gamble on reconditioning an old well, but they'll lease it and run it if she's going."

"Gamble?" Tom stopped, the struck match halfway to his cigarette. Nick's lower lip thrust out dubiously. "It doesn't always work?"

"What do you expect? Buying a house, nearly thirty acres, and a producing well for that money? You might not get it going at all. On the other hand, mostly they're clogged with mud or shale or wax, and you might find yourself lifting a lot more than you'd expect."

"How old's that well?" Tom eyed him intently.

"This little pool around here was opened in First World War, when they got wild for extra oil. Guess most of the wells on the farms around are say, twenty-five, thirty years old." Krimmer slapped peevishly at the back of his neck. "Too early for mosquitoes. Must be gnats. They always seem to find me. Why don't we go back to the car and talk—unless you'd like to look at the house again?"

In the car, Krimmer turned to Nick. "What do you say? Does it interest you?"

"Well—I want to think it over."

"I understand how it is. A man's buying a home, he wants his family to be happy. If you decide, and put a little money down to-morrow, of course that would fix it. Your son could probably get an F. H. A. mortgage. And I tell you another thing, the title was searched when Abel bought, and you could get in there right away, move in whenever you want."

Back at the crossroad, they got out of Krimmer's car, and Nick paused, leaning in the window. "I'll let you know tomorrow, sure."

"All right," Krimmer said cheerfully. "If you folks are willing to take the chance. That man was supposed to let me know before Monday. Of course, he saw it first."

2

THEY DROVE AROUND IN NEARBY towns for several hours, looking with desultory, half-absent eyes.

It was late, and they were on their way back to the city, when Tom pulled over to the side and faced back toward McRae.

"I want to find out if Krimmer was telling us a straight story on that oil well." For Tom it all hinged on that.

"But where could we find out? Seavey? Maybe he's a friend of Krimmer's."

"Guess we'll have to play it by ear."

Back at the gas station, Tom waited until he saw Seavey finish a conversation with a customer, then he went over.

"Well, Jack," Seavey's voice boomed, "come back for the rest of that beer?"

Tom guessed he might as well fling the cards on the table. "I wanted to ask you something. We've been out looking at part of that island—out on Beaver Creek."

Holy Cow! Krimmer had them to The Island! A joyful grin lit Seavey's face. And here, all along he'd been resigned to Abel raising the money and buying it.

"You run a pipe line, I hear. What's this deal about leasing? That on the level?"

"Come in, come in." Of course, Hube Krimmer must have something on his mind, too. Why sure, that county commissioner squeeze. Abel crowded him. "Come inside, Jack, sit down!" The jolly smile settled on Seavey's face.

"Well," Tom said, "wait'll I get my father."

Inside the trailer, Seavey put out three beers. Some days nothing went right. Other days made you glad you led a clean life. Like now—when the waves rolled up and broke just right on your beach.

He'd tell this kid all he wanted to know—give him a break. Except about Abel trying to set himself up as an independent producer. That might give these folks wrong ideas. There wasn't going to be any more of that around here.

By the time they'd finished the first frosted can and he'd put out three more, Seavey had answered their questions and begun to answer ones they were too dumb to ask.

"We got a lot of other interests around here besides the pipe lines, see, and when a well peters out, we don't bother, we let the lease die."

"But it's true, you'd lease it and run it, if we got it going?"

"Sure, sure. We got to fill our contract with the purchasing company. Ours are just gathering lines. And you don't even have to get a lawyer, there's a standard printed lease—what they all use around here." He opened a steel file, rummaged, then tossed a blank toward them. "Take it along. Usually the landholder gets an eighth. Out there on The Island, though, it's a little better. Dr. Purcell drilled those wells and ran them, and where you own the land and the rig, you get a quarter."

"A quarter." Nick looked lost.

"Royalty. Quarter of production. All you do is sit on your can and rake it in. Soft, eh?"

Tom picked up the lease and put it in his pocket. "Well, thanks, thanks a lot."

"Any time," Seavey said with an expansive gesture.

Outside, Tom said to Nick, "Sounds like a good deal. The oil well, I mean."

Nick said, "Yes. But—the ten thousand."

Tom tried to keep the irritation out of his voice, knowing what Nick's response would be. "Of course you could borrow. Or get a mortgage."

Nick looked worried. "No."

"Maybe we ought to have tried to get that price down."

"Do you think there's a chance?" Nick looked hopeful.

"We could try."

At first Krimmer beamed, seeing them, but when Tom finished he looked grave, a little shocked. "I may tell you right now the owner first asked eleven. And that man that's to let me know Monday is prepared to pay ten." Krimmer had a small feeling of uncertainty. What if Dorn didn't have enough and got away? No, I think he's hooked. He'll get it. "So—I happen to know ten is rock bottom."

17

By the time the Dorns arrived at Central Avenue, it was nearly dark. The odor of disinfectant and burned food met them in the hall and a closed-up, musty smell as they unlocked the door of the flat. Agnes felt something else, too, an atmosphere of dry anxiousness which she remembered from the other times when they must leave by a certain date and had no place to go.

In the kitchen, hurrying dinner, she moved around Tom and Nick.

Tom began to help her, setting the table in the dining-nook off the kitchen.

"What do you think, Dad?"

Nick hesitated. "I wonder about that price."

Tom looked up, the knives and forks in his hand. "You heard what he said. You won't get him lower."

"I was wondering if it was too low."

Tom laughed. "A fine thing to worry about." He scattered the silver on the table and bumped on the plates. When he finished, they sat in the nook out of Agnes's way. As they slid in, the dinette benches wobbled insecurely on their wall bolts.

Chin on hand, Nick said, "I been studying the Sunday real estate ads long enough, and watching farm listings and values on country places too. For years. Is there a joker somewhere? That price seems a *little* low."

Agnes turned the lamb chops under the broiler. "Nick knows, Tom."

"I know he does."

But Nick wanted to be argued out of it. "Of course, there's things might account for it. Leak in the roof, crack in the foundation—"

Tom helped out. "It's on a dirt road."

Agnes put in hopefully, "Some people might not like it being on an island."

"That's right." Nick absorbed these counterbalances.

When they ate, it was absently, as if dreams out of each mind moved around and around in the air above them, sometimes too fast.

They were nearly finished before Tom said, "Could we do it?"

Nick glanced over his shoulder at the scarred little desk in the other room. "I'll go over everything again. See if we could piece it out."

"Of course," Tom swallowed hard, "we could if we borrowed. Took a mortgage."

There was a silence. Nick frowned into his plate. "I guess I'll keep out of debt as long as I can."

18

After a bit, Tom began vigorously, "We'd need ten thousand, then, plus five hundred for the well." He made figures with his fork.

"That well," Nick said, "would be a mighty handy source of income. But all these years, I been figuring other ways."

"I know that, Dad, but the well makes it practical. Raising Belgian hares, or bees, or something you got out of a book in the library—that's okay, but—"

"But Nick can do it!" Agnes said. "He's got the go and smartness."

"I always planned to start small," Nick said. "Then spread out. Have two or three different sources of income. I got fifteen, maybe twenty solid work years yet. Just give me an opportunity."

"Well, sure, go ahead with those things, too," Tom said.

"I'd need five hundred to start, at least, and part of that'd be to live on till things got rolling."

Tom made more figures with the fork. "All right, then, we'd need eleven thousand."

"Yes," Nick said, "I'm afraid so."

Agnes lifted the plates to the sink and from the refrigerator slid out the tray of dessert. It had frozen too hard. She began to chop it.

Tom moved into the hall. "I'll be back."

In his room, he switched on the light, opened the top drawer, reached under the shirts and lifted out the black tin box. On top of his discharge paper rested the bank book. He thrust it in his pocket. At the door, he paused. Sitting on the bed, he opened it.

The entries extended over all the years he'd been in service. He could see Nick going to the bank with the allotment checks, putting them in.

I gave it to him, but he always said he was saving it for me.

If I used it myself, I wouldn't need to work part time after I get to medical school. Even with the G.I. bill, it'll be expensive.

From the kitchen, as Agnes hacked at the dessert, came the sound —chunk, chunk.

Chunk, chunk.

Chunk. He seemed to hear an echo from some other air, a long past day.

Chunk, chunk. Not in a room. Outside. Weather like this, too. Right after I graduated from high. Worked on the ice truck that summer. Some people still had ice boxes. I remember chunk, chunk, chunking out the square, slippery pieces.

I remember that afternoon, dropping off the truck as it passed our house. I was watching for the letter about the scholarship. Can see the rusty mail box on the porch. That Arnold Street duplex. Knew we'd have to move. We'd been no-money-for-clothes-or-movies poor. That time we were no-money-to-pay-the-rent poor.

How I felt, standing there, holding the letter. Nick in that old tan sweater, sitting in the Morris chair inside the window, looking out at me. Seemed strange to have him home middle of the afternoon. There was a new word in the headlines then—Recession. "First go the unskilled," Nick had said, "then the half-trained like me. Only ten left in the accounting department. Once you're past forty-five, not so easy to get in anywhere unless you have some regular profession."

Can still feel that smooth letter paper, see the precise type. "Due to diminished dividends on our endowment funds, we will be able to grant only one of our usual two scholarships this year. As the other candidate had the higher average, we regret . . . Perhaps next year . . ."

Nick pacing back and forth in that square room, lace curtains, the fern under the window. "Try for another." He sounded frantic. "There must be some place else."

"It's too late now, Dad. I'm going to get a job."

How he looked, near crying. "What kind a job could you get just out of high school? No training, nothing." Shouting at me furiously, "No, no! You're going to college. Going to be a professional man."

Anyhow, it didn't matter, because when I tried for a job, too many stronger backs ahead of me.

Agnes rattled the plates in the kitchen. In a moment she would be calling him.

He went to the door, switched off the light, but hesitated, then went to the window and looked out.

Who'd have thought Nick would figure that way out of the dead-end, taking a job as janitor. "It's no cash, but a basement apartment free, heated, near the university. Room for you—" And Agnes going off to her brother's up in Kirtleton to help out for her room and board. Don't think she and Nick were ever separated before.

That first year, think we lived on cornflakes. Of course Agnes came back after I found the night job as orderly in the hospital.

Anyhow Nick had that one day. That day I graduated. The way he looked. How hot it was. I felt like a sheep moving along in the line with all those hundreds. So hot we didn't wear any shirts under those black rented gowns. I had the letter from the draft board in my back pocket, I remember. I'd hidden it from Nick. He had that one day.

Agnes called, "Tom! Dessert."

Tom answered, "All right," but he stood looking into the dark.

If they knew I'm still thinking of it, they wouldn't get settled. Give everything they have to help. I know them. Then something happens to them, and I'd have to stop and start again. No.

His hand closed on the bank book. Once and for all, clean everything off the slate. Get them settled.

But he stood staring out into dark space.

Waiting for dessert, Nick had gotten from the desk the list of the hoarded Series E's. Under the light in the dinette, he was checking again the accrued value, using as scratch paper the backs of old calendar sheets. Writing recklessly on them, it was as though he were using the time he had not touched, because he had been waiting.

After she put the dessert on, Agnes stood, watching him. Then she went in to the little desk. Nick guessed what she was after. When she returned, she had them in her hand, the three shares of telephone stock.

It was her dower, come late, only a few years before, when her Aunt Flo's tiny estate had been neatly divided among six descendants. No matter what happened, Nick stubbornly would not let her cash them. Now, before she could lay them on the table, he shook his head, No. "We'll manage without. Better lock that drawer when you put them back."

Agnes stood, nonplused. Then she laid them on the kitchen shelf. She began to pour the coffee. "Tom," she called again.

He came and they finished eating.

While Agnes cleared, Nick took up the pencil, began checking.

Tom slipped the bank book out of his pocket. He laid it, opened, beside Nick's hand. "Might as well count that in."

Nick didn't say anything, but his pencil stopped in mid-air.

Tom went to pour himself another cup of coffee.

Nick said, "I don't like to use it."

Over his shoulder, Tom smiled. "It'll be my home, too, won't it?"

"Of course."

Nick touched the book and thought of the island.

He felt a deep urgency to fasten on to something immovable, become so fixed to it no storm could send him spinning.

He didn't know exactly the moment he had come to want this. There were all those years when he was so unthinkingly sure all that was required of him was to get Tom through school and let him become a surgeon.

He glanced at Tom's back as he stood, waiting for the coffee to re-heat.

For a moment Nick recalled a vivid picture. Tom's classroom and how it looked in the late afternoon sun, the pupils all gone. The shape of the teacher's middle-aged hands, the pattern of her lace collar, as she sat behind her little desk. She had asked him to come in. "You have a bright boy there, Mr. Dorn. You ought to see he goes to college."

That was a wonderful moment. One of the best. And the deep satisfaction stayed, a crystal bead glinting on a long dull chain.

Of course, the fixed goal of helping Tom become a surgeon had fallen in pieces after he knew about Tom's hand. It being his right hand, there wasn't any use thinking of that goal any more, was there? After Tom was discharged, they'd never even discussed it. What was the use of making them both feel bad?

He glanced at Tom again. He didn't know *what* Tom wanted now. All he *seemed* to want was for them to be settled.

Tom returned with the cup of coffee, but stood, looking over Nick's shoulder.

Nick had added up the Series E's. Six thousand nine hundred fifty-seven dollars and fifty cents.

Tom picked up the pencil and wrote under that the total of the allotment money—twenty-eight hundred forty one dollars. Then he drew a line, and added.

Agnes had come, and they looked at the total—nine thousand seven hundred ninety-eight dollars and fifty cents.

"There's the Christmas Club savings," Nick said, and wrote down, forty-seven dollars fifty cents. "And I still have some bonds in payroll savings I have to pick up at the paper company." He added a hundred twenty-four dollars.

They stared at the total. Nine thousand nine hundred seventy dollars.

Tom sat on the bench. "That five hundred for the well. I'll get that. I can do that much. I'll do it."

Back at the sink, two spots of color burned in Agnes's cheeks. Then she stopped washing the dishes, and found the newspaper, leafed through and, finding the page, her lips moved as she multiplied. She went back to the sink silently, but she poked the dish mop into the cups hard to work off her feelings.

She thought, It's like I been waiting so long to put down roots, something always asking, "Is it time?" If we had it, I could give the big yes.

They think I'm still sick. But I'm stronger now. That doctor doesn't know what's inside a person. I could learn to grow strawberries, make jams, nice, sell them. Or herbs. Little jars with bright labels.

Think what it would be like, living some place where we wouldn't have to move! Lost track of the places we've lived. That little house in Aspinshade, rented that a whole year, until the family owned it came back from West Virginia and wanted it. Seemed something always happened, rent raised, or like this flat, the building to be torn down.

Suddenly, she laid down the dish mop, dried her hands carefully, picked up the certificates and sat down on the other side of the dinette table.

"You listen," she said.

Nick looked up. He recognized the tone in her voice.

"I *want* to use these." She laid them down. "They're worth four hundred ninety-eight dollars. I looked it up. Write that down there. It'll be my home too, won't it?"

Nick looked at her a moment, mouth open. Tom smiled a little. "She's right, Dad."

Nick blinked for a while. Then he wrote it down.

Tom patted her shoulder as he got up. "Have to go. I have a date."

Finishing the dishes, Agnes could hear Tom in his room, changing his clothes. When he came out in gray flannel slacks, white shirt and the beautiful camel's hair jacket that girl had given him, she knew he was off for the night. She didn't like it. But he'd had a lot of troubles and she didn't blame him.

In the big double bed, Agnes stretched out carefully. Without being able to see the twists in Nick's face, without touching his body, tight as china, she knew how he was feeling.

"I'm checking those figures in my mind," he said, "to see if I made a mistake. Comes out the same. Pretty narrow margin. Is it too narrow?"

"Sometimes a narrow path is all right," she said. "If you can relax."

"Wait till I get a little more security, then I'll relax," he said tensely.

She thought, I've never been able to unshrivel him from fear. But then, I've had experiences he hasn't. Death, close, those times. In a way, I'm thankful for that. I can realize. Now, each moment, each man—husband and son—is wonderful. Nick. If I could somehow touch him to joy.

"I keep adding up columns," Nick said, "the good in one, the bad features about the place in another."

Nick's parents always worried, she thought. Can you inherit worrying? Even though I was an orphan, I had Aunt Flo, quiet, steady, working her garden. Not that we had much, but I never *felt* any lack.

Nick said, "I have to make that price spell—not too dear, not too cheap. Maybe the river floods the basement sometimes, and the land in back's not cleared."

"And it's far out for most people," she said.

"Yes. Maybe that's enough to account for the low price. But I have to be sure. Otherwise, I wouldn't want to use Tom's money."

"No."

They were silent. Then she said, "Seems like he's stopped wanting to be a surgeon. Or has he really? Maybe he wants us to be settled first so he acts like he doesn't care about going on."

Nick said slowly, "Is it right then for us to use his money?"

"He must have figured out that's best for him and if that's it, we ought to get settled, quick as can be."

They were silent again.

Agnes was thinking, Tom had that craze for sculpting, too, but he stopped. He has some of that worry, like Nick. But he's part me, too, don't forget. The shriveling back into fear and the surging forth into bloom. Tom. When he was hurt in the Army, he must have been close to death. Why didn't it come to him then—the wonderfulness of the moment. But young—a man, guess he has too many urges, women, and wanting things like a fine car and clothes, perhaps. He gets started—but he gets stopped.

Nick added sums silently. He was calculating one final resource. It came to three hundred seventy-three dollars. A secret hoard, saved by denial and stinginess. His answer to that always hovering, "Cash, please! What! You haven't it? What *good* are you?" His reasons for secrecy were obscure but strong. It wasn't as if he ever meant to buy a new suit or anything like that with it. But to be able to say, in some imminent, deadly breach, I can pay. If the demand were not too great. His dignity money.

Now, in the dark air over his head, he added it to the rest.

Then, as though drawing a mental line, trying to add up, he said tensely, "Well, what do you think?"

She hesitated. I know he likes the idea of the island, being on his own, dependent on no one. It's best for Tom too, if we're settled. It's not fair to push Nick, though. She made her voice almost colorless. "It seemed nice."

But her mind spun on. Thinking of the black garden soil, she could not keep the eager smile from her lips. She fell asleep thinking of how the light rippled on the porch ceiling.

Nick was still trying to make the columns balance. Then he saw that to him, the place seemed so dream-like in its desirability, that naturally, he'd be surprised when the price was one he could consider. Maybe the price was right.

He began to go over it all again.

3

TOM HURRIED AWAY FROM THE flat. The decayed rooming-houses looked gloomier at night and the paper-strewn gutters were reddened by the taproom neons.

He climbed Murdock Street, lingering at the top. Always every night going to Margot's, he found himself stopping here. Behind him, his daytime world. On the other side of the hill—soft as a black velvet box—the world of night. Even the pearls of light pendant from wrought iron lamps on the down-curving drive enhanced the velvet quality of the dark. And below, at the park edge, was the twenty stories of the Royal Princess apartment, ablaze with light. Margot had the penthouse.

He sensed the faint fragrance of a blooming forsythia, and Spring, lurking there, stabbed him. Something painful as guilt surged up to the wound. Ever since he could remember, he'd been breathlessly trying to catch up to time. "By this time you should be. You should have." Then guilt came with the smell of Christmas balsam or the sight of a first straw hat, forcing him to admit it was actually "this winter," or "next summer."

Spring. Coming over here to Margot's for five months, then. Impossible.

Five months all right. Out of the hospital August twenty-fifth, no, sixth.

Seems like just a few weeks ago. My last day at the hospital, can see that doctor handing me the mimeographed sheet.

"Look this over. You have the finger exercises. Here's a list of manipulations to get the hand supple."

Those two words, far down the list, the print blurred, but seeming to stand out.

"Clay Modeling?"

"One way, yes," the doctor smiling, "you might not be interested in that."

Didn't know he was talking to someone who'd once.

A nice little guy, that doctor. "It being the index finger of your right hand that's gone, I'd suggest you try to make the left hand dextrous. If you remember any Latin—dexter, right. There's dextrous and ambidextrous. If you try, you can become one and four-fifths ambidextrous. And that's not bad."

Not bad at all.

I could have worked with clay at the flat, but the idea of art school—liked it. Going into Gino's Cafe that night—why did I? Hangout for students from the Art School. Seeing that guy—what's his name—Eric, the perennial drama student, who never yet had a job and whose voice had begun to sound like the squish of a wet sponge. He paid for his drinks with news items from his world. "There's an evening class in sculpture just starting at Art School."

That very first evening, Margot.

Can't say I wasn't briefed. What's-his-name, Eric, in Gino's after class. "Everyone around school calls her shackjob. Her father's vice president of Firth Coal and she's been divorced twice for cause. She stalks the art classes to find a type she likes. You'll hear around the locker rooms how she—"

The fountains of forsythia sprayed accusingly.

All right, it's spring. But coming home then, Nick out of a job, doctor bills for Agnes, putting off med school again. That was a rough spot. All right, Margot's bad medicine, but I needed it. Like I needed the morphine that night in the hospital. "This will get you through till morning."

Five months.

All right, all right. But it's only decent to go over and say goodbye to her, isn't it?

26

If Nick and Agnes take that place, I'll have to go out there and get them settled. Means I'll quit at Netts, too. A good thing.

A slow flush crept over his cheeks.

Netts, where he worked as checker on complaints, built what he thought of as rash houses. Overnight, or so it seemed, a healthy looking meadow would be broken out in a rash of red brick cubicles as alike as pimples.

But after all, it being a bum right hand bars me from quite a few things. And I have to help out at home, don't I?

But if we go out there, quit at Netts. Quit with Margot, too.

He stopped at Gino's.

Almost as soon as he sat down, Eric, always hopeful of a picked-up check, slid on to the bar stool beside him.

"Well, still trimming the green leaves off the lumber every morning?" Eric asked, referring to the lumber Netts used in the houses.

"Oh, something's just broken for me," Tom said quickly. "My old man, rather. If I can get it cinched, I'll be in school come fall." Tom didn't know where that hard boastful tone came from in his voice.

"What's the big deal?"

"We found a place he can keep himself on—that is if I can get some money to recondition an oil well that's on it—" His tone changed to practical matter of fact. "By the way, this place is called Abel's Island. Ever know a girl named Abel? They say she went to Drama School."

Eric shook his head no, then, "Oh, that's the girl married Harry Winters, who was in *Cry No More*."

"You know her?"

"I know Harry better. He's in Charlesville, you know."

Charlesville. That was the mental hos—

Tom could see her slender tanned legs, her delicate head turning. Husband in psycho. The way I felt looking at her. Now, like hearing of a treacherous swamp in time to avoid. A brangle. Is there such a word? Don't know. Couldn't explain it to anyone, but to me it means tangled confusion, shoals, unsettled, involvements.

Going to get clear away. Out in the main channel. No more stopping, starting. No more brangles.

"So it's good-bye to Netts, eh?" Eric said.

"Yes, if my family can get this place, I'm going out and live there and help them get settled."

Eric stared at him speculatively. "Does Margot know?"

Tom decided it was his tone he didn't like. "Why?"

"I know Margot. She won't let you go. But what the hell, it's a soft spot."

Tom said angrily, "So she doesn't know, but I'm on my way now to tell her."

Eric was looking at him peculiarly. "If I were you and you mean what you say, I wouldn't go over there."

Tom reached in his pocket and slapped the money down hard. "Pardon me. I'm in a hurry."

He stepped into the night street.

Walking along Rankin briskly, he crossed and started out Barr.

He slowed down. It's true, though. Margot *is* a soft spot.

He left Barr and moved along College Street. University neighborhood. Rooming houses, shades high, light streaming, feeling of people living each moment as it came. Guitar music fell out of an open window. Ahead of him, a young couple walked, arms entwined.

Passing the corner, he could see, down one street, the dim white mass of the Medical School. He kept looking at it as he passed.

Yes! Get Nick and Agnes settled! Once and for all! Everything off the slate!

Then make my left hand dextrous. "Can't be more than nine-tenths ambidextrous," but that's not bad, brother. He clenched and unclenched his fingers with determination.

One thing, I always knew what I wanted. Well, maybe not always. Think of how much I wanted to be a sculptor. Got over it though.

Tom crossed the park, approaching the Royal Princess, approaching Margot.

Got side-tracked. Margot's a dead-end. Lingered too long. Tell her now.

When he stepped in the elevator at the Royal Princess he felt unreasonably angry when the man took him, without a word, to the penthouse. You'd think I lived here!

He let himself in with the key she'd given him.

4

MARGOT'S APARTMENT WAS dark. Through the great window that was one wall, the night sky flickered from rose to gold as with northern lights. It was the belch of sulphur from giant blast furnaces far off by the river.

When he touched the switch, the big room came alive, artful, soothing. The room was the creation of Margot's last husband, a monstrous fat man, owner of Thirty-two, the exclusive shop for women. The antique blacks and living browns, the walls textured like pale wampum, had been copied from a Braque painting. It was Felix when he lived here who had placed the slender yellow table where drinking or dining could come to life under the Klee drawings. It was he who had left the wall bare over the recessed fireplace for a Braque he had meant to acquire. He was proud of that virginal wall, sometimes dropping in with friends or current mistress, to boast of his disciplined restraint in not succumbing to a decoration not precisely right.

Tom, without thinking of it, gravitated toward the kitchen. Perhaps because the hard white tile walls, the vitreous sink, had been impervious to Felix. On the porcelain-top table there, Margot had left a mass of clay, partly thrown on the armature. "Ugh, worse than usual." Poor girl, it was her excuse, her entree, into the semi-bohemian world that suited her purposes. Tom had never gone back to the class after he started up with Margot.

Now he picked up a damp lump of clay off the table and worked it in his left hand.

What a feeling it had been, though. Working with clay again. Out of wet dust. To articulate an idea.

This damp clay odor. Like what? Like the smell in that loft Mazur used as studio.

Mazur was a well-known sculptor who, when Tom was still in high school, became interested in him after Tom won a local prize.

Those Saturday mornings! All the clay and plaster I wanted to work with. Sloshing. The exciting feeling of the stuff malleable under your fingers.

That same clay smell in the big barn-like classroom at the Art School. Absorbed people around you. Wonderful.

He put the clay back hastily.

Wonderful. But all the time that undercurrent in me. Anxiety. Or shame. Wallowing there, speculating on the million pliabilities of the material. Too easy to spend your time doing just that. Let yourself and you could easily get your kick in life that way. Those people in the class. Sure they were absorbed, but damn it, half of them fairies.

He strode back to the big room, giving the Calder mobile an angry push as he passed, so that all the tin fish tinkled.

"When I'm a plastic surgeon, I'll have the feeling of molding, building something up—and be able to buy myself a good car too."

He heard her key, and Margot came in.

"You're early." Her smile was never gay or amused but half-sleepy, half-derisive. Settling herself languidly into a low chair, she stretched slim legs, arching insteps swelling up out of exquisite sandals, as if she enjoyed looking at them. Her nose was large and her mouth wide, but her breasts and hips seemed to wing out from the slim mast of her body. Her clothes, since she bought them at Thirty-two, were what Felix insisted a woman's clothes must be—"amusing." Subtle, a little startling, as now, since it was April, she was dressed for June in several qualities of blue—the straight sheath of dress sea-blue, the wide belt cobalt, the shoes indigo.

"Let's have a drink, yes?"

Tom felt, for some urgent reason not entirely clear to him, it was necessary they talk now. After the second drink she usually—

He fixed them a drink. It gave him time to figure how to say it. He never liked to hurt anyone. People wouldn't have believed it, but she was vulnerable. Especially she needed to feel she was completely effective in that department. And, dammit, she was.

No use to be brutal.

He'd go way back and try to explain the whole thing. That would be easiest. She'd heard him griping in his cups enough about how he wanted his family settled. He could pick it up there. Then, without ordering his words, he told her about it, but when he finished, saying, "And it's a nice place and I want to go out there and get them settled," she was staring, her face blank.

"Why, they're adults!"

"Well, it's sort of complicated. My father has this phobia about debt. They'd use everything, theirs and mine, to buy the place. I'll have to get another small pot somehow to recondition that well. My father thinks he can make a living raising strawberries or something. You know—from office to cold frame in three easy lessons. I'd feel as if they were really set if they had the income from that well. After I get out there, I may be able to borrow it myself from the local bank and then get a job out that way to repay the loan."

"Well, for heaven's sake, is that why you're going?"

"Partly."

"Oh, that's foolish. You know I'll give it to you."

He flushed.

She sipped slowly, watching him.

"Just foolishly unnecessary, going out there, beating your brains out."

She went to the functional desk with the concealed drawer, and he felt somehow ashamed as he could hear her pen scratching, hear her blow on the check to dry it. She folded it in two, came over and sat down beside him on the love seat and slipped the check into his pocket. "There. Now, let's not have any more of this talk about your having to go out there. Give them the money. Now they're off your neck. You've done enough. I'd say you'd done everything any-one could expect."

Well, he *had*. "I didn't mean to borrow it from you."

"I know you didn't. But you have it."

Maybe he was foolish. She had plenty. He knew sometimes she'd spend nearly as much on handmade underwear or a couple of frocks.

"It isn't only the money. I want to go out there and help him get set. He'll need me."

"How old is he?" she asked drily.

"It's not that, he's not helpless, but—"

"I'm going to be very frank for a minute. I think you're sort of peculiar. Really I do. About that I mean."

Maybe she's right. He was a little blurred.

"Now, let's have another drink," she said.

Wash my hands of their whole mess.

She put an arm around his neck.

"Yes, but—" He struggled to get back to something that had seemed, at the time, fairly important. "It's not only the well. I want to be sure they're all right, then I can go back to medical school. Be out in the main channel, on my way."

31

"I can't understand that. Can't understand you at all. Look," she held up his four-fingered hand, "a surgeon."

"A plastic surgeon's different."

"Years of dreary work. And why? I don't get it. Life is awfully, awfully short."

He'd felt that way, often.

Suddenly the first notes of Brahms' Fourth chimed through the room—the door bell Felix had arranged when he lived here.

Margot, annoyed, moved toward the entry way. High chattering voices. A crowd. Felix among them, probably with his new wife.

Tom rose quickly. He wasn't in the mood. Maybe they'd go soon. He went into the kitchen.

He found a bottle of bourbon there, but when he took out the ice cubes, he let them form a small puddle on the sink as he stood staring into space. He filled a jigger and drank it quickly.

Margot was a good sort, she had plenty. She didn't mean to imply that he was no better than—

He poured another jigger and drank it quickly, but he still felt like hell.

If he could just shut out the high chattering voices in the other room. Go into Margot's room. Take a little nap. Yes. Take a nap. Quiet there. He picked up the bourbon and jigger glass.

Just as in the center of some women's lives stands a kitchen stove, the family dining table, or their own dressing table, in the center of this room, stood, importantly, on sheen of the gray rug, the enormous bed, with its gray-green silk cover. The bed was reflected in a huge mirror on the opposite wall. Margot enjoyed seeing herself in bed.

He sat down on the chaise longue, bottle in one hand, jigger in the other. He poured and drank slowly.

Will I have another? Better not. Feel blurry.

He put the bottle and glass on the floor. I'll take nap—

The downy cushions of the chaise pulled him into them persuasively. Not bothering about his shoes on the valenciennes lace-trimmed gray coverlet, he stretched out. From the cushions came the odor of pond lilies, half-asleep in warm mud.

Her perfume. Likes to drench herself with perfume when—Felix has it made up for her. Some manufacturer he knows. Pond lilies, half-asleep, wide-open-in-the-sun. Subtle, exquisite. Hate it. Don't know why. "Lilies that fester smell far worse than weeds."

32

Eric saying, "A soft—" Well, it's true. A soft ledge here all right. Wonderful. No responsibilities or worries.

And after all, I'm in control. It's a temporary thing, but fine.

I can hardly hear the voices in the other room. Shrill. Will I have another drink or—

He could feel his lids fall heavily.

He was lying on the ground where the broken plane was down, his right arm and shoulder ablaze with pain. Must have gotten the first burst. Never did know what happened.

Now, he half roused. Strange, lying here in this pond-lily smelling Braque-ish puddle I remember—

Lifting my head. Herby and Ben beside me. Twisted. They're dead. I must get up. Move. Get away. Roll over on my left side. Use my left arm. Push myself along. Can't. Crazy pain. Incredible agony. Wound tablets. Can't find.

I have to lie down again. What's beyond this puddle?

One good thing, I have the maps in my mind. A flat top hill, on the American side, a road. It'll be patrolled. By us.

The mud's soft. Must have rained not long ago. Mud's taking the curves of my body. Begins to feel warm. If I don't try to move—easy enough. Sort of a relief. Nothing I can do about anything.

He moved on the down-filled chaise, opened his eyes.

His hand closed on the bottle. He sat up, poured another jigger and tossed it down. As he leaned his head back, the check crackled in his pocket. He put the bottle down and stretched out again.

That hill—the plane tilted over, nose down. I remember I kept saying that tag line, "I wasn't fired, I quit."

His eyes closed.

Stay quiet. After awhile the enemy will come to investigate the wreckage. A prisoner. Out of it. Finish, go home. Out of their whole brangle. Or, don't move, maybe go unconscious again. Nothing to beat against. Just go.

He roused, blinking. Then he pulled himself up on his elbow on the chaise, frowning. A hand seemed to be knocking on a window bedewed with whiskey fog. Eric had said, "If you mean what you say, don't go—"

His head dropped back into the soft down. But his eyes did not close.

Back there beside the plane that day—no big decision or anything. No big heave of will power. But I remember each move, an

33

agony, dragging myself out of that puddle. The hill helped me. Could roll down. All the way—to the road.

He sat up, staring into space. It's like in those old movie comedies, when the carful of cops chasing the carful of robbers around and around the block, reverses. Staring at the carful of cops.

"She won't let you go."

He pulled himself to his feet, swaying a little. He could still hear the chitter of voices in the other room, in a high quarrel about something now. Then he moved toward the door.

He went into the bathroom and doused his hair and face with cold water once, then again. As he dried himself roughly on the thick soft towel, he knew what he must do.

He went back to her room, to the bed. He took out the check and laid it there in the middle, a small green rectangle in the gray-green sea.

He passed through the living room as if he were going through the men's room in a public building, without a word. In the hall, an elevator was discharging a passenger.

He stepped in, and as the elevator door was closing, the penthouse door opened hastily. Margot stood framed there, command and apprehension on her face.

The elevator started down.

5

TOM CAME HALF AWAKE WISHING he'd not been so friendly with the bourbon the night before.

From the dinette came the tinkle of spoons in breakfast cups, and as soon as his shade rattled up, Nick called in, "You up?" From his tone of eager impatience, Tom guessed Nick had come to some decision.

He stood, realizing.

I still have to figure a way to get money for the reconditioning. To me, that's what makes the deal practical.

Of course, anyone but Nick, they'd borrow from the bank. But not

Nick. No use arguing about debt. You can push him and push him and he'll give and give on a lot of things. On others you can struggle till you die or he dies. Impatiently, Tom rubbed the back of his hand across his face.

If only we could have gotten Krimmer down on that price. Well, we tried. No use thinking of that.

As Tom shaved, Nick came to the bathroom door.

"I was thinking," he tried to sound casual, "if you could maybe take another day off—"

"What did you have in mind?"

"We might go back out there, take another look around."

Best to go, and try to figure out the oil well deal later. "Okay."

"We'll get ready then." Nick disappeared.

Nick's earnestness touched some memory in Tom and, like a disappearing frost, his impatience vanished.

He shaved thoughtfully, remembering that time when he was in high school and Nick, so earnest, groping, talked to Mazur. When Mazur, the sculptor with a piece in the Modern Museum, had actually come to see Nick.

Tom could see Mazur, burly, in a rough wool sport shirt, hands on knees, leaning forward, talking to Nick. "I'd hardly have had Tom in my studio all these Saturdays, trying to help him, if I didn't sense a real talent. What's he want to go to college for, studying economics or Latin? I'll take him in with me, full time. Let him hang around, learn everything he can."

Nick, looking as if some basic rug were being jerked, saying finally, "Tom's going to be a professional man. Have some security—"

Mazur, stocky, forthright, looking back at Nick, saying, honest, resigned, "It's true, I have to carn butter for my bread doing church carvings, tombstones—"

Then, with a rare release of the springs of his feelings, Nick, trying to explain, "My father had seven children. With no training he was always the first laid off in bad times. Never in his life did he have enough money to buy an overcoat. He was never out of debt—"

Back in his room, Tom began to dress quickly.

His mother came to the door, an envelope in her hand. "A messenger boy brought it early this morning."

Margot's scent. Her handwriting. The "Thomas Dorn, Esquire" written with a lot of little curlicues, as if she'd put them there tongue in cheek.

He saw his mother glance at his face, then turn delicately and go.

35

He opened the envelope. Just a piece of blank paper. The check pinned to it.

He did not want to look at it or touch it.

I'm not going back there. So, how could I use it?

He finished dressing, putting the check in his shirt pocket, buttoning the flap.

Agnes was lifting the egg from the pan. Nick sat, elbow on table, waiting.

Tom half smiled at himself. My hands moving that way. Like I was shaping up clay, remolding. Nick—always want to rub out those three wrinkles engraved between his eyes.

Agnes put the plate down in front of him.

Never want to change her face. Her features nondescript, all in her eyes. You can't remodel fire.

They were waiting. He ate quickly.

"Okay. Let's get started."

They did not stop for Mr. Krimmer this time, but drove straight through the crossroad and out to the island.

It looked as it had yesterday—only better. A pleasant, unbelievable place.

Agnes walked around outside, as Tom, his eyes sharpened by the work he did, looked it over with care, peering, lifting, trying out, taking soundings, to be convinced finally of the house's honesty.

He and Nick circled it again. Their talk was of how the wall should be fixed, and the roof. Their voices were subdued.

They drove back to McRae. In the town, Nick drove down the business block and parked the car outside the one-story English manor type frame building that was Krimmer's office. He did not go in, though.

They sat, their breathing so tight and shallow it could scarcely be heard in the car. Occasionally, they stole a glance at one another. After awhile, Nick half turned in the front seat and looked back at Agnes. There was a deep importance, almost ceremonial, in his manner. But the words that accompanied the ceremony were only, "Well, Mother, what do you think?"

Agnes did not speak at once, as if recollecting the past, constructing the future. She looked at Tom and Nick, her dark eyes leaping up. They would not have to move again, ever. Then as if she knew the importance of the words she would utter next, she dropped her

36

eyes and said, steady and quiet, "If the rest of you want it, I want it."

Nick waited quite awhile before he turned slowly to Tom. "It'll mean using all ours, and your allotment money we saved for you. I want you to consider that." He did not go on at first. Then, like the next words of a clan rite, he said, serious and intent, "What do you say, Tom?"

Tom touched his shirt pocket and felt the paper folded there. So the money came from Margot. But if they could get set! It might free him. And he'd pay her back. He said positively, "I say yes!"

Nick let go a little shuddering sigh. "Okay."

And now the breathing was free, their faces lit by beginnings of smiles.

They went into the real estate office. Mr. Krimmer was behind his desk dictating to a middle-aged stenographer in rimless glasses. He rose, smiling affably.

"Well, well! Have you been out there this morning?"

"Yes."

"Have you decided?"

Nick Dorn felt many nameless things gathered for a long time rise up in a great wave. If you had a place of your own, what could touch you? "I'll take it!" he said.

6

ABEL WALKED BRISKLY TOWARD the Mansion House. The suburban train for the city would not leave for twenty minutes. He'd have time to tell Rena. Besides, it would be pleasant, announcing his good news.

Theirs was an old relationship. Like a garment worn for years, not cut quite right originally, it had been molded to an approximate fit. The garment had been put away for a long time, when Rena married and divorced, when his wife was still living. Now it had been taken out of the cupboard again.

Abel greeted the elderly operator at the elevator. "Good morning, Grover." He waited for him to fold his newspaper and place it on the chair. The man had at various times been involved in small businesses in the town, which always went broke, and here he was, reading yesterday's financial page and taking passengers for a slow ride in the creaky elevator.

Grover said, "Dow Jones up yesterday."

Abel nodded, "Yes." How sick and tired Grover must be, riding up and down, going nowhere.

At the top floor, as Abel got out, he managed very smoothly to slip the folded dollar into his hand. "Buy yourself a good cigar!"

Rena was waiting. She was small and rounded and forty-five. Her blue robe set off her dark red hair. He kissed her because she expected it. For himself he didn't go in much for kissing, unless it was going to add up to something and pretty quick.

His mind was on what was ahead in the city.

"The patent came yesterday!' His exuberance spurted upward.

The patent was on a compound for de-waxing oil wells. The idea had come to him long ago, when he'd been working around the Selport Gas field, not too long after he'd had chemistry in college. But in the atmosphere of the Selport boom, anything that promised less than a million seemed piddling. It wasn't until last year, scratching around to get secure on the island, he'd thought of trying to patent and make some money on it.

"That's wonderful, Glen," she caught his exuberance, "wonderful! You know, sometimes seems to me like maybe you'd be—I don't mean *better* off—but, well, *happier,* if you'd just stuck to making things, inventing them!"

"I know what I'm doing!" He moved impatiently toward the window, staring down into the street.

The way she talked was the way his father had talked too, the beauty of pure science, stuff like that. His father had been a technical man, or to put it plainly—one who got his brains picked. But his father never knew what the score was. Any more than Rena.

Like when I first came out here and used to come into the Mansion House billiard room after dinner, all the town's big men there then. How she kept needling me afterward, "Why don't you go any more? You need some relaxation." She didn't seem to understand when I'd tell her, "I'm not a good enough shot. What's the use of playing if you can't win?"

"I'm so glad for you about the patent, Glen," she said. "Is that why you're going into the city?"

"Yes. I'm going to sell it. To Weedon, of Weedon Company. He knows a good thing. I phoned him yesterday. Got the appointment right off!"

"Well, he remembered you from when you worked there—"

"He remembered I left there to start my own business! Put myself on the same footing. Glad I called ahead. It's more dignified. I think I'll ask ten thousand. Get five, anyhow. And then, and then," he rubbed his hands briskly, "I'll start rolling. With that I can carry out my plans for the island. All I need's a few breaks. A few? Just one. I'll sell the patent, then with that money, start the chain reaction! Lease all the old wells out there and recondition them like I did mine. Tell Clarence Seavey to go blow. I'll get the oil out by truck if I have to. Maybe form my own purchasing company—"

She nodded, realizing he was going over these things she knew to build up his own confidence.

"I'm more down to earth now," he went on. "I know I'm not going to be a millionaire."

"It's good you've changed that way, Glen."

"I just want what everyone wants. I don't want to be king of England."

And later, she watched him from her window go down the street. "A big courage to stay in there fighting. Never to admit he was ever knocked down."

The train sped swiftly under buoyant spring clouds.

Abel leaned away from the green plush seat, eagerly, rehearsing, "Look here, Mr. Weedon." No. "Look here, Weedon."

The snick of the conductor's punch advanced and Abel extended his ticket cheerfully.

An easy life a man like that has, Abel thought. But no adventure in it. No enterprise.

Now the train ground through a tundra of razed houses, slowing as the tracks fanned into a freight yard and then, inexplicably, pulled off on a siding and stopped.

Now what's the matter?

Abel looked at his watch. My appointment's eleven thirty. Weedon will wait. Won't he?

The conductor passed through, his face blank as a doctor who has no idea what is the matter but looks wise.

Abel glanced at the hands of his watch. Ten minutes. His collar began to feel tight. The inert coach seemed stuffy now.

What if Weedon doesn't wait? He has a big business, lots to do. I should have gone over last night. But the expense.

The train stood obstinately immovable. It's all out of my control. Dawdle here forever and I can't do anything about it. Why I like the island. Small, but I'm in control.

A switch engine on a nearby track pushed forward, shunted back. That engineer must get sick and tired of. Funny, an expression like that. Say the words without thinking, but underneath, they mean just that—sick and tired. A lot of heart and effort can be wasted, a fine head of steam get no place.

Let stuff like that come in front of your mind when you're trying to push forward, only makes you more tired, sicker. And anyhow, I'm on the right track now.

The train lurched, started slowly and picked up speed.

In the hall of the office building where Weedon Company had a floor, he paused and sniffed.

That odor of brass polish. I remember it when I used to report in years ago, from trips in the field.

He went into the anteroom.

I can hardly believe it's that same thin receptionist. Her hair mottled gray now under the net. She was here when I first came. What was I—about thirty-eight? Confident I'd be made vice president.

The receptionist rang Weedon's office and announced Abel.

My hands feel cold. Ask seven thousand for the patent. Get five anyway.

A beautiful young girl came out of Weedon's office. Her plum-colored silk dress was cut low in a heart shape in front. Her ankles, slim as a young colt's, woggled on two high heels.

"He said tell you he'd see you in a minute." Her air was half-smiling as if she were at a party. When she returned to Weedon's office, she closed the door.

The receptionist, manipulating switchboard plugs, was saying, "Why—Mrs. Weedon!" The note of dismay was quickly suppressed. "Thought you'd be halfway to California by this time. Grounded? Uh—he's busy on another line. Oh—wait. Hold on. Maybe I can get to him."

Her hands moved swiftly. "Mr. Weedon?" Emergency was in her low tone. "Mrs. Weedon's plane didn't take off. She's coming in to pick up the car keys." She listened, frowning, then lifted the other

40

key. "Mrs. Weedon, Mr. Weedon says just stay there. He'll drive out for you."

For a moment, forearms on the switchboard, she sat, as if deeply weary. Then she turned to Abel.

"He can't see you today. Asked if you'd mind coming in tomorrow instead? An emergency."

Must be getting old. Time was when I'd have laughed at Weedon's leching. Now I just feel irritated. So much at stake. So vital. Shrug pleasantly, act unworried, because everything becomes known to Weedon.

The young girl came out. "Say," she held an open appointment book toward the middle-aged woman, "what's these exes mean? Okay to give him an appointment then?"

"No," the receptionist was short and sour.

"Well, I can't be expected to know everything my first day!" When she approached Abel in a cloud of gardenia, he could see she wore no bra, and they stood out in little points. Her teeth, when she smiled, were small like a child's and everything seemed a joke, some game they were playing. "Same time tomorrow? Okay?"

He had started out when the receptionist asked wearily, "In case something comes up, where can he reach you?"

Not the Grimes on Fourth Avenue—cheap, barely respectable. "The Sunderland." A necessary investment. Dangerous to let Weedon think you could not afford the best.

But outside in the hall, he had a momentary shaky feeling.

A martini in the quiet oak-paneled Sunderland bar was expensive. Usually some of the courthouse crowd around. He didn't see anyone though.

Later, in the dining room with the discreet silk curtains, holding the menu with "charcoal broiled steak, four dollars," and seeing the price, he wondered if he ought not to have gone to the cafeteria down the street.

He had pared things very fine to get half the island and had been straining mightily to accumulate enough for the rest. Funds were a problem and this gave him an ashamed feeling.

But now he was glad he came. Look over there. Just paying his check. G. L. Marah. Still the number one man in the courthouse crowd, and looking it, even from the back. What if he passes me with just a blank nod, or even pretends not to see me?

Aggressively Abel ordered the steak.

41

This was a time to build yourself up. A doctor had warned him once about his blood pressure. "Cut out heavy meals." But the doctor didn't know what it was kept you in there punching. Think of the times in strange towns, after hassles with not one, but maybe three or four competitors, when a thick steak said to you, "Everything's fine, you're on the right track."

G. L. Marah was moving toward him. Abel wasn't going to act apologetic about what happened in the primaries last fall. Not his fault if Marah couldn't control the machine. They ought to have been grateful he let them use his name. It stood for something out there. Here he comes. Get ready not to see him, in case he doesn't—

"Glen Abel!" Marah's mouth opened like a purse into a cordial smile. "Long time no see. In the city on a toot alone, eh!" He went through the dutiful motion of a leer. "Say, any copper tubing around loose you could tie an order to?"

When Abel had been selling on commission for the jobbing concern, he could latch on to scarce materials occasionally. Marah was a building contractor. Maybe in the beginning, the contact was luck, but Abel had kept it oiled and running by energy and savvy. And Marah's chat ended by his saying, "Stop around at Headquarters some time. Always like to see an old friend."

Abel watched Marah's departing figure. Well! G. L. Marah does not shed sunshine when he means frost. They must plan to use me again on the ticket some time.

I never let myself admit it before, but not getting it cut me. I wanted it. Wanted to be commissioner. Part of things, the feeling of helping to run the show. Like my grandfather. I'd have made a good commissioner. I wanted it for Cynthia, too. Give her a niche, a feeling of belonging.

Grandfather. A man who understood what everything was all about. Sure, he lost everything, but that was a country-wide panic in '93. No one could blame *him* for *that*.

If he were here I could ask him—What's the clue? How did I miss? Who missed?

The steak arrived, exuding red-brown juice. Wonderful. Build yourself up. No one else will.

Good idea for someone to make a salt, colored, say red or green so the color'd show up. You could see how much you'd put on. When he felt good like this, his mind often went free wheeling around, coming up with ideas, some good, some bad, things to make. Interesting to work some of them out, just for kicks. Easy to indulge yourself, too easy, sitting around dreaming up that Rube Goldberg stuff without ever considering the important thing—what would the sales volume be?

After the avocado salad, he was full, but he passionately loved sweet things—cherry pie, cake, heavily sugared whipped cream. He ordered pastry.

Leave the waiter a real tip. They're not dumb, they know all about you, know when they're serving someone. Act successful and you are successful. After all, if I hadn't left Continental years ago, I'd probably be vice president now, assistant to vice president anyway.

The waiter stood, offering the tray. There were two eclairs, one small, mangled, its icing peeling off; the other large, its shiny brown curves glistening. Abel indicated the fat rich superior one.

As if absent-mindedly, but nevertheless with a peculiarly knowing expression, the waiter served Abel the inferior one.

Abel felt a choking rush of blood into his neck. Easy. Don't let him see you care. A foreigner. What could you expect? They did stuff like that, out of envy, because you looked as if you had everything.

The man, his face wooden, walked away with the tray and the first-class eclair. The build-up of the fourteen dollar room at the Sunderland, the martini, the steak and G. L. Marah was spoiled, just a little.

But don't let the mood slip. A good cigar. The girl in the sheer black dress behind the stand had large dark eyes. He took his time as she, indulgent, appreciative, regarded him sweetly. Then when she bent down to reach into the glass case for the ones he indicated, the sheer dress fell forward. Did she do that for every one? A girl like that, seeing hundreds of men a day, could pick the winners.

He bought two fifty-cent cigars. With a *Wall Street Journal,* he settled himself near enough to enjoy her. Rolling the oily greenish leathery Corona in his fingers, he inhaled its first fragrance. She bent over the case again, rearranging. He liked them like hers, perky, small.

Just looking, thank you. One thing with Rena, he'd always been straight.

He sat relaxed in the fat embrace of the leather chair. The smoke from his cigar joined the other smoke in the lobby.

A young woman in a red chiffon strapless gown, obviously party bound, stopped near him, as her escort went off to telephone. Around her hung the aroma of expensive brandy, and she cased the lobby with a scornful glance. He recognized her, an acquaintance of Cynthia's from that fool drama school. He didn't cotton to the way they acted. Too free with themselves. Time they got on, had a few disappointments, there was maybe some excuse. The escort waved now to Cynthia's friend and she moved off. Arrogant.

If only Cynthia had not gotten mixed up with people like that, it might never have happened. He could still see the smudged telegram—Harry and I married. That choking again. He'd only met him once before he went off to the Pacific. Perhaps he would not have felt so if it had been a man. But a boy, a silly boy.

Well, she was back home now. Where she belonged. Where—if he could make all secure on the island—she'd stay. What if she did talk occasionally about going back to the city, being a radio actress or some damfool thing like that? Mixed up with cheap phonies. Pansies, or men thinking of only one thing. She talked about it when she guessed he was low on funds. He never mentioned that of course—never let any woman know you don't have money. And if she'd just have patience, faith, he'd work it out.

Maybe up until the time I went out to the island, I was trying to build on turf you could roll up—like when the roofing company had that sales meeting, and put up a sample house and lawn right in the convention hall. When they took down the house, the workmen just rolled up the sod and took it away. A phony dream castle.

Well, I have a real one now. He smiled. Down to my last castle.

He leaned back, exhaling a few slow smoke rings. That day Cynthia came home. He could remember how he felt, standing on the portico. Mine as far as the eye can see. Inside, fire gleamed on mahogany, and Cynthia on a ladder hanging a Christmas wreath, in that fitted red wool robe, like a princess. That's when the pieces all fell into place.

He knocked the ashes off the cigar carefully. First you had to dream up the dream, then, make it happen. First off, sell Weedon tomorrow. Ask ten thousand. Then, recondition the wells, and—

Dream up the dream. To begin with, Cynthia would divorce that boy. Of course she felt sorry for him, but it was the only thing to do. Sometime—in the distant future—she might marry again. By that time, I'll own the other house there on the island. It's a tight little house, probably more livable than the bigger one. There might be grandchildren. He could see them in a wading pool, and Cynthia in a white dress, in a big fan-shaped chair, a thoroughbred dog—a collie —no, a Dalmatian—beside her under the trees. He'd come strolling by with his morning cigar, seeing all was in order. Have a caretaker and perhaps a woman to iron shirts and cook. Just as a hobby, have a laboratory in the old carriage house. Perhaps even, as a side line, form the Glen Abel Products Corporation. The house would all be in good repair, of course, brass polished, white paint gleaming. Put in a decent bathroom. Nothing made a man feel more certain of himself, able to tell himself every morning that he'd made it, than a fine bathroom, a chrome and glass stall shower.

Maybe go out for county commissioner again. He could see Marah's cordial smile. Have dirt roads in, the wells around producing. Like his grandfather, the earth would be working with him.

A colored boy in a white jacket? No, nothing la-de-da. Just decent comfort and the feeling your feet were planted on solid earth. One small firm place.

Tomorrow morning. The chain reaction.

7

THE RAIN PELTED DOWN, stopped, then showered intermittently the day the Dorns moved. The men had to put musty canvas covers on the furniture, carrying it to the van.

With the down payment safe, Krimmer had seen no reason why they should not move in at once. He had friends in useful places and had been able to arrange an early settlement date, and even though it was still two weeks off, he encouraged them to move in right away.

And since the Dorns must vacate the flat by the fifteenth, it seemed best to move now, ahead of the May first rush, when trucks of furniture rolled from one house to another as though the inhabitants were playing a game of musical chairs.

Their moving did not come hard. There was no one, especially, to tell good-bye. The people in the flat above had come only a few months before. Dorns had never seen them, only heard them moving about. One time, a man off their same hall had died and his body had been carried away and they had known nothing of it.

To Agnes, the process of moving had come to seem as familiar as

45

her frequent attacks of vertigo, "and I always get over them, too," she laughed.

To Tom, moving had become, during the fifth of his life spent in barracks, Quonsets, tents and hospitals, a wadding together of the few belongings, a ramming into the canvas bag, a shrugged "Let's go."

Nevertheless the day brought its peculiar exhaustion, not so much from the packing as from the confused strain of seeing a stranger walking out of a room carrying some familiar article, perhaps a chair on which one was accustomed to rest.

Agnes, watching the furniture hoisted and hauled, thought that it had been maneuvered around so many strange newel posts, it had taken on an abraded, characterless look.

Finally, even the laden packing boxes from Nick's old family home, stored over years in locker rooms of apartment and flat buildings, were on the van.

When the last piece was carried in at the island, it was dark, and cold hamburgers out of a bag made dinner for the Dorns.

As soon as the beds were up, they fell upon them, drugged.

Nick woke next morning to the smell of coffee. He roused, thinking it must be time to get up and go to the office.

Then he opened his eyes. Here was Agnes in the familiar bed beside him—but the room. Where were they?

At his stirring, Agnes roused automatically, thinking she must get his breakfast so he would not be late.

Then she realized. "We're actually moved in! The room's so big. Nicest we ever had."

"The way the sunlight flickers over the ceiling like that!" Nick said.

"It's from the water," she said.

It was probably that flickering light gave him this feeling of— now here—now gone, Nick thought as he dressed.

He put on a clean shirt, his shiny but neat brown suit and the black shoes with the scuffs well polished. At the mirror, forcing the narrow dark tie under the stiff collar, he stopped. "Why do I?"

"You don't need to," Agnes said.

"Habit, I guess. Like that butcher in the store on Bedell Street always wore that straw hat, winter and summer. And my brother Joe, years after he was out of the Navy, still wore his pea jacket." He half-smiled, knotting the tie securely. "My clerk's uniform."

From downstairs, Tom called, "Lazies! I made coffee! I'm off to

McRae. Want to see that Seavey about getting started on the well!"

They heard the car race up the lane.

Agnes put the final pin in her hair. "His energy's been held back so long."

Nick nodded. "It's loose now."

Even after they had coffee, Nick still felt he was moving in a recurring dream.

He crossed the kitchen and looked at the old oak veneer dresser they'd bought that time from Sears Roebuck. He touched the box of tools, its wood grayed with age, that had belonged to his father. They would not be in a dream.

"Nick, these cartons." Agnes pointed. "Lift them here."

Soon, knee-deep in emptied cartons and crumpled newspaper, she was stowing away pots and pans and dishes. "Strange," she said, "for quite awhile the kitchens always seem to belong to the woman who lived here before."

She put away the one-pound box of sugar, the two-pound bag of flour. "In a flat," she said, "you never have space enough to store large quantities."

Nick felt useless. He went outside.

After the rain a shimmering haze blurred the trees to unreality. The island, close circled by the vaporous river as by a sorcerer's ring, trembled in the golden light. It's like—what's that word?—a mirage.

Walking down the wet grass of the slight decline to the river, he quite unconsciously, with a circular motion, ground his foot into the damp spring soil.

He stood looking at the sky, the water. But after a while just standing, doing nothing, he felt guilty.

Didn't come to loaf. Ought to be getting busy.

When he returned to the house he could hear Agnes moving about upstairs, making the beds. He went into the main room, and, kneeling, unpacked with care the boxes of *Popular Mechanics* and *The Beekeepers' Journal*, long hoarded against this "some day."

That book I clipped the coupon for that time, *How to Be Independent Raising Belgian Hares*. He put it on top of a neat stack. Here's those text books, dark blue, gold letters. *Steam Engines*. And this one, *Principles of Electricity*. If I could have kept on at Tech Night School that time. Evening classes ten, twelve years to have a degree though. Fees and books expensive.

Now the books were all in neat piles on the floor. He looked around at the bare walls. Too bad, no book shelves in this house.

47

Not working makes me feel guilty. Guess I'm too used every morning to be going. Must get busy on a way to make some income. It can be small. But steady. He smiled. Independent income.

Bees. Yes. All those locust trees. An early bloom. Wonderful. Make a fine honey crop.

I'll need hives. Have to build wooden stands for them, like those pictures in the *Journal*. I ought to have a workshop.

He went out again to see.

The plain rectangular house stood on a slight slope, its basement only partly excavated. Under the porch, the basement was seven or eight feet high. He went in. It was dark. There were no windows in the foundation.

He went to the kitchen, rummaging in unpacked boxes for a flashlight. Finding it, he returned to the basement.

The flashlight picked up a long slanting crack. It rose out of the earth, crossing the stone of the foundation.

A shame. A shame. Ought to be fixed. They ought not to let that go neglected.

Then he felt something almost like a shock. The contact he had been trying to make with his feet had been made. They?

I'm They. *I* can do it. I have a *right* to do it.

He felt limp so that he wanted to sit down, not from weakness, more as if he could feel draining away a kinked-up tightness from years of the impossibility of doing anything about anything. I don't have to wait, feeling sore, helpless, for some landlord to come. I have a *right* to do it.

He moved briskly up the porch steps to the kitchen. Agnes was still upstairs.

He slid back the dusty lid from his father's tool box.

He found a trowel, and a steel measuring tape and went back to the basement.

He stood looking. Study it. Decide what I need. Probably cement. What else? Have to go into town. Get the stuff to fix the roof too.

With a fearful joy he put his hand in the crack and felt along it, figuring.

While Agnes was making the beds she heard Nick come in, but by the time she came down, he'd gone out again.

In the dining room, as she placed Aunt Flo's sherbet glasses in the wall cupboard, she was wondering where to put the piece of sculpture Tom had made that time. It was so big and heavy, two or three feet high, of rough red stone. As near as she could tell, it was a peep breaking out of its shell. Embryo—something like that—he called it.

Tom had such a craze for sculpturing that time. He'd forgotten it now, never even mentioned it. But she valued the piece as she would have his first scrawl in school, or a football he had played with.

Moving about, she began, in her mind, to visualize how to lengthen or shorten the curtains this time.

Then she smiled at herself. Why, I could think of buying curtains to suit these windows! Of course, the legal settlement isn't made, but it's not that. It's the times we moved gives me this half-feeling we're stowaways who'll be discovered.

What she was longing to do was to go outside and stand a little way off.

And anyway she ought to see if there were possibilities for a vegetable garden, or a chicken run.

Her shoes, made for city sidewalks which carefully insulated human feet from the voltage of bare earth, were not suitable here. An old pair of Tom's moccasins, with two pair of heavy socks to keep them on, would do. And the too-large shoes gave her a carefree hobo feeling, as she went out into the gossamer day.

The mist, running off, trailing mystic draperies, might be the daemon of the place retreating to a hollow to watch her.

The experience now was new. She had moved into cupboards and rooms, but never taken up abode on land. There was the possibility you might come to know each hazel bush or maple tree as well as, in the city, you did that woman you passed every day going to the grocery store, and to whom, like the tree, you never spoke.

As she crossed the narrow neck of land which tied what was called the island to the mainland, something moved in the sun-dappled water. A crayfish!

From the down slope on the first hillock, she saw the two oil derricks rising above locust trees in bloom. The creamy honey odor of locust and white clover lifted her spirits. Nick was sure he could make a small income with bees. She could hear them humming in the blossoms. He could do it. She always believed the day would come.

In the meadow, she passed a sink hole, ten or fifteen feet wide, half-filled with water.

A worm fence zigzagged casually along the edge of the property. Beyond it, a path had been worn, and startled, she saw a line of men approaching on it, single file. The caps with lamps, the steady purposeful walk, told her this must be the daily route of these miners from some nearby pit. Against the white May, their sooted faces stood out strangely.

Returning a different way, she came suddenly upon a little cemetery. The gravestones of Abels and Purcells blended mossily into the surrounding spring. Bordering them, like a circle of young dancers enchanted for a moment into motionlessness, dogwood trees bloomed.

Tired now, she sat down to rest. Bees worked in white clover growing over a grave. Contentment filled her. She thought how in the city, you rarely saw a cemetery, and people had no idea where they would be buried. Most of them, coming from other towns or cities, or countries even, never, or rarely, saw the graves of their parents or great-uncles. You never felt you belonged on the earth enough to actually claim burial space in it. But here! You could see what had gone before, and what was to come for you.

The buzz of bees was like sunlight you could hear. The sound shimmered with the serenity of an ancient summer sea.

The gravestones had taken on the stance of human aging, humping over, or slouching sidewise. One stone tilted upward, facing the drifting dogwood bloom which each year had come faithfully, and would come. She read on the pitted stone:

ALICIA ABEL BELOVED WIFE
The Only Sinner Is
He Who Hopes
Not.

Walking back then, a bunch of clover in her hand, and hearing the cardinals calling, she began, after a silence of years, to sing, a song remembered from childhood.

Rounding the river shore, she saw the chimney, the tranquil roof that was—theirs! The house seemed solid looking now. She thought how Krimmer told them the house had been built not for mere shelter, or gain, or to show off that it was bigger than its neighbor, but by a father, for his daughter. For love.

All the haziness of the morning had cleared away when Tom, with eager eyes, returned from McRae, bringing a steak for lunch.

"That Seavey!" His voice was exultant. "He's my boy! He's as much in a hurry to get started as we are!"

Agnes had not yet found the table linen, but the steak was thick and garlic-rubbed, and they were hungry. Nevertheless, before lifting the first bite, they three sat a moment, quieted by good fortune. They looked in silence at the river rippling below, at the clover in the water tumbler.

Before the meal was over though, talk came welling out of Nick about the repair job. Afterward, all three went to the front porch and down the steps on one side, to look at the basement.

"I counted on it for a workshop, but it's too dark," Nick said.

"Yeah, it is. But where else?"

"Funny, there's not a shed or garage or anything."

"Guess they had the use of the outbuildings of the other house at first."

"If I get working with bees, I'll need a workshop."

"Yeah. With light."

"Yeah."

The three stood looking.

"You could," Tom said, "punch openings in the side walls, and make windows."

"Punch openings?" Nick came face to face with a strange exciting notion. He stared at the stone wall. "Yeah!" he said breathlessly. "Why not? *It's our place!*"

"Yes!" Agnes said.

Tom was squinting at the wall. "You might start right there." He was pointing. "See?"

Moving briskly about now, they laughed over small things. All afternoon, Tom and Nick measured, drew plans and discarded them, arguing, so that by dusk, Nick was reaching into the tool box, ready to knock out the first stone.

Nick, who had never had a suit or a dwelling made to fit him, began to make a window in a stone wall—because he wanted it that way.

8

ON THE SECOND DAY AFTER Abel had gone to the city, Weedon did not keep his appointment either.

"Called away. Important meeting."

Probably off for the day shut up in some hotel room with Miss Purple Plum, the wife safely gone.

Careful not to let any concern at spending another fourteen dollars a day show. Weedon seemed to pay no attention, but they used to say if someone used an extra sheet of toilet paper, he knew it. "Moved to a cheaper hotel, eh?" Then the surmising Abel hadn't funds to get legal, the thought of snatching, of infringements.

When Abel went out into the hall, he had this flat, graveled feeling. Not only the resentment at wasted time, expense. More a feeling of being diminished. Of something important diminished.

They had installed new electric elevators in this building now. You got in and pressed the button, and then it was all out of your control. Nothing you could do. Closed in. Boxed. He hated the feeling.

But what if Weedon really meant to get rid of him? As if he were nothing, nobody—?

At first, as the elevator sank down, he felt just hollow. Then came that choking and a dizziness. Then a sudden blinding headache.

When he came to, he was sitting on the floor of the elevator, the door open. Must have blacked out. He sat there, dazed, scared. No one had seen him, thank goodness. He scrambled up, swaying a little. A shot of bourbon. Where? No place nearby. Here, in the building, a drug store.

At the counter, the sickly sweet odor of chocolate syrup nauseated him. "Can I get you something?" The clerk stared frightened. Abel could not speak. The clerk put a glass of water in front of him. "You okay?"

Abel nodded.

"There's a doctor there," the clerk nodded toward the prescription counter. "You want him?" Before Abel could deny it, he called, "Hey, Doc!"

A serious young man in rumpled seersucker came over, looking at Abel intently, unsmiling. "My office is here on the ground floor. Think you'd better come with me."

Abel knew, absolutely knew, he was all right. Still it was horrible, being treated in a drug store. A lack of dignity in it. And what if he'd blanked out in the street? Like one of those unknowns who dropped and were carted off to hospital or morgue, no one knowing or caring who they were. Fight all the time. I am something. Somebody. I am important.

The doctor's office seemed cool and shaded, and by the time the doctor unwound the blood pressure tourniquet, Abel felt absolutely okay.

"I'll give you a prescription." But he was taking a long time. He glanced up at Abel with troubled eyes. "No heavy meals, cut down on liquor and beef and too much salt. Take it easy." He seemed unwilling to hand him the prescription, to let him go. "Friend of mine died couple of months ago. Blood pressure. I used to say to him, it's all right to get fighting mad occasionally, but go on a diet, say one fight a day. Trouble was," he made doodles on his blotter, "he wasn't just fighting the world, but something inside himself, too." He cast a quick look at Abel.

"You want to give me the prescription?" Abel said.

He held it out, but did not let go. "And I'll tell you a better one. Don't think of your bad times. Think of the high spots. If you start getting mad, why think of the happy days. You know, the time you made the touchdown for dear old Eyewash, or the day the girl said yes—"

Out in the street Abel felt perfectly normal. That's how they were nowadays. You went in for some headache pills, and they began preaching at you. As if it were your own fault.

9

CYNTHIA, IN THE LATE AFTERNOON, would take a beach towel and go off on the west slope above the river to sunbathe.

She spread her towel on the grassy shoulder of the hill.

On Tuesdays and Fridays, she did not come here. The production man Abel had hired away from Seavey came through then to pump the well, and he was quite often drunk. On other days, though, she was alone, she was never afraid. Her years in New York—in and out of agencies, like as not with a casting couch in the inner sanctum if one were admitted—the years touring—taught her how to take care of herself. Except with a drunk. Couldn't tell what they'd do.

The sun on bare shoulders and legs warmed her to languor. In April she'd worn slacks and jersey. Now May had come, she could wear shorts and halter. She stretched out among wild strawberry and clover. Even reaching her toes to the end of the towel was easeful and sensuous.

Then, one arm up to shade her eyes, she squinted against the light into the charcoal black branches of a locust tree, a-burst with heavy hanging white blooms. Bees paid court, circling, disappearing into the flowerets. A light wind loosened the honey-laden odor, showering on her bare skin one or two blossoms. She picked one up, holding it in a delicate tanned hand. The curved pad of bloom enclosed, but not too secretly, the generating pistil. Every year then, more flowers. It was the same in the spring with humans, but instead of flowers, another generation of sons of bitches.

The grass under her body was warm now. Funny, how going there last month to Charlesville where Harry was, had driven all that feeling from her, as if she'd been sterilized inside with lye. Now, the scent and the sun and the wild business of May made her restless. And that was no use. It was no use.

The pale gold sky, the flash of a cardinal, the moving river sparkle were like players acting out a pantomime—but it was left to her to watch or not. She closed her eyes against them.

Why had she come home again anyway? Hadn't she hoped some-how everything would be changed? After all those hours hanging about in the wings and at rehearsals, as understudy for *The Tempest*, the lines of the play sometimes spun out of her without volition:

> Had I plantation of this isle, my lord,
> And were the king on't, what would I do?

She rolled toward the sun as shade reached the towel.

The way she felt cut off was what, when she first came, she thought she wanted. The only person she knew was young Leland, son of the local hardware dealer. He had gone from here, astonishing freak, to Art School, where she'd known him. Now they passed each other in the streets of McRae morosely. Prisoners who had escaped, been captured and brought back.

That wasn't really true of her. She'd come impelled by some vague wild longing. And Abel's letter, telling about the island, had arrived at that peculiar moment. If she hadn't just returned from the tour with the number two company. She thought she'd come just for Christmas.

But at first sight of the secure, shut-off island, defended from the world by the frozen river, sad, unnamed urges filled her. She'd walk about the house, touching furniture remembered from childhood, wander about the island.

She turned now to get sun on her back, propping on elbows, and looked down toward the other house on the island, foursquare on the river, speculating about the family that had moved in, and the son.

She'd seen from a distance the moving van, heard the hammering and shouting, recognized the family that she'd seen one morning at the crossroad.

Half-drowsing, she dropped her head on outstretched arms.

If only this island were like the one in *The Tempest*, magic, and she lived here with Prospero until some beneficent shipwreck. Then by a wand stroke all her past life—her marriage to Harry, the affairs in New York—would be made to vanish into thin air.

She turned over, blinking at the light. No wand had erased any-thing. She was still a tablet scribbled over with half-finished letters.

Some uneasiness roused her. She sat up. What would Abel say of their coming? Might be a good thing, perhaps, for now he could not go into debt for the rest of the island. They would not be isolated here so much, either. Healthier. He might, just at first, not like it.

She drew out full length again. This time in her half-waking fantasy, Prospero, rather than allow the cast-up mariners so much as footroom, caused the whole island to sink beneath the waves of a treacherous sea.

She heard splashing above the steady ripple of the river flow. She saw him, then, at a distance, the son of the new family. He had appeared around the bend of the stream, tugging at a boulder. Awkwardly. Using a knee, his leg, dislodging, getting it up, lugging it off.

He would disappear, then return for another. Engrossed in his activity, he was working his way closer to her, clawing, lifting, carrying, with fierce concentration. Why would anyone, how could anyone, care enough about something to be that intense about it? She watched him, wondering, a little repelled.

He was close to her hillock now, and after a time, he sat down on a boulder, smoking a cigarette. She wanted him to look up, give some sign he saw her.

Instead, he began a strange series of actions, so intently she could tell he was not aware of the blossoming trees. Holding his left arm extended, taut, he bent one finger, then another. He put his wrist watch on a flat rock and picked up a pebble, tossing it from right to left, catching it in two fingers. She realized he must be carrying on some discipline. Something remedial.

Torturing himself. Letting life go by. And if he got himself fixed up, didn't he realize he'd only be snatched back into it some way? She stood, wanting to remind him of that.

He saw her. He stopped, as if impatient at interruption.

How sad life was! People shut themselves off from one another. Perhaps he already had a woman, was married. She hadn't seen any girl around the other house though. She started down toward him.

He saw her coming. She felt not hurt, but astonished, when he moved off abruptly around the river shore toward his own house.

All night long then, alone in the Abel house, in the room where her great-grandmother Alicia Abel had perhaps conceived and borne a son, Cynthia had had disturbed, erotic dreams. She woke, crying out the name of a boy, the first she'd gone with. A conventional blond boy, whose face she'd almost forgotten. Wider awake, the incident that flashed into her mind was that boy inventing an excuse as to her whereabouts to save her from some punishment of her mother's.

Next morning she discovered, with the Abel mail, letters intended for the newcomers, who had as yet no box.

She could go up and leave them at their door.

Or—she might see him that afternoon along the river and hand them to him. But that was so obvious.

Well, what of it?

At first she thought one letter was hers. The return name on it was Eric Taggart, a boy she'd known in Drama School. Then she saw it had been forwarded and was addressed to Tom Dorn. How did he happen to know Eric?

The other Dorn letter was for Nicholas Dorn, bearing the imprint of The Workmen's Sick and Death Benefit Society. A letter for Abel too, from that brokerage firm, The Astoria Company, a familiar name. Their monthly forecast.

She'd seen similar envelopes with that firm's name on them, ever since she could remember. On the hall table in the house on Renard Street. In the mail box on the porch of the house in Edgemoor. As a child, she thought it was an astrology horoscope her father received, to help him manage the affairs that seemed to cause the sharp sudden quarrels, the long black hostile silences between him and her mother.

Tom Dorn now, he probably had seen on hall tables in his childhood this envelope from the Sick and Death Benefit Society. How different their lives must have been in all the complicated details. Yet, in a way, the envelopes stood for the same thing—their fathers trying to build a dike against the waters of incertitude.

Tom did not come to the secluded place that afternoon. Following the bend of the river toward the Dorns', she discovered him on a flat sunny rock. He was exercising his hand. He stopped when he saw her and half turned away.

She knew men liked to look at her, that she was physically attractive. How else had she been able to get any parts, even small ones? She knew she was not a good actress. His face did not move. He seemed to be wearing a mask which meant "I do not see you."

She held out the letters as she approached, as though he and she were members of strange tribes in a wilderness, and she could communicate only by a sign her desire to be friends.

He took the letters with an abrupt motion. As if the friendly symbol had been knocked from her hand, she stood, disconcerted. He stuffed the letters in his pocket, looking uncomfortable. "Thank you. Sorry you were put to the bother."

"It was no bother."

He glanced away.

"I see you know Eric," she said.

"Well enough that he probably wants to borrow some money." The mask was firmly in place.

Then, as if he wanted to have it out right now so there could be no misunderstanding. "I think he knows your husband."

Ah, so that's it. No fooling around with a buddy's wife. A boy scout.

Tears trembled up though, at the rebuff. He glanced at her, a fleeting look, but she saw through the eye holes in the mask, something harried and balked.

"I only wanted to tell you about the swimming," she began gently, and pointed beyond the neck where the river had gouged out a deeper bed. "There's a place there."

"Thanks." His voice sounded sad.

And as she looked at him, all she could think was, if only—What if she were just a girl who had lived here all her life, never gone to New York or been married. Nothing. And Tom Dorn had moved in. And it was spring, and she felt the way she did.

But she said in a voice she hated, sophisticated and slurred, "Why don't you drop up sometime for a drink, and bring me up to date on Eric." And she moved away then, fast, not wanting him to see that it mattered so much.

Tom stood looking after her. No more brangles.

But she was made so slender and so neat, and as she stood there, it had been as if she were about sixteen and had never seen a man before, and he was excited. He'd never thought of Margot since he left there. She and everything about her were done with. And he did not want to get in any more brangles. Not with some dame whose husband was in psycho.

Standing there, watching her disappear up the hill and through the trees, he wished he didn't have so much to do and so little time, wished Nick and Agnes were settled, wished he were out in the main channel. And the great wave of impatience set him again to exercising his hand viciously. He was never bitter about his hand. The only thing he was bitter about was the five years. The time!

58

10

ALL DAY ABEL WENT ABOUT the city in the ritual of seeing people to say hello. It might seem futile, but if there was one institution he supported it was contacts. Returning toward dinner time, he took a short cut along an alley in back of the hotel.

From fly-specked lunchrooms, the odor of rancid fat and old ketchup assaulted him, then the woolly steam from the ventilator of the Wile-U-Wate Dry Cleaners.

Inside, in a booth, Abel glimpsed a customer and gave an involuntary start. Stooping shoulders in old-fashioned striped green shirt, bald spot in fringe of white hair, long turkey neck. Professor Garfield. Abel found himself standing still.

Steam hissed, the presser raised the board and took over to the booth the pants of Elihu Garfield, Ph.D.

All his brains, all his science, and what good's it done him?

Abel walked away rapidly.

Who am I mad at? The professor? Myself? Rena? She's the one said, "Maybe you'd been happier, inventing stuff, making things." Like that old coot, eh? Waiting for his one and only.

He escaped through five o'clock crowds.

Why should seeing him roil me? Ought to be feeling lucky I had sense enough to wise up early.

That summer between sophomore and junior year. As early as that. Had all those courses in physics and chemistry. Good in them too. Else Father couldn't have gotten me the summer job in the metallurgical lab. Paid my expenses next year at school.

Peculiar odor in the lab—coal tar, sulphur, always liked it.

That day the works manager walked in. After him—J. B. Conovan. You knew he was head of the steel company. His daughter was with him, sightseeing. And a French Army officer. We were making steel for our Allies.

Beautiful girl. Conovan had so much something—dignity—not a man flicked an eye at her. I remember her serene look. My way is

59

smooth, my problems solved, it seemed to say. What I meant to do for Cynthia.

Conovan started low, worked up, then consolidated his gains by marrying the boss's daughter. But when I did the same, it didn't work out that way for me.

That lab chief—the job my father thought so big—I can see him standing, bowing to them. Father wasn't even expected to stand. Me, I could stare.

Professor Garfield was there that day for some reason. Why? Probably talking over a problem with the lab chief. For free. Actually.

Father always chuckling about Conovan, "He wouldn't know a benzine ring from a Bunsen burner," but that day, that moment, was the big wise-up.

I can see Conovan, the way he looked, raising an arm, finger extended as if he were calling, "Here, boy!" hardly glancing at the lab chief, starting to move off even as he gave the order. "Explain to Colonel Duval what I'm having done here. I can't be bothered with these technical details."

Next semester it was, I switched from physics and chemistry to business administration.

Father arguing. He never did know what the score was.

Now, Abel walking along the gritty pavement in the falling dusk, kicked an old newspaper out of his path.

And that night, in the fourteen dollar bed, sleep was a long time coming. And when it did come, he roused a few hours later, heart pounding, wakened by a nightmare. Its details had scurried underground, but lying there, eyes closed, a memory came to him. Strange, how vivid.

Winter. Yes, for his mother carried a muff, and on her dark brown pompadour, a fur toque. She was putting on Glen's coat and leggings. Odd how every glint of his father's hair, as he sat huddled, head on hand, seemed so clear. Glen could not remember the words, only the tone of his mother's voice. She was upbraiding his father. Money. There was no money. No money for the bills. She was taking Glen home to her mother's. And his father sat, head on hand, eyes down. Glen had learned two things then. First, that his father was no good because he had no money; and second, if you had no money, you would be deserted, and even something you loved, for his father loved him, would be taken from you.

He sat up in bed. That thick feeling. Scared him. Not do to be off-color tomorrow. He'd see Weedon sure. He must, must calm down.

Concentrate on the glittering crests of the waves, ignore the dark ground swell that kept coming, coming, ready to engulf.

He changed his position in bed. Think of Happy Days, that doctor said. If you can't think of something good, don't think.

He remembered going up and down the night streets in strange cities, hunting for a good movie, one you were sure was good, where the boy got the job and the girl. Now, walking up and down the dark streets of his mind, it seemed they were showing all the wrong films.

What would other people, trying to remember happy times, think of? Their wedding night. No, no.

But like a movie someone had started unrolling and didn't understand how to stop, the scene with Betty's father played itself out.

Her father had built out on Country Club Road, and Betty drove him out. Only a year or so after he'd graduated from Business School, he didn't even have a car of his own.

Her father wasn't angry, just objective. And her father ordered Betty, "Sit down, because I don't want any tantrums afterward."

He even offered Glen a smoke. "You know Betty's been engaged twice already."

"But Papa—"

"Now, when you came looking for a job with Wigwam Securities last summer, frankly, I wondered at a young man—I believe you told me it was your first regular job—selling oil stock."

A thick feeling of frustrated injustice came in his throat, as he thought, Wasn't it her father's getting hold of that gas field, forming a lot of small companies, selling stock, that built this pine paneled den, put the name on the office door, Wigwam Investments?

"Betty has what she inherited from her grandfather. She can do what she wants with that. But it might clear up your mind to know I don't intend to underwrite any young fireballs—"

Glen rose. That's why he'd mentioned the two broken engagements, meaning that when he knew, he'd fade. And you couldn't tell him off.

Betty, an extremely thin girl with a pretty face, certainly had seemed crazy enough about him. And he meant to make her happy. Later on, of course, after the wedding, when she cried all night, tired out and nervous from all the excitement, she said, Glen remembered other things. She'd become angry at long kisses. Later, when

61

it didn't matter, he could have spotted a lot of things might have hinted at how it would be. They had a word for it nowadays.

Yes, there was a lot of things wrong with the world today, but one thing they had—a word for everything. Frigid they called it. But it would have been easier if he'd known from the start, not have felt a boor. And always underneath, there was his feeling it was The Money. In her soul she must despise him because he had none.

Women had no power in themselves to get money. They had to find it through a man. Naturally they wanted a man who had or could get it. Mother, wife, daughter or mistress. He understood and didn't blame them.

Sleep did not come. He rose and took the fifth of bourbon from his grip and uncorked it. Then he put the cork in and put the bottle back beside the clean shirt. Tomorrow, he'd see Weedon for sure. No hangovers.

In bed, turning and twisting, he kept remembering how it had been when he blacked out in the elevator. Break it up. Happy days.

Happy days. The Day General Motors hit a Hundred Ten. How about that, eh? There was a day for you.

He remembered leaving his office, one of a row of ground glass cubicles—you were called a junior executive at Continental—to take a report into the office of the vice president in charge of sales. There was a ticker there. Standing in the empty mahogany and broadloom office, holding the tape in his hand, he read the figures—110.

Not that he was holding General Motors—he had a diversified list. But weeks ago, he'd decided at this point he would sell. He kept charts and graphs, covering a couple of years. He knew what he was doing. He had a contempt for the office boys and counter-men in the cafeteria who bought stocks as if they were betting on a horse race. Holding the tape, he had a feeling of triumph. He'd made it.

It meant not only the money. Freedom. Freedom from guilt. He'd never made excuses to his wife when the boom in the Selport Gas field broke. A lot of wise money had been in there. Sure, it had been a gamble. But—and the old feeling of frustrated fight swept over him —you had to. They blamed you if you didn't have it, and if you didn't take chances—how else?

But all her money had gone. It seemed ever since then he'd been lost in the Everglades. Losing her money had nothing to do with their unhappiness—that had happened long before. But now, she became the utterly injured. She even took sick. A nervous breakdown.

Even as he stood there, ticker tape in hand, he knew having that money didn't mean all his problems were solved. It only gave him freedom to decide.

Striving so hard to accumulate his wife's lost money, he'd put decisions off. Until he had it, he wouldn't dream of leaving. Rena knew that. And then, there was another question. Rena, after all, was not exactly the type who fitted in with the picture of a man who would be vice president. And yet, and yet, it wasn't just the usual, "His wife was cold and he met a redheaded girl." No one could know how it was. He remembered those days—how Rena left him with the feeling he'd done as much for her as she for him.

Of course, if he had Big Money, it wouldn't matter who his wife was. If you made it, enough of it, they knew you were a good man, and you could indulge yourself in other ways. People excused anything except failure.

The way it worked out though, his instincts were right in hesitating about Rena. Hadn't she walked out on him after the crash? Don't ever forget that.

He sat up in bed suddenly, as if he could reach out and click off the bad movie that kept unrolling, unrolling.

He could see himself going out that day, into the sunny early autumn street for lunch. Passing the City Club, he saw J. B. Conovan go in there, as he himself went down the block to the noisy crowded Blue Plate Room of the old Grimes. Afterward, along with many others on their lunch hour, he went to the broker's office.

There, the milling crowd was happy.

Trouble was, if he sold now, he'd be clear, but nothing over. Nothing to build on—ride on up with. Little Money. He'd still not be going into the City Club for lunch. Still not be able to do all the things he wanted to do for Cynthia. If he took the Little Money, he might let the Big Money slip. Charts and graphs were all right, but in the end—you had to take a chance.

He went back to the office without placing the order to sell.

Try to remember Happy Days.

After awhile something tranquil fell on him. A light. A late summer afternoon light.

Fanning himself with his straw sailor, coming home from the office. Must be about five-thirty, the way the light came through dry still trees, early supper smells from houses. He walked up that flight of steps from the bus stop and there she was, waiting.

63

"Daddy!" She greeted you like a little queen, but at the same time, your subject. Her hand was small and magic. What was she—five? She was perfect in all little details. How everything about her—face, dancing hair, round body, could be so perfect—but all in little. The feel of her hand, clinging with utter trust. That was the best moment, maybe the happiest moment, of all his life. Afternoon summer light.

Why was it so good? He wasn't doing too well, his job at Continental far down the chain of command. He didn't have any money. Odd, it should be that moment. But it was.

11

TOM AND NICK WORKED INTENTLY.

They had found a pile of dressed stone which, from the height of the weeds and shrubs around it, must have been acquired long ago by someone for a later abandoned project. But finding it, they became ambitious and decided to put up a small separate structure.

They had the sand and pea gravel and cement ready, but they needed more rocks to make a footing and shore up the earth on one side.

Nick swung the new plumb line they had bought as he said, "Man I struck up a conversation with in the hardware store said he blasted stones for his driveway."

"Yes?" Tom drove a stake into the ground with one final blow. "Sounds good!"

"He said farmers around use explosive to take rocks out of pastures, that we can buy it in Lelands. I might just get some." Nick laughed a little. "Makes me feel like a—not a farmer—but a real country fellow. Blasting rocks! Imagine me doing anything like that in the city."

Tom happily selected another stake. "We're getting to be professionals."

Working now from wet dawn to dusk filled with bird cries, Nick moved toward the dream, Tom like a man building a ladder out of hell. And Agnes felt as she had when Tom was a baby and Nick going to night school to learn to be an engineer.

Nick would not have believed it possible, but they were working with such absorption, the newly fixed day of settlement came upon them unaware. They had gone in the week before on the day originally arranged, only to find it had been postponed because Krimmer had been on jury duty.

Now they had barely time to drive, with Agnes in the back seat, into McRae.

In McRae, a smoke abatement program had been going on for some years, but the older buildings, like middle-aged coal miners, were still palled o'er with the hard cast of grime.

On the main street, some buildings had false fronts. Others, the Mansion House, the gloomy school, the Methodist church with the wooden cupola scalloped like a pie, were commonplace but honest.

One building, however, had an air of repose, of solid elegance, like a substantial citizen who knows his own worth. This was the bank.

Its monolithic columns of gray marble made a colonnade where customers, emerging through the bronze door, could stop, tucking away the bank book with the deposit entry in the same way worshipers coming from a cathedral might pause to dip a hand in the holy water font. And inside it was tranquil, too, the high-ceilinged chamber broken only by the swaying of the crystal chandelier, decked at Christmas with luxuriant greens, and at Thanksgiving with corn from the countryside. Even the tellers behind the cages moved discreetly, wearing their alpaca coats like chasubles as they bowed their heads over their little adding machines.

And like a chapel off a nave, the oak-paneled board room was dim and quiet. Krimmer and the others were waiting.

Mr. Smith, in charge of real estate transfers, looked askance at Tom's sockless feet thrust into dirty tennis shoes, at Nick without a coat. Both had the careless, hasty air of men who have been called away from more important things.

Krimmer was uneasy. What could be more important than a transfer of real property? There was a sort of affront in it. He was ashamed of them. It just didn't show proper respect. He didn't mean respect for him, but a wanton disrespect for—well, everything.

He pursed his lips and averted his eyes as a small chunk of mortar, loosened from Tom's dusty jeans, fell on the polished floor.

"Well," Krimmer kept his eyes thoughtfully down, trying to make the best of it, "we may as well get on."

After all, Mr. Smith could not, in any fairness, hold Krimmer responsible.

Afterward, while Tom and Nick went off with the clerk in the hardware store to get the instructions about the explosive to blast their rocks, Agnes went to another part of the store.

Just to enjoy it more, she shopped around with her eyes. She ran over the seed rack. Zinnias, four o'clocks. Annuals. They're here and they're gone.

She knew what she wanted.

There they were, twisted fine red-brown roots.

"Peonies?" the clerk asked.

"Yes."

"One dollar apiece."

She hesitated.

"These are deluxe variety."

"I'll take three," she said, thinking, It's all right. We're going to stay.

12

WEEDON SAT BEHIND A LARGE desk with a handsomely framed photograph of his wife in the center. "Oh, you're that Abel." He smiled. "Used to work here about ten years ago." He turned partly away. "Now, let's see," he was still smiling, "what did I fire you for?"

Abel could remember a time when he admired Weedon's ability to joke and at the same time knock his opponents subtly off balance.

He had to explain, "I left here to start my own concern."

But Weedon broke into any advantage gained with a vague, "Oh? And what did you say you were trying to sell?"

Abel, carefully casual, leaned back, refusing to be hurried. He had had to wait a long time to get this appointment. "As a matter of fact, I do have something to sell."

Weedon pawed for the phone. "I'll have the purchasing agent see—"

"A patent. A compound for dewaxing oil wells."

"Been a lot of those around." Weedon's smile was deprecatory. "Thing is to get one that works."

"It works. I've tried it." He'd cleaned out his own well with it last year.

Now they were, at least for the moment, on an equal basis.

Then he saw Weedon's eye travel downward, as Abel swung a foot from a crossed knee. Suddenly, Weedon raised his eyebrows and suppressed a smile.

What was it? What was the matter? His shoe? Ankle? Didn't dare look. Maybe nothing. Weedon trying to get the upper hand, somehow.

"A big operator like you, left to start your own concern, surprised you aren't manufacturing it yourself."

"I have a couple of things going. They'll keep me tied up."

"Is that a fact?" He glanced at Abel's ankle, then, tongue in cheek looked away.

What was it? Unobtrusively as possible, Abel put on his glasses. The cuff on the trouser leg was badly frayed. Why didn't I notice it before? Some little thing like that could ruin you.

"I suppose you claim the earth with a high fence around it on this patent of yours?"

"I've been allowed some good claims, broad, but safe."

"Well," he sounded impatient at Abel's dawdling, "let's see it."

Abel lifted from his brief case the copy the public stenographer at the Mansion House had made for him.

"Hmm." Weedon put on heavy black-rimmed glasses.

Then he settled down to read, pursing lips.

Finally, "How much are you asking?"

Abel changed strategy swiftly. "I'd like you to make an offer."

"Oh," Weedon smiled sarcastically, "I'm not *that* interested. Leave it here if you want. I'll have my patent man look it over."

Somehow the atmosphere had subtly become as it used to be long ago. Abel felt a compulsion to assert something. "Thought I'd let you have first chance," he said as if jokingly, "for old time's sake. So far I held off taking it to Argus."

"I hear they're about to go broke. But you might be happy doing business over there, at that. Didn't I hear, or read somewhere, that company you started went bankrupt?"

He'd remembered all right. He'd saved this.

If I defend myself with, "My partner was a crook!" it will admit bad judgment. But who could have guessed it of Parker, so quiet, secretive, steady, with such sound opinions on finance, everything? Abel stood up, letting his tension show in his brusque tone. "How long will it take?"

"Not too long. Phone in a day or so."

Abel moved to the Grimes then. By calling in every morning, he could avoid giving Weedon's office this information. "Moved to a cheaper hotel, eh?"

Next morning, the man at the Wile-U-Wate took Abel's trousers. "Sure can fix."

Waiting, Abel avoided the booth where he had seen the professor.

Maybe I ought to buy a new suit. But it'd have to be cheap. Classes you. I'll keep on with this one. Cost new a hundred dollars. More nearly represents me as I am.

Weedon had the specifications on top of the pile of papers on the desk. "I'll tell you how it is, Abel," Weedon's tone was disparaging, "the verdict is you have an item here," he tapped the sheet with his pencil, "that has *some* possibilities—"

"It certainly has," Abel broke in. "This compound can be used without shutting down the well, and that's more barrels per month from the producer's point of view."

"And it's a smelly, explosive mess to package, and that's from the manufacturer's point of view!" He began to stare, as if fascinated, at the clock on his desk, whose second hand whirled on, detached from struggling men.

"Of course," Abel thrust, "Argus Company has a better equipped plant to make this—"

"—and we have some products," Weedon bore in as if no one else had spoken, his eyes still on the clock, "that approach it."

That was a lie, or at least they weren't patented. The attorneys had made careful search.

"So," Weedon tapped the paper, "this little item has a certain nuisance value. Not enough that I care to get into any lengthy haggling, but enough so, if you assign us all rights for manufacture, sale and use, we'll offer five hundred dollars."

At that instant the phone rang and Weedon answered.

Abel understood now why Weedon had kept eyes on the clock. He'd instructed a certain call be put through at a certain moment, so the victim, instead of bursting into rage and walking out, had time to let the barb sink, to feel helpless. He used to admire Weedon for these nerve wars. While Weedon talked Abel reached across the desk, picked up the typed sheet, put it in his brief case, and moved toward the door.

Weedon, hand over receiver, said, "Think it over. It's cash in hand, and'll save you a lot of trouble, getting too close to products we control." The threat quivered through the air like a knife thrown into the wall near Abel's head.

Abel smiled grimly and went out.

On the street, he walked, not knowing he was walking. All the way downtown to the muddy river, along the cobblestone wharf, his brief case bumping against his leg. He stopped finally as if all the wheels in him had run down.

He stood there a long time, picking up all the cogs and putting them back in place so they were a man.

After awhile he walked steadily back toward the business section. What if—. What if—? Like an eagle blown to sea, he kept circling, darting, trying to find something to light on.

He went over, step by step, the way he had hoped to operate. Selling the patent was to have been the first step in the chain reaction. All right, that had failed. What about cutting across, directly to the second step?

In his mind's eye he could see his detailed notes:

Step 2: With capital from patent sale, begin leasing the abandoned wells in the neighborhood and set up as Producer.

What if he went directly to Fifield, the big oil company that bought from the small purchasing company to whom Seavey delivered out of his gathering lines?

Yes! Cut right across Seavey and everything else.

It was dangerous, though, to bring to Fifield's notice the possibilities of all those wells. Why hadn't they seen them already? Too small to bother with, probably.

If he could get a contract from Fifield directly, to deliver the oil from them. Be worth trying. He'd have no trouble getting a good loan at the McRae bank then, which had been difficult because of the bankruptcy. And then, start to spread out on the leasing and reconditioning.

Go now. Before I get nerved up.

69

On the walls of the spacious office with the blond-wood functional furniture and the gleaming water colors of the company fields, Mr. Reed Sheafer, in charge of new development, conducted business in a relaxed, dignified way. Intelligent eyes beamed from behind shell-rimmed glasses. In spite of obvious forty-ishness, there still hung about him an aura of good-gray-flannels-and-crew-cut.

Mr. Sheafer gave the impression of willingness to give as much time and attention as necessary to the cordial consideration of Abel's business, asking an occasional question, and smiling with appreciative interest from time to time.

Finally, Mr. Sheafer said, "I had the impression that little pool outside McRae was gathered by some local line—Seavey, isn't it?"

"Is that any reason," Abel leaned forward energetically, "why someone else can't do business there?"

Mr. Sheafer smiled. "A little competition's always good." He leaned back, his swivel chair squeaking sedately. "If, as you say, you have leases on some good reconditioning possibilities—"

A bluff was legitimate. How else did the big ones get started?

"—we might be willing to take them over from you."

"No, I want to be producer."

"I don't blame you." Mr. Sheafer offered a cigarette. "Of course, from our point of view, it's more economical, less bother, to take over and put in our own crew."

And it's out of my control, Abel thought.

Mr. Sheafer leaned forward, picking up a pencil, politely conveying that the discussion was ended. "Any time at all, Mr. Abel, you have a steady volume of crude and can arrange delivery at our trunk, why stop back and see us."

Abel picked up his brief case.

"Interesting to talk to you, anyhow." Mr. Sheafer shook hands. "We always like to know about a man who has ideas and energy."

Something inside Abel expanded, rose and floated gently in a warm soothing ground swell. He'd impressed this man.

"I may say, the type we're always on the lookout for."

What was he hinting at? Taking him into the company? If it were something on the executive level—

"As a matter of fact, just today at lunch, our Personnel Director was crying about what a problem he has finding a certain type of man."

"I have," Abel rested his brief case on the desk, "some affairs pending—"

"This mightn't interest you at all," he sounded almost apologetic. "One thing in its favor—it's out near you."

Out near him? The company offices were all in the city. "What's the position?"

"Well, as I said," Sheafer sounded tentative, "it mightn't interest you. The title is Field Agent."

The field agent, Abel knew, was the man who went around checking up on their stations. He wore one of the company uniforms, a neat khaki jumper, with Fifield stitched in flowing script across the chest.

In the sunny street, he stood a moment. Then he snorted, "The nerve."

Well, I'm not licked.

That over-age college boy offering me a place as field agent!

Not licked.

I'll make the damned formula myself! Out there.

Lot of bad features about that. I'll get around them.

Not licked.

I'll make it myself.

13

RENA STOOD LOOKING DOWN into the night street. She was waiting for Abel. He might come yet on the late train. He had been gone three weeks.

I hope he's sold the patent. I don't see why he didn't write.

The neon over the taproom blinked out. The street was lovely now, dark, deserted, resting up for another day of people endlessly seeking.

Away off on the hill above Wesley Manor, the Beaver Church bell grated out an empty midnight to stone ears.

Be fifteen minutes before the last train.

Along the street below an old truck moved with ghostly clank of milk cans, a farmer and his woman, forlorn phantoms, headed for the smog-choked dawn market on the bleak city wharf. Just so her father, in just such a rattling truck, would have bumped through here at night, loaded with cans or clucking chicken crates.

No use letting myself get blue. Anyhow, Glen'll be here tonight. *Do* something.

She looked in the mirror. In the overhead light, her make-up seemed to have faded out.

I'll fix my face again. He'll surely be on the last train.

With brisk strokes of cold cream, she wiped off the make-up, patted on new foundation, touched in the eye shadow and began on the mascara. Then she stopped with a rueful half-smile. Why do I bother? Three weeks. He could have called!

But she began on her eyelashes again, though slowly now. Why do I? Ha! I bet there's a lot of women in the world besides me that if there wasn't a thing called a bed, they'd never even *speak* to a man!

It's as if inside me there's two people having a jawing match. One's a real sweet dope who likes to climb into bed. All right, Glen holds me that way, I never denied it. The other one's this hard-boiled cynic, oh, a real wisenheimer, who calls the plays on him at every turn. I'd have married him when he asked me, after he first came out here, if it hadn't been for that wisenheimer and her, He has a sickness. Keep independent. Be your own woman.

She glanced at the clock. Seven minutes. She picked up the little brush and began to paint her mouth.

If I hadn't been through it all before with Paul, I guess this time I'd have gone ahead with Glen. But the minute he begins throwing his weight around, I feel this is where I came in. Too alerted to the symptoms, I guess.

She brushed in the lip curves expertly. Like I'm painting him a picture.

Well, maybe he'll change. Come off it, honey, you're too big a girl to kid yourself that way. To change, you have to admit something's wrong, and that's one of the symptoms—blindness.

Why don't I tell him not to come any more? Why? Homesickness.

She blocked in color on the cheeks.

That's not the word. Nostalgia. For our crazy youth. She smiled, remembering. How about it when I worked at Acme Steel and had that apartment on Cargo Place and he was sure he'd get his divorce soon?

And he's sweet. Yes, he is. Like coming up to tell me he got the

72

patent before he left this time. A fighter, too, gutty. Always admired that in him.

Finished, she examined the picture in the mirror critically.

If I'd married him when first we met again, like he wanted, I wouldn't be sleeping alone. And of course, now the daughter's there, everything's changed.

He thinks a lot of her. It's not that I don't give him credit for that. Her being there's temporary, though. Bound to be. Girl like that—lovely skin, pretty legs. She must be looking for a good steady man. That would be natural. She hasn't anyone now. Not that I know of. Well, times are tough all over.

She heard the train. She was at the window in an instant.

Passengers began to appear on the street below. Not him.

She went back to the dressing table then. Waiting, she looked at herself bleakly.

The cloak ticked inexorably. Ten minutes. He had not been on the train then.

Slowly, her hand went into the cold-cream jar. Slowly she wiped —one stroke, two strokes, three strokes—and the picture was gone, as if someone had removed a child's hopeful finger drawing from a steamed window.

She couldn't get to sleep.

Loneliness is a waste. Trouble with me, I ought to go out, meet people. Tomorrow. Anywhere. The woman's club. A notice in the paper today—newcomers invited.

The next day Rena put on her best black suit, calmed her shiny red hair with a net and went to the McRae Women's Club, newcomers invited. She looked around hopefully.

Somewhere among these buzzing women—that one there in an old coat and a new hat, sitting on the seat edge as if listening for the school let-out bell—perhaps there was one she could make friends with. She could see herself in a kitchen, helping with dinner, laughing, chatting.

On the platform, a woman whose nervous hands kept pulling down her bright green dress in front, reviewed *Mr. Blandings Builds His Dream House*.

Maybe all these women came longing just to talk to each other too. Why do they have to pretend to be getting uplifted?

She became aware of a pair of hands folded in a lap next hers. Thin, with a wide wedding band. Reminds me of my mother. This woman's paler. Her dark eyes excited, like she's out of the pattern, too.

Rena leaned forward, touching the card someone at the door had pinned on her. "I'm Rena Smith—Mrs. Smith."

The dark eyes leaped in response. Then, as if struggling with shyness and an unaccustomed situation, the other woman touched her ticket. It read "Agnes Dorn."

Afterwards in the room came a tidal wave of talk about baby sitters, garbage pails, new refrigerators and someone's husband who played golf all day Sunday.

I might wedge in with that story about Paul and the boys in his band playing poker a solid week in that hotel in Ashtabula. Guess not.

She moved off into the street, I'll meet the afternoon train.

But he wasn't on it.

An afternoon off, once your underwear's washed and ironed, is a problem. They say to get rid of the blues, do something for someone else. Who said that? Benjamin Franklin probably, he was always sounding off.

She decided to relieve Myrtle, who substituted as hostess in the dining room on Rena's day off. Myrtle's husband was waiting and they moved off through the lobby swinging locked hands.

Rena went into the almost deserted dining room. A man about forty, alone, spoke to her. She smiled noncommittally and moved off, pretending to fix a tired bouquet.

She was thinking about that hotel in Ashtabula. First time I tried being a dining room hostess. To work off our bill. Depression. I learned to play poker then, too, with the men sitting idle. Always thought it a pity it absorbed them though. They didn't talk or explain or console. Just got into competition over the cards. People never talk enough to each other.

She could feel the man watching. Dark pin-striped suit, tense hands playing with the silver.

I just have to walk past, settling my dress in a certain way. Easy enough to start the train of fire. Be someone to talk to. Loneliness is a waste. Three weeks. No word.

In the half-light of the red leather and chrome cocktail lounge, she sipped slowly, while he tossed his down.

"What's he?" His tone carried to the Puerto Rican bar boy who'd served them. "A chink? Those orientals all look alike. All sneaky.

74

Hate having them around." He laughed then. "At that this is better than New York. I have to go over there every two or three weeks. Mine Haulage Machinery's my line."

His voice went on and on. She couldn't throw so much as a chip on the flood. "—live in Cincinnati, through here every three months. You and I could be friends." She heard about his cleverness in pulling a deal, his hate of people who had more money, who voted wrong.

She grinned at herself. What'd I think? He wanted to *listen?*

She sipped her first while he had two more and by that time he was saying, his long nervous face vindictive, "Anything I hate's a woman more interested in her children than in taking care of her husband's real needs." He patted Rena's hand. "A woman that's any good ought to sense them, without being asked."

Rena withdrew her hand, and even, after awhile, her attention. It seemed he didn't even like his children. "—wouldn't think a fourteen year old'd try to spite you. I stopped his allowance, see, his grades were down. Then I say, 'Clean the basement and have it done Saturday or else.' He defied me. Come Saturday I hear him making this big date—whippersnapper like that setting up to think of girls—hear him getting all polished up. I let him. He comes down whistling, and I say, 'Where you think *you're* going?'"

Her mind wandered off. What if everyone in the world afflicted with hate should just die? Like when there was an epidemic. Everyone that was puss-full of hate just—died. Picking them off here and there, like polio, say. No one left but people who liked the world. Of course, there'd still be sporadic outbreaks.

What if there were labs full of men working on that? She could see a man in a white coat, and on a shelf in a big jar, like bacteria, all labeled— A big Foundation studying Common Meanness, or Sour Silence. Universities working on Acute Contempt, Hardening of the Heart, Atrophied Joy, Tumors of Smugness—

They'd put on drives, like "Give a dime. Help Wipe Out Infantile Prejudice." Have mobile clinics, an X-ray that showed it—

She realized the man from Cincinnati was staring, disgruntled. "I asked if you'd have another?"

"I must go." She rose. "Sorry."

"Alone?" She could see her name being added to his list.

Back in her room she laughed wryly. Well, the poor guy's a "Lonely, but" person too. Lonely, but he has to hate everyone. Maybe Glen'll come tonight. I won't wait up—and then, maybe he'll come.

75

But it was just the same, because even in bed, she was still waiting for the sound of the train.

No good lying here thinking how things could have been different. That's as much a waste as loneliness.

Strange how certain moments change everything. Never the same again. Like the time—

Must have been a week or so after the market crash. Yes, because he didn't call or come. The papers said his father-in-law had been cleaned out. I kept hoping Glen had gotten out at the last moment. All those days passed and he didn't come. Knew then he hadn't. I did all that thinking. Came to me like a light what we ought to do. I had to call him, though, ask him to come.

Autumn, yes, for the ginkgo tree outside the apartment window was all gold. When he came, haggard, but his head up, his saying, "I had a temporary setback. I'll climb out. I'll make it yet." He seemed to feel guilty, as if someone were accusing him.

"Glen, life's going by so fast. We could be happy. Why don't we go ahead?"

"Not until I recoup."

"Who says you must? We could manage. I have a job."

His whole body seemed to get rigid as iron. How well I know now he doesn't like to be told what to do—especially by a woman. I wonder if his mother was real bossy? "There are things besides money," I kept arguing, "like having a good laugh together." But I guess it irritated him when I'd wow out laughing at something you weren't supposed to be flip about. "So, what's money?" I kept on like a dope. "You still have two eyes, five limbs—"

Well, I had my pride, too. He ought to have been glad a girl with my looks and spunk offered. I remember how he stood glaring at me, like I didn't understand him. Well, he certainly handled me wrong, too.

If I hadn't met Paul that next week at the old St. George Roof where his band was playing. We moved too fast though. Married at Christmas.

She heard the whistle, forlorn, grieving, as the suburban train moved up the lonely valley, passing mine patches stuck on clay hills. She rose and went to the window.

Passengers from the train came under the arc and moved on. One more came toward the light. Not Abel, for this figure moved wearily, confused, a man stumbling up out of muddy, swirling water. The figure came under the light. Her hand flew to her mouth.

She switched on the lights quickly, hoping he would look up, see she was still awake. She was standing with the door open when he came.

His shoulders! I never saw them like that before. Rounded like the top of a question mark.

"Okay for me to stay?" His face had a turgid, bilious look.

"Of course."

"Thought better to go out to the island in the morning." He sat down, glum, moody. He didn't take off his hat. He was usually punctilious about things like that.

At least I know enough not to ask how things went, she thought. She took off his hat and loosened his tie. "Guess you're tired."

"Stomach's upset's all."

"A drink? Some of the Haig & Haig left."

"Okay," he said wearily, "let's have it."

She fixed the ice cubes behind the little screen in front of her light housekeeping arrangements. She handed him the glass. He took a long drink. "They can't lick me." His voice was defiant. "I'm still running my show."

Sitting on the arm of his chair after awhile, she said, "Tell you what, Glen, you'll have to get another little pot the way you got the money for the island." Snyder, number two boy in the courthouse crowd, after Glen did him a favor getting scarce material, gave Glen a tip, one worth money, for Snyder had fixed the race himself. Six thousand—enough for a down payment on the island.

He shrugged uneasily.

Guess he doesn't want to think of that—after all the gut-tearing, all he has—the island, came through a tip on a horse race. She said quickly, "Saved you the funnies! Li'l Abner in a complete file."

And later when the damp spring night rushed cool through wide open windows and the curtains billowed in the dark room and stirred the air to freshness, she thought that he still had for her a warmth, a solidity. He had never become flabby.

Then—something went wrong. It was bad.

And he went to sleep, deeply, with no teeth grinding afterward, like he sometimes did. She lay there, staring wide, hearing the elevator come up, up, never seeming to go down.

Strange that it should be wrong tonight when it's always good with us. What happened?

She resented his steady breathing, wanted to make a noise, turn on the radio, rouse him.

But no, let him rest. He must have had a hard time in the city. Must have been taken down a peg or two, maybe three. Left him feeling thwarted, as if he were hanging—

She started, then felt herself get cold.

Do you suppose—just because they hung him up, he—?

No! That's not possible. A man wouldn't spoil— And yet, he knew I was. Knew I would be till he did something, knew that might be days or weeks.

But no, a man wouldn't.

But some cold inner knowing persisted, like a harsh light.

I don't mean he'd do it deliberate, but.

One place he could have had some solace. To get himself crossed up there, too. The poor guy. What a horrible, murderous time he must have had in the city.

She felt a deep bruised sadness for everyone in the world.

14

ABEL'S HANDS CLUTCHED THE chair arms as he sat in Krimmer's office next morning. He was trying to look decent and calm and not let him see the news was a blow.

Across the desk Krimmer was remembering last August, at the beginning of the primaries. Remembering how earnestly he had pointed out to Abel that to cash in his political I.O.U.'s from the courthouse crowd in this end of the county was unfair. Remembering how Abel had paid no attention, even acted indignant. Now, Krimmer saw the working out of a religious truth he'd always believed —that the unjust man will finally be paid off.

Abel rose to his feet. Must get out of here. Out.

That May morning the first real heat arrived.

The Dorns had discovered that instead of hunting each stone, blasting speeded the work. Already they had nearly enough for the fill.

Now they were erecting a small cairn to hold the metal box of explosives. They worked with the manual of directions open before them, away from the house and near the water.

As the heat mounted, the river looked more and more inviting. To Tom it was finally irresistible.

Back in the house he found an old pair of bathing trunks and went down to the dock. The chilly water forced out of him an exhilarated yell. Nick came to watch.

By the time Agnes heard the shouted laughter and came down, Nick was sitting on the dock. His black city shoes, laces trailing, rejected, out of things, were in a heap beside his discarded tie and shirt. From his bare shoulders the bones stood up knobbily so that his flesh seemed peculiarly naked. With suit trousers rolled, he dangled his bare feet in the water.

Agnes, holding her skirt, ventured out on the swaying little dock beside him.

The Dorns' clothing, unobtrusive on city streets, against this landscape seemed makeshift, unsuitable, a little vulgar.

Nick, watching something in the water, decided it might be tadpoles. He tried to catch one in his hands. "Interesting to see it grow." Then Agnes fetched an old aluminum long-handled saucepan from the house and they tried with that. She took off her shoes too, and in the sun-warmed pools along the shore, she bent over, helping him.

The glimmering creatures eluded them. Agnes and Nick laughed, excessively merry. They were quite drunk on May.

They saw the neighbor's girl gathering something—watercress perhaps—in a pail along the shore. Working her way nearer, she stood up and waved.

Just then, a car stopped at the mail boxes across the creek. A man alighted. Handsome, silver haired. This must be the neighbor.

They watched him with curiosity.

Nick, saucepan in hand, sat looking, inert and open as well-laid logs waiting the friendly match.

So Abel saw them.

The taxi drove off, but he stood, staring. Although his lips did not move, a word echoed in the caves of his mind. No.

That woman, dress wadded up. And the man, with some kind of cooking pan, his bony shoulders sticking out. And that young one. Skimpy bathing trunks. Tugging at something in the water.

None of my business. Look calm. Walk on past. Polite, but keep dignified.

He moved toward the bridge.

Cynthia. Down there *with* them. In shorts and halter. All right for her to go around on our own grounds—. Coming down here—dressed like that.

That young one. What's he think he's doing? Tearing up a boulder. What they'd do, begin to pull the place apart. Without so much as asking if it's all right.

Look at him, standing up now. Taking her in. Too smart for any good. And her eyes, watching him.

He walked slowly across the bridge, swinging each leg with deliberation, shoulders and arms held rigid, feeling his chest constricting tight, tighter. His glance went up and down, taking in each detail of dishabille.

Unconsciously, the Dorns' bodies assumed a defensive posture as if Abel were a farmer with a shotgun, who had caught orchard marauders with fruit-stained faces.

Cynthia opened her mouth to call a greeting. Then she saw his face.

As he neared the other end of the bridge, words erupted into his mind like steam escaping from underground: Helpless in the city. Took that. Even swallowed Krimmer. But here! My island. Invaded. Overrun.

Don't let them see. Quiet.

Can't take. It's too much!

He did manage to keep his voice wearily patient. "Did anyone give you permission to use the dock?"

Cynthia's hand flew to her mouth, as if covering hers would silence him.

That young one, cool as a cucumber, "Do we need permission?"

So, they'll not only sprawl, but crowd.

I could have walked on if he hadn't brazened. "Is it yours?"

Robins, constructing a nest in the gnarled cherry tree on the river, proceeded undisturbed about their instinctive business.

Out of habit, Nick's tone was explanatory. "Well, we thought—we didn't know—"

Cynthia broke out bewildered, "What harm are they doing?"

"Cynthia," he called with tight control, "will you come up here a minute?"

He did not miss that her troubled glance went first to the usurpers and then to him. She came up.

80

Then his words seemed to eject of themselves: "That's a private dock."

When he tried to take Cynthia's arm to start up the lane, she pulled away, moving on alone.

He walked after her, keeping his back straight.

All a mistake.

The Dorns stood staring. Children, running with a large, gay, unbelievable balloon, if suddenly a match were set to it, might have this stunned look, finding themselves holding the quivering tatters of red rubber.

By the turn in his lane he was thinking: Sorry. Got started off wrong. Nothing against them really. Don't know them. Go back now, apologize, explain.

He did not go back.

Cynthia had gone ahead so swiftly he was nearly at the top of the lane before he caught up with her and reached to take her arm. She jerked away, then faced him, angry, bewildered. "Why? Why?"

Withdrawn, disdainful, like when she first came. Like she's lumping me with all the rest of the world.

He forced the words, "I didn't sell the patent."

Face softening, the threatening pose relaxing. What a woman's for, to understand without your having to say defeat.

"Come on." She started ahead. "I'll fix you some lunch."

Pity in her voice. Mistake telling her, telling any woman of failure. Never tell them anything of your income, your affairs.

They came to the house. The pumice of time had mellowed the bricks to rose. The decaying wood pillars that he'd repainted gleamed. In the high-ceilinged hall, amethyst light fell through stained glass on Cynthia's hands. She reached toward him fleetingly, as if to comfort him. But her hands dropped, sensitive to the impossible. Then she said brightly, in a good-news tone, "They brought the rowboat back! All painted and fixed."

"Where is it?"

"Moored at the steps."

Polishing with his finger a mar on the carved newel post, Abel wanted to ask, "What was the cost?" His taking the boat to a Sherrod carpenter for repair after finding it stored in the carriage house had been for her pleasure. Now he did not want her to think that its expense was the final harassing straw.

As though sensing his thought, she said, "You'll sell the patent yet."

He glanced at her and said, "I've decided to make the compound here." He sounded sober and determined. "Myself." Then he smiled. "Takes more than a bunch of middle-aged college boys back in the city to throw me. Your pappy doesn't shove easy."

He was moving toward the small room he used as study. "I want to get started. Lot of figuring and planning to do."

Pulling a pad of paper toward him, he began once again. Patiently contriving a ladder toward safety.

His fight began to flow back. Efficiently, he compiled lists of supplies, equipment. Where could he buy the raw materials in small quantities? Safety regulations to consider, but out here, ought not to have to worry about them.

And he must not lose sight of his real goal. To become an independent oil producer. Making the compound was merely to earn the capital for that.

He must recheck all his plans now. Everything had been thrown slightly askew.

Taking out his old notes, his eye fell on:

Step 1: Sell the patent.

He crossed that out and wrote:

Set up operation to make compound here (temporarily). Apt to be messy. Later, when operation bringing in sufficient capital, hire building outskirts of town.

His eye went on down the sheet.

Step 2: With capital from compound sale, begin to lease abandoned wells.

He glanced over the ones he had scouted already:

Farm of Geo. Bellows—two wells.
Jones property, Rider Road—one well.
Lot of S. Loney—two wells.

Step 3: Begin producer operations by leasing other well on the island. Contact heirs in California.

He sat back, tapping pencil to teeth. By the time he had that second one on the adjoining acreage producing, time to acquire his own reconditioning equipment and crew.

Step 4: As soon as sufficient capital on hand, buy remainder of woodland acreage adjoining my place, including well. This will give me two wells, owned outright, here on my own property.

Then, as if he had put weight on a broken shin bone, he felt a sharp biting pain. Had Krimmer sold these people the woodland and the oil well too?

What if Seavey got in there? Seavey and Krimmer. He had never thought of them working together, but perhaps they did. If Seavey had heard these people had bought the other part of the island!

The afternoon light had begun to make slanting shadows when he arrived at the idea perhaps all his worry was unnecessary. Perhaps they scarcely knew the well was there, or thought of it as an old derrick and had not even bought the woodland. "I'll go back and see if anyone's been working, or the weeds trampled down."

Perhaps Cynthia would have noticed if there'd been any activity back there. At the door he called her. There was no answer.

Striding through the daffodils in the back garden, past the old ivy-covered well-head, he came to the thick trees and shrubs on the slope. He always muttered, "Have this all thinned out, soon as I can afford."

What if I meet one of them on the path over there? Do I have to ask permission to walk on the land my own people settled?

He'd always respected his grandfather but now he had a feeling of puzzlement. He could so easily, being completely in control, have fixed it so the island must forever be kept in one piece. Breaking it up diminished its dignity, spoiled its purpose.

He went ahead doggedly, hoping he would not meet them.

15

PASSING THROUGH WEEDS ALREADY waist high, Tom returned from the Dorn well. He'd found Seavey's crew progressing.

Whistling, he rolled a pebble between index and middle fingers.

Then he saw her out on the river. She was moving along with the current, in a rowboat.

Trouble is, she's apt to be anywhere. I can't say she goes here, or there, so I won't. Having to figure all the time how to avoid her keeps her in my mind. Then at night—the wrong dreams.

Walk fast—pay no attention.

But she called him. He couldn't distinguish the words, only the tone of alarm. She seemed to be trying to turn the boat against the current.

Way she handles the oars, you'd think she'd never done it before.

She called again, in panic. The rowboat was a heavy one, freshly painted bright green, lettered in white "The Cynthia."

She got herself out there all right. You can say you're going to avoid everyone's brangles, but if they ask for help, what then?

Carefully he unbuttoned his shirt, a clean white shirt just back from the laundry, and hung it on a bush. One at a time, he kicked off his moccasins.

He swam out with the crawl he'd always used, but it was a little different now. He saw she was all dressed up. To work off his annoyance, he could do a little splashing.

When he was in the boat, it was not like that. Looking down into her eyes, at the soft hair, the lips trembling and childish as if she knew she were at fault, she didn't seem the girl who'd been in his thoughts last night and the night before—the dame out looking for trouble.

He'd never seen her in a skirt before. It made her look strangely exciting. Her sleek-fitted pale blue bodice had a rounded low neck, and her brown skirt swirled out in diaphanous folds. Quite a costume *pour la row*. Her hair, smoothed back under a brown ribbon with blue spots, gave her a trembling, ephemeral look, like a butterfly. Yes, a Monarch butterfly, brown with blue and gold spots, with those tawny little lights in her hair, and the slate-blue blouse, and milky beige skin.

Lifting the oars, he looked away deliberately. "Where do you want me to take the boat?"

"I rowed around to your house, at least the current took me. Your parents weren't home."

She certainly hadn't gotten herself up with care and bewitchment to fascinate his old man or his old lady.

"They went to town, Mrs. Winters."

"I wanted to apologize about the dock."

84

"What difference does it make? Only thing is—I'm trying to get them settled fast and my father lost a whole half day's work, stewing!"

The boat was swinging with the current. He righted it.

"I'm sorry," she said. "Something had happened to upset him."

"Yes. Like our moving in here."

"Father's not really like that."

"Good. I just hope he doesn't do anything else to get mine riled up and worried."

She kept on, as though she weren't sure he was convinced.

"All right," he said finally, "he's a prince. That suits me. I'll pull over toward the neck. You ought to be able to get home from there."

A little awkwardly he pulled in close to the graveled beach, and shipped the oars. "Now, take it easy." He stood, balancing.

Motionless, she sat looking up at him. Then her hand flew out beseechingly, as if begging forgiveness. What she said was, "Thank you for helping."

She kept holding out her hand. Finally he took it. It felt smooth and slender and warm. Right then he knew it was too bad the whole thing had happened. He would remember the warmth, and the way her hand moved in his like a butterfly you wanted to catch, tonight, when a dead sleep with no dreams was what he wanted.

Then he saw Mr. Abel standing on the path above.

No sound came but the lapping of the water. Abel's hands closed at his sides, his stiff body, his head thrust forward, all seemed to cry out, ordering Tom out of the boat, off the river, off the earth.

The fellow touched her hand.

Abel's breath came back, but now he seemed to be tasting a metal spoon with mold on it.

To use the *boat*. Didn't she know I wanted to take her out the first time? To *give* it to her.

He looked at Cynthia. "You didn't wait for me to take you out in the boat."

She flushed and averted her face.

Abel thought, All spoiled now. He said in a slightly jocular tone, "The river seems to be getting crowded."

Cynthia leaned forward quickly. "Father," one hand was extended to him, the other toward Tom, as if to make a bridge, "this is Tom Dorn."

85

Abel acknowledged the introduction with a brief nod. Then he was gone, only the bushes still trembled.

Wait a minute! Tom scowled after him. What was that crack about the river? Okay, okay, the dock, let him have it. Now the river! And even a hint she oughtn't to be associating with me.

He picked up an oar. "Want to go for a row?"

She looked surprised and then nodded yes.

Slowly he maneuvered back into the current, concentrating on oars and water.

After awhile he said, "A prince."

"Oh, you don't think so," she said, "but he can be nice, too."

Tom was silent then, rowing hard. He had a goal.

Her words came with a rush, trying to prove something. "Take this boat. He spent money he needed to fix it. I get restless up there. He's away a lot. Then I take the car out, drive too fast. I can't help it. He thought the boat would pass the time for me."

Silently Tom pushed toward his destination.

"He's really kind," she said.

But Tom didn't waste breath talking. He was out of condition. He wanted to get the boat to a certain place.

Finally, he arrived. They were in full view of the steps up to the Abel house. But he couldn't see Abel anywhere. Maybe he was watching, though. Tom meant to row the boat, and with her in it, right past the house, good and slow, so Abel couldn't miss them. The river now!

But he was out of breath, his hands were hot and blistery, and Abel was nowhere in sight.

He gave an exclamation of disgust. I'm bad as Nick, wasting time and energy. Here I am knocking myself out, when I could have been making those frames for the cement floor or going over the reconditioning contract. What do I care about Abel?

They were near the mooring post at the Abel steps.

"Want to tie up here?" He turned and caught a look on her face of withdrawn bleakness, as if home were the last place she wanted to go.

"No."

"I'll take you around then, to your private platinum dock in the front." It was a nice evening, and the rowing was, after all, good exercise. He could feel the muscles straining, very fine, in his shoulder.

She was quiet, huddled down. After awhile she said, "Did you ever have a feeling," her voice was sad, "that your parents are your children?"

He glanced up startled, then nodded yes.

"He's not a prince. But, when some people feel helpless—it's like an electricity that has to discharge."

Up to this moment, when their eyes met, there had been a silent battle; she, consciously or not, trying to entrap him into the sticky pitcher plant, he struggling against the allurement of soft hair, soft breasts, trembling lips. Now, they looked at each other with a surprised sense of being in league.

He didn't tie up at the dock. As he rowed under the bridge, they could see ancient wasp nests. He passed the woods at the first bend and finally shoved toward a little cove.

"Got a cigarette?" It was as if he spoke to someone who'd lasted with him through hard going and the commonplace words were meant for comfort.

They smoked as the water tapped gently. The world here was beautiful, fresh-springing with life. They, too, were springing with insistent life. But you couldn't stay here, floating, detached. There was that other world.

They rowed, finally, past the Dorn house. Sun set the windows eerily ablaze, and the dooryard, piled with stones, cement bags, window glass, had a poignantly vulnerable look, as though the humans engaged with their puny cares might have been spirited away.

Rounding the bend, water rippled over large flat stones. They stepped out of the boat and stretched on a dry flat rock with another cigarette. The sun was so low now it filled each wave trough with gold and turned her hair and face to warm rose. Locust blossoms fell in a shower. He brushed them out of her hair. It was like fine spun milkweed floss, dyed a deep tan.

When they kissed each other, it was good.

But the way she clung brought wariness. He stood up, starting toward the boat.

"Come on. We better go before it's dark."

She sat up. "What's the matter?" She was looking at him bewilderedly.

How to be plain and yet not hurt her. No use hurting her.

He came back a step or two, and stood, eyes on the ground. Finally he said, "A friend of mine was in psycho after Anzio. He was cured all right and got out." She rose and came toward him. He looked at her now. "When he came home he found his wife hadn't been able to take it. Now, he's an alcoholic and on the fast skids."

Her mouth opened as if he'd hit her a sneaking blow. Then she broke out, "You're making that up!"

He lit a cigarette with great care.

She walked away from him, then she turned angrily. "And what about me?" she cried. "What about me? Don't I matter?"

"I'm not going to help put those skids under some poor guy that—"

"Noble you!" she broke in bitterly.

Tensely he began to exercise his fingers, partly out of habit, partly to show her he wasn't getting involved. That way he didn't have to look at her. The friend was a good reason, a useful, handy reason —if not the true one.

Breathing angrily, she watched him. "What are you trying to do," she said sneeringly, "get yourself in tiptop physical shape again?"

"What's wrong with that?" he scowled.

"Why?" she demanded, as if he were out of his mind.

"Why?" He stared back. He didn't ask himself why. She kept looking at him, smiling, sarcastic.

Then, as if superstitiously reluctant to utter words that might call the attention of some mischievous power that would trip him again, he said, "Because, come fall, I'm going back to school." His tone was fierce now. "I'm going to be a surgeon."

She stared, almost with incredulity. "Getting yourself in shape for another ride on the merry-go-round. Sometimes I think Harry's the sane one. Saner to stay right where he is!"

"That's a queer way to talk."

"Probably so, for a noble boy scout."

His uneasiness made him furious. "What'd happen if everyone just said, I quit!"

"And the old trap didn't work any more. Let me tell you something." Her words seemed to come from the bottom of a pit. "They say people come from slime. They're bragging. They're still slime."

Tom seemed to hear an echo, to see the living room where the wall space waited for the Braque.

"I'm not doing it for people!" You had to push on, work out the pattern. He frowned stubbornly. "I'm going to do what I started out to do."

She whirled about, the brown skirt catching on a briar. She jerked it angrily so that it tore, and then walked away rapidly toward the bridge. Now she almost ran, her high-heeled shoes sinking into the sandy river edge.

88

"Good!" he thought. "Fine!"

Angrily, bitterly, he wiped the back of his hand over his mouth, trying to shut out the feeling of how her lips had trembled when he kissed her.

16

NICK SAT IN KRIMMER'S office. The chair was hard, and his hat hung between his knees, as he waited, tense.

He examined the advertising calendar from the First National Bank of McRae, he studied the large handsomely framed picture of Abraham Lincoln. Finally, his eyes came to rest on the bunch of bleeding hearts thrust into a glass of water on the secretary's desk.

The middle-aged secretary stopped typing to answer the telephone. Her face lit. "Yes, Mr. Krimmer. A Mr. Dorn is here. Yes, that one. Oh, Mrs. Krimmer called and asked would you be sure to get a price on the hams for the church supper. No other calls. Why," she flushed, "thank you, Mr. Krimmer." She hung up, and turning to Nick, her eyes behind her glasses looked a little dewy. "Mr. Krimmer's just the most thoughtful man I ever worked for. Always tells me to go home early when he doesn't have anything for me to do. Just nice. He said for you to wait, he'll be here soon."

"—so what I want to know is," Nick's voice was tight, "does he own it?"

"Well, now," Mr. Krimmer leaned back in his swivel chair and twirled a pencil in his fingers, "I'll tell you, Mr. Dorn, there are some men, and from what I've seen I wouldn't be surprised if Glen Abel were one of them, who simply like to bother folks!"

"But, why would he?" Nick broke out, incredulous. "The reason I came in is I want to *know*, because we don't want to use anything that's not ours! And I got thinking, I don't remember anything about the dock, one way or the other, in the deed. Does he own it, or not?"

"Well, now, I ask you, in common sense—where is it?"

"Well—it starts from under the bridge, but it slants out into the water on our side."

"Well, then. I tell you, Mr. Dorn, when something like this comes up, I ask myself, what would *he*," Krimmer swung around in his chair to face the picture of Lincoln, "say? He's always been a hero of mine. And I ask myself what would Lincoln say to a thing like this? And I'll tell you what he'd say." He swung back again sharply, looking at Dorn levelly. "He'd say, Don't let anyone shove you around!"

Nick blinked his eyes.

"You take someone like Abel, if he thinks he can get away with it, there's no end to where he'll stop. And if it were me, well, I'd do like Lincoln said. Of course you may be different and not mind being shoved."

All the way home, while the paint brush and the new spade and the bag of cement jounced around in the car, Nick was lost in thought.

Even by supper time the heat had not slackened and Tom watched the gray painted floor boards of the porch dry as quickly as he hosed them.

Then out of the open doors and windows came a gentle odor, melting, but powerful enough to stop all activity within its orbit. Warm yeast rising in wheat flour redolent with cinnamon, butter and sugar. It persuaded the blandished to come and sit, and wait.

Agnes was baking.

Tom came into the kitchen. "What's that revolting odor? It could be cinnamon buns."

Agnes, flushed with heat, closed the oven door and straightened up, smiling.

"You should be resting," he said.

"Nick went in to see Mr. Krimmer. If he hears something discouraging in there, to come home and smell the buns will cheer him up."

Tom's eyes crinkled. He broke into a laugh. "I've heard of women wearing Black Narcissus in their hair. You're deadlier."

Agnes scraped flour from the kneading board. "Maybe when you're young you want to find flowers in the hair. Later, cinnamon buns in the oven."

The car drove into the dooryard. They both became still, waiting.

Nick was not talkative when he came in. During supper, he seemed absent. Only after they finished, Tom asked, "What'd Krimmer say?"

Nick hesitated. Then he said thoughtfully, "He says go ahead and use it."

Tom moved in his chair uneasily. "Let's not have any trouble."

"If it's ours, we're the ones could say to him, use it. Or we could order him off."

"We're not going to, though," Tom said.

"No," Agnes said.

"Well, he did. I couldn't understand that at first. Maybe now I do. I guess I see why he flew off his handle. Remember that first day we came here to look, when Krimmer told me someone else lived on the island? I was surprised at myself, but, I resented it. I wanted it to myself."

Agnes put in, "And Krimmer said his grandfather settled it. His family's island."

"I was thinking about that, too," Nick said. "All the way coming out I've been turning it over. Guess I can see how maybe I might have acted the same as him. First, I thought we ought to have a survey made, find out just who owns that land it's on under the bridge. But then I saw no matter how the survey turned out, the best thing we could do would be to build another dock."

"But, Dad," Tom broke out, "what for? Sure we'll have a boat sometime. But we don't need a dock now!"

"We need it." Nick was earnest. "Not for the boat, but to let him know right off we'll keep to our own side." He rose from the table and walked to the window. "What do you suppose it'd cost to build one?"

"Oh," Tom protested, "but the time!"

"Still," Nick said, "he'd know right off we're not trying to crowd him."

Agnes picked up a dish and set it down again quickly. "If you do that, build another dock, that will crowd him!"

"No, how could it? It'd show him we—"

"You said yourself it was maybe only the way he felt that minute. That'd set it—like in iron."

"I don't know, seems to me two docks would say, We're here on our side, you're over there on yours. Let's go out and see where we could put it, Tom."

Tom stood still. "I don't know. Don't know if it's a good idea or not. The time!"

"Let's go take a look, anyhow."

Tom's eyes sought Agnes's, troubled. Then he moved after him reluctantly.

17

IT WAS NEARLY TEN NEXT morning before Abel stirred. He had figured at his desk far into the night. His brain must have been gnawing at his problems during sleep, for waking he knew he must find out at once if the Dorns had bought the woodland also. If so, he must try to cover the well with a lease.

If I'd just had a chance to get used to the idea.

He could see young Dorn in the boat with Cynthia, scowling at him with defiance. Would he have to do business with *him?*

Bannon. Yes. The production man would be here today. He could get Bannon to approach them.

Abel sat up, listening for the phwump-phlamp of the one-cylinder engine pumping his own well. No sound came across the woodland. Bannon was a good production man when he was sober. Abel sighed now. If Seavey had not fired him for drunkenness, though, Abel could not have hired him cheaply.

In the bathroom, he muttered as always, "Soon as I have the funds —modernize here."

The sun coming through the window soothed him. It would actually be fine to be out there making the product in the carriage house. At last coming to grips with something.

He was back in the bedroom lacing his shoes when he heard it. An explosion. Thirty or forty quarts of nitro going.

He threw on his clothes. Like a doctor who hears of a violated body, blood-bathed, he still must check pulse and breath before saying it is death.

He ran down the stairs, through the daffodils, around the carriage house. Through the delicate spring leaves, he could see into their dooryard.

Two cars. One, a small black coupe with lettering on the door.

The reconditioning crew would have an expert come in to detonate. That would be the explosives company man.

It was true then.

The feeling of helpless bafflement he'd had in town rose up again.

The treachery numbed him. If they'd given him a chance to talk it over. Standing there, hands clenched, the word that came up into his mouth was "beset."

Only Seavey would have moved in so fast.

A recondition job was a gamble. From visceral depths he prayed, "I hope to God it doesn't work."

Bannon did not come. Now Abel would have to go to town and hunt him through the taprooms.

As he drove down his lane, the small black coupe came up from the Dorn house with a careless swoop, gravel rattling, as though there would be no traffic except from Dorns. Near stone posts which marked the entrance to Abel's lane, he had to jam on brakes and wait for the other car to pass along the road to the bridge.

Waiting, a black depression settled on his face. They were using his road to further Seavey's interests. To get the other well going so Seavey could block him. A sucker! They were making a sucker out of him!

In town he went to Kelly's, the Silver Dollar, to Herren's. Bannon had been seen loading, but had moved on. He found him in the last taproom, saturated. Getting him home, finally, to his wife, Abel asked her to see he came to the island next day.

Perhaps Rena would have picked up gossip in the Mansion House about what was going on out there.

But she said, "Krimmer might tell you. He gets around everywhere." Take Krimmer's gloating again? Never.

Leland's. People went in and out for supplies.

Young Leland said, "Well, dear me, seems a lot going on at the island these days." Ordinarily Abel, finding him distasteful, would have cut him short, but not today.

"What sort of people *are* they?" young Leland broke out peevishly. "Not much like you folks, I'm sure. For one thing, the young one seems so *crude*. And the older one, well! Clarence Seavey's had a crew out there on that old hole in the ground, kidded them into thinking they'd get more oil out of it. Excuse me, you did get it from yours, but after all, they don't know from *nothing!*"

Maybe Abel's eyes were really seeking for it. But when he happened to see it, he had a sense of satisfaction. He picked it up,

93

from a table where metal and wooden and cardboard signs were displayed and in a colorless voice said, "I'll take this."

Wrapping it, Leland said, "I don't blame you! You must feel simply *overrun!*"

When Abel returned, Cynthia, in the big room whose high windows were draped in faded rose brocade, was playing the ancient Steinway. When she was eight or nine—his girl—the sound of her labored practicing had been a source of unnamed happiness. It gave him a feeling she was thriving, that he was providing the means for her to learn to play, that all was well with her. But now her playing seemed to cut him off. For one thing she played that same piece over and over. The notes from the scarred wood shivered out into the hall now like someone crying.

He took the sign and went down to where the road started up from the bridge.

Along the river, violets bloomed and clover scented the air. For just a moment, Abel had a curious hesitation. Then into his mind came the image of the black coupe swooping carelessly up his lane.

He found a suitable tree. Carefully he sank the first nail into the sign. He said half-aloud, "My grandfather built this road."

He sank another nail.

It seemed unusually quiet along the river. Even the water moved silently. The hammer blows echoed, expanding outward.

He drove in the last nail. "A lot of things I can't help, but *one* thing, I can keep from being a sucker on my own place!"

The sun, glinting up from the water, flickered over the neat black and white lettering, "Private Road. No Trespassing."

Bannon did not come. Abel had to go back to his own well to be sure the cock was open into the flow lines, that the gathering tank was not overflowing. He waited till evening. There would be less chance of encountering Seavey's smirk.

The path beyond the neck, as far as the cut-off to Abel's well, was a joint one. Thinking that while he was back there, he'd see about cutting a separate path, he took along a briar clippers.

All was in order at his well.

Returning, he noticed a particular tree because of the bees zinging angrily about as if their colony had been broken into. Then he saw the tree had been cleft as by a great knife and seemingly jammed back together, not quite evenly, the work of some Paul Bunyan with a mean streak.

94

Odd. There'd been no storms recently. Staring at the tree as he approached it, his foot sank into a fissure, three or four inches wide. The fissure—he couldn't tell how deep it was—ran up to the split tree and beyond. He had never noticed any erosion here before.

But it wasn't being momentarily thrown off balance by his foot slipping into the fissure that gave him the feeling of nausea. His stomach had been quivering all day, as if the nitro blast that morning had shattered the rock on which his island rested.

18

FEELING LAZY AND GOOD, TOM sat on the top step of the porch in the sun. He was watching Agnes happily troweling in a big flower bed he had just spaded for her.

Nick was all agog for letters these days, having written the supply houses in Florida for prices on bee colonies. He had gone to meet the letter carrier who would be coming along in his old touring car, lifting the little metal flags, stuffing the boxes along his route.

Waves of sound from the Dorn well reverberated through the woodland and across their dooryard. The reconditioning crew had trundled an eight-cylinder portable engine in along the path from the back road, and its phlang-phlang might go on for weeks. Until the regular pump could be put to the well, no one would know whether the gamble had paid off. But Tom, listening, thought the tension set up by the sound rather pleasurable. It was like the interval after you drop in the nickel and the ball rolls around in the pin ball machine.

"First thing, I'm going to plant those corms I found," Agnes called happily. Discovering the blades of gladiola in an overgrowth of hazel and poke weeds on the slope back of the Dorn yard had delighted her. Some woman must have put them there some long-off spring day, maybe like this. There's a going-on, unbeknownst. To flower a thousand years after.

Tom stretched back luxuriously on the porch boards, knees crossed

95

in the air, one toe swinging lazily toward cotton clouds scudding through the blue.

"You weren't fixing in your mind to have your idiot son keep that bed weeded, were you," he teased her lazily. "I'm bright enough to know where there's flowers, there's weeds. You weren't fixing in your mind to have your delicate little son get all fried under a broiling sun plucking plantain out of the daisyhocks, were you? That's what's known as stoop labor, and for that I get time and a half."

"Such as?"

"Oh," Tom stretched back lazily, "extra pancakes in the morning. Against my principles to pull the poor little defenseless weeds, anyway."

"Oh, you just haven't got a green thumb."

"I knew a woman had a blue thumb. It made the weeds scram."

"I don't know just how to do for gladiolas." Agnes squinted up into the sunny sky happily. "Guess I'm like an old maid left a batch of orphans. Just wanting them doesn't tell her how to care for them."

Chip basket and trowel in hand, she was moving into the thicket when Nick came quickly down the lane, the unopened mail in his hand, an astonished look on his face.

"What's he mean," he was bewildered, "No Trespassing?"

Agnes came back.

"What's the matter?" Tom stood up.

"There's a sign on the road. No Trespassing! He put up a sign!"

They looked at each other with consternation.

Tom lit a cigarette with deliberate motions. Finally, he made his voice calm. "Looks like we'll have to come in along the path through the woods."

"The back path?" Nick still sounded bewildered. "That's a quarter of a mile."

"Are you sure, Nick, you saw a sign?" Agnes looked a little pale. "Of course I did."

"It must be a mistake," Agnes said slowly. "Why would he?"

Nick looked astonished. "I don't know why."

"Well," Tom shrugged, trying to minimize, "let's not get in any fuss about it!"

Strange, five years ago, even two years ago, Tom would have been goading Nick on to do something, while Nick would be reiterating the futility of arguing with a landlord or an acid supervisor.

There was a small clinking sound. The trowel had dropped out of Agnes's nerveless hand, hitting a stone.

Tom took a worried step toward her. "I'll carry our stuff in the back way!"

Nick had glanced at Agnes, but now he was staring at the ground. His incredulity and bewilderment were fading.

Finally he said, "Of course *I* know we're going to build a dock so's he'll see we mean all right. But, *he* don't know it."

Agnes was pale. "Seems like if we could just talk to him. Neighborlike."

"But we don't even know him," Nick said.

"You could go up, nice, let him know."

Nick was diffident. "Would you go with me, Tom?"

Tom stooped down to pick up Agnes's trowel. He was remembering the boat that afternoon, with Cynthia and him in it and Abel standing by the bushes looking down at them.

"I think I better not go."

"I'd go with you, Nick," Agnes said, "but I think it's better you go alone. It's just man business. Let him know you."

"We-ell. Tomorrow morning, I'll go."

Abel was crossing the lawn when Cynthia came running up the lane, hand raised pleadingly, calling out, "No! Take it down."

When she was close to him, he began, "Your great-grandfather—"

"I don't care," she said. "Take it down."

He walked toward the portico. She followed. When he was on the top step she said pleadingly, "Father, take it down!"

How could he say it was to protect her? Her castle.

"Please!" He was astonished to see tears spring out.

"It seemed best to let them know. Once and for all."

"No! It can't be best!"

"I don't see why it should upset you."

"What do we care if they use it? It doesn't hurt us."

Abel licked his lips, realizing that the actual putting up of the sign had worked something out of him. His pain at hearing the explosion, at knowing Seavey was using his road—had lessened. He was even a little ashamed.

She was looking up at him, waiting. With that look she had when she first came. It was not worth that.

She smiled a little through tears, sensing his mood. Then she took his hand.

97

"Where's the hammer?" she asked.

"You'll hurt your hands," Abel said. "I'll do it."

He turned back to the road and she slipped a soft arm into his.

The next morning, Agnes laid out a clean white shirt, but when Nick came down, he had on his old clothes.

She looked at him questioningly.

"They're baling out the well this morning. I wanted to watch it." He sounded a little apologetic. "I'll go see him later."

She nodded, thinking, He's a little abashed at going. Putting it off. He'll come to it.

After he and Tom had gone back to the well, she walked off the porch, down the sloping yard, and along the rippling water.

Still can't believe it. Why would Mr. Abel do a hurtful thing like that? We wouldn't do a thing like that.

The fresh air was lilting and the leaves rustled with a gentle comforting murmur.

Violets grew in clumps under the alders.

She approached the bridge and went slowly up the slope to the road.

There was no sign.

She stood a moment, then turned quickly back toward the house. No need for Nick to go now. Better not. Better say nothing.

She moved as rapidly as she could along the path.

Later on, maybe when we're not so busy, when we're settled, we might go up there, get acquainted. When we're not so busy.

I guess I know that's an excuse. You can always find time.

I'm a little timid. With Nick there's maybe a little pride, too. Feeling Abel might have come to see him.

Next week, we'll go. I won't put it off. Next week. Or, maybe the week after.

19

A SUDDEN WIND-GUST FROM the rising storm flattened Cynthia's dress, so that standing on the river bank by the bridge above Tom, she looked like a ship's figurehead. Seeing him at work, seeing the lumber piled, she had stopped the car and alighted.

He came up to the bank finally for another plank.

"Two docks!" she said miserably.

"Yes."

She dropped her glance. "I'm ashamed."

"It *is* a little like something chalked on a sidewalk. We don't even have a boat."

"But—why?"

"It's Nick's idea."

Tom darted a glance at her. "He saw that sign the other day. On the road."

She flushed. "But—I—he—took it down."

"Yes, but Nick had seen it. It upset him, made him jittery. Nick wants to show your father we don't intend to bother him."

"All this work," she said unhappily.

"And time," he broke out. "At this rate, I'll be lucky if they're settled when school starts."

Nervously she fingered her wide belt buckle.

"I just came back from taking my father in for the noon train. He's gone into the city to buy chemicals for something he's doing. He won't be back for a couple of days. If you want to use the old dock while he's gone—"

"We don't need it."

Heavy clouds scudded overhead. A gust of wind impelled Tom slightly toward her as they stood together on the bank.

"A waste," she said.

Her hair blew back from her face, and her eyes, raised to his, pleaded. Tom suddenly thought of the expression "to strike in anger" or "to raise your voice in anger." Could you "make love in anger" too? What a crazy notion! And yet, and yet, it seemed almost as if the relief would be the same as striking some unseen enemy.

A tentative whirl of rain drops sprinkled their faces and in a moment rain pelted down with a rush, wetting Tom's shirt and her dress with dark lozenges.

"We better get out of the rain," she said.

With a lightning flash, the storm came, beating on the car roof. She sat behind the wheel, nervously stroking it, silent.

After awhile Tom said, "What's eating your old man, really?" His brows were knit.

"Well, one thing, he's upset because Seavey got in first and leased your well. Father's been trying to set himself up as an independent producer. Seavey doesn't like that."

Friendly Seavey!

"And then, there's a woman, in McRae. One of those things been going on for years. I guess she ought to be out here instead of me."

She turned toward him and looked up into his face and the rain had left her eyelashes moist. Her shoulder, so near him, was soft and round and he could feel her warmth.

"How is your husband?" he said.

The rain spat down hollowly. She was silent. After awhile she said, "I'm supposed to go to Charlesville next week. I go every couple of months." Then the words came like an involuntary escape of vapor from a deep, seething pool. "I don't want to go. It's all right, you don't dislike me for that any more than I do myself."

A tumble of thunder fell out of the ominous sky, and suddenly she said, "Let's go for a ride." Without looking at him, or waiting for his assent, she put the car in gear, and swinging around recklessly, went over the bridge and along the narrow road away from McRae, water flailing out from the wheels.

They flew over narrow black roads awash with rain, through sharp gullies, roaring up hills, shooting down steep inclines. Tom lost track of where they were, but he began to understand why Abel had tried to divert her with a boat.

I know how she feels. As if by going fast she might overcome the need. To love and be loved. Could I love her? Why do I even let such a thought hang around? Time! She's trying to hurry it, but I have to slow it down.

The rain had slackened as they rolled up a hill. He had no idea where they were. The top of the hill was flat, and had been marked out with tentative roads for some real estate development. "Pull over here," he said.

They bumped along until they came to the edge of a low hill, which fell off sharply. Below them was a little community of modest houses. She stopped at the edge of the hill and turned toward him. He put a hand out where her leg swelled up sweetly above the knee and under the warm silk felt her flesh start and quiver.

Just then, at one of the small houses below them, there was excitement and commotion. A car had driven up and a man and woman and a small child piled out hastily and ran with their parcels to the house. The man returned, running toward a clothes line, where blankets and winter coats had been airing, soaked now. They could see the woman moving about in the house and windows banging down. The man in the yard and the woman at a window called and gestured excitedly to each other. Laden, the man scurried into the house. In a few moments, he ran out and from the car took a large brown bag of groceries. When he went in this time, he closed the front door. After awhile in the half gloom of the rainy afternoon, a light was turned on in the kitchen.

"He has it, that guy," Tom said. "Me and mine and our house. The simple dream. A simple wife, a simple house, a simple baby, a simple trade. That's the beginning before a man can go on."

And as he said it, he thought of Margot's apartment and the perfume of pond lilies. No sir, he was not falling again into any complicated puddles.

"And who do you know it's happened to?" Cynthia was bitter. "As for me, I know only one, a couple, friends in the city."

One out of hundreds. And yet, the simplest of dreams.

"Maybe it only looks good from here," she said, smiling cynically. "He probably has ulcers and the wife spends her time thinking up ways to torture him."

Then he broke out at her meanly, angry that he could not say it had happened to anyone he knew. "You must have had a hard life!"

"Oh, I don't know."

"What were you, an actress or something?"

"Something."

"That's quite a career, isn't it?"

"Well, it can get you away from home."

"But you're back here now. Why?"

"It's safe," she said touchily. They sat in silence, then she began again. "My last week in New York, I'd been out on the road for months, an understudy in a company of *The Tempest*. I'd begun to make the rounds again."

Steam had formed on the car windows and she tried vaguely to wipe it off.

"The agent had sent me to see this TV producer. When I arrived, another program was just finishing in the studio. A cooking demonstration. A home economics woman had made a fancy meringue pie, with gestures. A couple of grips were watching her. We were sitting there in this tangle of cables and halves of living rooms and halves of windows. As soon as the show was struck, they moved in for the kill. One of them swooped up the pie and tasted it. He got a peculiar gritty look and he said to the other, 'This here tastes like burned rubber.' That seemed to sum up exactly the taste in my own mouth.

"Then the producer arrived. He was partly bald, the white carnation type. I started in on my usual, 'I was an understudy for Helen Hayes.' You said that automatically to snow them. They wouldn't call Hayes to check. A lesser name they might have. Then, of course, you told them you were sixteen. That's on account of the Age of Consent, which believe me, they all know about. Of course if you see them the next year, you can't get away with it, but then they rarely lasted in their own jobs for a year. This one knew Harry. Knowing your husband was away, they assumed that went with the job like the agent's commission. And the trouble was, I didn't like him. Maybe I was stirred up because I'd just had a letter from Father, and was carrying it around in my shoulder bag, wondering what to do.

"It was Christmas week. Christmas is a terrible trap. You get the mistaken notion everyone else is happy, and safe in the bosom of a family, and you feel lost and unwanted. I decided to come home— just for Christmas. But when I saw the island, there was something about it, shut away here. Then, the little graveyard, with Alicia Abel's name on the stone in the snow.

"In New York, there was plenty of love. I thought I wanted to get away from that. But, there's this thing called Nature." She tried futilely to wipe the steam from the window in her path of vision. "And now, I ask myself, 'What else is there?'

"That stuff you were dishing about that house down there," she gestured to the small dwelling, where lights glowed now from another window, "that's an ad man's dream, or some movie you saw. It ain't necessarily so."

He moved away from her in the seat. "I'm going to make it that way."

"You can't make a leaf on a tree."

"One thing I know. I'm not going to have the kind of life my parents had. Scared all the time."

"Who isn't?"

"I'm going to make it different."

"You know what you remind me of? A little ingenue, fresh out of the American Academy, tearing her guts out in an audition and already, the redhead chewing gum in the second row is sleeping with the Director."

What was the use of saying these things out loud? It only made it harder. It was too easy to not stir.

The rain had stopped. He opened the car door abruptly, went around to her side, and opened the door. "I'll drive." She slid over and he got in and started the car.

The sky was gray and washed-looking, but there was a luminous freshness in the air rushing into the open car windows. The trees looked unbelievably green and new, as if life were at this moment just beginning. It was cool, and in her thin silk dress, she shivered, and pressed against him slightly for warmth.

He put his arm around her and kissed her, while the car was still moving. He was thinking, she's right. Maybe better to snatch what there is, when you can get it.

The rain began again with a gentle, insistent beat. By the time he brought the car over the bridge and up under the Abel portico, it was late afternoon. "There's some bourbon," she said.

In a shower of blown rain drops from the dripping hemlock trees, they ran for the pillared entrance.

They came into the room with the faded rose damask. The light slanting through windows reaching from floor to ceiling shimmered as if in a castle sunk under water.

She turned on the radio to the local good-music station, and after a moment came a brilliant splashing of piano notes. She went to the kitchen then, and he could hear the slish-stich of ice cubes.

On the piano the black notes of *Orpheus and Eurydice* flowered across the white pages. The glass doors of a black walnut bookcase stood open, and there was a novel on the faded brocade of the tufted sofa. Waiting, he opened it. A colored frontispiece depicted a young man, with enormously broad shoulders and high collar, kneeling in front of a girl with a haystack of bright gold ringlets, her ruffled skirts held in one dainty hand as she held out the other to be kissed. On the flyleaf, in Spencerian penmanship, was written "Myrtis Abel. 1893."

Abel's bourbon was good.

She came toward him, took the old novel out of his hand and turned a page. "I was reading it. It ends something like, 'Then he took her in his strong manly arms and that spring they were married in the vine-covered church by her mother's minister and lived good and useful lives forever after.' That's you!" She laughed.

But in showing him the page, their hands touched. Suddenly the book dropped to the floor. She felt him pressing her, hard.

It came with the sharp suddenness of the electric storm, and exploded in them with the same force, long gathering.

There was an odor in the room a woman used, maybe from her powder or perfume, and it was her, and it did something to you whether you liked it or not. Tom thought of musk in a room in Africa. He remembered the pond lily sleepy odor in Margot's room. But here, the windows had been left open, and outside, locust trees, sopping wet, loosed their damp fragrance into the room.

They did not close the windows.

Later, the odor of drenched spring blossoms flowed over them. Cool, almost too cool, shiveringly, deliciously cool.

Lying there, the blue wisps of their cigarettes came together and rose like a campfire in some overpowering wilderness.

Outside on the red tin porch roof, rain had beaten down the flowerets into a thick layer. A watery sun appeared just in time to sink, a sunset of purplish blackberry stains on creamy linen.

And just as the rain had come, steady and loosing, after the first electric storm, so now talk poured out of them.

Cynthia's skin, where her shorts and halter had covered it, was like pale satin. From the lower floor, where they had left on the radio, came a wave of Haydn, swelling up to them, radiant with kindness.

Thinking about the damp blossom odor, about the other odors, had started Tom talking. "—we'd been on this long stretch, eight missions, bad flak, and a fellow I'd trained with got it. I'd been with him here, in Africa, in Italy. They gave me a week's leave. I was all set to shack up with this girl. A nice girl, a music teacher before the war. Her family'd been killed. Somehow she'd saved this negligee. Pink, with some feathery stuff. She was trying to make it nice for me. I'd bragged how I wasn't going to get out of bed all week, but a funny thing happened. There was an odor in the room. Musk I think. Perfume, but stale and dirty. Suddenly I realized I didn't want to be where I was. Not my dish. I moved out of there fast."

And after awhile Tom said, "I don't see his picture. Your husband I mean. Do you love him?"

"I guess I can't love anyone."

"What'd you marry him for, then?"

"We thought we'd be good for each other. We're the same age. We both came from mixed-up homes."

"Oh, that. Who doesn't?"

"But it was really difficult for him, he was gifted. Not like me. I had the lead in a play at Souverin High, and went to Drama School. I liked the life, the way you really know people, everyone changing clothes, bumming carfare. But I never had a gift the way he did. He was just beginning to get parts, too."

"Was it any good with him?"

"Maybe if we had more of a chance. We never knew, really. We married just before he went over. There we were, in this tourist house, just before they embarked. Harry, well—he was always too intense. I remember that last night. They weren't supposed to tell us, but I knew he was going. After he left me, I could hear them, all night. Marching through that little town, down this macadam road from the camp, where they were loading onto the ships. In the dark street in front of this house I could hear those clumping shoes. Feet in the night, seemed like millions of boys' feet.

"In the morning when I went to the Red Cross desk where we were supposed to inquire, this woman on duty, I could see she felt sorry for me when she said, 'Gone.' But I was all right. In the night, listening to the shoes, I'd had time to get used to it.

"And then the strangest thing happened. All that time he was overseas, a year and a half before he caved, he became changed in my mind into—The Strong Man. Poor Harry, he never was. I built him up, I don't know how or why, into that."

"Well," Tom buttoned his shirt, "maybe he'll be okay yet. What about that?"

She did not answer. Keeping her head down, she slid into a pair of gray flannel slacks.

"How is he now?" Tom asked.

She entangled herself, pulling on a white jersey over her head. Emerging, she moved toward the wall. She pointed to a small water color of a woman with aquiline nose and chestnut hair. "I figure that's my great-grandmother, Alicia. What an easy time she had. Knew what was expected of her and did it."

Tom was stepping into his moccasins.

She glanced at him, then away quickly, tightening the belt. "Father's away a lot."

Tom stood up. "I'm not coming up again."

"Why not?"

"On account of Harry."

"I told you," she said drearily, "I don't love him."

"All right," he said, "then why don't you divorce him?"

"The way he is?"

"What way is he?"

She circled away nervously. "All right, don't come. I'm not begging you."

"Either you love him or you don't. You want to stay married or you don't."

"Oh, you're so righteous!" She picked up the hair brush but forgot to lift it to her hair. "I pity him, I ache for him. Does that help?" She turned to face him. "This isn't hurting him."

"Well," he said stubbornly, "why don't you divorce him then?"

For a moment hate sprang out of her eyes at him.

"I'm not going to help put the skids under some guy so he ends up like that friend of mine," Tom said doggedly. "I would be if I went on with this. I'm not going to."

It was such a reasonable excuse.

He could not look at her as he said it.

20

THAT MORNING, AS SOON AS Abel alighted from the train in McRae, he went to see Bannon. Bannon was an all-around handyman. Abel made the deal include this quarter-ton truck in which they were now riding out to the island, and also Bannon's seventeen-year-old son. The son was riding in back with some of the supplies.

Feeling amiably expansive, Abel touched the order in his pocket.

It meant he had to get the new operation set up quickly, but he could do it.

Even the sight of Bannon's sour countenance did not lessen Abel's magnanimity toward the world.

Confidently he reviewed Step Two in his long-term plans: Make the compound out there temporarily, six months, a year. With more orders, rent a small building outside McRae. Keep Bannon and hire someone with a little technical training to take over the operation. That'll free me to go out for more business.

The truck seemed to ride buoyantly through woods rampant with May.

Abel leaned out of the truck. He was watching for that place trees had been cut out for a transmission line and he could see the island.

There! Sun glinting off the slates. See the other house too, sun on the gray shingles. That crew-man in McRae telling me those people are hanging by a thread. If they don't get production, they may have to go. Well, that'd be hard luck for them.

One of the things I'm going to do soon as I get there—soon as there's an opportunity to do it offhand. Tell them to use the dock. Not apologize. Just say, "Use it."

Across the stream he saw sun flashing from a white dress, as she sat, head bent, in a wide lawn chair. The image—house, imposing trees, charming figure in the light dress—was like something he'd seen before, or dreamed.

Grandfather must have dreamed it up like that. Made it come true, too. Starting from scratch. They say he was one of eleven children. His father a little grocer in Philadelphia. Say he started out, worked his way on foot over the mountains. Started as sandboy in the glass works, fought on up. How he must have felt, losing it through no fault of his own. Shirtsleeves to shirtsleeves in three generations. Well, this is America, why not well-off to well-off in three generations?

He glanced across at the island, at May morning sun on roof, moving clouds, girl—and smiled as he touched again the order which brought the picture closer to permanence.

Nothing'll stop me this time. Unico's not the biggest jobber, but reliable. A little luck in everything. That manager being an old oil-well man, seeing the possibilities. Taking the rights to sell in West Virginia! Everything worked out! Even being able to get credit for supplies, having this signed order.

He leaned forward in the truck.

They came to the bridge.

Abel saw the glaring newness of the second dock.

Why couldn't they have let it die? Given me time to come around.

A slow flush crept over his face.

I don't like it.

Bannon and the boy squinted up at the carriage house roof as Abel pointed to the fancy wooden cupola. "—fire hazard. We'll take that down right away. Gave my promise to have this first order on hand at the truck loading station in McRae by June fifteenth. Have to get going."

Bannon drew down the corners of his mouth.

"The zinc sheets'll be here Monday." Abel pointed toward the back. "Put in vents for the exhaust."

Bannon spat and glanced away as though the prospect of working for this madman were profoundly depressing.

"We better start now taking everything out," Abel said, moving briskly.

Bannon went to the door and looked in. His morose face was long, as chewing slowly, he gazed at the lumber and debris piled inside. In one exclamation of "pssht!" he managed to convey sarcastic outrage, that the task was impossible and that he was being imposed on.

Just as when Abel had first seen his house this afternoon, it seemed his reverie come true, but when he came closer, all the needed repairs showed—so now, at dinner, Cynthia, even in the candlelight, did not seem the girl in that picture on the lawn chair under the trees.

She had a ravaged look. Her congratulations on the order seemed detached from what was going on inside her. Eyes down, face pale, she turned her food over listlessly.

Something about Charlesville, Abel thought. But she won't talk about it. Makes her angry if I do. He felt helpless.

Still, think I ought. Finally, he asked gingerly, "Did you go to Charlesville while I was gone?"

"Why do you ask?" Her voice edged him off.

Couple of weeks before she goes there, always looks worried. "I just thought it was about time for you to go."

She burst out as if he were torturing her, "Why do you keep nagging?" She jumped up, and he heard the screen slam.

He sighed.

For a few days she went about with a white scared look. Then she announced she was going.

He drove her into McRae. Before he put her on the train he touched her shoulder reassuringly.

After she left, he worked night and day. But sweating long hours in soiled coveralls, urging on Bannon and the boy, sometimes going on all night by himself, was satisfying as any work he'd ever done. Not having to wait for someone else to give the nod. To be able to seize a problem, make things move. No one to make you small. And now, passing under the picture of his grandfather, he felt unabashed.

He even noticed as the countryside smiled its way toward June that the rhododendrons next to the house had burst into bloom, and that evening, watching a sun go down behind honeysuckle just coming, he thought of Rena. He had an impulse to telephone her. She might come out tonight, if she were in the mood.

But what if Cynthia came back while Rena was here? Making decisions about the compound, he could do that all right, but women and their feelings!

Besides he had his hands full. Bannon, the cranky craftsman type, was unwilling to cut corners, everything must be done as though to last a hundred years. And he had to watch the son, bright but too eager. Abel had warned him it was dangerous but he went right ahead and washed out a drum with water, and of course got a snoot full of gas.

So, actually, with all the press of small decisions, of daily problems, Abel did not know the exact moment when the water supply stopped.

No water came from the tap in the carriage house. A pail sent down the well-head, left as a picturesque touch, brought back no water.

Abel could not understand it. This artesian well had served the house since Dr. Purcell had it bored to supply the high-legged tub hauled out from McRae.

Mysteriously, unreasonably gone. And of all moments to go! No sense to it. Why should it fail now, when any small hindrance could tip the scale for him? He'd shaved costs too close anyway.

He had to let the boy stop pasting labels and put him to carrying water in buckets up from the river, up the high stone steps, to fill the tank which had supplied faucets, toilets and baths. Drinking water had to be boiled.

He was glad Cynthia was not here.

He had to go into McRae and hunt up a man to come out and find out what was the matter.

After silent exploration, the expert, squatting down on his hams, his old straw hat on back of his head, gave his diagnosis. "Looks like she's caved."

"But why?" Abel's voice rose a little.

"Lots of rocks, loose dirt in there."

"Why should there be?"

"Somethin's done it. Can't say what. God makes, God takes."

Abel had to go into town again and find out what might be done about a new water system. Coming out of the contractor's office, the figures, seven hundred and fifty dollars, wavered in front of his car.

But he couldn't! All his cash, his credit, had to go into having the compound packaged for market.

He felt a sense of injustice, like a man squared for a fight and ready to give a good account of himself, who is suddenly shoved from the rear by some unseen opponent.

In Leland's buying heavy cord for packaging, Abel's face, though he did not know it, wore a black frown.

"Well, Mr. Abel," the elder Leland straightened his sleeve garters, "I hear you got new neighbors. Miz Leland tried to sell them a ticket to the last church supper, but they never showed. Fur as anyone knows, they don't go to any church. A funny crew!"

"They don't bother me," Abel said.

"That so? I thought you looked sort of upset."

"My well caved, that's why."

"Yeah? What happened?"

"Lot of rock and dirt, they say. Don't know."

"Well, that Dorn, the older one, came in here awhile ago buying things, I declare like a madman. Wanted explosives to blast rocks for some project or other and bought enough to blast us all to kingdom come. They just don't seem to know what everything's all *about*! Might have jarred something."

In the car, Abel sat, staring for a long time before he started the engine.

All the way home, sunk in gloomy thought, the figures seven hundred and fifty kept coming before his eyes.

A strange thing that a good and faithful well, that had served—. And then, suddenly, to go. And at the worst possible time.

Explosives to blast rocks.

One thing he wanted to know. As soon as he arrived home, he went around to the back where, through a space in the shrubbery, he could look down to the Dorn house. To their water supply.

There he stood, a long time. He had not been paying any attention to their doings. Ignored them. It was the first time he ever watched them.

Nearly as he could make out, the woman was scratching around in what was evidently a flower bed. No one else in sight. She went into the house but returned carrying a dipper, and began to carry water from a pail near the door and spill it on the flowers. They did things in such a stupid amateur way. But it didn't answer his question, for the pail of water might have been carried up from the river.

For a moment, he had an impulse to go down and ask her straight out, Is your water well gone? But what if the man, or that son, came smirking?

He returned to work.

He had to push harder than ever now. The water loss slowed the operation.

And he had to figure where to get seven hundred and fifty dollars.

He was showing the strain by the time Cynthia came home. He was glad she was back, glad her bag was in the hall. She looked tired, in a dress rumpled from the train journey and he did not at first mention what had happened.

As usual, on returning from there, she looked pale. Now, in addition, she had a curious set look as though she had made up her mind to something. As usual, she did not talk about it.

By the time dinner had ended, Abel could not keep his troubles in any longer.

"—and they tell me if I have a new well bored, it might cave too." He tried to keep his voice matter of fact, not wanting to upset her. "If I use the river, it means a new pumping system."

As if suffering with him this harassment of fate, she was gentle. "Too bad it happened just now."

"One thing I'd like to know," he was scowling at a mended place in the lace table cover, "is whether those people still have water."

"Why?"

He did not say anything for awhile. "I just wondered."

She glanced at him quickly. "You look tired, Father. I think you're working too hard."

He went into the study.

Perhaps what she had just been through at Charlesville gave her a heightened awareness and compassion for anyone with trouble. She managed her laundry, dishes and bath on the carried water as sparingly as possible so as not to disturb him and in the afternoon, instead of sunbathing, she typed letters for him on the old Underwood he had saved from the partnership office.

Sitting in the wan light of the study typing, "Dear Sir—call your attention—able to deliver—ship from our plant," she would stop often, lost in labyrinthine thoughts that had nothing to do with this. She wanted to see Tom.

Next morning she overslept and, rising, stood in the window, looking out into early June. Cardinals flashed against fountains of spirea. Across one corner of her high window, dew pearls hung netted in a spider web. The sky, garden, birds, all seemed blended into one great shout. "There's such a thing as Nature," she had told him, and she could hear his stubborn voice, "Not until—"

She wanted to talk to him. She rehearsed how she would say it: "I went. I told Harry I want a divorce—"

She looked down there. No one was in sight.

Then Abel came into her path of vision. He stood on the lawn. She could not see his face, but the back of his neck, his shoulders, his clenched hands, were those of a man watching a cave out of which some dangerous thing—a snake, a wild animal, might emerge. He turned momentarily and his face had a dark purplish look. She thought of the expression "bad blood." He was working too hard. Too much strain.

Hastily, she dressed and went out. He'd gone. By the time she had coffee, he was out again, standing there.

Quickly, she went toward him.

He did not glance at her. "What I ask is," his face was dark, "would she be watering plants if they had to carry the water?"

"Why is it any of our business what they do?"

"None. But I can't help wondering. They've been blasting rocks for something they were building. Maybe that did it."

"Oh, Father, way down there, cause trouble up here?"

"I don't say they did it on purpose."

"Of course you don't."

"But I *do* say they were blasting."

She watched him return to the improvised workshop. Back in the house, she could not settle down to typing again. She had a sense of some hovering menace.

112

She'd go down herself, quickly, simply, and ask Mrs. Dorn, Did they have water? Just be natural.

If she could talk it over with Tom—.

It seemed so simple to go down and ask for him.

Or—.

Weeks ago, she'd thought of offering Mrs. Dorn the use of the Abel telephone if she needed it. Like everyone that year, they'd have to wait months for a new phone. But she rejected this excuse for going down. She might not see Tom.

It seemed so simple and yet. Something told her if Abel, harassed as he was already, found Tom and herself talking privately somewhere about the island, it might disturb him.

Finally, she put a letter to Tom in the Dorn mail box, asking that he let her pick him up at the bridge that afternoon.

Tom could see, through telling him, she lost some of her own worry, but he began to have a churning in his stomach. Not fear exactly, but an uneasiness as if he ought to be doing something—he didn't know what—but at once.

When he lit a cigarette, he flipped it, after one puff, through the car window. They were parked a mile or so down the dirt road. Then, absently, he lit another cigarette.

"Isn't there," his brows drew together, "a cistern up there at your house?"

"No. The water from the well was stored in a tank."

"Probably because our house was built later, after bathrooms, we have a cistern. Water enough, actually, from our well."

"Enough from ours too, until now."

Studying the problem, Tom began automatically to work his fingers. "If the extra water from our well was stored in our cistern, and if that water could be brought to your tank. Need a pump. That shouldn't be too expensive, and it'd be okay until freezing, anyway."

"Oh," she breathed a long sigh. "He'd appreciate it, Tom. Especially now."

That's what Tom thought. Perhaps this would stop anything that might be creeping up here.

"Let's go back!" he urged restlessly. "I know it'll be all right, but I want to tell Nick about it."

She made no move to release the brake. "When are you coming up?"

He turned surprised. "I thought I explained how I felt about that."

She fumbled with the gear shift, sensing this was not the right moment to tell him. Wait until he's in a better mood. After this is straightened out.

He said, "I'll have to come up to make the offer, of course. As soon as I talk to Nick and explain about hooking up the cistern. Soon as I can."

21

TOM WAITED UNTIL NICK was alone and outside the house. If Agnes heard, it might disturb her.

Nick looked up as Tom came through the elderberry bushes. A pile of ashes and cinders from the coal furnace in the house had been dumped there by the former occupants.

Nick had made the sifter out of a crate by tacking a piece of coarse wire mesh across the bottom.

"People here before certainly wasted a lot of coal." Nick rattled the sifter and the ashes fell through. He lifted out three coal lumps and placed them on the salvaged pile.

"A mean job," Tom said.

Nick nodded at his pile. "Nearly a quarter ton already. If I can salvage even a ton, that'll cut down on what I have to put aside for next winter's fuel." He shook, then lifted out a couple of good-sized lumps with satisfaction. "Whatever I save means more outlay now for my bees."

Tom smiled. "Everything for the bees."

Well, what's wrong with that? Nick thought. "Want something, you have to work for it."

And he kept on sifting the choking ashes as Tom told him his idea about the water.

When he finished, Nick did not say anything.

"Don't you think it'd be a good idea?" Tom demanded finally. "The way I see it, it'll set up a better feeling."

"It might, and it might not."

114

"What are you worrying about?"

"I'm not worrying. Just being cautious."

"But, Dad, best thing we can do is be friendly to him."

"I guess if he wanted to be friends he could have come down. I been right here."

"What do we care about that? What we care about is not having any trouble."

"That's why it seems best to be careful."

"Careful—but not stingy!"

Nick lifted out a lump slowly. All right, son, I see you looking at me, disgusted, impatient. But you don't know. All the times without, the things I gave up, the piece of pie in the cafeteria, the stogies I liked, the shirt collars turned, the pants de-shined, the fishing trip to Idlewild with the others.

Tom's face had clouded angrily. "You're not sore on account of the dock and that sign on the road? Not letting that stop you?"

"No. Of course not. That's not it."

"Then I don't get it. It's not like it would cost us anything."

"Not now, it won't. But what if something happens to ours?"

"Let's worry about that when we come to it."

"He'd have put all that money into rigging up to my cistern. Think he'd like it if I needed it? I have to think about tomorrow."

"You're always worrying too much about the future, about things that never happen."

"It happened to his."

Tom's silence was full of impatience.

"Things aren't the way I wanted them," Nick said. "I wish they'd been different from the start."

"Then let's start them over! Make them different!"

"It's not the way I thought it would be. We're both aiming at the same thing, but he's not the same as me. I had a little more experience than you, son, and I know it's better to keep away from people when you don't understand them. Not get mixed up with them."

"We could offer it to him!" Tom broke out impatiently.

"I give it to him today and there's not enough for us tomorrow. How about that?"

"But, damn it, Dad—" Tom broke off and let out a long exasperated sigh.

Better drop it now. He gets set on something. Maybe later, I can make him see.

115

Cynthia waited. She typed for Abel, she waxed the handsome old buffet in the dining room, trying to keep busy.

It disturbed her that Abel, two or three times a day, broke off work and came out to stand staring down at the Dorns. It made her wish anxiously Tom would hurry.

He did not come.

One evening, as the fireflies appeared in the June dusk, her loneliness became unbearable. She felt she must talk to him. Aside from the water, there was what she had come back from Charlesville all poised to tell him.

She went down the steps and untied the boat. Once before she'd found him by letting the current take the boat around to his side of the island.

She came upon him before she expected, near their house, at the river edge. Not exercising his hand, just standing by himself, gloomily smoking.

She had learned how to manage the boat a little now, and took it in to the shore, but even after he was in the boat, he looked morose. He let the current take the boat. Near the neck he stopped and lit a cigarette. Vast flamingo colored streaks flared across the sky.

He broke out, "That Nick!"

"What happened?"

"You'd think letting you people use a little water was going to hurt him."

So, that's why he had not come up.

"I don't know where he gets that stuff."

Her head drooped as she studied her bare toes in the brown leather sandals.

"All day I been fighting," he broke out, "arguing and fighting!" The boat bumped the gravel, going no place. "He can't see it." His voice was empty. Then he hurled his cigarette into the water with baffled fury. "Sometimes, even if he is my old man, I can't bear him!"

She leaned forward and touched his knee gently, knowing there were no words to say.

The birds began their evensong, filling the river.

After a time she said, "I don't know why you let it throw you. I told you—it's just people."

The birds' cries sounded melancholy as dusk deepened. They sat still for a long time. She thought, We have one thing, anyway, if he could just see it.

116

"Listen, Tom," she began then, "you said you wouldn't come up unless—I got clear."

He made no move.

"And so I did."

He sat up, staring at her.

She went on then, hurriedly, eyes down, as if reciting a dull lesson. "I went to Charlesville and I told Harry I would get a divorce."

Tom sat back from her abruptly, incredulous.

"You oughtn't to have done that!" he cried in consternation.

"But," she was puzzled, "he doesn't care. It makes no difference to him."

The sky was opalescent now, a few stars gleamed. Honeysuckle just coming out scented the air. "I wasn't thinking of him."

She looked bewildered.

With a shuddering breath, he slumped down as if unable to cope with something.

It seemed a long time before he began to talk, staring up at the sky, his voice low-geared, burry and unmodulated.

"After they fixed up my shoulder and hand—this was quite awhile after the plane came down—back at base, there was this doctor. He asked me—I was just coming out of the anesthetic, Well, how do you like life? and I remember mumbling, Can't say, haven't tried it yet. The only reason I tell you that's on account of Donner, so you will understand what I mean about him.

"He was no special friend of mine, I swear he wasn't. Because our names began the same, we'd been falling in or lining up in alphabetical order since we'd started training, and that's why he was always beside me. The greenest kid. Talk about not having tried anything yet. Never seen anything. Never even had a woman. Anyhow, when he didn't come back from this mission, they gave me his personal effects—he had no folks. There was a diary—."

He moved uneasily to escape some memory.

"Anyhow, that's when this crying jag hit me. I'd never bawled in my life before. They thought it was on account of Donner. As if I didn't have sense enough not to make friends when anyone could turn up missing. Anyhow, they gave me a leave.

"Of course, I got over the crying. It wasn't for Donner. I was crying about everything—." He laughed wryly. "Did you know I once thought of being a sculptor? I was bawling for the time I didn't get a scholarship I counted on; for getting drafted just before med school, for a lot of stuff about Nick and Agnes. Was I sorry for myself!

"That was the leave I spent with that girl I told you about, re-member? I said it was the musk and thinking about guys she'd been with stopped me. I guess I knew it wasn't really that. It was because she was a Girl with a Load of Woe. I didn't want to get tangled up with her. Sure, she'd had a gritty time generally, but it was more than that. She was all screwed up in her mind. What I was scared of was, I might get involved with her, feel I had to help her. Me, a guy hanging by his finger nails to a cliff."

Over the river, the sky was deep midnight blue, pierced by stars cold as icicles.

His voice went on, doggedly.

"So, when I told you I wouldn't go on, I wasn't being a boy scout. It wasn't really that I wouldn't do any fooling around with a buddy's wife, wouldn't go on for that reason.

"Maybe I have a sixth sense about such things, but I can smell trouble a long way off. And you're one of them—A Woman with a Load of Woe." His voice now had a desperate note. "I got too much to do, too little time to do it. I can't carry someone else's pack! I never thought you'd go and tell him you wanted a divorce!"

"But we can help each other!"

"I can't marry anyone!"

"Marry!" she stared at him. "Did you think—? Oh, you fool!" she almost wailed in chagrin and disdain. "Did you think I wanted to get *married* again? I wouldn't marry *anyone!* To me, marriage means children, and maybe I have a Load of Woe, but," her voice sounded as if she recoiled from an abyss, "do you think I want to pass that on?" She put her hands over her face a moment, then took them down. "Oh, what's the use? It doesn't matter. You don't understand. You just don't understand. Let's go back!"

He rowed around to the mooring post by the Abel steps. They did not speak.

He tied up the boat. They sat there, sad, confused, not wanting to leave each other. When she spoke, her voice was sorrowful.

"For me, I say, get drunk, make love, do what you have to, nature gave us the appetite, didn't she? If you find someone you can wash it all away with, even for a couple of hours—. If you find it, take it, like a good meal, or a good drunk. Better than liquor, isn't it? Liquor can make you mean."

The stars burned down, inescapably beautiful.

They went up the stone steps.

118

22

THE AIR AROUND THE DORN house seemed to dance in the glinting light from the river. The oil well was producing.

All that slow-gathering tension, mounting through weeks of the noisy portable engine, had gone. There was a new sound now, fainter, steadier—the phut-phut of the one cylinder pump. The Dorns' voices were relaxed and they held their bodies buoyantly.

The rustic table on the porch overlooking the river had been there when they moved in. The chairs were makeshift, one from the kitchen, some from the living room. But give them time.

Seavey, perspiration staining his white shirt, leaned heavily on the table, grinning at them. In front of him, the oil lease, stiff, important-looking.

Across from him sat Nick, in rumpled khaki trousers and mud on his shoes, beginning to look as if he lived in the country. But he still wore his necktie and his hair neatly plastered.

Agnes sat next to Nick, for she, too, was to sign. Her starched dress of red and white print was fastened high at her thin throat by a small gold bar pin. Though she might want to, she would never be able, nonchalantly, to wear the blue jeans she saw on women in the doorways or yards she passed on the way to McRae.

"Looks like a barrel a day, maybe a barrel and a half," Seavey said. "She won't be a big producer, but I'd say she'd be a steady pumper and that kind can go on for years. All you lucky folks got to do is sit with your feet on the rail and collect the royalties."

Nick laughed right out. He'd be busier than he'd ever been in his life. But, doing what he wanted to do.

For weeks, he'd been poring over bee catalogues. In the new workshop, he'd made the lower tiers to hold the frames. Tom wouldn't help. He'd been mean since that time they argued about giving the water. When Nick drove to the Bee Yard, ten miles down the road across the state line, for supplies, Tom sulked. "You oughtn't to put any money in that stuff till you know about the well," he'd said.

Nick hadn't figured on the well to make a living, the way Tom thought he had. Nick meant to make a start with bees. Then, get under way with hares. Maybe later today, drive over, get the rest of the things he needed for the bees. The supplier had over three hundred colonies. What a place!

Tom looked happy and relieved now, as if he'd forgotten the argument they'd had about the water. Tom certainly had counted on the oil. Now they had it. A small but steady income.

In the city, they'd never had guests. Occasionally, when Tom was in high school, he'd bring someone. But they'd always been too worried—or about to move. Or something.

Now Nick's eyes were warm and eager as he said heartily, "Mother, don't we have some beer on the ice? How about a drink, Mr. Scavey?"

Seavey smiled. "Fine." They'd signed the lease.

By the time they'd finished, Nick was in full flower as host—even bragging about improvements. He went into details on the workshop, the hives. "Be glad to show them to you before you go," Nick said cordially. Seavey might know about running a gas station or gathering oil, but he, Nick Dorn, knew about bees.

Seavey went out with him good-humoredly. As they stood on the slope in back of the house Nick expanded proudly, "Have to place the hives just right. Calculate the sun and the wind. Bees are real interesting, the way they manage, with a queen and workers and nurse bees for the young brood. They're very ancient, too, long before the Bible. In some ways, they're smarter than we are."

Seavey was looking up at the Abel house as Nick ran on happily, "—already have my colonies ordered. Thought I'd start off using Italian queens—"

Seavey, near Tom, said softly, with a jocular leer, "Speaking of queens, see anything of the lady up there?" He motioned toward the Abel house.

Tom stared back but did not reply. Nick was running on. "I ought to get, say, twenty-five pounds of honey to a colony in a season, and the honey brings about a dollar and a half a gallon—"

Seavey moved off, restlessly. Agnes, to buoy Nick up, declared, "Bees are nice!"

Nick needed no encouragement. "Then, there's the beeswax. A valuable commodity, much sought after in industry. And you can rent out your colonies. Put them in a fellow's orchard for pollination, get eight or ten dollars, just for that—"

"I must be pushing." Seavey started toward his car. At Tom's side, he said in a low tone, with a grin, "One of the boys on your well told me he saw her one afternoon in a littly bit of shorts and one of these halters out on the hill taking a sun bath." He peered up the hill. "Just my luck to come on a cloudy day!" He clapped Tom's shoulder.

They were beside Seavey's car now. "Say," he kept looking up at Abel's curiously, "what's he doing up there? Looks like smoke or something coming out of that old carriage house."

"I don't know," Nick said. "I got too much to do down here to pay any attention!"

And it was true, and Tom breathed a sigh of relief.

Seavey still peered at the house above. "I guess Abel's all right, but," he grinned, "he can pull a fast one, too." Now that the Dorns had signed, and weren't apt to get any notions, he could safely say this. "I brought my recondition crew in on his well, like I did for yours. Didn't use nitro on his, but some stuff he'd cooked up, and baled her afterward. And then what do you think? Wouldn't sign a lease. Says he'll be producer! He has to turn it into my gathering lines, only way he can get it out, but he likes to play big shot. Calls himself a producer! Him and his one well!

"And when I'd heard he'd pulled that about the dock, I thought, There he goes again.

"Well," Seavey was starting his car, "so long, folks."

After Seavey left, Nick, with confidence now, sent off an order for additional colonies. And next day he went to the Bee Yard at Green Hill again—he loved the place—to bring back more supplies.

The first small order came the next morning. Against Tom's will, Nick had sent it in some time before.

The carrier, across the river by the mail boxes, honked his horn to attract their attention. Nick knew what it must be. He ran over.

The bees arrived in three-pound packages, their syrup can dripping in the middle of the wire mesh, and inside, in a delicate little cage of her own—the queen.

Nick, like a young interne, who, having gotten an A in Surgical Theory, is confronted with punctured flesh and spurting vein, was confident and worried at the same time. Hadn't he pored over pictures, text and directions?

Afterward, Tom, bringing Nick ice for the sting on his hand, said, "You're okay, Nick. Those bees haven't read the right books."

121

"I'm a little nervous. They just don't know me yet."

To his surprise, Tom got a big bang out of the bees. They were so neat and self-contained and as soon as Nick had them transferred, began to set up housekeeping. All the buzzing and whuzzing gave a feeling of purposeful energy.

Agnes's sense of festival materialized into the need to bake some gala dish. With unwonted color in her cheeks she said, "Tom, you get me some of those pie cherries from that tree across the river and I'll bake a cobbler."

What with the bees and the smell of honeysuckle, there was a joyousness in the air.

Nick, who was in business now, had purchased a ledger.

He began the record: "June 11," but then, his pen ran on, spilling his feeling onto the new page.

Got the bees. I never thought the day would really come.
Hasps for frames—.40.

Tom stood on the porch.

Think I'll go swimming. Try that deep hole around the bend. He got into his swim trunks.

His moccasins moved almost without sound through the still green woods.

The river loosed a fresh smell of water washing over sunbaked rocks.

I like it here around the bend. Water looks deeper. Remember Cynthia saying it was.

The grass feels thick and soft under my bare feet.

Then, the plunge. Didn't expect the water'd be so cold. After a little, the numbness was succeeded by the invigorating tingle.

But the shock had shaken him free of the dark woods, the houses, of Nick and Agnes.

Swimming there, feeling detached from the shore, he realized it. Agnes and Nick! They're set!

The well's in!

He turned over on his back and floated.

When he came out, the grass invited him. Why is it a cigarette tastes so fine after a swim?

The pleasant light of deep summer touched the water soothingly.

Be nice if Cynthia were here, just walking around the bend there, or gliding along in the boat.

Well, she won't be. Not now. Not after I had to go and put on that boy scout act.

What got into me?

He finished the magnificent cigarette and stretched back on the thick grass.

That girl needs me.

And she was wonderful. Wonderful!

All the small leaves in the locust tree over his head stirred gently.

The odor of wet locust blossoms on the roof that day, through her open window. The satiny way her skin looked.

He sat up.

He put on his moccasins. Then he stood awhile looking at the shimmering peaceful water.

Why not? I'll go up and see her. Tell her. Everything's different now.

Even the pebble he skipped over the surface of the water seemed buoyant.

23

FIREFLIES GLINTED IN THE blue-green light as Tom walked up the Abel lane.

From his own house he'd glimpsed her moving on their lawn.

She came around the house as he approached. Her thin pink dress and high-heeled white slippers made her look the way you wanted a girl to look.

They walked around to the chairs under the elms. Abel was in McRae.

The twilight was heavy with the odor of honeysuckle.

Not as easy to say as I thought it would be. Especially after me telling her I wouldn't.

She seems glad I came, though.

He smoked to see if that would help. Then he threw the cigarette away and went over and sat on the wide arm of her chair. Her hair—always want to touch it. Soft and silky under my hand.

"I'm the guy who didn't want to get involved with you."

She smiled. "That's what you said."

"I was carrying a pretty heavy pack then. But our well's in. I feel different. As if I could do what I wanted. And I guess you knew all the time what I really wanted."

She looked up at him, smiling provocatively. "Were you trying to show me or yourself just how strong-minded you were?"

"Maybe it did seem as if I were trying to show off."

"And now, everything's different?"

"Well, it is," he said. "I feel free now."

Her eyes crinkled up, amused at him.

"I didn't say it before," he said seriously, "but I was really touched when you told him you'd get a divorce."

Her hair slid out from under his hand as she turned her face away. Her voice sounded flat. "Was it so important?"

"It makes it all better. You're doing what you can, trying to get free."

She was at the far side of the chair now and when he touched her to draw her back, she felt tense.

Her face was still turned away. "What's the matter?" he asked.

Her voice was dull. "I started to tell you that night we were in the boat. But I didn't. It didn't seem to matter."

"Tell me what?"

"I went to Charlesville, but I didn't tell Harry anything. I lied to you."

"But," he stammered, "why would you? There's no sense to that."

"No sense to what you were asking, either. But you were such a boy scout I thought I'd make you happy and tell you I did."

Tom stared stupidly.

She broke out angrily, "Why inflict misery on him? Isn't there enough in the world?"

He was silent. After awhile he said gently, "But you have to straighten it out sometime."

She eluded his hand and jumped up, stumbling over the grass in her haste as she moved away from him.

He was startled. Then he followed her.

He even tried to take her in his arms. She pushed him away and returned to her chair.

She took out a cigarette, tapping it frantically. He could not see her face, but she was breathing rapidly.

He went over and sat on the grass at her feet.

"What goes, baby?"

She burst out finally, as if to hurt him or herself—or someone. "If you want to know the truth, I didn't even keep the appointment with his doctor."

"I didn't know you'd made one."

"Well, I did. Even wrote ahead for it."

"Then why didn't you keep it?"

"Look," she sounded frantic, "I'm not asking you for any advice or any help. Skip it. I don't want to talk about it."

He tried to put his arms around her again, to kiss her, make her act naturally, just through his tenderness, but she pulled away and her voice had a persecuted note. "Look, how did we get on to this? I don't want to talk about it."

"Okay, if you say so. But if you tell me what goes, maybe I could help."

"I was all right before you came. Why did you have to stir this up? Accusing me like this."

"I'm not."

"Why don't you go home and leave me alone?"

Tom sighed. "All right."

He walked across the lawn in the dusk.

Talk about a woman with a load of woe. She *does* need help.

He went down the lane slowly. If I knew how.

By the next morning, he was thinking: Just as well she sent me away. Bad tendency I have, causes me a lot of trouble. Trying to help people.

But by evening, when soft dusk was settling, he got to thinking about her. He was seeing her as she looked, smiling provocatively.

It's not good for her to be up there brooding over things.

I could try to see her around the island casually. Just meet her accidentally. Let her know I'm standing by.

All next day he watched for a sight of her light dress through the trees. He did not see her.

By next evening, he knew he *wanted* to see her. Missed her.

Guess I'll have to go up there by the front lane. Probably be better if I wait till Abel's not around. Go when I see him drive toward McRae.

Then, that afternoon, on the path near the back road, he did meet her accidentally.

At first it seemed she would turn and go back. Then, she stopped

125

and looked at him so that he had a feeling she had missed him too.

When he came up to her, he took her arm. She could not escape this time. He walked along with her.

"I tried that swimming hole the other day. It's fine. They say no one ought to swim in a lonely place alone. Might get a cramp or something. How about you coming tomorrow?"

She looked at him, sucked in her breath, then looked away mutely. Think she wants to. She acts like she's scared or something.

He held her arm. "I promise not to say a word about—anything." Her smile was a little tremulous.

"How about it?" he pressed. "Say about three? It's going to be a hot day."

"If you promise not to talk about—that."

"It's a deal."

The water was not so cold and invigorating and the air was milder. After they swam, she sat on the grassy bank, knees drawn to chin, sad and withdrawn.

Tom looked at her. Hard to talk about—us—without mentioning Harry and the divorce. So, better be quiet.

After a long time she said, "I guess you think I'm really crazy—not wanting to talk about that."

"No, I don't. But I'm not going to say anything about it because I said I wouldn't."

"I know. It's me. *I'm* talking about it. I guess I need to."

She was silent then for a long time.

Finally, he said, "I remember once in Italy I was on a three-day pass and a town I was in was hit. I was caught in the street, pinned down and helpless. And afterward, I didn't want to open my eyes or take my hands off my ears, or even move."

She twisted a lock of her hair. "I meant to see his doctor this time." Then she broke out as if he'd been arguing with her, "Why else would I write ahead for the appointment?" Her voice was sad then. "When the time came I sat there in that little hotel. I know every leaf on every rubber plant. I just didn't go."

He wanted to ask why not, but he was silent.

She jerked her hair viciously. "I despise myself. I haven't acted right—about Harry."

"You mean sleeping around? Well, as to that—"

"Much worse," she broke in. "I—everyone talks to the doctors. But not me. Oh, never me. It's not that I don't feel pity, ache for Harry, that I haven't shed lakes of tears, all useless."

If I could just ask her what she's afraid of.

She began to cry softly.

At least I can do something about that.

When he put his arms around her, deep, shaking sobs came, and it reminded him of something.

It's like a long gathering. Like that time after Donner, when I wasn't really crying about him. She's crying for something I don't understand.

After awhile she straightened up. "I'm ashamed of myself."

He kissed her on the forehead.

She said, "I guess I better not see you any more until I get over this silly nonsense."

And as they walked home, she was hectically gay.

She's in trouble, he thought. Inside her. And I care. A lot. But I don't know what to do.

24

THINKING OF CYNTHIA, TOM strayed off the trodden path returning from the Dorn well. He wandered absently through the dense grape vines, hanging like thick draperies. He passed a small ravine on the back edge of their land and on impulse walked up it. A dog growled. Tom stopped, then moved ahead cautiously.

He came upon an ugly little shack, cunningly hidden behind the broad-leaved vines. A young man about nineteen, in dungarees, sat in its open door, smoking a corn cob pipe.

A wash basin, still dripping, hung from a nail by the door. Candid brown eyes gazed at Tom from a ring of soot, evidently the wash-up from a day's grimy work.

"Hi!" Tom raised a hand in greeting, as though he were the intruder, and requesting right of entry from a man on his home place.

The boy looked at Tom with frank curiosity. The dog growled

and he put a hand on his collar. "Hi!" he said finally, as if permitting friendly entry.

Tom approached the doorstep slowly. "Quite a place you have here." He eyed the hut of ingeniously put-together flattened steel drums and rusted corrugated iron.

The boy's face lit with pride, but his tone was deprecatory, "Oh, I just got enough done so's I could move in last week."

Tom sat on a stump. "Hope you're not drinking from the brook. That's surface water."

"Sure I am. I ain't no sissy."

"How'd you happen to settle on this spot?"

"Well, it's close to the plant. I unload cars at the Chain Works. That's until I begin to make a living here."

"You're going to stay?"

"You don't think I'd put in all this work if I wasn't? Had to carry in every stick on my back. I bought this ground from George Green. You know him?"

"No."

"He's always around Herren's Tavern in town. I used to eat there. Can't understand anyone like him. Sold all his land the other side of the road, bits by bits, to get booze. His father farmed it, George just inhurrited it. Then he sold me this piece over here."

Tom bent over to pat the dog.

"Are you sure George Green owned it?"

"I got a bill of sale. Paid forty dollars. I know it's all right cause George signed it."

Tom glanced at him. His face has such a relaxed openness. His eyes are so trusting. Then I tell him he did all this for nothing. Green slicked him. Will he still have that trusting look? Tom thought of Cynthia. "People are—"

"I got it around here somewhere," the boy said. "Say, you wanna come in?"

Something simmered on a kerosene stove. Pine boxes nailed together made two chairs and a table. An iron cot, neatly made up with a khaki blanket, stood in a corner. The whole hut was tidy with the neatness of a clean animal.

The boy hauled out an old duffel bag from under the cot. Dusk had fallen and he lit an oil lamp.

"That's clever." Tom admired the match safe, a sardine can wired to the wall.

128

"Oh," the boy's face lit up in the lamp glow, "I ain't finished with the place yet.

"Sit down," the boy said cordially, motioning to a wooden box. He rummaged in the bag, pulling out a metal box with a lock. "I knew I had it." He opened the box. "It's here somewhere." He lifted a folded stiff paper. "This ain't it." He laughed a little. "Me college diplomer." He held the paper toward Tom, smiling.

"Yeah?" Tom smiled, taking it.

It was the baptismal certificate of Alfonse Josef Gilbert. Of the St. Ignatius Orphan Asylum.

Tom remembered the stark buff brick building with the high iron fence and a playing field baked dusty in the sun. "That's the one on Route 51, isn't it?"

"Yeah. I dint go in there till I was eleven."

"How was it?"

"Oh, all right, I guess. Jeez, I can still hear the noise when we'd come in the dining room to eat. First, a nun would read from the Bible, then we'd go to it. We had these here tin dishes, and metal top tables. Holy cow! Some music!"

He found the other paper then, a receipt for forty dollars, signed by George Green.

"You like some soup? This ain't no old canned stuff. I bring in fresh vegetables."

"Smells good," Tom said.

The boy moved quickly, but happily, about. "These here's plastic." He put out two red bowls. "Got them in the dime store. You like some coffee?" he asked eagerly.

Tom smiled, remembering Nick on the porch, playing host for the first time, offering beer to Seavey. Extolling his little place. Some deep hunger satisfied.

"Why, sure, I'd like some coffee." They sat on the boxes, the lamp lighting their faces, and the boy watched him anxiously to see if he liked the soup.

"Swell!" Tom said. "Pretty cozy."

The boy looked around complacently.

He made, he said, eighty cents an hour loading at the "Chainy." With that, he'd build a real place here later. And make a living raising hunting dogs. "You ever hear a story called Nora and the ark? Sister used to read it to us. Nora brought in the animals two by two. You got the start of something there. I got Betty here," he stroked his dog's head, "she's named after Betty Grable, a girl in the movies, you may have seen her? I'll get a dog to mate Bett. Then I can train the pups as huntin' dogs, see? Sell them. Earn good money that way."

Tom almost laughed out loud, thinking: Here's a neighbor for Nick! What am I worried about? Nick'll let him stay. And if I have to tell this boy Green cheated him, at the same time I can tell him Nick is decent. Cancels. Perhaps if someone had been with Cynthia. She wouldn't look that way.

The boy was running on, expansive now. "Later on, I'll do some farmin'."

"You ever farm?"

"No, but jeez, I used to look through the fence at St. Ignatz, at a farm. Farmer'd stop plowing, look at the sky. No one to boss or watch him, only the sun. In there, everything went by the clock and you never owned nothing."

Sure Nick will let him stay.

Now the boy was the generous host, urging more soup, a little more coffee? They sat relaxed, elbows on table, smoking. Tom looked around as the lamp threw shadows, blotting out the corrugated iron, making it just walls enclosing a human shelter.

"You'd never know it was there unless I showed you the place," Tom told Nick.

"Can't be very big," Nick said. Under the circle of lamp light, he had his catalogues and accounts spread out before him on the dining room table. "Might buy some of these patented honey combs. Save the bees time."

"I bet a bee worries a lot about time."

"Sure," Nick smiled, "busy bees!" He carefully erased some figures, put others down. "Busy doing a thing interests you—maybe that's the best thing of all."

Tom thought of the boy, finding it hard to convey to Nick in words the other fire and light, the other embodied dream. "I told him I was sure you'd let him stay."

Maybe Nick saw. "Guess he's just trying to get along," Nick underlined an item in the catalogue, "like the rest of us."

"I'll tell him it's okay then."

Nick nodded, carefully copying a figure into his accounts.

25

TOM'S SCRAPER RASPED ALONG the window frame and the old paint fell in flakes. Then he began to chip out the broken putty. He reached the second floor windows on the Abel side.

From there he could hear the tinkle of a piano. It came through the Abel French windows and sifted down through the trees.

It intruded disturbingly. He did not know the music which she played over and over, but it had a forlorn sound. He felt as though he heard someone crying.

He worked the fresh putty around another loose pane, trying not to hear.

He saw Abel and his helper drive off in the truck toward McRae, but the piano notes sounded over and over.

She never comes out doors any more. That's not good either. She's alone. Really alone. I'll bet she can't spill anything out to Abel. She's talking to the piano.

I don't know how to help her, but at least I could be someone to talk to. She had said, Leave me alone, but even as she said it, an undercurrent seemed to cry, Help me.

He put down the paint scraper.

When she came to the door her eyes were dull and she had on no lipstick.

In the lawn chair, her shoulders hunched forward dejectedly as though she were physically tired.

How can I help her when I don't even know where to find her. "I worry about you." Might as well say it right out.

She glanced at him quickly, her eyes full of trouble.

What do I do now, he wondered.

He began then, not quite knowing why, a long, detailed account of the time he'd been on the three-day pass in the town when it was hit and how, afterward, he could not find the man he'd been with. "Piles of rubble all around. I knew he must be under one of them. I'd call. No answer. Then, some stones moved. I knew where to begin to dig."

She looked at him and her eyes said, Help me.

He picked up one of the heavy chairs and moved it over facing her, penning her in. Sitting there, he took both her hands simply, with a good firm hold.

"If you began digging a little yourself, I could see where you were," he said.

Now she would not look at him.

He said quickly, "I know a lot myself about playing dead. More than you might imagine."

Her eyes fastened on him, now, intent.

"Sometimes I get a feeling," he went on, "that I want to say, I wasn't fired, I quit. It usually comes, I notice, when I've laid me down somewhere in a spot that's comfortable enough, at least where I'm not bothered. Mighty like being dead—real comfortable." He stopped, not sure enough of her feeling for him to tell her about Margot and the brackish pond. Anyhow, how explain the urge to get up and move? Don't understand it myself. Something needling me, but something else saying, Why not shut your eyes and forget everyone and their troubles?

Long bars of summer light fell through the moving trees.

Her voice was sad. "If I could just shut my eyes to the people, and see only the other part, the world around."

"You know, this may hurt your feelings, but sometimes that's what you—. I mean, you're so beautiful, so—sort of untouched looking. But when you talk—and act—it's like you say people are."

"I despise myself most of all."

"You ought not to. I don't. I care about you."

He was surprised to hear this. It's as if trying to help her I got a vested interest.

"You think I ought to go and talk to that doctor." She was staring at her hands now.

"I don't, baby. I don't know what you should do. The only thing I do know is that at some moment, you have to make yourself take your hands off your ears, open your eyes and get up and move."

She looked at him pleadingly. "How?"

You'd think to hear me it was easy, or that it never happened to me any more. And she's looking at me as if I had the answer.

"You just do it," he said.

She twisted her hands together. "With my brain, I know you are right, but doing it—that's different."

When he left, he kissed her.

Halfway home, he smiled ruefully, realizing what a different feeling he had kissing her. Before he had just wanted her. Now, he wanted her to be all right.

Next morning, as he drove toward Green Hill with Nick for more bee supplies, they saw the flag up on the Dorn box.

A letter for Tom from Cynthia. He stuck it in his pocket to read when he was alone. When they arrived at the Bee Yard, Nick went inside.

Tom took it out and read: "I'm on my way to Charlesville. Only please, just when I first come back, be there waiting for me."

26

A DEEP SENSE OF SATISFACTION welled up in Abel. He had just delivered the first shipment to the trucking station in McRae.

I pulled it off. On time! In spite of no water. In spite of Bannon's stubbornness. Having to drive him, work night and day myself.

This is just the beginning!

Everything on the upbeat. Even Cynthia. Deciding finally to get clear. Hating to go to That Place, but going, to straighten her affairs.

He drove along the road and stopped at his mailbox.

An order! Small, but another order. Quick delivery, they say. He laughed. I put up a big front. They don't know the stock on hand at "Glen J. Abel Specialties" is zero. Means I have to start right in again.

He drove up the lane. The water lack slows me. His brows contracted as he glanced toward the Dorn place.

It might very well be. Especially their being inexperienced. Not knowing what they were doing. Probably used too much, far too much, blasting a few rocks. Upset some strata up here on my place. If so—what about that seven hundred and fifty dollars?

Next time I'm in McRae—go in and ask at the courthouse who'd look into someone damaging a water well.

Not now. Have to press on with this new order. Bannon, damn him, just because we got one off, going on a drunk. Have to manage with the boy. He needs training, but he's coming along.

Tired.

He went to the carriage house at once. That June had been hot and the fumes in the carriage house had been sickening until he found a heavy duty fan in a second-hand store. It pushed the gases through the vent in back. After that, the work went more easily. The exhaust didn't help the vegetation, but that couldn't be helped.

He started the fan and he and the boy began the operation for the second order. Heat or no heat, had to push on. As he worked, he heard excited voices coming up the hill through the trees.

He went out and stood peering down through the shrubbery.

Now what are they up to? Always something. What are those square white things? Bee hives? Might know it'd be some cockeyed thing or other.

When he went back in, the boy had, in spite of warnings it was dangerous, dumped the rest of the drum of dry material into the mix all at once. Abel had to concentrate on that small emergency.

Later on, in the heat of the afternoon, waiting for the boy to carry up water, he went out to the edge of his lawn. He stood looking down at the Dorns, at the bee hives.

A sensible man'd be careful using explosives. But someone that'd take up an outlandish hobby like that? A word he had been groping for came into his mind. Screwball.

When Cynthia alighted from the noon train in McRae, she felt as though if she could just get to Tom quickly, she'd be all right. But the taxi man who carried fares to outlying points would not return for half an hour.

She had not eaten all day. She went across to the Mansion House. Confronted with a large noon menu and the fat gray-haired waitress, the idea of actually taking in a healthy normal meal gave her violent nausea, a rebellion at swallowing.

Then she saw Rena, on duty, in her black dress, her mass of red hair shining. Cynthia had forgotten she might see her. Or had she forgotten? Maybe something told her to come in so she would see Rena. A warning of how easy it was to end up, like Rena, half-

134

starved for life, for love. Unless you seized, accepted, swallowed. Nauseated or not.

Cynthia stared sickly at the menu, wishing Tom were here. Wishing she could phone him.

She ordered milk and a sandwich.

As she ate, her hands trembled.

Finished, she sat there. Before she left, she'd been so confident she was not going to let herself play Sleeping Beauty any more. Now, she had to get up and go forward. If only she could get to Tom. Her knees shook as though she were too weak to walk.

She saw again the sun parlor at the hospital in Charlesville with its washed-out chintz. Saw the doctor leaning forward earnestly, hands on the arms of the creaking wicker chair as he talked to her.

"—if there had been no organic injury. There's always hope if it were not that. But you knew the shell fragment had pierced the brain covering. Progressively deteriorating—incurable. It's healthier for you to accept this about Harry. Not feel guilty if you want to marry again, rear a family, make a new life."

The dining room seemed to black out a moment. Of course, she had known about the injury. For a long time, in the dark caves of her mind, the fact the doctor announced had been waiting. Yes, she'd known it. But as long as it was kept back of the threshold of the cave, she did not have to do anything. It was the permitting it to be said to her openly that left her scared and defenseless. She'd let herself be wakened out of the frozen sleep. And coming out of it, she wanted Tom to be here, to help her.

The doctor, of course, had been full of sympathy for her.

He thought it was Harry she was scared about. But she'd felt sorry, achingly sorry for him so long it was all built into her fibers. She no longer quivered about it. What she was scared about was herself.

If you were waiting for Harry, no one prodded you, no one expected you to marry, have children—to eat a hearty, wholesome meal.

You could not, with eyes downcast, and bitter self-excusing mouth say, People are slime.

I took my hands off my ears.

But now—I have to act as if I had heard.

I have to get up and go on. And I can't.

"You just do it," he said.

Perhaps when he talks to me again, I'll *act* different, too. Act as if I really were all right.

Maybe then I'll be able to take up my bed.

27

NICK, BEE VEIL ADJUSTED AND wearing canvas gloves, came through the grass.

A mid-June morning, sunny after rain—could a man ask for more? Just about this time, he'd have been disappearing into the office—for years that gloomy building full of the odor of old lunches near the rail yards—knowing when he'd be through for the day, the sun would be too. And here he was! Sky, wet leaves, river scintillating.

And wasn't he becoming an expert! Yesterday morning, when the last shipment of bees arrived, he'd been able to hive them quickly before the rain broke. In the afternoon, when he'd been up to look, there'd been no activity. But then, worker bees never went to the fields in rain. Ahead, the glisten of white hives looked beautiful to him. Ten colonies already. He was proud.

As he approached them, he wondered about the quiet. No sound or motion. Early of a sunny morning, the workers should be going out and returning with loads.

Delicately he examined the first hive. The bees were in the colony. He stood, staring. Then, frantically he ran from one hive to the next. They were in there all right, in dark clotted masses.

All dead. He gave a great cry, "Tom!"

Tom had come running. Now he stood panting, breathless.

"All dead!" He looked at Nick just standing there, like a man in a crash that doesn't know it yet. "What did it?"

Nick stood stunned.

"Maybe it was that hard rain, Dad."

"For thousands of years bees've lasted through rain."

At least he's talking now.

"The hives are dry," Tom said. "Must have been something else."

He looks now as if he knows there's been a crash.

"Might have been some disease, Dad. Come on, we'll go over to Green Hill, ask that guy. A bee fever or something."

The bee man came back with them. It was not only that Nick was a promising buyer of supplies. There was a bond between Nick and him, as between people who collect Chinese victrola records or go in for marathon walking.

The man peered at the ground, sniffed the air.

"Ain't no farms nearby, is there, none I noticed."

"No, why?"

"Wondered if anyone was dustin' crops. But no farms near, so it ain't that. You been fumigatin' anything yourself?"

"No."

He looked at the trees, then pointed up the hillside. "What's that?" Halfway up, the leaves hung curled. Closer to the carriage house they were dead.

"I'd say," the man nodded toward the shriveled leaves, "they was gassed. Is that a fan I hear runnin'? That could have drove it. Someone blew out a gas."

"That can't be right," Tom said quickly. "Wouldn't we notice?"

"A little could kill them bees. You wouldn't have felt it."

After the man left Nick just stood there by the hives.

"Might as well come back to the house, Dad. Have some lunch."

"You go."

Can't leave him standing there. He's looking up the hill.

"That fan's still running." His voice was strained.

"If that's what did it, it was accidental."

"But it killed them."

"Guess he's making something. It could have happened without his knowing."

"I'm going up and talk to him."

Not the time for him to go, all wrought up. "What for?"

"If he's doing something hurtful and he knows, he'll have to stop, won't he?"

"We don't really know what happened."

"If he did it, and killed"—Nick's face crumpled up—"all my bees—"

"An accident."

"All right, an accident, but he'll want to make it right, won't he?"

If I go instead of him, might not be good either. The way Abel looked that day when Cynthia and I were in the boat.

Nick started up the path.

137

"Well, wait. Wait a minute! I'll come too!"

Nick went on, head down, hands clenched at his sides.

Tom followed.

Glad Cynthia's not here! What if something got started, and she heard—. That look on her face, recoiling contempt.

Tom called, "What's the hurry?" Nick moved ahead doggedly. "Wait!"

They came out on the Abel lawn.

Cynthia! She's home. Standing there talking to Abel. Must have come on the noon train. Still has on her city suit and shoes and stockings. I can't let anything ugly happen.

"Let me do the talking, Dad." Tom's whisper was urgent.

"I can tell him."

Her face is so pale. And she's looking at me so pleadingly.

"Good-day, Mr. Abel," Tom said.

"Hello." Abel looked questioning.

"The bees are dead," Nick said in a flat hurt voice.

Abel looked puzzled, as though to say, "Why bother me with that?" But he didn't say anything, just looked at Nick, waiting.

"All of them." Nick's voice rose a little.

Tom put a hand on his arm.

"We were wondering, sir," Tom's glance went to the open door of the carriage house, "what you were doing?"

Abel gave a little incredulous start, then stared at him. "Why do you ask?"

"We want to know what made those leaves wilt," Nick broke out.

"Well," a flush rose in Abel's face, "I don't know as that's anyone's business but mine, what happens on my place!"

"It's my business if it kills the bees!" Nick cried.

"Sir, we thought that if we knew, we could—"

"The bee man said some gas or other killed them," Nick broke in.

"What's that to me?" Abel burst out, a tried man.

Nick's mouth opened, astonished. "You don't *care?*"

"Are you trying to come up here and tell me what I can make on my own property?"

Nick, his mouth still open in bewilderment, looked at Tom.

"And I might say I'm a busy man," Abel said impatiently. "I ought to be working right now, not wasting time standing around here arguing. I have an order to fill, and you come up and worry me because some crazy hobby of yours doesn't pan out. If you learned what you were doing before you did it, maybe you wouldn't cause so much trouble—not only to your own property, but others'!"

"Other property?" Nick gasped. "Who caused trouble?"

"Blasting when you don't know what you're doing! And then I have no water!" Abel's face worked now with righteous indignation.

Tom glanced worriedly at Cynthia.

"What are you talking about?" Nick's body gathered into a tense knot.

"I'm talking about my water going, that's what!"

"Your water! What have I got to do with that!"

"You could have had a lot to do with it."

An incredulous look was growing on Nick's face. "You don't care about my bees, on account of your water. You're trying to get back at me. That's it."

"What do you mean get back at you?" Abel demanded.

Incredulity had spread on Nick's face. He could not speak.

"What do you mean get back at you? I want to know!"

Tom's glance was at the ground, his face was miserable as he licked dry lips. What will I do? Tell him Nick was too stingy to give him the water?

"I want to know what's this about the water," Abel's voice was harsh now. "You and your bees! That water was serious business. Seven hundred fifty dollars worth!"

"And if we needed the water ourselves," Nick said defensively, "you wouldn't care!"

Cynthia had moved swiftly to Tom. "Tell Father."

Abel looked at Cynthia's hand on Tom's arm.

Tom glanced quickly at Nick, then at Abel. "I wanted him to give you water from our cistern and he wouldn't. That's all."

Abel's eyes stayed on Cynthia's hand,ʹ resting on Tom's arm. "How'd you know so much about it?"

"I told him," Cynthia said.

Abel stared at Tom a moment blankly. His words grated out. "I didn't ask you for anything."

Outraged bewilderment had been mounting in Nick. "I want to know what about my bees. You'll surely want to make them good."

"Me, make them good!" Abel broke out, angrily astonished.

"Even if you don't care—"

"Perhaps that's why you came up here, crying around about your screwball bees so I wouldn't do anything about my water!"

139

"You're surely going to pay!"

"Pay! Pay! Pay seven hundred fifty dollars!"

"Shoved around long enough!" Nick glared back at him now. "I'm going to begin to shove too. You'll pay!"

Tom grasped Nick's arm firmly, turned him toward the house. "Come on."

"He *has* to pay!"

Shakily, Agnes put the wooden salad bowl on the table.

I knew it was bad, hearing their voices up there. Now seeing Nick's face, all twisted up, makes me feel dizzy.

"Come, Nick. Lunch now," she said.

Nick did not move. He sat staring ahead with bewildered incredulity.

"I put bacon dressing on the lettuce. Tom coming?"

"No. She didn't go in their house either. That girl."

Nick came to the table. He did not lift his fork.

"Tom blames me, thinks I shouldn't have made any fuss, I could tell."

"Well, it's over now." Her hand wavered as she put the salad on his plate.

He put down his fork, staring ahead. "I could have gotten over it about him not wanting to make good, I wouldn't have been mean. He didn't *care!*"

"Maybe he just didn't show it."

Agnes put her hands in her lap to hide their shaking. I'll go up there myself, talk to Mr. Abel. He'd care if he understood.

A long sly crackling, rustling sound came from somewhere.

Nick's clenched fist slacked open. "What was that?"

He ran upstairs first. Then down. When he did not return, Agnes followed him.

He was standing in the basement, looking at a crack opened between the wall and the new concrete floor.

"Never mind, Nick."

"Maybe he was right saying I didn't know how to do **anything**! Even the floor I made!"

"You can fix it!"

"Yes." A new look of sullenness hardened on his face. "I'll fix it."

"Nick, don't look like that."

Agnes clutched her shoulder with a spasm-like movement. That pain!

"I'll fix the rest too!" Nick broke out. "Never had anything to fight for before. Now, I'm—not—going—to—let people—shove—me anymore!"

Tell him it's like his fussing and fighting cracked it open. Can't get breath. Can't see Nick. Waviness. Blackness.

Nick must have carried me upstairs here to the sofa. Must not have been out long. Just a few minutes. Nick has no meanness in his face now. Scared looking.

"The medicine. Look in the shelf where the cups are, in the kitchen."

The medicine's helping. Just stay here awhile. Feel better. Sit up and show Nick I'm fine.

"Please, don't move!"

"I'll rest awhile. But I'm all right. I'm fine."

Something I must do as soon as I get up. The medicine dulls me. Try to remember. Yes. Go up and talk to Mr. Abel. Explain how we are just like him. Meant to go long before now. Ever since the dock. Don't feel up to it now. Just as soon as I feel better, go.

Tom stood, his face lowering.

Cynthia kept her eyes on him all the time, anxiously.

Sunlight was a glare on the water where they stood at the bend. He turned away from her to look at the houses with angry disdain. His eyes—rejecting everything, she thought.

"Sorry you came back to this," he said, still looking at the dwellings, repudiating them. "Everything they need to make things go here, and they have to start this!" His voice was edged with contemptuous exasperation. "I'd have worked to pay for the bees. I tried to shut Nick up. Not that your old man was any better!"

"He's been alone. Guess he got brooding about his water."

"The whole thing just makes me want to go some place and puke."

You hardly know I'm here, she thought. You're as accusing as they are. All a waste. A waste. Those words I used to parrot, never knew till now what they meant— The expense of spirit in a waste of shame is lust in action.

Tom, as if trying to remold a stone, kept working his fingers. "Just when I thought I had things rolling." His eyes were cold and his mouth bitter. "You'd think some part of them *wants* to spoil things."

Blackberries hanging ripe like bits of coal. Sun on honeysuckle.

141

High noon of the day, of the year. It could be high noon for us, too, she thought.

His voice was dull. "What's the use of trying to do anything?"

I won't *let* it be wasted. Not now, just when I. Want him up here with me. Not just our love-making either. There's something else. Don't waste. I have to find a way. Have to *do* something. Find the words. Have to.

For the first time in a long while she felt strong and steady. Her voice was calm. "Tom, I talked to Harry's doctor."

"Oh." He turned to her, contrite. "I'm forgetting about you. See what this stuff does! Eats into everything. Tell me. Was it bad?"

"Not in ways you'd think. I guess I knew it underneath all the time. Knew there'd been an organic injury. They couldn't help that. It was the letting the doctor say it to me. That Harry won't be better."

"Oh, baby."

"I'm trying to be honest now. And I'm going to get a divorce or annulment or whatever is needed. Father'll help me. It's not that I don't pity and ache for Harry, always will. But I was using him as a shield—for me. The world seemed so bleak."

"Maybe you had something there."

"But," she went on quickly, "all the time I was waiting for the doctor, all the time since, I hung on to one idea." She took his hand, clasped it firmly. "You."

Took up my bed, she thought, surprised. Walking!

"It was on account of you," she repeated.

He kissed her.

But because he was still angry at Abel and Nick, or because she was exhausted from what she had been through, the kiss brought no physical stirring.

They stood a moment.

Then, he looked back at the houses.

She took his hand, held it. "Are we going to let them waste what's between us, too?"

But he did not return the pressure of her hand. Still with the bleak angry look he started toward the houses.

28

THE COUNTY ATTORNEY HAD kindly nearsighted blue eyes. He peered now into Nick's troubled face.

"That'd be a civil suit, out of my jurisdiction. But I always like to help folks if I can, so I'm going to give you some advice." The attorney had just been appointed circuit judge to begin next term, fulfilling a life ambition. He had a mellow feeling toward the human race.

"First off, figure the lawyer's fee, figure you might lose the case. Against that, put the figure of how much the damage—what was it to? Bees?—figure the cost—and you'll see what I mean."

Nick's clothes began to look like those of a country fellow come to town, rather than the other way around. Nervously, he moved his hands from the chair arms to the pockets of his khaki pants.

"Lots of folks get mad and don't stop to figure. Why don't you talk it over with your wife?" The attorney's lenses seemed too small, so that his kindly eyes seemed always to be squinting. "Maybe you figure it's worth it to cause Abel some trouble. Make up your mind whether you're doing it for that, or to recover damages. Then, weigh your chances."

Outside the office, Nick sat in one of the varnished oak chairs in the corridor, staring at the pattern of the tessellated marble floor.

Talk it over with your wife, he told me. Didn't tell her. Didn't tell Tom I was coming. How could they understand what was going on inside me? Always before I took it. Never stood up for myself.

The attorney says out of his jurisdiction. There ought to be some justice.

Hubert Krimmer, in a freshly pressed dark suit, came out of the Recorder of Deeds office, and walked, his shoes squeaking, briskly down the corridor.

"Well! Hello, Mr. Dorn."

Nick glanced up. "Hello," he said morosely.

"You look sort of down. Anything the matter?"

"Maybe."

"How's everything out at the island?"

"So-so."

Krimmer sat on the edge of the chair next Nick. "Having some trouble?"

Nick found it a relief to tell it.

Krimmer leaned forward sympathetically as Nick poured out in phrases still bewildered at injustice, the death of the bees.

"Tch! Tch!" Krimmer commiserated. "All I can say is let someone get away with one thing, they keep on." Then he said helpfully, "I can give you the name of a good lawyer."

"Well, thanks, but—"

"His office is just across the street. I'll take you over and introduce you."

Why is he so eager? Easy enough for him to urge me to spend more money than I can afford. Get tangled up in the law. "You got something against Abel?"

"Not at all. But I can tell you if you have a suit, act at once. Evidence tends to disappear."

"Um. Thanks just the same. Guess I'll think it over awhile."

Krimmer rose. "Up to you, of course," and his shoes squeaked complainingly as he moved off down the corridor.

Nick sat a long time, staring at the floor.

Putting a hard coating of words around it set it, as if a stone had formed inside him.

Hubert Krimmer paused on the steps outside. A client was waiting in his office, but Krimmer stood, studying his nails, thinking.

Far as I'm concerned personally, he thought, be glad to forget all about Abel and his doings. But as long as he hangs on there at the island, can't afford to. If only I *knew* whether or not he's had his craw full and won't meddle any more on the county machine ticket. If only I could be *sure* he's had enough. Does he still have his city connections? One thing I know, the more firmly he entrenches himself on the island, less chance of his foot slipping, of his moving back to the city. He plays such a lone wolf. Never know *what* he's up to. That's how it happened before. The first thing I knew, orders from the courthouse crowd and Abel's on the ticket.

Krimmer sighed.

Not counting on that Dorn to do anything. He'll go home and

talk it over with that dumb wife and son, and they'll argue him out of any law suit. I remember them all right.

But on the other hand, is it right for Abel to be messing up the countryside with fumes? I'd heard rumors before this. Buying supplies, hiring Bannon. Manufacturing something out there. First thing you know, be established, hiring hands, throwing his weight around.

Some chemical stuff he was making, they say. That's not right. There's some kind of an ordinance. A nuisance ordinance.

As if reaching a decision, Krimmer turned and went inside the front door, down one flight of steps to the basement, along a corridor, to a door lettered M. J. Flanagan, County Constable.

Who got Flanagan his job? I can just suggest he check to see if an ordinance is being violated.

29

"THAT'S WHAT I WANT TO know!" Standing beside the improvised laboratory, Abel glared at the constable. "Who did it?"

Cynthia, at the altercation, had run out and stood nervously twisting a lock of hair.

"Who?" The constable stood on solidly planted feet and glared back. "Don't need to be anyone. It's the law."

"Someone had to start it! You can't tell me!"

Cynthia moved worriedly toward him.

"We don't say who!" The constable chewed stubbornly. "But I'm telling you—just don't do it!"

"Who's going to stop me?" Abel's eyes darted around baffled, seeking a foe to come to grips with.

With mock patience, the constable took from his blue serge coat a folded paper. In a deliberate, maddening voice he read:

"Ordinance seven six two—No person shall make or use within the said county fumes of a noxious nature within three hundred yards of a human habitation." He pointed to the Abel house, to the Dorn house. "You could hurt crops or a pet or something with them fumes." He looked at Abel reproachfully.

"You mean to tell me on my own place—"

"Look, Mr. Abel, you being a respectable citizen, I didn't bring any injunction, nor warrant. I'm putting it to you as a warning."

"I'm trying to carry on a business and I'm not going to be interfered—"

"They's a fine of three hundred dollars, and furthermore, confiscation of materials. So I am telling you, don't—do—it!"

Low ward-heeler!

Wrathfully he watched Flanagan go down the lane to his car and drive off.

On the island my grandfather! To try to stop me! Away out here in the country. No one for miles around. Except the Dorns. If it hadn't been for them being here, the constable couldn't try to stop me. They're the only ones near. Just *being* there! That's the interference!

Was it Dorn who told him?

He found the pencil in his hand broken in two fragments, so hard had he clenched it, trying to keep from shouting out his enraged frustration.

I can't afford to stop! Have to push on! Have to take a chance!

For three generations, the county attorney's family had lived in McRae. The Abel family had moved away from the vicinity before that. Now, the county attorney shook hands with Abel, and made cordial chit-chat, ending up with, "I watched your try for the commissionership last fall with a lot of interest." He smiled, "Don't think Hube Krimmer enjoyed it quite so much though!"

Was he a friend of Krimmer? Abel swallowed hard. No. Think not. "It's about some screwball that's moved in out there on the island that I came to see you," Abel said.

The county attorney looked at him quickly, then dropped his glance, waiting. What was going on out there anyway?

"He was dynamiting around and I think he loosed the rock strata and hurt my water supply. Upshot is I'm out seven hundred fifty dollars. Now my question to you is—if he did that, isn't he responsible? Doesn't he have to bear the damage?"

The county attorney came down on the front legs of his chair. "Be a little hard to prove."

"I know he bought the explosive in Leland's. I know he was blasting."

"As I understand, you're not thinking of a criminal action, not accusing him of doing it deliberately?"

"Deliberately or not, I'm out seven hundred and fifty dollars! And

146

a peculiar thing, and pretty hard for me to take—his own well is intact."

"Umm." The attorney stroked his plump cheeks philosophically. "Often see that. Someone's carelessness will damage another's property, and not hurt their own. See it sometimes in automobile accid—"

"My question is, is he liable?"

The attorney rose and went to the water cooler and had a drink. He offered one to Abel, who refused impatiently.

"There's a lot of tricky points." He returned to his desk. "Do you want me to send a man out from this office to check around, see what happened?"

Abel moved uneasily. Someone like Flanagan out there snooping. Not until I get this second order out anyhow. Can't stop. "Oh, that might come later," Abel managed to sound casual. "My question now is simply, in a case like that, isn't he responsible?"

"Well, like I say, a lot of tricky points." He was drawing an apple on the pad in front of him, putting in careful details. "I might tell you if this came up to a grand jury, they'd be bound to wonder. Dorn was in here awhile back complaining about you."

"Me!" Abel was astonished. "What about?"

"Claims you damaged *his* property. Bees, I believe."

Abel's heart pounded. Dorn! That *was* how the constable knew!

"There's a record of that," the attorney said.

Abel felt the thick choking. Here I am tearing my guts out, breaking my heart trying to get out the compound, and they pay attention to some nut and his bees. The injustice of it.

"Of course, if you want me to send an investigator—?"

Abel rose, his chair scraping back noisily.

The attorney stood up and insisted on shaking hands. "It's a little hard sometimes, but I find we just have to take people as we find them."

Abel had finished and consigned the second order. He did not have the same deep joy in it, though. And the first money received in payment had to go toward the new water system. He'd held off the contractor until the shipment was off and the carriage house padlocked. The workmen might carry gossip back to McRae.

Now, the men, ditching, fitting pipe, installing the pumping unit on the river, were all over, and the demands for actual cash were agonizing.

Since he couldn't make the compound with the workmen about,

he should have used the time to go to the city and drum up more business. But, an odd thing had happened.

His oil well suddenly went off. On the fourth of July, Bannon had gone on a drunk. He was still away. So, all that miserably hot week, Abel searched and puzzled for the cause.

Bannon's boy tried to help. Abel had taken him firmly in tow now, and had even thought, if he were well supplied with funds, he'd enjoy helping this boy get an education. But he had to content himself with giving him advice, and taking the trouble to make of him a devoted follower.

Together, they checked the rig as best they could—the casing, rods, the pump itself. Bannon, a crafty and experienced hand at nursing the old wells in the neighborhood, whose margin of profit was small, had been, Abel must admit, doing a good job. The rig seemed all in order. Perhaps the well had paraffined up again on the sand face.

They spent a day using Abel's own compound, and then three or four days baling out the loosened refuse. No return. If only Bannon would sober up.

Abel held down his panic, but a bleak memory shoved its frightening face above a dim horizon. Hadn't he heard—somewhere—? No, he wouldn't let himself think of it.

He *had* to have the income from the well. He threw himself frantically into checking the rig, putting new cups on the sucker rods, running a hook.

When Bannon did return, on a sultry day in the middle of July, and found Abel had been "messing in his work," disturbing the delicate arrangements he had set up, a surly look settled on his long face. He moved in ugly silence, with an expression which said, "I know what's the matter, but I ain't talking."

Finally, his hostility to Seavey overcame his surliness. When Abel and Bannon met Seavey on the joint path, Seavey, passing, laughed as he raised a hand in greeting.

Bannon turned, staring after him. Then his sullen mouth opened, as if to spew forth all the bad liquor he had soaked up, all his resentment stored against the world: "You ain't going to get no production no matter what and I'll tell you why. They're takin' it."

Abel's own fear put into words. "But Dr. Purcell, the original driller, he ran both, and at the same time!"

"When Purcell run them they was still in the flow stage. It's a different story now."

"What makes you so certain?"

"Look at the log. When did they put the pump to her? June twelfth. When did this one begin to wean out? June seventeenth. I hear from the crew they're liftin' three barrels a day and that includes your two barrels."

"But can they do that?" Abel's tone was reasonable.

"They are doin' it."

"After all—"

"What you going to do?"

"I don't know." Abel stood baffled.

30

IT WAS A HOT NIGHT AND TOM walked out under flashes of heat lightning.

Two whole weeks. Wanting to see her, and holding back. All this arguing with myself. What good's it done me?

Her words, "Are we going to let them waste what's between us?" seemed to repeat themselves endlessly. Sometimes guilelessly. Sometimes dragging implications after themselves.

Because she's right. There is something growing between us. It's good. It's wonderful. But.

Why do I hold off and stay away from her?

Getting in too deep. Didn't intend it.

He looked up the lane. He thought, or imagined, that he saw a white dress moving in the dark.

It's this ache I have all the time.

I want to see her.

He went up the lane.

She walked with him across the dried-up daffodils. She didn't ask him why he had not come. She was glad he was here.

She talked to him eagerly, as if the words had been waiting. "—and it's like all that business about Harry, me hiding my head—it's working out of me in bits and pieces.

"That day when I had just returned and they quarrelled about the bees—I still don't understand just how it happened with me, but I seemed to see you sinking and I got this strength. I don't know where it came from."

"I guess we both know," he said.

The heat lightning flickered above the trees as they stood there together.

31

HOMER SWINTON GAZED APPRECIATIVELY around the high-ceilinged room at Abel's Island. Lamplight glowed on the faded rose damask.

Homer, thirty-six, unmarried, lived in an apartment in a made-over house in McRae with his widowed mother. She had been a dressmaker who helped him through law school, and they had no social life. Now, the wide nostrils of his nose quivered as Cynthia came in. He had few chances to brush up against a girl like Cynthia. She was beautiful all right. And, he'd heard things.

He wished Abel hadn't arranged it this way, that she would have come to his office. But, he guessed from the way Abel looked at her, he kept her close when he could. He'd been afraid, when Abel talked on the phone, it'd be something simple like desertion. But as they talked, he found it was more complicated.

Cynthia leaned forward under the lamp, soft hair falling forward, her head turned to look at him. He was rather squat, with black wiry hair in a crew cut and he blinked now behind enormously thick-lensed glasses as he spoke. "In this state, divorce from defendant with unsound mind can be complicated. Naturally, there are ways. We may have to make it annulment. I'll look it up, Mrs. Winters. Could you come into my office, say Thursday?"

"We'll be there," Abel said quickly. "And if that's all about that, I know Cynthia won't be interested in this other business." Abel didn't want her to think of the island as anything but a serene castle. And it would be.

Cynthia moved through French doors, her pale dress floating away from the lamplight like an escaping moth.

Abel's tone was calm and reasonable as he told Swinton about the draining of the oil.

Swinton had graduated from the law school in the city only six or seven years before, but he had been doing well. Aggressive enough to jostle on to the primary ticket as county solicitor through city connections, and defeated, like Abel, by the same means, he had, nevertheless, been retained by a couple of local oil and gas companies. That meant he'd be up on leases.

"Interesting." Swinton rolled the bourbon around in his glass as Abel finished. "But, there is an odd legal aspect to consider."

Cynthia drifted back in.

"We're just talking business, Cynthia," Abel said.

But she lit a cigarette.

Abel was about to suggest he'd finish in Swinton's office, but Swinton, with Cynthia there, seized the chance to exhibit a photographic mind that could reproduce whole pages of dusty law books.

"You see, Mr. Abel, whatever one may think of a certain ruling," his voice had a pedantic note, "over the course of time, the law sets up precedents."

Abel broke in. "I'm just interested in what's right."

"Yes, but judges and lawyers, like the rest of the human race, tend to accept, with relief, any answer that's been found to a knotty problem. Now, it has been ruled that oil is by nature fugacious—"

"Say it in English." Abel was short.

"I had occasion to cover this on the Krider case. It has been ruled that oil is by nature migratory, and is in the same category as a wild animal. If a fox leaves your land and goes to your neighbor's, you have no redress if your neighbor catches it and sells the skin." He set his glass down carefully. "It has been ruled, and sustained, if oil escapes from your land to your neighbor's, you have no legal redress."

Abel's hand gripped the chair, his eyes seemed to shoot angry light. If a man can't claim and feel secure in the earth and what's beneath it, what can he count on?

"I could institute a proceeding, you understand, but you might well be out of pocket the costs of the litigation."

"There is a possibility," Homer straightened some books into a precise pile, "an arrangement worked out in some places I've heard of. Owners of adjoining leases overlying a single reservoir get together and work out a pooling agreement."

"Hanh!" came from the depths of Abel's being. "You don't know the type of people I have to deal with here. A screwball, and Seavey."

Cynthia took out a cigarette, tapping it with staccato jabs. She opened her mouth to speak, but then said nothing.

"There is one possible legal action, but it's no remedy, really. You want—or so I believe—a reimbursement for loss of production and a stay against further loss."

"What's the action?" Abel said with impatience.

"In certain cases—I'm thinking of Jelef versus Warren, a dispute over leases—you can cloud a man's title. The refineries are alerted on these title liens and won't pay out money unless a very heavy bond to indemnify them is posted. So, while a writ of estrepement would not reimburse you, it prevents, in effect, your opponent collecting any money. Now, in this case, of course, there is no indication for such an action."

Cynthia, moving about the room jerkily, broke out angrily, "Well, why did you mention it then?"

"I have not advised it."

"It's stupid. Mad!"

"Professionally," Swinton blinked behind the thick lenses, "I must show my client the whole picture. It's not exactly nice, but sometimes when you are dealing with the devil you use a long-handled spoon. Naturally, in summing up, I would advise which course I consider best for him to pursue."

"All right." Abel was curt. "What?"

"If we wished to play that angle—to put a nuisance lien on them, the advantage is this: It might force them, by cutting off income, to close down. You could thus make them come to terms with you."

Abel said heavily, "What do you advise?"

"Considering all the pros and cons, I believe your wisest course would be to accept it as an unfortunate piece of luck and do nothing."

Abel sat down, his head thrust forward. He glanced at the picture of McRae Abel.

Swinton had risen. "I can expect you then, Mrs. Winters, on Thursday? In my office? Good night!"

32

AUGUST POURED SMOTHERING heat out of a gray sky. If a breeze rose, it came from the direction of Jupiter Number Three, bearing sulphurous odors.

Now that the workmen had finished the water system and gone, Abel could have started manufacture again. But he hesitated. If he stocked up on more materials, hard enough to get delivered because of the safety regulations, he might lose them. So he kept the padlock on what he had, and began to look for a small isolated building. But always, inquiring, there was a bitterness in his mouth. Was he to be interfered with, then, on his own island?

And all day, every day, there was the sound.

It came mockingly through the woods. The pumping of his oil, sucking his strength and the resources of his island.

Then it was stepped up. Not only each dreary sultry day, but at night, now, too.

Sometimes in the flat stretches of the night if the heat were great, he paced about the house, clad only in shorts. Once he turned on the light to look at McRae Abel, who had the clue. But he got no help there.

Perhaps if the heat and the sound had not kept him from sleeping at night, he would have seen some other way out.

Priding himself, though, he had reasoned it all through calmly, by the middle of August, he had decided. It seemed the only course. He went in to McRae to see Homer Swinton.

When the writ was filed, the elderly clerk at the court house complimented Homer on its quality. He liked to see a really tight document.

"Seavey's going to be sore," he chuckled, "and whoever this Dorn is. Kind of stymied, aren't they?"

"Any document I draw is sound and will hold." Homer prided himself on his work.

And then, one still night, Abel, sleepless, seemed to be trying to raise over his head a heavy mass marked Accounts Payable. He went down to the study to check again over bills and invoices. Sitting there, very late at night, it seemed to him he heard stealthy footsteps approach, cease, then begin again.

Hastily, he put out the gooseneck lamp, thinking that under it, he made a target. He listened. He could not be sure, but he thought he heard the steps stealthily retreating. Perhaps it was only his imagination, like the cracking sounds he often thought he heard in the black of night.

It was too hot to sleep.

The first few days after the writ was filed, he had at least the satisfaction of not hearing the sound. But now, it had begun again. Swinton said they were pumping and storing the oil. The refinery knew better than to pay out money on a clouded title—they'd been caught that way before. So, the oil was being run through the Seavey lines to the small nearby refinery, into storage tanks. At least no cash came back to them.

Sitting there in the dark, Abel thought of his own well, far off in the woods, unprotected. What if they tried something? Probably not, but—.

Just to reassure himself he took a flashlight from the hall closet, made his way through the dark woods, checked, found nothing amiss. He'd come again in daylight, and ask Bannon to look too.

He started the return. As he left his own narrow path, he saw ahead on the joint path, another flashlight.

Coming toward him, held by some unknown hand.

Who would be coming along here so late at night? In spite of himself his heart pounded, his hands dampened with cold sweat. The other light seemed to hesitate, then advanced.

Abel, muscles tensed against attack, inched ahead.

Restless from the heat, Nick had wakened, and, groping for his watch, remembered he had left it back at the well. He had taken it off when the production man had asked him to hold a board he was hammering.

Can't sleep in this heat anyway. I'll go back and get it. Might rain tonight.

He was nearly to the well. He saw another light. Who would be back here in the woods?

154

Slowly, waveringly, alert for hidden pitfalls, the lights groped back and forth. White canes tapping through a jungle.

Then he saw it was Abel. They were quite close. Their circles of light blinded them.

The night seemed to listen achingly. They passed in silence as though speech had not yet been invented.

Next day, Abel, standing near the crest of the slope at the rear of his house where he could overlook the Dorn dooryard, watched, for a long time, the activities below.

They were carrying stones toward the front of the house. Mixing something. Cement? What now? You couldn't guess where they'd light next.

His night meeting on the lonely path; the strange crackling sounds he heard sometimes in the night; the activities below which he did not understand—disturbed him deeply.

Two or three days later, in McRae, in Leland's hardware, when he saw a good one, with a fine scope, reasonable because it was used, it occurred to him he had been foolhardy not to be able to protect himself. It was a question of being sensible. It would have, he felt, a clean healthy effect all around.

The island was far from town. No policemen walked a beat out there. He didn't know why he hadn't thought of it before, taken the precaution.

He arranged for the permit, and complying with regulations, left it at Leland's to be picked up later.

Then he went to see Rena. He wanted to forget all his worries. He wanted comfort and solace.

She was glad to see him. That is, at first.

Then, she failed him. They'd spent a peaceful enough evening over a highball or two. But then—. He got up and dressed in the middle of an argument and left. At one o'clock in the morning.

That was a woman. Everything going fine, and they were all right. But let things get mean for you, and a different story. Well, what did he expect? How was it after the market crash?

Now, driving home in the night, he felt he had no place to turn.

33

THE HEAT IN THE CITY HAD a peculiar stickiness. Tom boarded a street car to the University.

He had remembered a professor he had known there, a Dr. Garfield. A character. Several times, Tom had been one of a group of students the professor led on nature expeditions. Talking about rocks. Tom could still see him, white hair blowing in the breeze. It was extracurricular work for the professor. He enjoyed it. But Tom remembered he was supposed to be an authority on the geology of this region, too.

Summer session was going on and Tom had written for an appointment. The professor might know, Tom felt, whether their well really was robbing the other, and what might be done to get unsnarled.

The street car left the center of the city. It stopped to load passengers near the high white sides of the Royal Princess Apartments. He had an uneasy feeling. He had not seen Margot since the night last spring when he walked out. He ought to go up and tell her he meant to pay back that money, just as soon as—. Then he felt a tightening all over his body, thinking of what he had allowed to happen, the tension somehow generated out there. But how could he have prevented it?

He thought of Cynthia. That, too, had happened.

The science building was fairly new. It had been donated by a man who'd acquired wealth manufacturing tin plate. He had imported much art to decorate it. In the great hall, dim and cool, were parts of an eleventh-century Norman church brought over piecemeal. Off this arched hall were small rooms, not chapels, but laboratories. Tom could see two shirt-sleeved students bending over some work on a bench, engrossed, watching a test tube. Near where he stood in the great hall, a pretty student with bushy blonde hair and a low-necked blouse sat eating her lunch out of a brown paper bag. She had probably come in that morning on the street car from one of the nearby industrial towns.

She sat eating and reading, under the gracefully elongated statue of Saint Eustace, pockmarked softly with the wear of centuries. Relaxed, she munched her sandwich, a bright red and blue and yellow comic book propped up before her.

The professor was showing his age. Instead of standing in the hall after his lecture, gesticulating, talking to his students, he had come into his little office to rest.

He did not really remember Tom, although he always claimed to remember everyone. You belonged to the Human family, didn't you, and he knew a lot of that family, from away back, so he probably knew you.

He was interested at once in Tom's problem. It touched his fancy and his knowledge. And he was vain enough to like being recognized as an authority.

He knew all about those oil reservoirs, and showed them to Tom on the quadrangle maps. He talked about the Upper Devonian sands as though he were talking about Renard Street.

That the one well was probably draining the other he had no doubt. It could easily happen in the marginal stage of stripping. "Of course," he said, "the other man has a recourse."

Tom listened intently.

"He can drill an offset well on his property."

"That would be expensive, wouldn't it?" Tom asked.

"Very. That's why the arrangement's often made to pool the oil in a reservoir. It's just good sense. An agreement is made to pump in a certain way, at specified times and pool production. An engineer can work it out for you."

A tentative surge of hope rose in Tom. "Pool it! Sure! I see that!"

The professor was so old, knew so much. Tom wished he could ask him, but you oughtn't to burden him with your personal gripes, too.

"I guess," Tom said, eyes down, hesitant, "it's sort of a question of personalities, too." He stopped. "It means a lot to me. I—got sidetracked. Been trying to get back to med school."

If only the professor would go on, give you the word. Give you that distilled drop of wisdom, from all the facts, the people he had known. "Sometimes things get a little rugged," Tom said, "you might even say—discouraging."

"Yes." The professor nodded. He rose, and with his benign smile, swung out two light wooden doors. Behind them was a recessed area, an alcove, five or six feet deep. He snapped on some hidden light. On a platform sprang into vision a model, clay and papier mâché, of Time curving backward, in a beautiful sweeping coil, like the shell of a nautilus, each age, from Pre-Cambrian to Cenozoic, a different delicate hue. And on each the hand of man had written with precision a name. An antique monk working with loving care on a statue of his patron saint might have set it in a niche like this, and colored it, too, and devoutly embedded it with cloisonné and lapis lazuli.

"Just here," the old man placed a finger, as though indicating a crossroad in some neighboring county, "we stand. And back here," he touched a delicate mauve band, "fairly recently, probably less than fifty million years, that oil pool was formed."

"And," he touched with reverence a rose-colored band, "here we find the first organic fossils. Quite young, you see. Hardly more than half a billion years old."

And now, when Tom did not ask him for the word, it came.

"When I look at that," the professor said, "I think there is perhaps only one sin life can commit. Not to go on."

34

COMING OUT OF THE PROFESSOR'S office, Tom felt almost as buoyant as he had the day the bees came. Nature may have thoughtlessly neglected to put a fence around the oil reservoir, but here was this common-sense solution.

Jubilantly, he dropped the coin in the pay station. When her voice came, he could guess by her tone Abel was with her. Tom told her what train he would be on.

He came out into the glare of the crowded street.

Being away from her turned some lens to sharp focus. He missed her and it was not only the physical longing. He began to realize what they had. What if I lost her? What if someone else came along? She was not walking with downcast eyes any more.

He hurried toward the station. It was as though two halves of him had been pulled apart and wanted to come together.

He milled with the crowd of commuters as the train was announced. He found a seat. By the time the train was passing through the yard, he knew what he wanted.

It's been good. I want to keep it. Make it even better. Deeper. More solid.

And she needs me.

He grinned ruefully. If it isn't some force outside you—your parents, a Recession, a war—it's Mrs. Nature. You're cooked anyway. He could see Cynthia leaning toward him, her soft hair and trembling lips.

He'd never been "met at the train" before in his life. He had never wanted to be. Being met carried implications, the taking up of emotional responsibility.

But I sure don't want anyone else to sleep with that baby.

When the train chuffed in along the hollowed-out bricks of the McRae platform, she was waiting. On her face was the look of withdrawn disdain that had been there the first time they talked.

Then she saw him and he watched almost with fear a spontaneous flash of eager trust, that, now he was here, everything would be fine.

Then she told him why she had been worried. Not only because Abel had been working furiously, which meant the possibility of fumes carelessly made, and that she didn't know but what Tom's father might be working with the hives again; there was something else.

Abel had begun to talk about the bridge a great deal. The bridge his grandfather built.

But the way her hands stayed with him, warm and returning his pressure, the way she looked at him, Tom felt the wave of buoyancy again. When he told her about the professor's suggestion of pooling, she was happy and excited.

"That'll work fine," she said, "because the night my father talked to the lawyer, he mentioned pooling, and Father said, 'Oh, but they'd never agree to that!'"

She caught hold of Tom's arm. "We'll go and talk to him together—" She broke off, biting her lip. "No, guess that wouldn't be too good."

"I'll talk to him myself," Tom said. "I'll fix it up right away. To-morrow!"

He sighed then, as if a long tension were leaving him. "I feel better, baby, than I have for a long, long time."

"Me too."

He drove. When they were outside the town, he stopped. She settled down, head on his shoulder, as he kissed her hair, her eyes.

Then he could not hold it in any longer. "Do you remember that time we were sitting in the car in the rain? That little man with his house and wife and kid? I thought then if things had been different, you'd have been my girl. Well, they're going to *be* different. And I think you and I ought to take what we have here and make something out of it. Something permanent."

"If only we could."

"Why not?"

She kept holding his arm. "Do you remember that first day on the island, when I handed you your mail? I had such a strange sad feeling —that if only we had met then all fresh, with nothing bad having happened—Harry, or any of those people in New York—it would have been wonderful. Perhaps we can act as if that were the way it really happened. As though we came together now, unused. As if even those times with us before didn't count!"

"The way I feel, baby, we got to do something about."

"But this will be altogether different. It's like this would be the first time."

"It'll be our wedding night."

"Yes."

"Well," he suddenly held her tight, "you just be sort of walking along the road tonight about sundown, and I'll just sort of happen to come along in the car."

That evening as soon as she was in the car, Cynthia said eagerly, "Did you ask your father about the oil pooling?"

"No. I think better get Abel's consent before I mention it to Nick."

"You're afraid Father won't."

"If I miss, and Nick knows, it'll make everything uglier. Nick stews. Better if I work everything out, then go to him."

"I hope Father sees it."

"Isn't it to his interest?" Tom argued, reassuring himself.

"I wish it had been his idea," she said. "But—why are we being so gloomy? He'll do it."

"And Nick will do it. It'll be fine." Tom's brows drew together as he said it.

"Anyhow," she reached out and touched his hand, "we'll think so. For tonight. Not let it spoil that."

"That's right. Everything's wonderful—for tonight anyway."

After they left the black road, Tom angled left and here they were running along in back of the Abel and Dorn properties. He parked where the path began through their woods.

A sagging township bulletin board marked the place. Notices of tax delinquencies, election and bond campaigns had been put up and torn down haphazardly for decades. In one corner, faded blue and yellow paint showed the head of a doughboy in a 1918 hat and the word Buy! A nail had riveted part of a poster on the word Atomic.

They followed the rough path, and after a while, climbing a slight rise on the mainland side, reached a spot Tom had marked before as a fine place to come with her some day. The hill top was rounded and the grass dry and wiry.

Carrying the blankets and the bottle of wine, he said, "Of course, it ought to be champagne for a wedding night."

"Oh, but this is to be a folk-type wedding! *Vin du pays!*"

They stretched out on the blankets, propped on their elbows, looking across to the west where the sun had just set, leaving a rosy stain.

Except for the robins, it was very still, for the Dorn well had been shut down temporarily. They were putting new cups on the rods. No workmen shouted to disturb the serenity.

The locust leaves had thinned out. Their sound was not the soft moist rustle of May. It was in a higher key, a violin note, light, sharp, urgent, reminding one of time and its disappearance.

Autumn rains had not fallen, and the leaves on the ground were not sodden or sour, but yellow, full of sap, with no odor of decay. Their exhalation was like a sniff of wine—exhilarating.

In fact, the evening atmosphere was like a bottle of wine, glowing, glinting, ready to be uncorked and enjoyed. Not a drop of it must be carelessly spilt, but all savored and used.

Mint, dusty now, grew nearby, and pale asters, fragile as crystals. Grackle clicked and chuttered in the seeded dry grass.

The light was changing slowly from rose to amethyst and the island floated before them in an opalescent glow.

"Light, lumen. I've always loved that word. Look, the shingles on the west side of your house! All glistening!"

She was wearing a sun-back dress, for it was quite warm, with no stockings and open sandals and he knew she had only a bra and panties underneath. But somehow they were in no hurry to make love. They wanted first to savor the moment, the light, the leafy odor.

As they gazed, Agnes came into the Dorn dooryard. They could make out only the woman's figure, bent over, puttering at the flower bed probably. Then Nick came around the house and stood there.

Oddly enough, at that moment, Abel came out to the top of his steps. He did not see the Dorns, he was on the other side of his house, the river side.

They were so far off one could not tell if there were tension in the faces, or sharpness in the voices. In the afterglow, the little figures stood out, detached, not like anyone they knew, but as if they were studies, one entitled "Man and Wife, Dooryard," and the other "Man, with House."

Cynthia stretched out on her stomach, elbow propped, gazing off at the little figures. "If things weren't so mixed up and bitter, I'd have gone down to see your mother. She seems nice."

"Yes," the son said. How could you describe your mother? "When they first came here, it was fine, like they were, you know, starting over again. Sleeping together and everything. But now, I don't think so. My old man's too worried again."

Abel disappeared behind the trees, but in a few moments appeared at the top of the hill in back of his house. He stood, seeming to peer down at the Dorns.

"He's always doing that!" Tom said, frowning.

"He's worried."

"What about?"

"I don't know. I guess he was used to having the island to himself and it makes him uneasy that part of it's out of his control."

Tom flopped over on his back then, gazing up at the opal sky. "You know what, baby? I think there's going to be a nice corny moon."

She turned over and gazed up too. "Look!" She pointed at a line of bees disappearing into a high locust tree.

"Yes. Must be a swarm in there. Bees are the darnedest things. They work, and take care of their young, and every once in a while, a gang of them swarms up and sails out and founds a new colony. Strange."

"Why do they do it?"

"I don't know. I don't know why they do."

"What date's today?" she asked suddenly.

"August thirty-first. Why?"

"Well, this will be our wedding anniversary. Oh, later on, after the annulment, we can get a license, and stand up and swear, but this is our real wedding day."

"Bridal night."

"Yes. Only instead of saying, 'With this ring I thee wed,' I'll say, 'With this act of love I thee wed.'"

"I guess this is the best time I ever had. Right now." She put her hand in his. She did not have to say anything, he could see it was for her too.

"I don't know why it's different from any other time. What I have that I didn't have before."

And so they stayed quietly, watching the light fading, almost sensing the earth moving on. They talked fragmentarily. Tom told her how it had been in the city.

"—and this professor, he's a real old man. Written on his face, like on a rock, are the thousands of things that have happened to him, thoughts he's had. And do you know what he said, out of all that? He said, the only sin in life is to stop going on."

Suddenly she sat up, startled. "How odd he'd say just that! Because that's what happened to me. There'd been so many things filled me with revulsion. So, I stopped. But then, after I began to love you—well, that was a hard time, too. I was fighting inside myself. Something urging me to stay quiet, stay where I was, to stop and be quiet—like death. But something else, tearing and barking and screaming at me, urging me to go on."

"You were fighting that all out yourself?"

"No, not myself, not really. For what we have between us, something I never had before, is—" She searched for a word to express a new feeling, and then said, sort of surprised, "Why, I guess it's—trust."

For a moment he felt as he had when her face lit seeing him in the station, felt again the responsibility he had assumed. And yet—and yet—hadn't he been thinking that what was good about their relationship for him too was—trust.

They lay there, serene now, as the light moved subtly from amethyst to mauve, and the last of the bees went in their steady line toward the tree. "Look at those bees, bringing back their loads of honey, keeping the whole thing going."

"Something makes them."

For some reason Tom began to think of the time the plane came down. He had never talked about it to her. Always for him, two ways—

one toward the easeful dark puddle, the other the hard bright surge forward.

"What are they doing now?" Cynthia asked lazily.

"Oh, Nick and Agnes are just standing, looking out."

Cynthia did prop herself on elbow then to look down. They could see Abel silhouetted against the evening sky.

"From here, everything looks so peaceful and easy," she said.

"If only Abel will go along tomorrow. Nick's pretty sensible," his face tightened, "but sometimes he gets queer notions."

"Why are nice people sometimes such bastards?" she said.

"Maybe if everyone had what they really wanted in life, they wouldn't be," he said.

"You think so?"

"Well, they'd be too busy enjoying themselves, wouldn't they?" he demanded.

"I'd like to try it out, give everyone what they want—if I knew what it was!"

"That oughtn't to be hard to figure," he said. "As the lord king duke of this island, I decree each and all are to have what they want. We'll begin with you. What, my beauty, dost want? Dream it up, kid."

"What I want," she smiled, "you can't give."

"That's a hell of a way to talk to the king of the island."

"All right, king. Fetch me this. Insight. A woman has to be daughter, wife, mother. Touch all those lives. So—that's what I want. To be good *for* people."

"It will come about," he said.

"Well—thanks."

"How do I know?" he asked. "Well, with most people I want to remold their faces, to take away, or add, but your face, no. I never want to change it, like everything was there already, just waiting to come out."

"Funny about you," she said. "I noticed it before. You don't seem to think like a doctor or surgeon would, don't seem interested in the liver and lights, and how the big bone's attached to the little bone. You just want to change people's faces!"

Tom shifted elbows uneasily, and he sounded cross. "Oh, I'll think about that stuff all right. When the time comes."

"You told me once you wanted to be a sculptor."

"Yes. But that was a long time ago."

They were silent and then he began as if some memory had stirred.

164

"I remember how I felt first time I laid hands on modeling materials. In Aspinshade High, in Miss Hicket's Arts and Crafts room. I went slightly crazy. Some of the fellows spent their time fixing up jalopies, or fooling around with a C melody sax. I hung around her room every minute I could, modeling. She'd stand behind me sometimes, not saying anything. But it was she who entered a piece of mine in a local show and it won a prize. And that's when Mazur—you probably never heard of him—"

"Yes, I have! His sculpture's well known."

"He let me work in his studio, wanted me to study with him, not to go to college. Even talked to Nick about it. But Nick wanted me to be a professional man. And to Nick being a professional man meant being a doctor."

"Oh." She smiled half-absently, as if joining two broken strands together. "And that's how you became intent on being a plastic surgeon. It was a compromise."

"Well, yes, I guess so."

They were silent for a few moments.

They watched Abel stroll to the edge of his lawn, looking down at the river.

"Glen J. Abel," Tom said. "What is it *he* wants?"

"Sad, isn't it. Because whoever wonders, what does my father want out of life? For so long we think of him as put there to provide for us, we assume that's all he wants. But I guess I know what he wants all right. He thinks it's money, that he has to buy happiness, but when you cut away all the crud, what he wants is—an acceptance of his dignity. I guess he'd have been happy as patriarch of some tribe."

"Well, it has its points."

"Like if I had a son, he'd get a real bang if it were called Glen second. Stuff like that. He likes to be the head."

"Chairman of the Board. Well, some people need to be given a title. So—all right. I decree it. Tomorrow, he'll agree to the oil pooling, of course. Then, say we start out with our two wells, form the Consolidated Amalgamated Oil Well Company of the Universe, Inc. Make him president."

"Okay. But how about your father? Would he agree to that?"

"Why sure. That's the beauty of this giving everyone what they want. What Nick wants is hundreds of beehives."

"Is that all?"

"It's what they represent to him. Underneath what he really wants is not to be scared or worried."

"Give them to him, your kingship."

"Okay. Take a gander over there! See! Hundreds of beehives! Too many for the island. They're spreading over on the meadow. Ooops! Hey! Stop! That's enough!"

"All right, my father's Chairman of the Board. Yours has millions of bees. Now what does your mother want?"

Tom rolled over on his elbow, and looked at Agnes's figure in the afterglow.

"Every time I see her, like now, detached, I realize she's a walking miracle. How many times she's been given up for dead—and there she is. She gets real passionate about things growing. I decree rows of tulips and carrots and raspberries and daisies and tomatoes. What she'd want would be—watching them grow."

"Let it be done, oh, king."

Tom's voice was sad. "If that were all."

The lightness had gone out of her tone. "It's not so easy."

"They expected a magic island. Unshakable," he said, "and where they going to find that?"

"Except maybe inside them," she said.

He let go a troubled sigh. "That's not included in my concession. Takes plenty heap strong magic for that."

"Guess they have to accrete," her gaze at the houses was wistful, "like coral."

"Guess so."

She smiled again and made her tone light. "So far, oh, king—if you're interested in constructive criticism—your magic has been strictly road company. Too easy. High-class magic ought to be simply impossible."

He cupped a hand on her shoulder and she lifted it to fit more closely into his hand, looking up at him.

"Name it!" he said.

"Magic this! A house for us. A fantastically modern house. Up here on this hill—not too close to the others, but not too far away. One side all glass, open to sun, terraces free to light and wind, the house part of the earth. My friend Jody—I told you about her—her husband studies architecture—you should see the mad ones he dreams up—impossible, but wonderful, exciting."

"House, materialize! Look! See the sun shining on the glass!"

"You going to put it here on this hill, without even an argument?

166

You forget when you're a doctor, a surgeon, you'll have to be in town. This is too far from hospitals, patients."

"Yes, but," he moved uneasily, "it could be a week-end house."

"Okay. I like the house over here rather than on the island. Something sort of—not right about retreating to a cut-off place. A hating. For children, I'd want them over on the mainland, free to come and go, open, easily accessible, more connected with everyone else."

"We'll have to build a road from here then, connect with the highway. Second thought." He clapped his hands sharply. "Hey! Turn the house around, face it that way! Hmm . . . look at that! Chip out of the glass down there in the corner. Slave 419! Fix that!"

They turned over then, and with clasped hands, looked up into the sky.

"If only it could be like that," she said wistfully.

"It can be. Don't you know that what beautiful women like you dream up, great big strong brave intelligent lusty men like me— make?"

"But—"

"But me no buts. From now on, you might as well begin to accept the possibility of happiness. Because that's what you're going to get."

In the warm dry winey dark, they turned toward each other, knowing love did not have to be snatched or grabbed but was there waiting.

Then a sound came shattering through the night. The moment splintered into a thousand irrecoverable fragments.

For a moment they were frozen, terrified.

The sound came again. In the still countryside it echoed through the woods.

Cynthia sprang up.

"What is it?" he asked.

Her breath came in little gasps. "I know."

"A rifle. But who? What?"

The sound came again, tearing apart the tender night.

They froze again.

Then they were running.

Panting, they reached the neck. Tom saw lights flash on in the Dorn house. Lights already streamed from the Abel place.

Cynthia ran toward her house, Tom went crashing and stumbling down toward the Dorns'.

Ten minutes later, he came panting back up the slope. He saw Cynthia's dress moving toward him in the dark.

"Tom?" she whispered.

"Here!" She came to him, and they stood, their breath coming in sick gasps. "They're all right down there," he said, "turned the lights on to find out what happened."

She pointed. "I didn't go in, I didn't have to."

Inside the Abel house, in a small downstairs room, Tom could see Abel now. Sitting in the circle of light from a desk lamp, the rifle in his hand. Then he placed it on the desk in front of him. Tom wanted to cry out, "What's wrong?" but something about Abel's grim face, the way his shoulders hunched, kept him silent.

"Soon as I saw him, I knew," she said. "He says he hears prowlers out here at night," she whispered. "He must have thought he heard someone and fired."

"Yeah." Tom felt nauseated. Like that time as a kid when he fell down the basement steps in the dark and sat there, not hurt badly but not knowing whether to cry or be sick.

Cynthia began to cry softly. "Everything inside you gets thrown back on itself every time it wants to come out."

Tom tried to swallow away the backed-up feeling of shock and frustration. "Always broken off. Interrupted."

35

THE NEXT MORNING, ONE NEW colony of bees arrived. Nick planned, as he could afford it, to replace the dead. He did not feel as he had when the other bees arrived. Now he was not so sure the world around was friendly and would be glad for him.

Tom said uneasily, "Let's put them as far as possible from Abel's exhaust vents." He helped Nick carry one of the wooden hives away from the slope and down toward the river.

Carrying, Nick said, "Don't know why I should change from a good location to a poor, just on account of *him*!"

Tom glanced at Nick's face. Not the time to talk to him about the pooling. Best wait till it's all set.

Perhaps he ought to talk to Seavey first. His consent would be needed.

I know him better now, though. He seems to think and talk only of women, but when the chips are down, he'll do whatever means money in the Seavey sock.

Tom did not rush up to Abel's house immediately. It was too important, too much hinged on it. He must slow himself down, consider the angles, decide best how to suggest it. If Abel understood rightly, he'd agree all right.

By mid-afternoon, Tom was shining his shoes. He put on a clean white shirt, a necktie, and even though the day was sultry, a jacket. He did not take the short cut up the slope, but walked formally on the Abel lane. As he came to the house, the view along the river, with the boat bobbing at the foot of the steps, was serene.

Abel, his back to Tom, was at the far edge of the front lawn, nailing, at shoulder height, a piece of pine board to a tree. He did not turn.

Tom, crossing the lawn, called out respectfully, "Good afternoon, Mr. Abel."

Abel turned swiftly. He stared a moment before he spoke with a rising inflection. "Good day." Then he turned away and carefully marked a place for a nail.

But Tom said confidently, "I'd like to talk to you, sir."

Abel turned and glanced with seeming indifference, over his shoulder. "Go ahead and talk." He loosened a nail to straighten the board.

As Tom had visualized it, he and Abel would be sitting down somewhere, perhaps in the big room with the red damask, perhaps outside on the steps. But he tried to sound easy. "Or are you too busy at the moment?"

Abel appeared absorbed in straightening the board. "Not any busier than I'll always be." As he took a nail out of the bag on the tree crotch, the hammer dropped. Tom sprang toward it, but Abel bent swiftly and almost snatched it up.

Tom remembered something. That time on the river when Cynthia and he were in the boat and Abel came along. That same look.

Tom took a deep breath. Wouldn't do to get rattled. After all, he was offering the guy something, wasn't he? He lit a cigarette. "It's about the oil."

Abel stopped hammering quickly enough then. He swung around and faced Tom, staring at him levelly.

"This way," Tom said quickly, "none of us are gaining. I talked to a geologist, an authority. He said people often get together and work out a pumping schedule."

Tom took a deep puff of cigarette, glancing at Abel, trying to judge his reaction. "They pool the oil. Seems like the sensible thing to do."

Abel was not looking at Tom. His eyes, through narrowed lids, studied the ground. His mouth was open, but one hand stroked his cheeks slowly. Then through still narrowed lids, he shot a quick appraising glance at Tom. He said not a word. Deliberately, he turned, and finished putting the board on the tree.

Tom, nettled, felt the blood rise to his face.

Finished, Abel strode, ignoring Tom, to the portico. Tom swallowed hard. Then he followed him.

At the portico, he saw the gun. It had been under Abel's coat, on the top step. He hadn't noticed it as he passed. The barrel shone in the sun.

Abel picked up a pad of target paper, went back to the tree, and fastened a sheet to the board.

He returned to the portico and picked up the gun, sighting the target.

Tom took a long deep breath and said in a controlled voice, "I wonder if I made myself clear?"

Abel peered through the scope.

"About pooling the oil, I mean." Tom sounded on the defensive.

Deliberately, Abel put shells into the gun. "Yes," he said drily, not looking at Tom, "I understood you."

Tom lit a cigarette, trying to keep his hand from shaking.

"You're not interested?"

Abel took time to cross and straighten the target and return to the portico before he answered.

"I didn't say that."

He sure can make you feel like a fool, Tom thought.

"You *are* interested then." He forced an unemotional tone.

Abel lifted the gun and aimed at the target. "I put good money into reconditioning my well. You come here and drain my pool." He pulled the trigger. The bullet hit the edge of the target and the sound racketed back and forth along the serene river. For a moment Tom lived again the sick feeling of last night, when he and Cynthia had heard the gunfire splintering the night.

"Maybe I didn't make myself clear." Tom's resentment escaped. "I'm offering to share our production."

Abel's tone was savage. "Your production?" He took aim. The sound of the shot broke the air into bits. This time the bullet struck closer to the center.

Abel peered at the target. Looking at his grim face, Tom had a flash of understanding. Must be pretty barbed for him to swallow, at that. Our coming in and taking it. I'd feel the same way!

Tom's cigarette had gone out. He tossed it away and lit another, his hand not shaking now. His tone was conciliatory. "It would certainly be better than no one getting anything. If we got together with an oil engineer, we might work it out."

Abel lowered his gun and turned to face Tom but he did not speak. His narrowed eyes and hard glance said it for him—Why are *you* trying to sell it? What are you trying to pull?

Without being accused, Tom broke out angrily, "I'm making an offer."

"Stick to facts," Abel said shortly. "Offering what ?My oil?"

He raised the gun and fired quickly this time. And when he hit very close to the bull's eye, he had a look of almost animal satisfaction.

Tom threw away his cigarette. What's going on here? What's he trying to do? Have to use my head.

He shoved down his anger, studying Abel as he deliberately sighted the gun.

I got it. He's trying to keep the upper hand, so that when we get into discussion, he's not the one that asked. Yes. Okay, I'm not proud. Give him plenty room to operate.

Tom asked quietly, "You'd like to think it over, then?"

"Leave it that way if you like," Abel said stiffly.

"Do you want me to come back for an answer?"

"Up to you," he shrugged, and Tom walked down the lane slowly.

Next morning Abel drove to McRae.

"I think it's your best out," Swinton said. "All you can hope to do with the writ is create nuisance value. It's bringing no results. So I'd go along."

Outside in the street, Abel decided to go up to see Rena. He'd not been there for the last couple of weeks. Now, he felt alone.

Not a bright woman, sometimes she'd say something, or see things you didn't see.

"Why, that's a good thing," Rena broke out. "You've not been yourself, Glen. All that quarreling!"

"There's been no quarreling," he retorted. "I'm just not going to be crowded."

"Better to settle things."

"Well, I don't know," he said. "I feel it's really my oil they're taking."

"It's not doing you any good this way. You haven't been yourself, Glen."

"Yes, yes, you said that before," he said, a little edgy.

He had planned to stay the night, but strange, the way a woman could irritate you, drive it away. Just by acting so big and trying to run things. He had a good mind to go. But, finally, he stayed the night.

Next morning, as he drove to the island, thinking of what Homer had said and what Rena had said, he guessed, in most ways, it was best to take the offer.

There was something, though, some feeling that made him hesitate. It *looked* all right. But—why were they offering? He narrowed his eyes a moment as suspicion prickled a rasping hand down his spine.

At the house, Cynthia was not about. He went in the study and sat a long time, very still, in frowning thought.

Even if common sense said, settle the mess, there was this something he couldn't quite put a finger on. He thought how wrong everything had been since they came. He went out, pacing around restlessly.

Them, offering *him* his oil back.

He saw them passing easily and carelessly back and forth over the bridge. The bridge his grandfather built. As if they owned everything in sight.

Later he saw Dorn come and stand on it. Smoking and just standing, looking at the water. Using it now for a lounging place. Abel rose abruptly from the lawn chair and went in the house.

He wondered where Cynthia was. Perhaps if he talked to her—or did she already know? Sometimes, he wondered if she and that young—.

If I talk to her, it might bring into my mind what seems hovering just out of reach.

She was not downstairs. He went up to her room.

The door was partly ajar, a window curtain stirring out in the breeze. He knocked, and getting no answer, pushed the door wider. Not there. A dress she had stepped out of hung across a chair. A pair of panties were tossed on the bed. Then, his eye riveted on something.

A bright object. He stared at it, transfixed. A necktie. One he had seen before. He remembered thinking it flashy and in bad taste when he had seen it on him the day before yesterday.

Last night, while he had been in town. And right here, in this house! He wanted to rend the necktie, grind it under foot. Instead, he stood rigid.

Back on the lawn, in the chair, he felt spent and sick. He sat for a long time, brooding. After awhile, the thing he had been trying to grasp, the answer about joining them in a pool or not, came to him.

Perhaps Homer Swinton was smart. But not smart enough. For Abel had seen finally what to do. It might take a little patience.

He remembered the stories he'd heard in McRae, that the Dorns were operating on a shoestring, had to have some income to stay there. For a little while they'd been eating high on the hog with their three barrels a day. But not long enough to have given them much of a reserve. If he went in the pool with them, that income'd resume, even if reduced.

He rose and walked about.

Then he sat down and wrote a letter to the Dorns. He intended to put it in their mail box, but before he could finish, Tom, anxious for an answer, had come to the Abel front door.

Tom's face was strained.

"I didn't mean to hurry you, sir. But if you had a chance to consider, I wondered—have you thought it over?"

"Yes," Abel said flatly. He did not invite Tom in, but stood inside his own door, looking at him bleakly.

"And what was the answer, sir?"

"No."

36

AGNES DID NOT TELL TOM or Nick she was going. They might not see how it could help.

Soon as Tom told me about Abel not wanting to pool the oil, seemed to me I knew why. Doesn't trust us. Because he doesn't know us.

The girl hasn't come to call. It's polite to wait. One kind. But there's another kind.

Take it up carefully, wrap it in an old cloth, dampened, so if she's not ready to plant, it'll keep.

She put on her good blue dress, and brushed and braided her hair anew.

That it would maybe clear the air. All that air between the houses at first was sunshine and morning mist. Now seems like it shivers and rocks. Not only from the rifle sound.

I ought to have gone before. Put it off. Timid from not knowing *him.*

Should I go up the front lane? No, the path's more neighborly. Show myself. Show him I'm someone he doesn't have to keep peering down at.

At the top of the path, she was abashed at herself. A sprout coming out of a plant doesn't know what's going to happen to it either. The feel of the dampened cloth enclosing the ball of earth gave her confidence.

The girl saw her and came swiftly across the back garden. "Oh, I'm glad you came."

"Is Mr. Abel at home?"

"No, he's in McRae. Will you come and sit here, under the trees?"

Agnes held it out. "It's a lily. White with pink spots."

The girl took it in her two hands.

"Oh, thank you."

They looked at each other.

She and Tom. I know, way he looks and acts. How lovely she is, twinkling delicately on a slender stalk like a wind flower.

"We could plant it now, if you like," Agnes said.

The girl fetched a tool eagerly. They knelt as she dug a hole, and poured in the water. Agnes placed the root in. Together they patted the earth over it.

On their knees, they looked at each other again, troubled, waiting for words to come which would make a bridge. None came.

It's like the bridge is there, though. Like we're meeting out in the middle of it.

"Would you like some daffodil plants?" the girl asked.

Agnes's eyes gleamed at the thick-sown blades. "I would. Yes!"

Afterward, carrying the daffodil plants home, Agnes thought: Never said a word of what I meant to.

But as she moved down the path the air seemed just sunshine and morning mist again.

It was nearly midnight and Abel had not returned from McRae.

Cynthia waited.

If he'd talk, tell me. Then I could know what's in his mind. Don't like the way his eyes evade.

Not to pool the oil with them. Seems against his own interests. Worries me.

Abel came finally, gray-looking.

She sprang out of the chair. "Father, are you all right? You look—"

"I'm fine. I've some work to do." He moved toward his study, went in and closed the door.

He's closing not only that door. All his doors and windows.

Next day, he left early but he returned in the middle of the afternoon. She stopped him as he went toward the study.

"Father!"

He turned a closed face to her.

"I'm worried about you," she said.

"You needn't be. I've been working on something I believe will clear a lot of things up. Settle them. In the courthouse, hunting through the records."

Oh, please, heaven—

"What I should have done long ago. Establish our place here so that we—"

"You're going to close the bridge!"

175

"There's no public record of its being built. It's private. My grandfather built it."

"Oh, don't do it."

His face set. "It's a business matter."

"No, no, it isn't. Any more than not pooling the oil."

Slow painful red crept up his face. "Oh, you know all about that, do you?"

Does he guess that Tom and I?

"Don't let everything become distorted for you, Father!"

"Distorted for you, I think." He seemed to be holding back terrible rage.

Yes, he knows.

Abel said, "If I'd posted it long ago, everything would have been all right here."

It must not happen. I've only one weapon to stop him. A treacherous knife.

"My problem is to protect what I have," he said. "And that's one way to do it."

"No, no. It will only make things worse."

His eyes were full of baffled helplessness that she did not understand him. "It's for you."

That's why my one weapon's so sharp. It's necessary to him to feel all he's struggling for here has meaning.

He went on doggedly. "From the moment those people came, has there been anything but trouble?"

"Then let's not make any more."

"That's woman thinking. A man fights for his own. And I'm going to, no matter if everyone's against me!"

He looks so queer lately. Like he needed to cry out but wouldn't.

"One fact seems evident. I've been derelict in not taking measures."

Must jolt him. For his good. For everyone. Maybe I'll only have to threaten. Tears came to her eyes. I don't want to use the knife. I don't.

"Father, I can't live in the midst of all this meanness and hate. If you block that bridge, I'll have to go."

His eyes striking back at me, putting me with the everyone against him. Maybe the threat will deflect him.

He turned away and she could not see his face, only his rigid back. "I listened to you when you said don't post the road. That was a mistake."

"No, it wasn't."

"I know what I'm doing."

"And I mean what I say."

Abel walked across the portico, down the steps, across the lawn toward his car.

What if she did? Nothing to work for. She's just threatening. Don't like that. Man ought to be master in his own house.

At the car he lifted out the sign the carpenter in Sherrod had made. He looked at it with a sense of satisfaction. Good job. Letters three inches high. "Private Bridge. No Trespassing under Penalty of Law."

Then he laid the sign down. What if she meant it? His arms hung at his sides impotent. The air seemed bleak.

He closed the car door slowly and turned away. It could be that she's right. Make things worse.

As he walked back across the lawn, the Dorn well began to pump. Draining out what I counted on.

He went in the house, got out his rifle and targets and began to shoot. The sound, at least for awhile, broke up that mocking rhythm. He liked the feel of accomplishment as the bullet cut cleanly into the target. A deed begun and finished.

As he stopped to reload, he saw a figure crossing the bridge. He put down the rifle and went to the top of his lane. It was young Dorn.

Crossing the bridge, so matter-of-fact. As if he owned. For one searing moment he could see the necktie, carelessly, across the bed. As if he owned. Everything!

A fool. I've been a fool.

She's wrong.

Letting them use my bridge. I've been actually helping them to stay. To drain me. Of everything.

He saw their car come out. The father and son were in it. They drove across the bridge, turned down the dirt road.

This was the time to do it.

He went to the car and lifted out the sign. From his workshop he brought a chain. He went down to the bridge. He fastened the chain securely across the bridge and attached the sign by the hooks the carpenter had put on. As he looked at it, his face relaxed for a moment, as if in relief from frustration. No one could claim they didn't see it.

He went up the lane and returned with his gun and targets to a spot where he could overlook the bridge.

After awhile, he saw their car drive up, waver, back down to the road. He could see them sitting in the car, talking with excited gestures.

He became very busy adjusting the target.

This was much the best, most dignified way to handle it. Maybe he should have consulted Homer Swinton before. But no, Homer hadn't been smart enough to see what should be done about the oil pooling.

After awhile, their car turned and moved slowly off down the road.

She stood in his study door, her hair wild from the wind, her jacket unbuttoned. She's been to the bridge. Or—seen him.

"Take it down!"

"I guess in some matters you'll have to let me use my own judgment."

"Tomorrow morning! When I wake up tomorrow, if you haven't taken it down, I am going!"

He was silent.

That night, she didn't sleep well. It was strangely sultry. She heard, too, the rustling, crackling sounds she'd heard before and could not place.

She heard the first fall winds come before she fell asleep.

She woke early, just after daylight, with a sense of trouble.

With a raincoat wrapped about her against a blowing rain, she went down. She stared incredulously at the sign rattling madly in the wind.

He thinks I won't go.

She went back to the house. Abel was still asleep.

Quietly, she telephoned the McRae taxi, and packed a suitcase.

An hour later, as Abel still slept heavily, the taxi picked her up as she waited near the mail boxes.

37

TOM UNLOADED THE GROCERIES on the kitchen table. He had carried them in his old army pack along the path from the back road.

"Near as I can learn, Dad, there's no boatyard near. Lelands' said they could order one from the wholesaler."

"How much?"

"A hundred fifteen."

"For a rowboat?"

"And it'll take six weeks to get it at that. If we ordered one un-assembled from the mail-order place, it'd be about a month, and cost around seventy dollars."

"Seventy dollars!"

"If we could just find a used one somewhere!"

"That ad I put in the McRae *Star* comes out Tuesday. Said we wanted a second-hand boat."

Tom and Nick waited in the county attorney's anteroom.

The attorney, returning from a leisurely lunch, was cheerful. "My, my, chilly enough for a top coat already. Autumn's really here."

They went into his office. He leaned back, relaxed. He liked folks, liked to hear their troubles. He'd already heard about this from Hube Krimmer. Think Hube has it in for Abel, though, on account of the primaries last fall, and he's probably colored it.

Nick nervously declined the smoke. He had a folk fear of the law, springing from old wives' tales ending "—and then he fell into the hands of a slick lawyer." All the way in, he had beaten down this fear with the bludgeon of a bigger one—the fear of being shoved off.

"Ah, me!" the county attorney sighed as Nick finished his story about the bridge. "Why can't you folks get on out there without all this?"

"But—it's him!" Nick broke out.

"We-ell, Glen Abel's a taxpayer and a respected citizen. He probably had his toes stepped on some way too." He leaned back and arched his fingers into a church steeple. "Aside from the legal angle, my personal advice is for you people to act like folks. Just sit down together and be willing to give a little. Get on."

Of course he means well, Tom thought. He's sincere. You can see it from the way he looks at Nick. But Nick moved impatiently and got the tight look that spelled "Nick versus the world." Tom could understand that. Easy enough for that man back of the desk with his cigar and probably a new house in Stratford Heights, to be smug. What does he know about hanging on a cliff and having someone stomp on your hands?

The attorney said, "I wish there were a way you could arrange it without getting us into it. Just be friendly, you know. In my experience," he turned to Nick, his kindly eyes peering, "it's better for the law to keep out—if it's private spite."

Nick's jaw snapped shut at that.

The attorney spread his hands on the desk. "Mr. Abel, awhile back, was in here complaining of you."

"Of me?" Nick was dumfounded.

"He seemed to feel some blasting you did may have injured his water supply."

"He's crazy," Nick stammered. "Plain crazy. He has my wife scared to death. Walks around out there banging away with a gun he has."

"Is that so?" The attorney was concerned. "Well, that's not right. What's he do that for?"

"You're asking me?" Nick broke out.

"I don't like that."

"It's not the gun, but the bridge I'm worried about!"

"I can assure you, Mr. Dorn, no one is going to break any laws if I can help it. If the bridge is county property, that's one thing. I'll have my clerk look up the record and let you know. You might come in another day."

Nick flushed and Tom said hastily, "Since we can't use the bridge, it's a mean trip in, especially if it's been raining. We have to leave the car and walk a long stretch through rough woods. We'd appreciate it, sir, if it's possible, if we could find out today."

Nick went to the *Star* to see if there were answers to his advertisement. Tom had something else on his mind. He was worried about Cynthia. He hadn't seen her for two days; nor caught any glimpse of her at the Abel house. With the tension in the air, he did not think it wise to go up. The Dorns were still awaiting their telephone. Now, Tom went to a pay station.

The voice that answered was dignified, deep.

In spite of himself, Tom took a fast breath. "May I speak to Cynthia?"

There was a pause. "She is not here."

"Do you know when she'll be there?"

"No," the voice said shortly.

"All right. Thank you."

Tom was disturbed. Where could she be? Or, was she really up there and Abel would not let him talk to her?

When he and Nick returned to the attorney's office, Tom still felt a puzzled uneasiness.

"It appears not to be a county or township bridge," the attorney said. "But I've been thinking it's not a good idea to let a thing like this simmer on, causing trouble." He began to pace about. "I think an easement has been established."

"What's that?" Tom asked.

"The bridge has been used by everyone for a long time. So it's established by custom as a public way. That puts it in public domain. You have, in other words, an easement."

Nick looked relieved and bright. "Well! When can we start using it?"

"It'll take a little time for me to check into it more carefully and if necessary, prepare a proceeding. If I were you, I'd not use it until we do that. No use stirring up trouble."

"No," Tom said quickly.

"You just sit tight. I don't think it's a healthy thing for Glen Abel to believe he constitutes the law and the prophets in my county. No, that's not right. Don't you worry. Just leave it in my hands."

Nick rose. "Thank you."

"That's all right. And in the meantime," he slapped him on the shoulder cheerfully, "don't go building any spite fences or anything like that!" he chuckled.

Nick started and then flushed.

Tom said, "I told him not to."

There was still an hour of light when they returned from the county attorney's office. Nick doggedly resumed the work that had occupied him for days.

It was built of timber he'd found. "Too much outgo already."

At first he wouldn't even say why he was collecting it. Finally Tom had prevailed upon Nick to tell him.

"Seven, eight feet high. Just across the dooryard. It'll keep him from over-looking us, seeing everything we do." When Tom had refused to help, Nick became stubborn.

His face looks like that quirk beginning again, Tom thought. Way he looked refusing Abel the water. Like he's feeling alone. Go out with him now, help him hunt wood. Make him feel better.

There was still a little light. They went toward the back woodland.

"I haven't combed up those ravines yet," Nick said.

That boy in the hut, back here somewhere. Can't even remember which ravine. Haven't seen him for a month or more.

Then Tom heard Nick, somewhere ahead. His voice was loud. A dog barked fiercely.

When Tom came up, the boy, angry, bewildered, was holding his dog back as Nick, hands on hips, red faced, was glaring at the shack and shouting, "You take it down, stick by stick, and get it out of here!"

The boy looked at Tom in bewilderment. "What's a matter with him, he crazy?"

"Nick, don't you remember—?"

"I won't have it," Nick shouted. "Got to keep your eyes open every minute, pushing you from one side, sneaking in on you from the other!"

"You said it was all right when I told you—"

"He could set fire to the woods, dry as they are, or do a hurt to the oil well! This is my land. Don't watch out, can't call my soul my own!"

"You said it was okay," the boy accused Tom.

"You hear?" Nick broke out. "Thinks he has a right! You get that thing down and get off this land and by tomorrow night, or I'll get the constable in here to help you!"

The boy hung on to his dog as it strained toward Nick, barking fiercely.

Tom spoke through clenched teeth. "Come on, Nick! You want me to hunt wood? I'm going!"

On the path, he turned on Nick, outraged. "What in hell got into you?"

"Shoving and pushing at me from all sides! There's a thing called squatter's rights. Leave him go on, he'll be claiming them!"

Tom glared and set his jaw to choke back ugly words.

Nick walked on, head down, muttering to himself.

Tom stood there, realizing what he felt was shock.

What's happening to him? Of course, he's worried about his place. But no place is worth that. All that's been happening here—he's letting it get to him.

I ought to try to talk to him.

Sobered, Tom moved toward the house. Better let him cool off first. Then, talk to him.

At dinner, Nick looked harassed, but was silent.

Then, something drew Tom's attention to Agnes. In refilling the water glasses, she dropped one, shattering it. She stood, then, dazed, staring at the pieces.

He realized guiltily all this about the bridge, unsettling them, must be doing things to her. He made her lie down while he washed the dishes.

He did a fast makeshift job, thinking of the squatter.

I'll go back and see him. I don't want him to get to feeling that people—.

A pearly afterglow lighted the world. Approaching the place, Tom purposely made a great noise through the dry leaves.

The oil lamp behind the boy in the open door made him seem larger than life. "Oh, it's you. Come on in."

Pictures cut from magazines were pasted on the walls and some plants grew in a box.

"Say, what's a matter with that little coot was with you, hollerin' around here? He offa his trolley?"

"That's my father."

"Oh." The boy stroked the dog's head. "You tole me I could stay," he said slowly, "that your father said so."

"He's had a lot of problems lately."

The boy was silent. Finally he asked, "You want some coffee?"

"Okay."

As they sat waiting for it to boil, Tom said, "I'll try to talk him out of it tomorrow."

"You think you can?"

"Sure. Sure I can. He ought to listen."

They sat, elbows on table, drinking the coffee.

Tom admired the pictures, the boy told him he was making ninety cents an hour now, and after awhile he said, "Does your old man know about that crack on the hill?"

"Yes. Yes, I guess he's seen it."

183

"I was walking around the other day, over on the island where youse live and all over the place, and I seen it."

"I wonder what does that," Tom said.

The boy turned to look at him. "You mean you don't know?"

"Do you?"

The boy looked at him, blinking. After awhile he said, "Before the war, my old man was killed in it, you know—he was a coal miner and we lived up at Mt. Ephraim. I seen them there."

"Oh," Tom said quickly, "Mt. Ephraim's a long way off."

"Crack looks the same. It means the ground's hollow."

Tom's heart seemed to stop. Then he said, "Oh, we'd have known that."

"Less it was someone like George Green, wanted to slick you."

But that was impossible. Hadn't Abel bought the land too? Tom's heart began to beat regularly again.

"Comin' from up there, guess I thought everyone'd know what those cracks meant," the boy said.

It was a little while before Tom said, "We always lived in the city."

Abel had come from the city, too.

Tom was thinking of something he'd seen two days ago that had worried him. The back door, under a cracked lintel, had pulled away from the house and sunk an inch or so.

The boy said, "I guess I see them cracks 'fore anyone else, account of my brother Willie. Me and him lived with granma—my mother died, I don't even remember her—and me and," he swallowed hard, "jeez, it scares me even now to say his name, me and Willie lived with granma. Real old, she was, over eighty. This here evening, a nice summer evening, just dusk. I remember the bats were out, flying around. They always scared me, cause they seemed so crazy, zooming around in the half-dark. Willie was about nine and I was ten and we was playin' in this vacant field with Johnny and Dan Vitski. Playin' war because there was these round sink holes and we was playin' they was foxholes.

"I could hear, far off, across the lots, granma callin', just like she always did, 'Come in, boys, and wash your feet before bed.' We always played in bare feet."

The oil lamp flickered across the boy's staring eyes. "Willie stooped down to hit a mosquito on his leg, and all at once, the ground went from under his feet. I began to go too but his head was down to my feet. I began screamin' for Dan and Johnny. They come and could help me."

Tom sat rigid and cold.

"They was old workin's under that field. The pillars in the eight-foot seam had been took and she'd been lettin' go, sinkin' and pot holin', and that evenin', she went. They couldn't find Willie."

It was impossible. Impossible.

That fissure in the basement floor.

He rose hastily. "I'll talk to my father and try to fix it up for you here."

He moved through the woods quickly. He wanted to find the crack now, look at it again and reassure himself it was nothing like that. But it was too dark to find it.

At home, he found a letter from Cynthia. The Dorns received little mail and often a day or two went by without their looking in their box. Especially now, when they must drive around.

The letter was from the city.

> —and it seemed best for him, the only way I had to try to stop
> him, that I go. I'm with Jody and Bill, people I went to school
> with. Telephone me the next time you're in McRae. Must talk
> to you—

He put the letter in his pocket and went outside, pacing up and down. His worry grew as he paced.

That cracking sound he had heard.

Professor Garfield. He might know. He would know.

Anyhow, he could see Cynthia if he went in. He was uneasy about her. He decided to go tomorrow on the early train.

Next morning, when Tom tried to talk about the squatter, Nick was still obdurate. All Tom could do was say, "Promise not to do anything until I return." Nick would only repeat, "I don't like it."

Tom was gone for two days.

On his return, he had a lot on his mind. But the boy back in the woods was on his conscience, too. "Dad, let's go back and talk to that boy."

Nick's look was peculiar. "I told him to go."

I should have done something more before I left. Set in Nick's mind now. But I had to go in to see the professor, didn't I?

And he thought of the professor's portentous words.

Maybe by this afternoon Nick'll have softened up. I'll go back and see the boy myself now.

At the ravine, Tom stood staring at the scattered pieces of aspiration. The constable had been there. The oil drum stove was in a briar patch, a dent in its side. And Betty Grable's smile had been stepped on.

Standing there, looking at this tangible evidence of a mushrooming in Nick of something strange and ugly, the flame of Tom's anger guttered in a draft of fear.

It was not the best moment for him to meet Nick then, as he did, face to face, returning on the path.

Tom's revulsion leaped up. "You acted fast! While I was in the city!"

Nick looked grim and dogged. "Everybody shoving me! I'm going to shove back."

Tom's anger released itself with a shout. "Because there's bastards in the world, you have to be one?" He stopped, horrified. Now *I'm* yelling at *him*. It's spreading.

Nick licked his lips. "I waited a long time to get this place."

"You could have given him footroom," Tom cried.

"He could do a hurt to something. I have too much to worry about, to have that too."

Nick glanced up at Tom now for the first time, and Tom's revulsion vanished because he could see in Nick's eyes, suffering, a reaching out for something to hold on to.

"Nick," Tom began patiently, "you're letting this get to you. About the bridge and all. Sing your own tune."

Nick said doggedly, "It means so much to me here."

"I know. Dad, before it's too late, let's go find that boy. He used to hang out around Herren's Tavern in McRae. He might still be there. A boy like that's always on the ragged edge of being a bum. He might just say to hell with it, and hit the road. I don't like to think of him in some hobo jungle."

Nick hesitated. Then he said, "All right. Let's go."

Tom drove fast on the state macadam, but he had to slow where the traffic flowed into the broad United States highway. Waiting, he caught his breath.

He saw a figure walking on the road, coming from McRae. Carrying the duffel bag on a shoulder, his dog beside him. Heading toward the highway.

He wasn't trying to hitch a ride.

"There he goes," Tom said unhappily.

They drove across the intersection and stopped beside him.

"Hi!" Tom said.

The boy stared stonily. Tom thought his face was worse to see

186

than the scattered shack. It made him think of a jumping tooth nerve which hasn't quite died.

"You leaving?" Tom asked.

"What's it to you?" But the mask of arrogance he was trying out was like an inexpert black-face job at Halloween. It did not quite reach to the edges. Behind it, cowering, was horrified realization.

"If you want to come back there on the place, it's all right," Tom said tentatively.

"Who you kidding?" the boy said, with hard arrogance.

Tom felt helpless. Then he said, "Well, can we give you a lift?"

The boy's eyes sharpened with cold suspicion. "You can't turn *me* in. You go to hell."

They sat, watching him go.

Nick said finally in an almost fearful voice, "I didn't think." It was as if someone in fever had a non-delirious interval.

"It wasn't like you," Tom said.

"The bees, the bridge—Abel—!" Nick's voice edged upward again as though the fever waited. "If it weren't for him!"

Tom said patiently, "Better stop and take a fix on yourself, see how far you're getting off the beam."

As he drove home, Nick said, a little stubbornly, on the defensive, "He *could* have started a fire."

Tom thought, he's covering, because he has to live with himself. I'm not going to say anything more. Maybe it'll be warning enough.

38

ABEL WAS TARGET SHOOTING when the car stopped across the bridge. He lowered the gun, watching.

A man got out.

Abel came to the head of his lane. The chrome on the green car glinted in the September sun.

Halfway down the lane, Abel saw who it was.

What's he want?

He moved faster to forestall the county attorney's coming up the hill.

Snooping around to see if I'm still making the compound? Or have a safety permit? I do have that raw material stored in the carriage house.

He walked faster.

From the other side of the swinging sign, the attorney raised a hand in greeting. "Good day, Mr. Abel."

"Good day."

The attorney waited until Abel had crossed and stood near him. "I hear you've been having some trouble out here." His voice was casual, betraying only sympathetic interest.

"No trouble!" Abel was short. So! Those people had run crying and sniveling, trying to gain an advantage.

The attorney nodded toward the sign. "I see you have the bridge blocked."

Abel's jaw squared belligerently. "It's my bridge."

"Is that so?" The attorney's tone was friendly and as though interested in a piece of information. "You know, Mr. Abel, everyone used that bridge a long time."

"Too long," Abel was grim.

"Yes, that's what I mean!"

"I don't care what you mean," Abel said. "I'm not going to be taken advantage of."

"I don't blame you for that, but, after all, it's no money out of your pocket to allow its use."

"What's it to you, anyway?"

"It's been my experience a chat will sometimes avoid a lot of trouble. My sworn duty is to keep the peace. If it can be done with a little talk, that's best. Saves the taxpayers money."

"My grandfather built this bridge."

"A long time ago. And everyone that lived on the island and folks that had business here have been using it. In fact, Mr. Abel, an easement has been established. You know what I mean?" His tone was calm and pleasant.

"It's my bridge."

The attorney sighed. "I have a paper in my pocket, an injunction, but I don't want to serve it. I don't believe it's necessary. Why don't you think it over, now that you understand about the easement. Talk to your family. I'm going to keep the writ in my pocket. But," his tone changed subtly, and for the first time he looked hard at Abel, "you know it's there ready to be used."

"Facts are facts," Abel broke out. "My grandfather built it!" Coming around here with his holier-than-thou airs. A man has some rights.

"Now, now, no use getting heated."

Abel did not say anything but his mouth set grimly as he thought: Rather than lay down and let those people walk on me; rather than let you come out here and trample on me, I'll blow it up! Blast it out of the water!

The attorney was running on about what nice weather it had been. "Oh, that reminds me, something I wanted to mention. Thought of it after the day you came in about your water supply. By the way, I hope you were able to get it fixed up?"

Abel's tone was clipped. "It's fixed."

"It occurred to me afterward, there might be some subsidence going on."

Dim bells, jangling, made a discord to drown out a hideous knowledge which must, at all costs, be blocked off.

"It can happen, you know, where the land's been mined out."

"What do you mean, mined out?" Abel's look was fierce.

"Why, where the coal's been taken out. A squeeze can start underground years later. I remember a case over in Steffel Township—I was assistant county attorney there at the time. Case where a farmer's well went, but another fellow down the road had his. Seemed the one that disappeared went in the stratum below from sandy shale above old workings. The other one must have been just far enough beyond not to be caught in the pull. The cavings'll usually move outward in concentric rings, if it's been chain pillar. How was this mined out, do you know?"

Abel violently, fiercely, rejected the idea.

"What makes you think it was mined out?"

"Oh, I'm pretty sure it was. They took out the four-foot vein around here a long time ago. They probably came through later and took out the top vein. That may leave a shallow cover."

Abel felt cold all over.

"In that Steffel Township case, part of his house went. One night about eleven o'clock. The kitchen wing just disappeared. He kept living there, hanging on the edge of the fissure. This subsidence is an eerie thing, erratic, but most interesting."

Abel just looked at him.

189

"Sometimes they can stop the caving, or help it, so they tell me"
—you would think he was talking about the nice weather—"by pumping in culm. Pretty expensive though. Of course, when your neighbors
are sinking too, which they probably would be if you were, why the
expense can be shared."

His neighbors!

The attorney started back across the bridge.

"I must be getting on. Nice talking to you."

He unhooked the chain with the swinging sign. "If I were you,"
he looked levelly at Abel, "I'd just forget this." He put the chain over
the railing.

The attorney was in his car now. He slammed the door and drove
off.

Abel stood awhile, the words Never, Never, boiling inside him.
Then he refastened the chain.

Inside the house, he stared at the crack. It ran from first to second
floor. The stairs had pulled away from the wall a fraction of an inch.
You couldn't pass up to rest without being aware of a force gnawing.

Those people might have done a mischief to the water. This,
inside the house, they could not have done.

He went out and walked back to where the fissure ran across the
ground. He stared at it a long time, depressed.

Then rage took its turn.

Who dared? The foundations! Grandfather planned it as a rock
for the Abels. He must have.

Who dared? Must be a law. Have to leave support under a man's
house.

Homer Swinton. Guess I'll have to go to him. Consultation fee, a
hundred dollars. Besides—he'll know I didn't ask him about the
bridge. Have to go to him.

Whoever's responsible'll answer to me. I'll fight!

"Of course," Homer fussily tapped a pencil on his desk, blinking at
Abel from behind his glasses, "it would have been wiser if you'd
consulted me before taking action on the bridge."

"I tell you I found it in my grandfather's papers. I *know* he built
it."

"Yes. Well, as to the county attorney's claim the bridge was used
without protest or barring. How does he know? Can he prove it in
court? The people that lived out there over the years, the renters,
have scattered. He'd have a hard time proving no protest was made

by the bridge owners. We can claim a protest *was* made. Go ahead and bar it!"

At Swinton's pleased look, Abel had a flash of doubt. Swinton would want to make this into a case, especially if it could be pumped up with publicity. No better way to get notice politically.

It was not about the bridge Abel had come, but—the idea he hated even to mention—subsidence.

Afterward, Swinton said, "I'll look into this subsidence. I'll call you."

Abel went home and waited.

All day, all night, he found himself tense, listening for the sly cracking sounds, in his imagination seeing the rocks faulting beneath his house.

Finally Swinton telephoned and Abel went in.

Swinton's notes were spread on his desk. "Here we are. The manor house and seventy-five acres, known as Abel's Island, was put up for forced sale, 1896."

"What's that have to do with the cave-ins?"

"Just a minute." Swinton picked up another sheet. "I discovered a separate instrument dated 1895—that's the year before McRae Abel sold the house. A hundred year lease."

"On what?"

Homer read, "McRae Abel, party of the first part, leasing to Rumbert Coal Company, all the subjacent estate—"

"What's that?"

"The underlying coal."

Abel felt sick. "But—why would he do that?"

"There was a country-wide panic in '93. Perhaps he was in financial difficulties. Perhaps he did it to try to stave off selling the manor house. Or perhaps he knew the house would have to go, and was scratching around trying to get what he could. Sold out the coal rights before the house went."

Abel broke in fiercely, "Well, that doesn't mean— They still have to leave support!"

"It's a peculiar type lease they used then and fairly common around here at the time, I believe. I copied this so you could see."

Abel's unwilling eye read: "—the right to mine out all coal in veins at, near, or under the surface—hereby demised without leaving any support whatever for the surface of said workings—" Abel sat motionless, staring at the paper in front of him until the flourishes on Swinton's writing began to look like snakes writhing.

There must be some way out! "What about those people that took the top vein? That's probably what caused it!" he broke out aggressively.

"The Rumbert Company later demised all their rights to the West Grove Company, and it was the same type of lease."

At first Abel could not seem to gather himself together. Finally, his voice came hollowly. "There must be something I can do!"

"Unless you have some information which you haven't disclosed, I don't know what it would be."

But all the way home Abel kept repeating the simple facts to himself, trying to accept them. And back on the island, he walked about touching things. He felt numb.

In the room with the rose damask, he looked long at the portrait in oil of McRae Abel. A handsome, bluff man, with white hair. Abel had prided himself, always, that he resembled him physically.

39

SITTING IN THE CAR, TOM took out the notes he had made yesterday in the professor's office. Even looking at the hasty scrawls brought back too sharply his own feelings as the professor had talked.

He had greeted Tom with warm interest.

"And were you able to make an arrangement for pooling the oil out there?"

"Not yet." He did not meet the professor's glance. "Something else I wanted to ask you about." He told him of the crack in the concrete, the steps pulled away. "Perhaps I imagine it but the corner where the plaster's cracked looks out of plumb. Gives me the jitters to think of it."

The professor stroked his chin slowly. "I know the bottom vein was taken long ago. If they've mined the top vein, you could get caving."

"But, no mining's going on!"

"Sometimes cover subsides at once. Other times—ten, fifteen, even twenty-five years later."

Tom felt as if an icy wind was passing through the room. "But—why would it start now?"

"A squeeze, a creep, an underground flood, a fault, who knows? Man does not control everything in the world."

Tom's brain seemed to spin. Nick! He went numb then, not able to face that.

There must be *something* to do! They couldn't just sit and let the bottom drop out!

He tried to concentrate on the technical information the professor was giving him, but he wrote automatically, too upset to take it in, or ask questions. Even his fingers seemed numb.

In the street, he had one thought, "Have to call Cynthia."

He remembered his half-scornful ridicule, hearing some barracks-mate, ill-favored, not-too-bright, being so sure he mattered, having such a sense of importance, when something bad or good happened to him, saying, "Got to call my girl."

The young married couple where she was staying were old friends, she'd said.

The coin reverberated in the box and a girl's voice answered. "She's not here. Is this by any chance Tom Dorn?"

"Yes."

"She's gone to Charlesville."

"Tell her I was here and I called."

Charlesville. Meant she was pushing through the ugly legalities. But even in the booth, the professor's words gnawed at him.

Now, sitting in the car, absently twisting the wheel, studying the notes, Tom could see he must get the answers to questions the professor had raised.

He started the car toward McRae.

The clerk in the Recorder of Deeds office said, "Funny, your asking about that. Someone in a day or so ago, inquiring."

"Mr. Abel?"

"No, a lawyer. Homer Swinton. I can lay my hands right on it without hunting."

Tom, seated at a small oak table with wobbly legs, read: "McRae Abel, party of the first part, to Rumbert Coal—"

"You should have heard Swinton when he sees it's one of those old no-support leases."

"No support?" Tom felt sickish.

193

"Yes. See?" The clerk put a dirty finger nail on a line.

Tom finished reading.

"You want to see the other one? Had them both out for Swinton."

Tom read the second lease. Then he asked, "Do you know if West Grove has an office in McRae?"

"Used to be upstairs in the bank building, I think."

The clerk in the bank said, no, they'd moved to Greendale. The chief engineer, George Richardson, still lived in Wesley Manor.

The woman who answered the telephone said he wasn't in but was expected.

As Tom drove up to the house in Wesley Manor, a car swung in the drive and a man around forty, in high-laced boots with red-topped socks turned over them, got out.

He invited Tom up to the porch, though he said he had to leave soon.

Tom felt as quivery as the springy metal porch chair he sat on, as he asked the questions.

"Yes, West Grove took out the top vein," the engineer said. "Quite a while ago, before I ever worked for them. What's the trouble? You getting some caving?"

Tom swallowed. "Yes."

"Usually comes along, sooner or later. I've seen a cover hold up twenty years. Other times it'll go as soon as the pillars are pulled. It's mean. You can't do much legally, though. It's been more'n six years."

"Six years?"

"You can't file a suit for that in this county after six years."

Tom knew the engineer was in a hurry, that he ought not to sit here.

The engineer looked at him sympathetically. "One thing you might do. Pump in silt or culm. You being on the river there, you could get silt. Of course," he glanced at Tom quizzically, "it takes money. There's a company around here does it. If you want to look into it, I'll put you in touch."

Tom rose. His mouth was dry but he managed to say, "All right. Thank you."

Tom drove down the tree-lined street. "Takes money—" How much? Should have asked.

But anything was too much for the Dorns.

Go see Seavey. Ask if there was any hope about the oil writ, about getting anything there.

194

Seavey was in the trailer, talking on the telephone. He motioned Tom to a seat.

"Cracking and caving!" he shouted angrily. "You mean back there by the wells?"

"No, not there."

"Oh." He wiped perspiration from his forehead. "For a minute, you had me worried. I was sure the workings didn't go in there."

So he had known all the time the ground was hollow.

"We might have culm pumped in," Tom said. "Is there any chance of getting at the funds from the oil?"

"Swinton has us boxed. We can't seem to unfreeze that writ." Seavey leaned back and put his fingers together. "Come to think of it, maybe this is a good thing."

Tom stared, taken aback. "Good?"

"The workings run under Abel's land, too, don't forget. Maybe he'll take himself back to the city where he belongs. Coming out here trying to push into a business we had set up for two generations! He's stepped on other toes, too."

"What's that got to do with our house?"

"Well, now, you can't always look at things just from your own self-interest. Yessir, it may be a good thing. I think he'll go."

Tom swallowed hard and when he could speak, his words were clipped. "Is there anything I can do about the funds from the oil?"

"Not a thing," Seavey said cheerfully.

The Mansion House was nearest. In the dim cocktail lounge, the empty glass before him, Tom knew this was going to be no help. Not even another and another.

Nick. For him it would be like waiting a long, long time to marry a woman, to discover she'd been raped.

In the almost deserted lounge, he sensed someone looking at him.

Oh. Cynthia had pointed her out once. Not a bad-looking dame.

What if I went over and sat down beside her and said, Listen, tell your fine friend Abel to take that writ off our oil payments!

What's she doing? Picking up her drink. Coming toward me!

He rose as she approached.

Rena looked hesitant. "Mind if I join you?"

"Happy." He did not smile. She sat down.

They sipped their drinks in measuring silence.

"How's everything out on the island?" she asked finally.

What a thing to make light conversation about! Like to open up, tell her—tell someone.

She kept her tone casual but her eyes were anxious. "Haven't seen any of you folks from the island in town. You—or Mr. Abel."

That's why she came over. Trying to find out what's up with her boy friend.

"Everything's fine." Tom was not smiling. "Just fine. Last I saw of your friend Glen Abel, he was shooting off a gun and telling my father and mother they couldn't use the bridge."

She flushed. "He's had a lot of things upset him. Glen, I mean."

"Who hasn't? Me, I just learned the coal under the island was mined out and the house is sinking."

"Oh, no!" After awhile she asked, "The Abel house, too?"

"Yes, I guess it is."

She looked more anxious. "It means so much to him."

"You think we don't care?"

"He's put up such a fight."

"Fought us enough anyway."

With a troubled glance, she traced circles on the table with a finger. "He's been changed lately. Sometimes if too much goes against a person, they give up. Others keep fighting but it makes them mean. Guess I've been pretty impatient with him, too."

He drank in silence. Finally he said, "I've been told if we could pump culm in there, might stop it, the sinking. Not guaranteed, but a good chance. But your kind friend, Mr. Abel, has put some legal thing on our oil money."

She was staring at her drink with sad eyes. She said, "I might talk to Glen. Usually he's rather bull-headed, but maybe he'll listen." Then she asked, "Is Mrs. Winters still there? His daughter?"

"No. She's gone."

"He's there alone. Not good. Not good for anyone."

But Tom was thinking about Nick. And he knew that sitting here drinking, he was just putting off the question, How will I tell Nick?

When she rose, saying she had to go on duty, he had no excuse. He paid for his drink and left.

Slowly he drove toward the island.

At the intersection where they had to turn off now for the back road, he was in such a dark mood, he slowed almost to a dead-stop, thinking, Have a good notion to drive up and across the bridge. But Abel's always around target shooting. Might just make things worse.

In the dooryard, Nick glanced up morosely. "Oh, you're back. Trying to get this job finished." He struggled to pull a nail out of an old board.

196

Tom stood looking at him. "Why don't you forget it, Dad?" Couldn't Nick see this was part of what was pulling him off the beam?

Nick glanced toward the kitchen door. "It'll stop her crying around, saying he's staring down at her." His tone was peevish. "Stop that anyway. *One* thing I can do something about."

Like when a battery leaks and the acid runs over everything, Tom thought. He felt an aversion to the island, to everything connected with it. He walked away quickly.

Along the river he saw something white fallen in high weeds,—a hive fallen off its stand. The last colony Nick had received. "They might work the goldenrod crop," he'd said. I ought to pick it up. Oh, what the hell. What difference?

Dejectedly, he moved along the shore toward the bridge.

In the stone abutment on the island side, above the swirls of willow branches and sticks lodged there, he noticed a crack. Nearly two inches wide. Could that be from the subsidence? Him and his precious bridge. Serve him right if it collapsed. Don't say that. Bad for everyone.

A car was approaching from McRae. Abel. He slowed, then kept turning to stare at Tom as he drove up his lane.

Tom saw the flag up on the Dorn box.

Should have driven up there when I was on the other side. Have to go back through the woods, drive around—if I want the mail that much.

He walked over the bridge. If he takes a pot shot at me, let him.

In the box, two letters.

One envelope, smooth, creamy, engraved with the name of the University Medical School.

Strange—feeling this paper—reminds me. That sticky August day, year I graduated from High. Lifting the letter out of the mail box on the porch. Way I felt, reading: "Due to diminished dividends—we will be able to grant only one of our usual two scholarships. We regret—." Can even see the date. Nine years ago.

He opened the letter. The machinery he'd started last June, when everything seemed possible, was in motion. "All prospective registrants whose names begin with letters A to N inclusive will present themselves October three at nine in the morning—"

He broke into a laugh. Imagine me actually believing—. How could I have kidded myself like that? A plastic surgeon!

He wanted to thrust the letter from Cynthia in his pocket out of

197

sight. Don't want to think of. Don't want to be in communication with her. Not now.

He read the first few lines:

—I love you. I just began to. Before, I didn't, though I didn't know that. This is all different—.

He crumpled the letter into his pocket, feeling sick.

How could I have dreamed of such a thing? Letting myself think I could marry. Actually thinking I was off the ground, everything set. Ought to have known by this time!

Into Tom's mind flashed an image—that boy, that walking-away boy.

Moving down the road, away from mistakes and responsibilities. With a long sigh of relief to say, Okay, I quit. Drifting.

For that matter, I wouldn't even have to hop freights or sleep by the road. Margot.

I wasn't fired, I quit.

He went in the house.

Agnes rose slowly out of her chair. "Tom, I think you'd better drive me in to that doctor in McRae. I was waiting for you."

"Nick would have—"

"He has enough to worry about."

"We'll have the doctor come out."

Her voice was matter of fact and calm. "That costs fifteen dollars and I'm not bad off."

It took them awhile to get to the back road because she had to walk slowly.

As they drove along toward McRae, Tom looked off through an opening in the woods. He could see across a valley, where the United States highway rolled off and away, going toward Postville, Arden, Lentel and on west. Away. If the boy got a hitch, he was past Riggton now. All this behind him.

"Tom, stop by that locust grove. Here!"

He stopped.

"Last time we went in when Nick slowed here, I thought I saw bees flying in and out of that dead locust. Might be a good swarm in there. If we see signs, we can tell him. He might be able to get them."

Tom looked at her a moment, but he kept the impatience out of his voice. "He doesn't care about that now."

"That's now. He will."

198

"What's the use of it?"

"Will you get out and look for signs of them?"

He got out grudgingly. Simplest thing to humor her. When he came back he said, "I couldn't see anything."

They drove on.

Bees for Nick. Was she blind? Not only the bridge. The caving. The professor said the subsidence might stop, or it might go on, might be gradual or sudden. The uncertainty of it could drive you batty.

"Last time I was in," Agnes said, "this doctor said, Do you worry about your condition? It's not like that at all, I said. I couldn't explain. Each day, life begins."

Maybe it begins, but it gets stopped before it gets very far, he thought.

"Sometimes I wonder how you pick up and go on," he said.

"You do it yourself. I've seen you."

They drove through Sherrod, stopping at the light.

Well, maybe. That time the plane came down. The disappointment about med school. Margot. All right, I got up and went on. For what? I'm tired.

They drove along without talking. They were almost into McRae.

"Sometimes," he said, "I just don't see why you *want* to go on."

"Maybe a person doesn't have anyone to love could feel that way. I have you, I have Nick. What would happen to him if I said, it's too hard. It's a sort of trust. I trust God, I guess. Whatever it is up there, to be there when needed. I've had all that help. It's stored up inside me. I'd feel ashamed not to pass that on. What if Nick trusted me and I'd given up? You, you'll go on. You have love now. You'll find out how it is."

She went into the doctor's white frame house. He waited in the car.

After awhile he took Cynthia's crumpled letter out. He finished reading it. "—I went to see Harry and I feel strong, as if I had even extra strength to send you."

He got out of the car, pacing up and down in front of the doctor's house.

There must be *something* we can do.

He paced, eyes on the pavement.

Krimmer.

He's been in business around here a long time. He must have

known or guessed the coal had been taken out, that there might be trouble. And if he did, was that fraud?

There *must* be something.

Krimmer wouldn't assume any loss. But those heirs in California? A wild chance.

Even if we could recover a part of it. Perhaps start over then. And I can tell Nick, now that there seems *something* to do.

He reread the letter from the medical school, absorbing it now. October third. There might be time.

They were sitting in the dining room. Outside bare branches moved with a stricken sound in a small chill breeze.

Nick sat, hands hanging between his knees, staring ahead, as Tom told him. He sat still for such a long time, Tom was frightened.

Finally Nick said, "His grandfather. Yes, his grandfather."

"Oh, don't get off on that again. It's what *we're* going to *do*."

"Sold out, undermined his own island."

Hubert Krimmer looked up as they came into his office. What did *they* want? They looked like trouble.

"Well, yes, I'm busy," he said, "I'm due to meet a customer in ten minutes, but what's on your mind? I can spare a few minutes."

"That's good. That's real good," the father said, and it seemed to Hubert that his tone was rather ugly.

The son broke in then as if he wanted to keep the father quiet. "We're having some trouble out there, Mr. Krimmer, that we feel you as the agent should do something about."

"Abel?" Krimmer leaned forward.

"No." Tom told him. As he finished, he looked at Krimmer with a level glance. "We feel you should have warned us."

"I remember distinctly your asking me what that pile of old slag was and I told you. That meant there'd been mining in the vicinity. After all," Hubert could feel a sense of annoyance mounting in him, "you're adults. I can't pin up the diapers for everyone wants to buy a piece of property."

"But who would have thought of cave-ins?"

"You don't actually *know* it *is* that, do you?"

"What else could it be?"

Krimmer shrugged. Was he supposed to figure that out, too? His annoyance deepened. Next thing, they'd be thinking of asking for their money back.

"We don't expect you yourself to take any loss, but"—Well, now that was big of him, Krimmer thought—"you ought to make those people that sold us the land give back our money."

Hubert stared.

"Or at least part of it," Tom said. "It being a cash deal, we have to rely on some good faith."

Hubert thought that in all the years he'd been in business he'd never heard anything so plain silly, so full of gall.

"Naturally, we've been living there all this time, we'd expect to pay for that," Tom said.

"But the rest of it," Nick broke in grimly.

"Or at least part."

"And after all, you were the agent, and if you put it up to the people who sold—"

Hubert was recovering from his shock, but a feeling of outrage was taking its place.

"I've had about enough of this," he said indignantly. He went on with righteous wrath, "In the first place, if it *is* a cave-in, it might go on for years without getting a lot worse. In the second place, don't forget you got that oil well. And it's not undermined back there, is it?"

"No."

"I understand it paid off very well. And don't forget I made it possible for you to get that!" The sense of their ingratitude actually made him sick. The nerve of them.

Nick broke out wildly, "Don't you know Abel's got us stymied with some kind of writ?"

"Well," Krimmer said crossly, "that's your problem. If you can't get on with *any*one!"

It was a funny thing—and Hubert felt a kind of admiration for him—but Abel didn't come running in here like these crybabies, asking for his money back, as if they'd been playing with doll dishes. It was ridiculous. For all his big head, Abel was folks.

"You mean you won't do anything for us?" Nick was glowering as if the caving was Krimmer's fault.

"*I* do something?" Krimmer had about enough of this. "Didn't I hear from Leland you people bought a lot of explosives for blasting? There must have been some cause for this to happen now, you know. Been a long time since there was any mining there. It's likely with all your rooting around and blasting, you stirred it up! What I'm wondering is if Glen Abel has thought of that?" He glared right back at Nick.

"You're just trying to find an out! You can't get away with this! Then just leave us—"

No use trying to be decent to people like this. Krimmer put on his hat. "I'm not going to listen to any of your abuse. I'm sorry. I have to meet a customer. I'm late now."

He had to walk out on them.

40

AT SUNSET THE AIR WAS STILL motionless, although all day the radio had been warning of a hurricane moving up the coast. As Glen Abel walked across his lawn, the fading light induced a mood of subdued reverie.

Last summer, Cynthia sat in that chair in her white dress. Now he was alone. She'd put the telephone number where he could reach her in that hateful letter, "Write me when the bridge is opened." He could go in out of the sad, shimmering light, pick up the receiver and say—.

But was it his place to? This was her home, he her father. Besides, she'd have to come to confer with Swinton about the annulment, wouldn't she?

How could she have gone like that? She was gentle. It was so unlike her, he could even wonder if someone had influenced her.

He was very lonely.

Of course, there was Rena. But there was a certain danger there he feared. An exquisite humiliation.

Walking along the path now, he dreamed for a moment his old dream—the prosperous kindly man, a well-trained dog at heel, settled, secure.

The Dorn well was not pumping. The island was quiet.

At the brow of the hillock he looked back. His roof and the Dorn's were touched by the sunset to the same rose, and for an instant, seeing them so, he thought, if only they had been reasonable. Someone you could figure out.

Returning, he almost stepped into a fresh fissure, which ran, heedless of boundaries, under the split rail fence.

After he went to bed in the lonely house, he lay rigid, listening.

Finally, he turned on the radio. The hurricane was advancing up the coast, it was a quarter to two. He rose and stood at the window. In the Dorn house, a light came on. Not a wide shaft, slicing the gloom. A small, worried light, as if someone might have heard a cracking sound. He stood a long time, looking at it.

He'd not forgotten the county attorney's mention of culm packing. It was expensive. But—if it were shared?

All night, he'd been searching for a way. Perhaps that was the only one.

He'd have to allow them, probably, the bridge. But Cynthia would return then.

When he went to bed he fell asleep promptly.

He woke next morning, heart pounding, roused by a nightmare. It was fading, but there'd been something about a large man behind a desk. J. B. Conovan, furiously demanding why Glen did not have something. Money. Glen had stolen Conovan's daughter. He was running down a long road with her, but she had changed to Cynthia.

Blankets, hastily pulled out of the closet last week in the first autumnal chill, were suffocating. He kicked them away and sat up.

Unbearably sultry this morning.

At that moment the island's quiet ended. The Dorn well ruptured the stillness. Running it again! Sucking up his substance.

And last night he had thought he might work something out with those people! How could he have believed it possible?

He dressed slowly. If they'd just give him time, he'd make it yet. Keep your guts, hang on, never let your adversary see you'd been wounded.

Afterward, he tried to work in the study, but it was stifling.

He went outside. The boat, tied below, moved scarcely at all in the water. He went down and stood looking at it. How lovingly he had readied it for her. The bright lettering, "Cynthia," was mud-flecked now. She had deserted him.

He pulled the boat up on shore and turned it over. Bannon would help him put it up for the winter.

All day, as he went in and out, their pump pounded at him.

In mid-afternoon, back in the house, he heard a car drive up.

Cynthia! A wave of tenderness and triumph filled him. He ran out.

It was Rena.

"I just had an impulse to come," she said. Her soft green dress set off her hair. She was vivacious and gay. She had not been here since Cynthia's advent.

He felt uneasy. Her coming of her own volition slid the situation out of his control. What if she offered now?

If only things could have remained the way they were—Cynthia here, Rena in McRae.

They walked around outside and she went down the steps to see the boat.

Her figure was still charming. And because she looked desirable, he was angry. Because also she threatened a humiliation. The cross-pull was unbearable. It gave him a deep weariness, a yearning to be freed, at last, from all conflict.

After she went in the house, he stood awhile looking at the leaden river.

When he turned he saw Dorn standing on the slight rise over on his place. Just standing.

What if now? Propose the culm packing. It wasn't certain. In those old workings, who could tell? But often it worked. Then, at last, release from conflict.

He almost made a gesture to hail him.

Better if Dorn came to him.

41

TOM HUNCHED OVER ON THE top step of the porch, chewing his thumb.

Not guaranteed, that culm packing, but a good chance. The workings wouldn't be divided between his side and ours. It'd have to be a one-piece job.

Mr. Glen J. Abel, the man who wouldn't pool the oil.

Cut it. I'm off that stuff. There must be a way.

He wouldn't pool the oil, but he'll feel differently about this, won't he?

You have to ask yourself, is a man a specific bastard, say about one pet peeve? Or a general bastard?

For a long time, Tom sat. His thumb nail was down to the flesh. Dimly at first, finally with surety, he grasped something. What Cynthia and I have between us, is trust. That's what's missing.

Vividly, a moment came back, a harsh image. Abel's face, seeing Cynthia in the boat with me, the way he looked, seeming to order me off the earth.

And the way he looked that day I put it up to him about the pooling, and he kept on target shooting. Tom winced.

And his eyes staring at me from his front door as he said no. Suspicious.

The acid that leaks over everything.

Anybody else, I could put it up to him—take the writ off the oil first. Then we'll share the expense of trying to do something with the culm. Anybody else, yes.

But if I put it up to him to first take off the writ, he might think we're trying to trick him into unblocking it. The acid.

No, the thing to do's not even ask him to. Just hit him about the culm packing.

I could get a job. We could pay our share on time.

How much will it cost, I wonder? I could go in to that engineer, get the dope from that company he mentioned. But why discourage everyone throwing around some big sum before they even agree?

I can't do anything anyhow until Nick agrees.

Nick, the man who wouldn't give Abel the water. Don't think of that. Nick'll see this is for everyone's good. He's not stupid.

Unless he gets scared.

First, Nick.

I better walk pretty easy, feel my way. Figure out how best to put it to him.

Then that afternoon, Tom was lucky.

They were working in a mess of plaster, filling a long crack from first to second floor between stairs and wall which seemed to taunt them with, "Close me and I will open."

Nick, disgustedly slapping plaster in, gave him a chance. "You'd think engineers with all their inventions would have figured out some way to do about caving!"

Tom laid down his trowel. "Well, there's culm packing."

205

"What do you mean?"

"That mining engineer, that Richardson, said they pump silt or culm in."

Nick's eyes lit. "Why didn't you tell me?"

"It'd have to be a one-piece job. We'd have to get Abel to go in too."

"Fat chance of that."

"Well, I don't know." Tom straightened up, rested his hands on his hips and looked steadily at Nick. "How about you?"

Nick turned his face and carefully wiped up plaster dust from the stair with an old rag.

Tom didn't hurry him. Taking out his cigarette pack, he tried to loosen a cigarette without touching his dusty hands to it. "I can go in and look up this engineer. But—no use doing anything, unless you agree."

Nick sat down on the top step.

Agnes came into the living room, glancing up at them, and turned on the radio. "Looks like to storm. I want to get a weather report. Comes on at one." The radio blared up. A hillbilly voice announced the Sunshine Hour, and the Reverend Billy Williams nasally intoned his text for the day. "Be not deceived. God is not mocked. For whatsoever a man soweth—" Agnes, hunting the weather, turned the dial. An announcer's synthetic voice informed the world that "The hurricane, now off Cape Hatteras, is moving up the coast. It has already inflicted severe damage, bringing floods and—"

Tom was lighting a cigarette, not looking at Nick.

Nick rose. "I guess I'll go outside for awhile. Think about it."

Restlessly, Nick moved through the woods, batting with annoyance at the gnats circling in the sultry air.

Culm packing. That must mean filling in the hollow places with slag or sand or something.

Look out! A new fissure. Almost stepped down into it! A gape, a wound.

If only the oil money were not checkmated.

Then Nick came over the top of a little rise. Across on the Abel place, he saw him. Standing at the top of his steps that led to the river. And beside him, a woman. With red hair. They were just standing there, looking down at the river.

Nick stared at them with a little shock. He had never thought of Abel as someone who might enjoy food or drink or want a woman.

She moved away then and went in the house.

206

After a few moments Abel turned and saw Nick.

The moment stood out, seeming for some reason weighty, more important than the sleeping, eating, walking of weeks and months. A long moment, trembling on the fulcrum of the time beam, with past at one end, future at the other.

Nick had a notion to go over there. To say, "Look, it's what has to be done—."

The notion seemed to jet from what he saw, or sensed, or maybe imagined. The embryo of a gesture, like the swelling of the rigid cylinder of a plant stalk before the leaf bud breaks through. Perhaps sensing the rustling, sliding hollowness beneath, Abel's hand pushed outward toward Nick with a longing for equilibrium.

Nick wondered what would happen if he walked around to the steps. Tell him I'm willing.

Why not? It's to his interest.

But wait. I ought to get more facts. Maybe better if Tom talked to him. Handle it better.

The time beam trembled on the fulcrum and the moment moved away.

Nick sat down beside Tom on the top step of the porch.

"Well," Tom said, "what do you say?"

"I say, all right."

A surge of strength rose in Tom. There was a way. Always some way. "Fine."

"But, first, we have to get Abel to unblock our oil."

Tom swallowed hard.

"I'll get a job. We can do it that way."

"But he'll have to give us our oil. You go ask."

Tom looked at a knot hole in the floor. "That's not the way to handle it."

"But ask him!" Nick reiterated.

"I tell you, we have to forget about that. Go after the culm packing first."

"Why forget it?"

Tom shook an imaginary pebble out of his moccasin.

"You could go see him," Nick insisted. "Ask him."

Of course he'd think that was what to do because he hasn't had the same experience with him I have. "I already did," Tom said slowly.

"Oh." Nick's hands dropped to his sides. After a while he asked in a flat voice, "When was that?"

Why does he keep hitting this? I'm scared of it.

"Something you didn't tell me?" Nick had begun to look tense.

Tom made the cigarette lighting last as long as he could. Guess it's best to tell him how it was, then he'll see himself that's not the way to handle it. "I didn't say anything at the time because I didn't want to get your hopes up, but I asked him to pool the oil and he wouldn't."

"Pool the oil?"

"That first time I went to the city, Professor Garfield told me about it. Abel could drill an offset well, but it would mean a big investment. People often do this pooling, arrange who is to pump when."

The three lines appeared between Nick's brows. "And he wouldn't?"

Why did we have to get into this? Finally Tom said, "No."

Nick's body was tense. "That would have un-stymied us—but it would have been to his interest too?"

"Well, yes, if he took off the writ, we'd have shared the proceeds."

Nick seemed to be withdrawing to some bleak swamp.

"Now, don't go imagining anything," Tom broke out.

"Imagining! You said yourself, it would have been to his own interest!"

"That's all past. Let's concentrate on the problem we have now."

Nick's legs were crossed and his arms wrapped around his body. Finally he said flatly, "Where'd you get this information? About the packing?"

"From Richardson, that engineer."

"He a friend of Abel's?"

"No. I don't know. What difference?"

Nick's eyes narrowed. He stood up then, looking off toward the woods and his oil well. He started to say something but his lips thinned. He went down the porch steps.

"Now, wait, Nick." Tom rose hastily.

Nick did not turn around.

"Don't begin to—. Wait!" Tom called after him, angry, not only at Nick, but himself, because he had not handled it better. "Let's talk about it!"

Nick kept going doggedly, walking away from the house toward the river.

Lunging blindly away from the house, something seemed to be

208

swelling inside him like a great wave, which must break, must find expression.

Soon in the tall weeds, he passed the lone beehive. His one hive, and that man had caused him so much disaster, he'd neglected even that! As he set it to rights, he was thinking of Abel's face, that day the bees died. "He didn't care if he killed them. A murderer at heart!"

The wave pushed him on restlessly. He passed the cairn of rocks they had made as a storage place for the metal box of explosives. Last spring—the spring far off—bathed in golden light. How hopefully he'd blasted the rocks to make the workshop. His workshop, which was to have helped him earn a small living. Bring him the joy of making. If it had not been for him.

He sank down on a log, his shoulders hunched forward and his eyes on the ground.

Tom didn't see straight. On account of that girl. Sweet on her.

But how could I have been so soft-headed as to think, even for that one moment, we could work out anything with Abel? Someone who would go against his own interests to hurt us!

He could not understand anyone like that. It made him afraid.

A whirl of raindrops struck as though some sower had scattered a handful of cold ghostly seed. The temperature dropped suddenly.

Nick walked back along the shore, hardly knowing where he was. Now he was under the bridge. He stopped, transfixed. He was staring at a crack, nearly three inches wide in the masonry. Beautifully wide, jagged, ominous! The wave that had been gathering in Nick rose high and broke, as he stood, staring.

He glanced up at Abel's house. Abel was standing up there, looking down.

The rain seemed scarcely to reach the ground before the wind took it. Beyond McRae a flash of lightning tore open the sky, and after suspense came the thunder groan.

The equinox, with manifestations of power, was carrying away the failing year.

42

THE STORM WAS APPROACHING, but in the big room, the damask curtains still hung limp in the humid air.

Rena was chatting gaily.

Abel narrowed his eyes. She's thinking of it, waiting a chance.

Fixing the drinks and serving them saved him from talking. Afterward, he entrenched himself behind the writing table.

She was running on, "—been three weeks since you were in."

"I've been busy."

"I was worried about you."

"I'm fine."

"Why don't you come back to town with me? We can have a good time. Do you good to get away for awhile."

She had never understood about the island, that he was committed to it. "I can't go now," he said. "Things are happening here."

She glanced at him quickly. "You look jumpy and tired."

"I told you I'm fine," he said.

"Well, it worried me when I knew you were out here alone."

How did she know that?

She looked at him with troubled eyes. "Especially if things aren't going right."

Watch out. A woman is always looking for a chance to get close. Then—the knife stab, the disemboweling.

"Everything's going fine."

"The taxi driver didn't know whether to come over or not. Why do you have the bridge closed?"

"There are good reasons for it."

She put her drink down, and moved to a chair closer to his.

"It must make it hard for you."

"Why should it?"

"Such an ugly atmosphere."

"Perhaps, in the circumstances, that's a good thing."

"That can't be, Glen. You look tired. One of the best things you could do would be to take that sign down!"

"Why do you say that?"

"You'd be happier."

"I'm happy."

"With Cynthia gone? You can't tell me. And if you hadn't posted the bridge, she'd be here, you know that as well as I do."

He scowled. "Have you seen her?"

"No."

"Who told you?"

"Young Dorn."

Young Dorn! Abel felt thick blood in his throat. The only way Dorn would know was from Cynthia herself! Not the kind of thing dropped in a casual street meeting. After an intimate conversation, yes. In a room, somewhere, alone.

"Where'd you see him?" His eyes seemed to dart fire.

"In the Mansion House."

Abel felt as if he could not get his breath. He was seeing an image of Cynthia's bed, a garish necktie carelessly—.

"You'd be better off, Glen, really, if you forgot the whole thing."

"Forget!" He glared into space. "I'll never forget it!" He was thinking of the boat, and discovering them in it.

"It's not as if it cost you anything," she said.

He broke out with strange vehemence, "I'll blow it up before I'll let them use it!"

She looked startled. Instantly he was on guard, aware from the movement of her hands toward him, he had revealed too much of his agony.

He sat there broodingly.

Cynthia, with Dorn. Treachery.

Perhaps he had enticed her.

The coming storm made the room murky. The half-dark gave Rena too much of a chance to say it.

He stood up abruptly and switched on the harsh overhead lights. A few moments later, the storm must have struck somewhere close by. The lights went out.

Sitting there in the flicker of the candles, he could see, trembling up to her lips, ready to spring at him, the words he dreaded.

He had a fleeting frenzy of wanting to silence her even by choking.

In the half-dark, she could not see his face. She said, "When you first came out here, before your daughter came, you asked me to marry you. I wanted to, how I wanted to, because I was in love with you. I've always been. But I said no. Now, I think we might. For each other's sake, we ought."

He moved away and stared through glass dark now with driving rain. The storm at least could lash and beat down anything and anyone.

What if she came on purpose to tell him of Cynthia's betrayal, thinking when he was still quivering, she would—.

She said softly, "If you're worried because you are out of funds, why that doesn't—"

He turned on her, goaded, in rage.

"How do you know so much about that?"

The rain blasted against the house and drowned out her words. When the steady downpour came, she said, "I don't. I just guessed from the way you looked, things weren't going well."

Yes, he thought, and you hoped when I was down, to give the deep cut, force me to admit I have nothing.

He came toward her menacingly.

"Glen, dear, don't look like that. I love you."

"I don't need sympathy." The gale banged the shutters wildly against the house. He raised his voice over the wind. "I don't care how many are against me. I have faith in myself."

"Yes," her voice was sad, "but in what else?"

The window shades rattled and the candles went out.

There was an ominous lull in the storm.

He stood rigid, staring.

Then the wind rose suddenly. A sharp loud report came through the storm, followed by a long dull roar.

Frightened, she turned to him. "What was that?"

His hands clenched. "Maybe it was his house. Blown clean off the island!"

She went to him quickly and stroked his face, tenderly as one would a fever patient.

He jerked away from her and went to the window, trying to see through the wall of rain.

The sound had not come from their side.

What if—?

"Where are you going?" she cried, frightened. "Put on a raincoat, anyhow!"

He was struggling to open the door against the wind. Rain blew in as he forced it. Then he was on the outside and the wind slammed it shut.

The maniacal fury of the storm beat down the trees, flattened the bushes. He ran down the lane.

The dull roar had come from there. He had to know.

He could hear the stream hissing with a harsh sharp sound as if meeting obstacles.

He was soaking from the rain but he did not feel it. A lightning flash showed him, like a nightmare he had dreamed once, the bridge. Rena had not given him the final blow.

Another lightning glare inflicted the scene on him again. The floor of the bridge on the island side was down three or four feet. The earth had caved from under the abutment on this side. He heard repeated dull thuds as the torrent hurled branches and debris against the bridge floor.

He stood stunned. This could not have happened to him.

He remembered, almost at once, he had seen them, the son, and the father, down there in the last day or so. The bridge had been there a long time, had withstood other storms. Why would it have happened now?

It would not. Unless someone had *made* it happen.

43

THE STORM SEEMED TO BEWILDER Agnes.

Tom watched her a little anxiously as she moved from icebox to table, putting out the salad, the cold meat, the bread and butter on the supper table.

"Where's Nick?" Her voice was faint.

"Oh, he'll be in soon." Tom lifted the heavy meat platter out of her shaking hands and put it on the table. When the lights went, he located two plumbers' candles and lit them.

Nick came in. Agnes stared at his wet clothes, confused. Tom said, "Better change. We're ready to eat."

Worries me that Agnes looks like that. She's bothered by the

213

storm, but it isn't only that. All this trouble is getting to her. Way she jumps at every thunderclap. Never bothered her before. Guess I better not stir anything up now, by asking Nick. Bad enough as it is.

They ate in silence. Only their magnified shadows on the wall moved as their hands reached out for food.

When they finished, Tom said, "I'll clear away. You better rest, Mother." But she refused, moving back and forth like an automaton.

Afterward, they could not settle to read or work. The storm's rage could not be shut out. And in lulls, they listened, intent, for a sly, dreaded sound.

Stealing in over the gloom of the storm, came the darkness of night. The three sat silently by the shivering candles.

The wind and rain stopped momentarily, began again. Then the sound came. Not the one they were expecting.

A sharp terrible crack, followed by a dull roar. They jumped up and stood staring at each other.

It had not been in the house. Outside, fairly far off.

Nick's hands clenched at his sides and a wild look came over his face. "It's down. It was cracked already! I saw it! It came from there! It couldn't have been anything else. The bridge! I hope it's wrecked, ruined!"

Tom moved toward Agnes quickly as he saw her sway a little, cringing away from Nick. Then he turned on Nick in a sharp, low tone. "That's no way to talk!"

Nick flared. "I'll talk what way I want!"

Agnes sat down and covered her face with her hands, to shut away the storm breaking inside the house.

Tom's voice was low, tightly controlled. "Let's keep in mind why we came here."

"I know what I came for!" Nick broke out. "A little peace, a little security. Not to be shoved around!"

Tom tried to keep his voice down, but the storm rose with renewed frenzy, and he had to almost shout over it. "We had bad luck sure—"

"Bad luck! Maybe it's about time for him to have some bad luck! Man like that. Going against his own interests to hurt us. Not pooling the oil. You said so yourself!"

Agnes said shakily, "No, don't think that way. It'll only—"

"If he hadn't been here, everything would have been all right!" Nick cried out.

Tom tried to keep his voice reasonable. "He didn't cause the cave-ins."

"His grandfather did. Selling out that way. Fine grandfather to spring from—a seller-out, a gutter, an underminer. And he's the same. I hate him!"

"No, no—" Agnes began and Tom ran toward her as she slumped in the chair, crumpling up, and slowly slid down, her head over her knees.

For a moment Tom raised his fist at his father, then at Nick's look, his hand fell.

Nick's voice came wearily now. "It's worried her. I know it. I didn't mean things to go this way. I can't help it. I can't help it."

After they gave her the medicine, she seemed better. Nevertheless, they watched with her far into the night.

Toward morning, the storm died down.

And after awhile Agnes fell into a natural sleep.

44

AN HOUR EARLIER, THE STORM had slackened, but now at midnight, as Abel crossed his grounds, he had to push against the driving wind and rain. He was not going in until Rena had gone to bed, and he was watching for the light in an upper room to go off. He did not intend to face her.

Laughing. They had all been laughing at him behind his back!

Cynthia had deserted him.

When the light remained on, he plunged into the woods, heedless of rain, feeling even a satisfied vengeance in the wind lashing the trees.

A lightning streak revealed the Dorn house, unhurt. His bridge, but not their house. He remembered how it had been with his water well. His had gone but theirs had been fine.

As though lit by a lightning flash that did not flicker out but glared on in his mind, a frightening terrain had appeared from below the surface. The terrifying series of traps he had walked through was clearly lit now. How could he have been so stupid not to have seen? Everything that happened had been planned.

Not only the bridge hurt, but the draining of his oil. They must have been in league with Seavey and they knew he'd have a hard time staying on without that income. They were hoping then for the one little shove. He'd fooled them!

Of course their water was intact! They'd not hurt *it*. Hadn't Leland said they'd bought an extra lot of explosives, much more than they needed? He'd been away a lot about that time, too, they'd have had plenty of chance to do a mischief. They must have hoped he'd have to go then.

And sending the constable to keep him from making the formula on his own place!

Probably that whole gang, Dorn and Seavey and Krimmer, were in with the county attorney and put him up to suggesting the culm packing. Wouldn't they have loved it if he'd gone more into debt, poured it in, trying to hold up the land, and all for nothing.

In the new glaring light, the pattern stood out at last. They had been trying to shove him off!

The rain beat on his face and he cried out, "They hurt the bridge, but they can't crack me!"

When finally he came back toward the house, the light was out. But Rena must have heard him struggling to shut the door against the wind. She came hurriedly halfway down the stairs and stopped. She stared at his dripping clothes, then at his face.

"Something's wrong. What is it?"

"The bridge is down."

"The storm."

"Not the storm. You don't know what's been going on here."

"Glen, don't let yourself—"

"Twice I saw them, the father and the son, at the exact place. They had plenty of explosives."

"Glen! Those people wouldn't do that!"

She was quick to take their side. "You seem to know."

"If they did," she said sternly, "it was you shouting around about blowing it up gave them the idea!"

He could not until this moment really believe it. But her saying so confirmed it.

"It certainly throws a light on what happened to my water."

"Stop it! Next thing you'll be saying they caused the cave-in!"

216

A chill look settled on his face. "They did all that blasting."

"The caving's on their land too!"

"It might have backfired, caused more damage than they meant."

"Glen, this is all wrong. Stop it. Young Dorn is as worried about the caving as you are."

"You're mighty thick with him all of a sudden."

"I just happened to see him in town."

"I'll bet." He smiled strangely.

"You're angry at me for some reason. You didn't like me offering that way—"

"I'm not angry. Just seeing a lot of things. Seeing it was like that other time you offered. You knew I wouldn't, then, too, with nothing. Gave you a chance to pull away. Think I didn't realize when you married so fast afterward, that you had that guy on the string all the time? You never fooled me."

She came down to the bottom of the steps fearfully. "Glen, you never said or thought a thing like that before. You know it's not true."

"You thought I'd never figure it. I'm a lot sharper than you give me credit for!"

She came swiftly toward him, frightened.

"Glen, dear, you're letting this make you sick. This suspicion. It's bad. It can grow. When Paul was drunk, he'd get like that. And you know what happened to him. I tell you, it's dangerous. It can push everything out of focus."

"Are you trying to dictate to me?"

"I came to help you."

"I don't need help."

He moved swiftly to his study and went in and locked the door.

Abel sat at his desk.

Then he paced up and down. He was seeing the details, realizing what had been going on. But he'd figure ways to combat them.

Near daylight, sitting at his desk, he fell asleep with his head on his arms.

It was broad daylight when he wakened, stiff and weary.

He went down to examine the damage. Standing there, he saw the crack in the masonry. Sheared off. No storm did that!

He did not feel rage. Just cold self-possession.

He had immediate problems. His car was on the island. The only

217

way off now would be down the back path—through the Dorn property. He smiled sardonically. You couldn't tell him!

When he went to the house to call about the bridge, he discovered the phone dead. Rena was still asleep and he went out again.

His boat. He could not take his car over, but he could use the boat, and not use their path. And just let them touch the boat. Just let them.

Fetching the oars from the pump house, he managed, heaving and tugging, to right the boat and float it again in the flooded stream. The current took him swiftly to the fallen bridge.

The flag was up on his mail box. He'd forgotten to collect his mail yesterday. Cynthia.

He rowed to the far side, landing the boat with difficulty. The letter was an inquiry as to whether he wished to renew his option on the old garage building outside McRae. "With a further payment, we—" He tore it to shreds.

He recovered the sign from the slanting bridge. When he rowed back to the island, he had to find a tree stump, once far up the bank, for a mooring post, for the docks were under water. Fastening the boat there, he hung the sign, "Private—No Trespassing," over it.

He went back to the house.

Rena was not there. She must have walked out the back way through the woods.

They all did that, if you were in trouble.

He sat down on the top step with the feeling he'd had before—of not being able to come to grips with an enemy

He sat there a long time, his house a great shell behind him, and he a small legged insect come out to ruminate on a horrifying world.

45

IT WAS VERY EARLY IN THE morning. Agnes opened the door of Tom's room. He was asleep.

The receding storm had clarified the world, left it still and cool and spent.

She pulled her flannel robe around her, looking down at him. A good son. Ought always to consider you might not have a chance tomorrow to tell him that. So tell him.

He never wore a pajama top and the cover had slipped off his shoulder. The mended tissue stood out like a star.

She smiled faintly, remembering a time she'd looked at him this way. He'd been about eleven, home from his first trip away, two weeks at a boys' camp. She'd come in after he was asleep, to see what had happened to him.

Considering his face now, in sleep, she felt a serenity. He'll be all right. He'll surge up.

Under a carelessly flung-down soiled shirt, partly covering it, was that piece of sculpture. A free form, it was called. On the bureau, the papier mâché dog with clasped paws, holding tie clips and odds and ends. That had been with him since he was little. Then she saw the letter stuck in the mirror. "Those whose names—October three—"

She sat down in the straight chair, feeling a return of weakness. All the time, he had been hoping.

His eyelids fluttered. Still sleep drugged, he sat up. "You all right?" He looked a little frightened.

"Yes. I just want to talk."

He sat up shivering and pulled the covers around him. Then he reached into the pocket of the shirt hanging on a chair for what might make this stark world bearable—a cigarette.

"It's Nick I'm thinking about," she said.

Tom expelled some smoke. "Yes."

"It seems hard he should have had all this trouble, when all he wanted was one small place he could be sure of."

"Listen, Mother," Tom said quickly, then broke off, trying to find words. "You never got to know Abel, did you?"

"I always meant to, but I kept making excuses, putting it off," she said.

"Well, just now, your saying that about Nick—I see something. It may sound crazy, but it makes me want to laugh. Like when something is completely cock-eyed. Because, that's all Abel wanted too! One sure place. Now isn't that enough to make a sane man laugh?"

"If some good comes out of the laughing, if it leads you to feel for them, yes. But laughing to scoff, what good's that?"

"I know, I know. But you'd think it would make them understand! Instead what do they do?"

"Nick says everything's Abel's fault—"

"And Abel does the same. I know that. Says everything would be fine, if it weren't for *us*," Tom said.

"I guess it's been such a torment to them, blaming it on someone eases it."

Tom ground out his cigarette, frowning. "It's like they've infected each other with a disease."

"Fear's a terrible sickness. It changes people." Agnes held her robe closer.

"I'm scared too," Tom said. "About Nick."

"I know. It's as if—looking at someone with hate, filling his mind with them, he gradually becomes the same." Her eyes were troubled.

"And there seems nothing to do."

"Except love him. And never forget that good can happen."

Without moving, she could reach a hand and touch the letter in the mirror. "I didn't know. Neither did Nick. You go now, Tom."

"It's no good, pulling out. First, we're going to make it work here, some way."

"Yes." She nodded, even smiling a little. "Some way."

As though he could stop struggling for awhile, he fell into a heavy sleep and did not rouse until nearly noon.

He went to find Agnes. She was puttering in the kitchen.

"Oh, I'm better this morning." She looked drawn and her movements were slow. "The bridge is down! Nick was out early to see."

"That noise last night!"

"He said the land's caved on this side."

Tom gulped his coffee. The bridge caved! Abel would have to use the back path himself.

"Where's Dad?"

"He went back to the car. If it got through the storm all right, he had to go to Sherrod on an errand."

Her voice came with an effort. Tom reminded himself she'd been like this after other attacks. But he wished Nick had not taken the car. He'd have gone in for the doctor. He persuaded her to lie on the sofa.

Outside, in a clean gray day, he took a long inhalation of cigarette. Perhaps he ought to telephone to McRae for the doctor.

But that would mean going up to the Abel house and asking for the use of the telephone. Well, why not?

He went first to see the bridge.

He stood staring at it. That was a storm!

As he stood by the fallen bridge, Rena came along. She looked like she'd taken a beating. Not a physical one, though her red hair was wild and the green dress she wore made her face, without make-up, look ghastly.

This would save strain. Asking her to phone from Abel's would be much simpler.

As soon as they greeted each other, he said, "My mother's sick. We have no phone. Will you call on the Abel's? It's a Dr. Benson in McRae. He'll know her. Will you ask him to come?"

"Abel's telephone's out. The storm blew down the wire. Say, have you a car? I want to get out of this place!"

"My father has it. I don't know when he'll be back."

She looked like she'd plunge in the water racing past, swirling heavy tree branches about.

Every once in a while a chunk of earth dropped away from the treacherous tangle around the bridge.

"Even if you got over," Tom said, "you'd have to walk to the cross-road before you got a hitch. Hardly any cars pass here. That dirt road'll be mean this morning."

"I have to get away from here."

They moved around to the other side of the bridge to see if it would be possible to clamber over it. They saw the boat and the sign.

She started through the mud toward it. "I'll use that!"

"Do you know anything about boats?"

"Never rowed one in my life!"

"The water's pretty swift."

"I don't care!"

They heard a car churning along the dirt road. The mail carrier came into view, slogging slowly through the mud. He stopped at the mail boxes across the river.

"Hi, there!" Rena shouted.

"Hi! Say! Bridge's down!"

"Will you give me a hitch in?"

"How'll you get over? Can't wait long. Late now."

"I'll get over all right!" With reckless haste she untied the boat. The carrier stepped up his idling motor a little, to express his impatience.

She was struggling with the oars.

"Oh, here!" Tom said. "I'll take you over."

"I'd appreciate it. I don't like to hold him."

In the middle of the river, she glanced back. "Eliza crossing the ice."

On the other side, she looked at the Abel roof above the bare trees. "I don't know," her face was troubled, "perhaps I oughtn't to go, no matter what he said. He's all alone."

The carrier had finished putting mail in the boxes and was holding the door open. "If you're comin'."

Tom leaned in the car window. "You'll call the doctor, won't you?"

"Yes," she said, "and—thanks."

The car ground, trying for a start. Tom watched it, mud and water spraying out behind, disappear down the road.

Their flag was up. Cynthia?

The letter was for Agnes. An announcement of some sort. From the Woman's Club of McRae. It seemed incongruous, but he realized he had no idea what she was like, really. Perhaps she had longings, all the time, for such pleasant, womanish conventional things.

Thinking of her alone, he moved quickly to the boat.

The current was vicious. He felt good, though, the way his hand obeyed him. Then he realized Abel was coming down the lane.

Striding rapidly, swinging his legs. He'd felt this tightening up before as Abel's commanding figure bore down on him. He had a flash it was tied up with Cynthia. The avenging patriarch.

He pulled in and moored. I'll just explain I took that Rena, or whatever her name is, across.

He climbed over the crumbling bank. But what if I'm messing in some private fight between them? Better say nothing.

He had started off down the shore when he heard Abel's voice, loud, cold, measured. "I want to tell you something."

He turned to go back. I'll explain to him. But he had gone only a step or two when Abel said coldly, "You touch that boat again, and you'll—be—sorry!"

Then he saw Abel's eyes. Queer, staring. You could not explain anything to eyes like that.

He shrugged and turned away, moving swiftly toward his own house.

46

ABOUT THREE THAT AFTERNOON, Agnes began gasping for breath and clutching at her left shoulder.

Tom knew about propping her with pillows. He knew about the sedative. After it began to take effect and she dozed, he felt panic again. They were so cut off.

Nick had been in two hours ago, but left. He hadn't gone to Sherrod. He'd been all morning on the back road trying to get the car started. "I didn't have the right wrench. Took me hours to work over the plugs. Then that wasn't it. I'll try filing the distributor points this afternoon. I hope it's not mud or water seeped in."

Agnes had seemed fine when he left.

Now Tom paced around the room, darting an occasional worried glance at the sofa.

Rena must have arrived in McRae, by, say, one-thirty, two anyway. If she'd called the doctor right away— He might have been having office hours, though. Or out on a call. If Rena had known it was urgent. But this morning, it hadn't been. Tom gnawed his thumb.

Half a dozen times he started out to fetch Nick. If one of them stayed, the other might try and find a doctor, any doctor. I can't leave her alone. Nick'll be coming any minute.

At six, Nick, greasy and mud spattered, returned. "I finally got it started."

By then, Agnes was quiet, her breathing easy.

They fixed supper, warming up leftover baked beans they found in the refrigerator, and ate hurriedly.

"Mother seems all right now," Nick said in a low worried voice.

They ate dispiritedly.

"Dad?"

"Yeah?"

"What'll we do if something goes wrong with Mom tonight? I think we ought to try to get her to some help."

"Yeah. You'd think that doctor would have come. Who was it you asked to tell him, did you say?"

"Some friend of Abel's."

Nick's face tightened and he was silent.

"We have to do something," Tom said.

"Yeah. Trees down all over, it'd be terrible for her to try to carry her back through the woods."

They ate in silence.

"One of us could drive the car around to the front of the island," Tom said.

"What for? With the bridge down?"

"We could take her across in the rowboat, Abel's boat. He has it tied under the bridge."

Nick said gloomily, "He probably won't want us to use it."

"I'll ask him. He can't refuse." Tom started for the door. "Don't go for the car till I come, so she won't be alone."

Nick nodded.

Tom moved through the dusk. Last night, the storm had torn the world apart. Tonight the island was still as a photograph. The moon was rising. The low hills, only a few hundred yards away, were a phantom mauve. They seemed miles off and mountain high.

He went up the Abel lane hurriedly.

He lifted the knocker and let it fall. Within, echoes sounded. No step responded.

Waiting there in front of the closed door, he thought, We have to get a sick woman across the river! This is wasting time!

He ran down, taking the shortcut through the shrubbery.

When he came in, panting, Agnes had roused.

She seemed all right, except that she made no attempt to rise as she might have another time, to clear the dishes.

"He wasn't there," Tom mumbled to his father.

"Now what?"

"We can't stand on ceremony. We'll use it."

Nick took his flashlight from the kitchen closet. "I'll go back and drive the car around to the front road."

Tom made it sound casual to Agnes. "We thought, seeing we're so cut off, best get you into town."

She nodded quietly.

Then Tom stopped. "What was that? Listen!"

An auto horn sounded faintly.

"The doctor!" Tom cried.

224

The horn sounded again.

"Across the river!" He ran out.

He moved swiftly toward the bridge. Across the river, the small coupe was outlined in the light of the risen moon. Its headlights shone on the tangled bridge.

"Dr. Benson?" Tom cried.

"Yes!" came a voice. "Bridge down! Your mother bad off?"

"Last night she was. We haven't a phone, and our car's back through the woods. We didn't like her being here tonight."

"If you can get her over, I'll take her in to the hospital. Best place."

"I'll have to bring her over in a rowboat. Don't know what else to do."

"How is she now? Breathing all right?"

"Pretty well."

"If I come over, we'll lose time. You have some medicine?"

"Yes."

"If she acts worried, give her a little. Wrap her up in blankets. Bring some pillows."

"All right." Tom felt almost a sob of relief well up.

He sped back to the house.

Agnes was not heavy. They wrapped her in blankets plucked off a bed. Nick carried her.

Tom ran ahead with the pillows.

He dropped them in the boat and pulled it up as far on shore as he could.

Nick put her down gently, with the pillows behind her.

Tom had to keep his mind on the current. It seemed even stronger than it had been in the morning.

Anxiously, at the edge of the flood, Nick stood watching the boat.

Halfway across, Agnes began to gasp for breath. It terrified Tom. What could he do here in the middle of the river? Then she seemed to relax and was all right. He had a guilty feeling he'd never done enough, paid enough attention, to her.

They made the other shore. The doctor helped carry her to the car.

"Not room enough for you," he said, wadding the pillows and blankets expertly. "It'll crowd her too much. You have a car, you say?"

"Yes. On the back road. We'll be in as fast as we can make it."

"The hospital's on State Road."

"Okay."

"Well, Tom," Agnes's voice sounded normal, only faint, as if coming from a distance, "I wonder if I'll get to see my pineys bloom."

"Why, sure you will, Mom."

"Yes."

The doctor had started the car.

Tom stood watching until the tail lights disappeared.

He felt like crying. But she'd be all right. Wasn't she always all right?

Across on the island, he could see Nick's blurred figure as he hurried toward the house, anxious to start their trip out the back way.

The sound of the doctor's car died away. Tom wiped his face with the back of his hand.

He started back across the river. The moon was higher now. Its shimmer coated the water. Like silver plate, he thought. Hard to believe the river underneath is muddy.

Then he came aware of the figure standing on the other side. Near the boat mooring stump. Not Nick. Nick was halfway home by this time.

Tom saw the moonlight sparkle on the gun barrel.

Abel felt the world rock under him. Except the man in the boat. He was fixed. Him, in the boat.

If I could rub out that image.

Must! Everyone, everything, trying to down me. Never on top.

Nothing right since they came. Enticing her. Must have. Probably part of the plan.

I warned him. He took the boat. Took everything. Defied me. Makes me nothing.

Abel felt a convulsive overpowering need to blot out the image in the boat.

I warned him.

He raised the gun.

He heard the scream cut the moonlight as the figure leaped, fell. The image was gone.

The world was rocking again and he was running.

Inside my study. Don't know how I got here.

His chair, as he sank down, felt real. He rubbed his hand over his face confusedly.

They have cracked me.

Nick, hurrying toward his house, rolled ahead of him little marbles of worry—where'll we stay in town?—ought I to pack a bag with Agnes's things? It kept his mind from sinking under the large stone of worry about her condition.

His house in the moonlight was gaunt and patient looking. Climbing the porch steps he was thinking—Must be sure the water and gas off, might be gone—

The moonlight was shattered by the sounding and re-sounding detonation of the rifle bullet, jarring and rattling the windows of his senses.

A scream.

He froze with dread. An animal-like scream of pain.

His heart pounded wildly against his ribs. Tom. Tom, in Abel's boat! What if—?

Nick ran, heart pumping madly.

Rounding the bend, his gasping breath sucked in the sulphurous odor hanging in the still air. But he did not see Tom. Or anyone else.

"Tom!" his anguished cry rose. "Tom!"

He ran on, appalled eyes searching the empty river ahead. The deserted scene bewildered him. Calling, distracted, he ran until his breath was out of his body, until his legs, on the slippery clay of the flood's edge, were leaden.

Then, out in the middle of the racing current, he saw the boat. It was passing him swiftly. The oars were gone.

There was no one in it.

Premonitions of evil burst forth in a tortured cry, "Tom! What happened?"

But maybe he hadn't been in the boat. Had gotten to the shore. Slipped somehow in the mud, fallen.

Nick ran again, to where the boat had been moored, crying frantically, "Tom, where are you?"

The only sound was the rush of the water in the serene moonlight.

Scarcely knowing what he did, he ran back and forth along the water, searching in frenzy above the bridge, below, beating through clumps of rushes, weeds, calling, incoherent with fear.

Finally, he sank down on a log jutting partly out of the water.

Gone! Abel had shot him and he'd tumbled into the flood! Gone. Then a word framed itself in his mind. Murderer. The man who had killed the bees.

He sat rigid, as something rose and beat against his ear drums.

If I had a gun, I would rid the earth of him.

Hunched over, he sat outwardly as still as the moonlight. Inside,

227

like acid distilled in drops for a long time in a vat, there was a seething and boiling.

The bees, the road, the dock, the bridge—not enough for him! Now —Tom!

As if the acid were vaporizing, rage blinded him.

Blow him off the island! Cleanse the world of him. That evil man. Like all the others that have pushed and worried and squeezed. And I could never hit back.

Rid the earth—. Blow—. Blast—.

Hunched over, he sat staring inward. There'd be a sound and the trees would reel—but the cruel and all their works and dwellings would be rooted out of the world.

As though some demon pushed him erect, then started him forward, he moved swiftly. Past his own house, across the stretch of grass, through the cherry saplings, along the river to the cairn.

Maybe the sticks would be wet from the rain. For an instant he knew relief. If he hadn't the means, how could he? But the demon urged him. He thrust his hand in and touched the metal box. Dry. Five or six sticks left. He took them out, with the fuses and caps. He didn't bother to close the box. In a madness of haste, he ran as though he must do it while the demon possessed him.

His shadow in the moonlight moved on the high ugly fence as he approached it and passed around it, running.

Moonlight, lacing through the bare trees in the wood, made stripes, and he did not see the tree root. He fell, and falling, the sticks flew from his hand.

In the two or three seconds before they hit the ground, before he knew if they would strike a rock, or be somehow detonated, he lived a long agonizing lifetime, long enough to know if they went here, his own house, everything, would go. The sky seemed to shake with fearsome light and the river to foam darkly. He lay there, cold with fear.

Then he rolled over and opened his eyes.

He was staring up into a vast sky, serene and deep with moonlight. The tranquil woods seemed only to shelter him. Finally, he struggled to his knees.

He felt cold and weak and empty as though he had vomited out of him all the acid and spleen.

I, Nick Dorn, could have been a murderer! I, Nick Dorn, who used to wait on the corner of Bedell Street to catch the 8:13 street car, who got weak eyes from a hard case of measles as a child. Like the terrified wretches who stare out of smudged news headlines, to whom you say, "How could you have done such a thing? How could it have happened?"

He rose, shaking, to his feet. Slowly, he walked down to his house. There it stood, whole and sweet in the moonlight. The island looked indescribably beautiful so that he was almost moved to get down on his knees again.

"I don't deserve it."

And he saw how the moonlight fell, touching everything with exquisite tenderness. What if there was, as they said, up there, a Kindness, who had somehow.

Maybe he should not have given up searching for Tom. What if he were alive, needed help?

He replaced the sticks fearfully now, in the cairn. Then he walked, beating through reeds and bushes, away from the island in the direction he had seen the boat disappear.

After a long time, Abel raised his head from the desk.

A terrible idea was forcing itself into his consciousness.

It was not a nightmare. It was he who had blotted out the image in the boat.

The scream sounded in his ear. The figure—falling.

He stood up. What if I killed him? Me, Glen Abel. No. Such things don't happen.

But what if?

He broke out in a cold sweat. Accusing eyes stared at him. Cynthia!

A murderer!

Could I really have done it?

Verdict, guilty of murder.

Who would care if the pressure cracked me? Temporarily insane—but guilty.

Cynthia, staring, horrified.

I'll kill myself before I. He grasped the gun.

No, not a coward, too. Face the music.

Rena saying, "You have a sickness, Glen. Have to be in control—"

Face it. Go back, search the river. Maybe he needs help.

If only I haven't killed him.

If only.

The storm had blown down many lines. The crew in the repair

truck worked after dark, using the flood light. They had supper in Sherrod and started out again.

As they neared the crossing where the dirt road took off, they had heard a shot.

It was impossible to tell where it came from.

They finished repairing another broken line. "Wonder what that shot was," one of them said.

They moved on down the road and repaired another wire. After a bit, they started again.

Driving slowly, looking for storm damage, they saw the figure staggering along the road toward them. The headlights picked up the white shirt with great dark stains.

They ran toward him.

"What's the matter?"

"What happened?"

"The boat," Tom mumbled. "It stopped right there in that cove. The cove where Cynthia and I were."

"The guy's in shock, Joe."

Quickly they drove him in to the hospital.

47

THE GAS STATION AT VALLEY Road was open. Nick telephoned the police from there.

The calm operator who took the report questioned him in an unexcited voice.

Nick wanted to protest angrily that it was not A Missing Person. It was his son, who'd fought in the war, who had—who had—but no one would care he'd finished second in his class.

By the time he reached State Road, coming into McRae, it was midnight.

Should he go to the hospital first to see if Agnes were all right? Or to the police to see what they'd done? The hospital was closest. He ran up the steps.

Dr. Benson was coming down the corridor. The little hospital was understaffed and he had been called into Emergency. It had been a busy evening. The heart case—looked like she'd be all right—then the frightened young mother halfway along to her first-born, and now this gun-shot wound.

He saw Nick, disheveled, wild-eyed, come in. The doctor held up a warning hand. "Shush. People sleeping. He's all right."

Nick stood panting. "He? My wife—?"

"Your son's here. A couple of linemen brought him in. Didn't you know that?"

"And—he's—all right?"

"He will be. I'll have to do some probing, soon as I get the X-ray. Just hope a tendon's not cut."

Nick leaned against the wall and put his hands over his face to squeeze back tears.

The doctor waited, giving him time to get together with this news. "The nurse'll probably shoo you out, but you can see him for a minute."

Nick trembled. "My wife?"

"Resting quietly. Think she'll make it."

Nick opened the door. The nurse glanced impatiently over her shoulder.

"Not now."

But Nick, seeing Tom's eyes gleaming at him, had the feeling he'd had on the island of, I don't deserve it.

"You all right, son?"

"Okay. How's Mom?"

"He says she's all right."

"Don't tell her about this."

"No."

The nurse reached pointedly in front of Nick for the gown. "You can come back later."

Outside in the dim corridor Nick sat on the hard bench. He had a strange feeling he was in church and realized it was because of all the flowers and potted plants, put outside the patients' rooms for the night, lining the walls.

48

TOM WAS STIFF AND SORE next morning. Considering the nurse's report that they'd worked on him last night for a long time, he probably felt as well as could be expected.

Quite early, the doctor came in. He had a hearty cheerfulness that made Tom uneasy. After the small talk, he came out with it. "We had some trouble with the tendon. We'll have to go in later. But we'll get it fixed up if it can be done. Don't you be discouraged!"

He began to scribble on a pad on his knee.

"I have to make a routine report to the police on any gun-shot wound. They'll probably come around to question you. Me, I have more important things to think about, like getting you well."

When he left, Tom stared bleakly at the ceiling.

A report on a gun-shot wound. To the police. Abel would finally get his. Shooting a man. That would mean jail. Let him pay! He deserved all they could do to him and more. He had it coming. Give it to him. Soak him hard.

The nurse came in. "The shaving things." The tray rattled as she put it on the bedside table. "You probably want to shave yourself. But, later, when I'm not so busy, I'll do it if you want me to."

She went out.

He kept staring at the ceiling.

He could have asked her to call Cynthia. But why?

He didn't want to see anyone. Especially not her, with her expecting him to know the answers, be a strong man out of a circus. He didn't want to see Nick or Agnes either.

That doctor was so cheery. Not a bit discouraged. No, sir, not a bit.

Why should he be? It wasn't his life.

Tom's face felt gritty. The shaving things were right there. He had only to sit up, reach out a hand.

Why bother? If the nurse thought he ought to be shaved, let her do it.

He closed his eyes.

He didn't give a good goddam, if anyone should ask, about anything.

No, the doctor was not discouraged. It was not his left hand. Not the hand he needed. Counted on.

In a way, there was something very comical about it. If you cared enough one way or the other to laugh.

All the striving wasted. The exercises lost.

He'd tried to build up the clay on the armature, to make a full rounded figure. Something kept knocking it off.

Shave? He was going to stay here stretched out. He didn't even care whether he opened his eyes or not.

Fleetingly, he thought of Nick and Agnes.

He guessed they'd manage all right.

Agnes, with all her saying, "—have to go on." What use?

That time he took her into the doctor's office in McRae, she saying, "What if Nick trusted me and I'd given up?"

He suddenly felt too warm. He could hear Agnes, almost as if she were in the room. "You, you'll go on. You have love now. You'll find out how it is—."

The room seemed suffocating. He kicked back the covers savagely. "It's a sort of trust."

He was burning up. They kept these rooms too hot. Then he felt sick. He wasn't sure where. He braced himself against the foot of the bed as if to keep from sliding down a precipice, every muscle as tight as a jammed-on brake.

Nothing but worry, ugliness, waste. Don't care about—He licked dry lips.

Hold on!

Off that stuff. That to-hell-with-everything way out. I swore off it!

For what seemed a long time he lay there, tense. His heart pounded as if he were helpless but must fight someone.

His defenses were slender. Her hand—and the way he felt then.

He broke out in perspiration.

Just because you said you were off that way didn't mean you wouldn't try to use it.

So—this is what it'll be like. And many times after this. I have to keep *on* saying, Not that way!

After awhile he sat up, shivering.

That doctor'll fix things up. He let go a long breath. Sure he will.

233

And if he doesn't? He stopped shivering. Something—he didn't know what, helped him. There'll be some way.

He was exhausted, as if he'd been through a battle. Well—he had been.

But it had been easier this time, he had not gone down so far, wallowed so abjectly. The struggle had been shorter.

After awhile he began to shave. Once he got going, he went on automatically. The routine even steadied him. It could be, he thought, that with time, a person learns evasive tactics, gets to be a wily fighter.

Suddenly he wanted Cynthia to be here.

He was tired and still shaky, but it was physical fatigue. He knew what he wanted. Cynthia. He needed her. He had to tell her, What a battle! What a terrific guy!

No, he needed *her* to tell *him*.

His fatigue made him peevish. You'd think Nick could at least have offered to call her.

Her phone number was on her letter. I'll call her myself. But there was no phone in the room. Make that nurse wheel me out to a phone booth! I want to *talk* to her!

When the nurse came in he demanded, "Bring me the things out of my pocket!"

She glanced at him quickly. "You ought to try to relax. Not go tossing around. Just be quiet. Let things heal."

He glared at her fiercely. "Look, will you get my things?"

The edges of his wound seemed like jagged metal that rasped together.

"You ought to rest." But she went out. After a long time she brought his wallet, stiff from wetting.

He looked through it. Not there.

"Bring me the pants, will you?" His voice sounded fretful. His whole arm and shoulder felt hot, his mouth cottony.

She finally brought the wrinkled pants. "They were hanging to dry. You must have waded through water last night. Now you just stay quiet. What is it you want? I'll find it."

"A letter."

She fished it out and handed it to him.

The water had washed out most of the ink. The number was a blur.

The nurse was looking at him accusingly. "You'll be getting a temp on me. Can't I look up this number for you?"

234

"I haven't the address." He wished he were six so he could cry. At Jody's, in the city. That's all he knew.

The nurse said with professional cheer, "Now, don't worry or your wound won't heal. If it's a girl, she'll turn up."

But he needed her now.

The nurse was going out the door. "Just try to sleep."

He tossed miserably. He kept trying to visualize the number on the letter. An SU exchange. The rest he could not recall.

Time passed. When the nurse looked in again, she said, quickly, frowning, "Doctor left orders you were to have some medicine if you didn't lie quiet. You're going to get it!" She disappeared and returned in a few minutes with the dose in a glass of water. "Take this!"

Tom was swallowing it, when there was a tap on the door. The nurse went out, leaving the door open a crack. He could hear her in the corridor, expostulating with someone.

"Doctor said he was to rest!"

A man's voice answered, and Tom thought he recognized it. It was the County Attorney. "Did he tell you who did it?" He remembered the doctor scribbling, "Routine report to the authorities."

What a mess! He wanted Cynthia to come, wanted Cynthia to love him, to say, What a terrific guy! And if she came, the Dorns would be having her father put in jail.

If the nurse lets him in, what'll I do? If only I had time to figure.

The attorney was asking, "Didn't he say anything about what happened?"

She sounded tart. "No, he didn't."

"Hmmm. Well, anyhow, I think I know. People that go banging around with guns! Something like this bound to happen! Is his father around? I could get the story from him."

"He was here all night, but he left a while ago."

"Where'd he go?"

"Home, I suppose. He'll be back."

"If I could talk to the boy just a minute."

"But he's had a sedative," she protested crossly. "You'll rouse him."

The door was swinging in. If I had time to think—Tom closed his eyes.

He could hear the attorney's heavy breathing over the bed.

After awhile he heard the door close. When he opened his eyes, the room was empty.

He'll be back, though.

235

The medicine made him fuzzy, but his muscles were still tense. If only Cynthia were here. Must decide what to do.

The attorney stood on the front steps of the hospital. He took the doctor's report from his pocket again and squinted through his glasses at it.

He remembered their saying that time, "Abel's always threatening around with a gun."

A slow angry flush crept over the attorney's face. He was thinking of Abel and the bridge.

Perhaps the time's come, he thought, to show him whether he's stronger than the law. It's more like he thinks he's above it.

Might have a little more respect for it if he finds himself arrested for assault with deadly weapon, or attempted murder.

He stood, lips pursed, staring into the street. Wonder if I dare arrest Abel on suspicion, before I get their story? I'm sure he did it, doesn't seem to be much risk.

Law-scoffer. Like to show him.

As if deciding, he went briskly down the steps, along the street.

When he reached his office, he telephoned.

Abel didn't ask questions or bluster. It was almost as if he were prepared to take whatever was coming to him. He agreed to come in.

Half-opening his eyes, Tom sensed it was dusk. He felt tense as if, even under the sedative, he had been fighting.

He heard someone move in the room.

"I think he's waking up now."

Cynthia!

It was Cynthia's voice!

He heard the nurse. "He needed to rest. He had a rough time last night." She was farther off now, at the door. "You going to be here awhile?"

Cynthia took his hand. "I'm going to stay right here."

The door closed.

Cynthia's voice seemed to float in the air around him, loosing raw nerves and muscles from spasm. People that had polio bathed in warm waters that relaxed them so that their muscles—. This was the way it worked. He closed his eyes for a moment. Going to be all right. Everything.

Then he clasped her hand firmly and opened his eyes.

She bent over him quickly. "Tom!"

The room was half-dark now, but they did not think of turning on the lights.

"All the way out," she did not let go of his hand, "I kept telling myself—Whatever happened, he's alive."

She said, Whatever happened. Then she doesn't know yet. That it was Abel.

I'll have to tell her, because that attorney'll be back. Quickly, because I—we—have to figure what to do.

"Cynthia!" He held her hand firmly. "Listen! This is important. Your father did it."

"Oh, no!" Her voice recoiled. He could hardly see her face in the dusk. "And yet," she sounded sad now, "even before you told me, I guessed it. When I heard of the storm, I tried to telephone but the line was out. I called Rena. She'd heard you were here. I guess I knew why. I'll *never* go back now!"

"That's not it! Not the way. I've been wrestling with it, but I'm full of medicine and my thinking may not be straight. Remember that time Nick wouldn't give Abel the water? How disgusted I was with Nick when he couldn't see it was to his interest to give it, stop whatever might be building up?"

"But you! Your hand!"

"I'm not trying to be a hero. I'm telling you straight out what I'm thinking about is—us."

He could not seee her face at all.

Then she began to talk in a low breathless rush. "Tom! *I* begin to see something too! What made me so bitter before was all the waste. Hope wasted, love wasted. We'd be just as bad, if we kept on with that."

He said, "What worries me is—it—it's out of our hands."

He heard her quick intake of breath. "Why?"

"The doctor made a report and that attorney came. I didn't talk to him, but he'll be back."

"Oh, Tom!"

"It won't be so easy."

After awhile she said, "Couldn't you just—not talk. Not tell him anything?"

Tom took a long breath. "If that were all. There's Nick."

In the dark room there was no sound for a few minutes.

Then Tom went on. "Nick's changed. That's the trouble. Time was, when I'd just have put it to him. But now. Things have happened to him."

"Yes, I know."

"He's been in a strange mood lately. And to tell you the truth, this morning, before I understood what it would do to *us*—I felt pretty vengeful myself."

After a bit she said, troubled, "Maybe it will be all right. Try not to worry."

"Yes."

She stood up to go. "The nurse told me about your mother. I thought I'd go in before I left."

"Yes—that would be nice."

"Rest now." She kissed him lightly. "I'll be here first thing in the morning. And—don't worry."

He heard the door close softly after her.

No, I won't worry a bit, he thought. Lying in the dark, he was remembering Nick ordering the squatter off.

Cynthia stood beside Agnes's bed, hesitant.

Agnes's face looked gray, but her eyes still burned with a quiet steady flame.

Sensing the hesitancy, Agnes said, "Don't be afraid to talk to me about Tom. I already know. I heard the nurses discussing it. I know it's his left arm."

Tears sprang to Cynthia's eyes, but she fought them back.

"Sit down a little," Agnes said.

Cynthia sat down. "It's like he's holding all that in! But when he realizes, what'll happen? What's to become of him?"

Agnes's voice was gentle. "I don't know."

"If he hadn't had the plan for being a surgeon so long!" Cynthia let the tears come now.

Agnes nodded slowly. "Yes. But I'll tell you, sometimes I had a feeling about that. That he wasn't really meant to be a surgeon. It was more as if he decided to do it, and was beaten down a lot and just got stubborn about it."

Cynthia looked up with startled recognition, as though some inner knowing of her own had come to the surface.

Agnes said quietly, "Once, a long time ago, he wanted to be a sculptor."

Cynthia let out a sigh. "What if that doctor can't fix up his hand?

What if he gets to not caring about anything again? That's what I dread."

Agnes was thoughtful a long time before she said softly, "He'll be all right."

"Perhaps I ought to try to talk to him about it." Cynthia looked worried again. "Remind him he could be a sculptor. He could do that, even if his hand doesn't come back. *Make* him see."

"Don't worry. You never know what's going on inside a person. Best leave it alone. All he needs he'll find stored in himself. Everything's there, waiting. Maybe more than we could ever imagine."

Cynthia looked quickly at the face on the pillow. It could be so, she thought, because that's the way it was with me.

Shall I tell her about the attorney, she wondered, and about Nick? Ask her what to do? No, not right to upset her.

But after she had said good night and was in the hall, she repeated the words, as if they were some incantation that might blunt ill-luck, "maybe more than we could ever imagine."

49

NEXT MORNING CYNTHIA ARRIVED at the hospital before visiting hours. Waiting in the deserted little lounge off the corridor, she heard heavy steps coming along the hall, then a voice.

Abel!

Before she could move, they had passed the lounge—Abel and the attorney! They were going toward Tom's room. She flew to the door. Yes, that was it.

Standing there, heart pounding, she felt desperately sorry for Abel. She stood, irresolute. Ought she to go in? No, better not.

She began to pace about the lounge, feeling helpless.

Morning sun fell across Tom's bed.

It ought to be nearly ten—time for Cynthia. He rolled the bedside table toward him and picked up his wrist watch. Fifteen minutes yet.

There was a tap on the door, it opened and the County Attorney came in. With Abel!

Seeing Abel, Tom's heart pounded painfully. I'm scared. Not scared of Abel. Scared of what can happen, if Nick comes in.

If I could have kept it between us—Nick and me. There was a chance then. But bringing Abel! Hope to God Nick doesn't come.

The attorney asked, "Has your father been in yet?"

Tom seemed to have no breath in his lungs. "No."

Abel just stood there. Usually he put up a front of being at ease in any situation. Now he just stood there.

The attorney motioned to a chair facing into the light. "Sit down." He himself was standing with his back to the window.

Abel sat down.

The door opened hastily. The nurse came in, flustered, a little angry. She opened her mouth but the attorney said drily, "Don't give me that before-visiting-hours rigmarole. This is important. Have you seen Mr. Dorn around?"

"He's in Mrs. Dorn's room."

"Will you ask him to come here?" the attorney said.

The nurse was beside Tom's bed now and leaned toward his ear. "You want me to call the doctor? Have them thrown out?"

Tom looked at her. Then he sat up slowly. He was seeing it had to be done. The chance taken.

The nurse was looking inquiringly at him. He swallowed hard. "No. Crank this bed up, will you? I want to sit up."

She did so and went out.

The attorney, as if to forestall any conversation, turned away and looked down into the street.

Abel looked at the linoleum.

For a moment Tom wished Cynthia were here, with her hand warm in his.

No! Too much in the air already. Complicate things.

Then the door opened. Nick came in.

Seeing Abel, he gave a start. Then he looked inquiringly at the attorney.

The attorney said, "I wanted to get some things cleared up, Mr. Dorn. Sit down, will you?"

Nick hesitated, then sat down.

Tom, with the bed raised in back of him, seemed to be floating above them, detached.

He wished it were over. He held his muscles tight to keep from shaking.

The attorney's voice was slow and important. "I received this report of a gun-shot wound. I'd like to know what went on out there."

Abel spoke now. "You didn't have to bring me here for that. I'd have told you."

"Just a minute. I'll run this." The attorney turned to Tom. "Tell me just what happened. Who shot you?"

Tom looked at Nick, sitting with downcast eyes so that anyone might have thought he were the guilty one. If only he would go along. End this crap. *End it!*

Tom took a long breath. "It was an accident."

Abel started and glanced at him quickly. Nick opened his mouth, then closed it.

The attorney reddened angrily. "Oh, come now. That's hard to believe. You mean you shot yourself out there in the boat?"

"I didn't say that. It was an accident everything happened just the way it did. An accident."

The attorney turned almost petulantly on Nick. "What do *you* say?"

Tom's breath seemed to stop. He wanted to shout at him, "Shut up! Let it die!" If there'd been time to pour out to him his feeling of a whole lifetime of stops and starts, maybe Nick *would* have understood. But it was too late now.

Nick was looking at him. Tom could only look back, dumbly. It seemed a long time before he heard Nick's voice. It came rustily, as if he needed to clear his throat.

"Nothing. I have nothing to say."

Tom's breath came back now. He felt as if he were really floating. He wanted to yell in relief.

The attorney turned on Abel angrily. "I know you did it. I'm no fool."

Tom broke in quickly. "No matter what happened, if we don't make charges, then it has to die, doesn't it? If we don't accuse anyone?"

The attorney squinted at him awhile, trying to understand. He rammed his hands in his pockets finally. "If you don't know what's for your own good."

"What makes you think we don't!" Tom realized he was tired now.

The attorney turned on Nick again, almost pleading. "What do you say?"

Nick sat drooped over as if he were the accused. Tom saw him swallow hard. "We don't accuse."

The attorney sighed, nonplused. Finally, he shrugged. He started out, but stopped, looking from one to the other, puzzled. Then he went out.

Abel went to the door. He stopped. His lips opened, but no words came. Finally, he said, "Well, I'll be seeing you around."

Tom said to Nick, "Crank this bed down, will you, before I float off into space." His tone was brusque. By the time Nick finished, they were both in control again, could speak unemotionally.

Tom stole a look at his father.

In the straight hospital chair, Nick, his arms hanging in front of him, looked at the floor.

Finally, he said, "I guess you wonder what got into me."

Tom said, "I'm glad you didn't accuse him."

"I had no grounds to." He took a long breath.

"I meant to tell you about it sometime, anyway." Now he looked up. "After it happened out there, and I hunted and couldn't find you, after I thought he killed you, I wanted to take that explosive and blow him up. I almost did. Almost did! I'd have been a murderer." He stopped, but went on. "I have no grounds to act as if I'm any better than him, or wouldn't have done what he did."

Surprised, Tom sat up quickly. A cherishing fondness for Nick warmed him.

Then, into his mind's eye came the face of Abel and the way he looked as he had left the room. And remembering, he felt uneasy.

Tom said, "Dad, I wish you'd—but of course you couldn't—not with that attorney there. But I wish Abel *knew* how you felt."

"Abel?" Nick looked up from under his brows. "Why?"

"Because—well—he's beholden to us too much. I was watching his face. Be better if things had been left more even."

"I don't know as we're called on to worry about *how* he feels!"

Tom flushed. "His feelings *do* matter. And I say, let's get smart. I don't mean you should go and make a big production of it, but I do say, let him know how you feel. That you don't think you're any better than he is."

Nick's lower lip thrust out. "Well, I don't know."

Tom started to speak hotly, but took a quick breath, and licked his lips. Let him alone.

After a moment he said in a quiet voice, "How's Mom?"

"Doctor says she'll be all right."

"Tell her," Tom began. "No, never mind. Just tell her I'll be up in a wheel chair and in to see her tomorrow. Tell her to bake a cake."

Cynthia paced between window and potted palm.

An image kept thrusting into her mind. What if the door of Tom's room opened, and the attorney came out holding Abel firmly by the arm? Surely no more than that! But she thought of Abel's pride, his arrogance. Tears came to her eyes. He couldn't stand it!

She lit another cigarette.

Then she heard the door open. She seemed cold all over.

Only one man walking. Then the attorney, head down, passed the lounge. Alone.

Warmth flooded her again and she could move. Impulsively she wanted to run to Tom's room, to find out what had happened. But Abel was still there. What if she burst in at the wrong moment, jarred some delicate filament?

She couldn't bear it any longer. That attorney would tell her. She hurried down the corridor. He had gone. In the street, she could see him, walking rapidly toward the center of town. She hurried after him. At the traffic light she was held. She lost him.

Slowly she turned and started back to the hospital.

Before she arrived, she saw Abel come out. He stood, alone, on the steps. Just stood there, looking up at the brilliant blue of the sky in a way he seldom did.

Then he came down the steps, and stood again, at the curb, looking around as if he were in a strange town.

She wanted to cry out to him, joyfully. Instead, she moved ahead faster.

Then, she stopped. Tom's father had come out of the hospital. He was on the top step and he was looking down at Abel. He descended one step, but stopped, irresolute. Then he moved down the steps slowly, toward Abel.

He spoke, and Abel turned.

Clear sunlight poured over them, so that every move and gesture stood out sharply.

The two men were not standing close together. In fact, passersby on the street walked between them. But in spite of this, they remained welded into a conversational unit, were still in communication.

Abel, though taller, did not look down at Nick. Nick did not look up at Abel either. Instead, talking, they gazed soberly at the ground.

After awhile, their heads rose as if the conversation were concluded. It seemed they were going to shake hands, but a group of teen-age girls walked chattering between them. The two men merely nodded good-bye but stood looking at each other a moment.

Then, Nick crossed toward his parked car, and Abel went on down the street, alone.

For a moment Cynthia thought of calling after him. Then she realized he was headed in the direction of the Mansion House.

Tom! I'm going to Tom!

And now she felt so light-hearted, so buoyant, it was hard to keep from running.